A GARRISON CHASE THRILLER

A THIN LINE

D1403573

CRAIG N. HOOPER

For Mom and Dad

ISBN 978-1-7333755-1-1

Connect with Craig:

Website: http://craignhooper.com

Email: craig@craignhooper.com

The power of choosing good and evil is within the reach of all.

—Origen

CHAPTER ONE

THE MAN WHO taught me two different ways to kill a person with my index finger showed up on my doorstep at twenty past six on a blustery, overcast Southern California morning.

I opened the door and gasped when I saw his face, which was beaten to a pulpy mess and unrecognizable. I knew it was my mentor, Hans Schlimmergaard, aka Slim, because of his 6'6" frame. The man was as thick as two men and built like a giant Lego block. Slim wasn't a blend into the background kind of guy. He was the background.

"What? Don't you recognize me, pal?" Slim stepped forward as he smiled.

At least I think he smiled. It was hard to tell.

I stepped onto the porch, mesmerized by his car wreck of a face. It was pinkish red and swollen in every place a face could swell and covered with lacerations too numerous to count. His right eye was swollen shut and a golf ball sized nodule protruded over his left. The jagged cuts on his face went every direction, creating a jigsaw puzzle effect. Some type of clear cream, which I assumed was antiseptic based, oozed from the wounds on his cheeks. The early morning light cascaded across his glistening face, drawing even more attention to the carnage. With his short, red hair, his head resembled a half-eaten peach. No kidding.

Since I was such a wizard with words, I managed, "What the . . ."

Slim didn't miss a beat. He used his right hand to circle his face. "Plastic surgery gone awry. Let me tell you who not to use."

I laughed. "Your looks may be gone, but at least you still have your sense of humor."

We did the guy thing and leaned in and tapped each other's back. I pulled back first. "Seriously, buddy, what happened to your face?" I motioned toward the two Adirondack chairs on my porch and walked to the farthest one. "And it's fine you came by for a visit, but why so early?"

Slim didn't sit. "Well, I'm still on East Coast time and I know you're an early riser and would be awake. I have some news to share. Two big things, in fact." He looked left and right, then back to me. "Can we, uh, maybe talk inside?"

Something in his eyes got me moving. It wasn't paranoia, necessarily, more like uneasiness. I waved him inside and quickly closed the door. When I turned back and saw Slim wringing his hands, I knew the situation was more serious than I'd originally thought.

I peeked out the small window on my front door and scanned the area. The wind swept down the street and swayed the palm trees. No people were around, and nothing seemed out of the ordinary.

I looked at Slim. "You think you were followed, don't you?"

"No, not necessarily." He sighed. "Okay, maybe. I'm not sure actually."

I glared at him. Normally the man was incredibly decisive and not the wavering sort.

"Are we in danger, buddy? From whoever bashed in your face? You know Simon's here."

Slim hung his head. "I knew you'd gotten weekend visits back. Since it's Monday, I hoped he wouldn't be here."

"He's sleeping right now, probably for another twenty minutes. Gina picks him up at eight on Monday mornings. You wouldn't bring danger to my house, right?"

"No," he shot back. "We're okay. I'm pretty sure I wasn't followed. I'm just being extra cautious, a little paranoid maybe. Like I said, I've got big news. And I'm on edge."

"Well, now I'm on edge, too. That face would put anyone on edge. Tell me what the hell's going on."

I ushered Slim through my two-bedroom beach home toward the back of the house. When we arrived at the kitchen, I offered him a chair, which he struggled into. I sat in the chair across from him, waiting for him to speak.

Slim took a deep breath, then said, "The Rat's alive, buddy. He's alive. And he's been captured."

He kept talking, but I didn't listen. Hearing that name shocked me. I leaned back and looked up at the ceiling. Slim was right; this was big news. Huge news, in fact. I ran both hands over my bald head, thinking about the Rat, whose real name was Anurat Wu.

The Rat was a former general in the Royal Thai Army, though his infamy came from the ruthless warlord title he achieved later in life. The man was responsible for a vast human trafficking ring. Many of his victims were trafficked through the Long Beach port, which is how Slim and I got involved. We'd both been successful in our military careers, so we'd been recruited to work for a government black ops organization called, *The Activity*. On my final mission with *The Activity* we were commissioned to take out the Rat.

To make a long story short, we traveled to Thailand and worked in conjunction with the Royal Thai Army to capture or kill (preferably) the Rat. Slim and I acted in haste on some faulty intel and got into a massive firefight with the Rat's soldiers. The mission eventually became public and rumors started swirling about the Rat's death in the shootout. The Thai government, however, never confirmed or denied the mission or mentioned a thing about the Rat.

Slim and I weren't convinced the Rat was killed. We believed the speculation over his death added to his criminal credibility and infamy, which was why he never came out of hiding. Anyway, we didn't have proof he was alive until now.

"Crazy, huh?" Slim leaned forward and shook my hand to snap me out of it.

I looked at him and swallowed. "We knew it, didn't we?"

He nodded. "We did. And the feds asked me to testify against him. Which, of course, I agreed to."

I pointed at his face. "So the Rat found out you were testifying against him and paid you a visit hoping you'd rethink your decision."

"Well, the Rat didn't, but his goons certainly did." Slim gestured at the full French Press on the counter. "I'll pour us some coffee." He clawed at his belly as he struggled out of the chair. "Hopefully it will help my bellyache. My pain meds are wreaking havoc on my body, or maybe it was the room service breakfast I had."

"So where'd they find the Rat?"

While Slim poured the coffee, he said, "Holed up in some run-down crack building on the east side of L.A. A few months ago, the feds received a tip concerning his whereabouts. Once they confirmed via facial recognition that it was the Rat, they arrested him. But the Rat claimed to be someone else and lawyered up. He wasn't an American citizen, and he'd never been arrested, so the feds had no fingerprints, no DNA, no dental records, absolutely nothing to identify him with. The only way to confirm his identity was to approach the Thai government for help. Except the—"

I pounded my fist on the table. "The Thai government wanted to keep everything under wraps, wanted nothing to do with the case."

Slim nodded. "Right, but eventually they acquiesced, agreeing to send over his fingerprints as long as our government kept the Rat's capture secret."

I scoffed. "Of course."

Slim slid a cup of coffee in front of me and eased back into his chair. "Buddy, we're talking super-secret stuff here. I mean hush-hush orders issued straight from the executive cabinet. Specifically, the attorney general's office."

"That high?"

"Yup."

I thought about it for a moment. "A win's a win, I guess. The only way this could've been better is if you or I caught him. Then the Rat would've never made it to a private trial in some federal judge's office."

"There may not even be a trial," Slim said, leaning forward and grimacing in pain.

4

I furrowed my brow. "What? How come?"

"Since the Rat's lawyer knows our government needs to keep the situation quiet, the lawyer is trying to broker a deal with the attorney general. The lawyer said the Rat will formally admit his guilt in the Long Beach murders and take the death sentence in exchange for not being sent to Texas and prosecuted for those murders."

"Why would he do that?"

"The Rat doesn't want to die. He knows if he's sent to Texas, he'll fry. If he gets the death penalty in California, he'll never fry. Not even close."

"Right. When was the last time California killed a death penalty convict?"

"2006," Slim stated. "And Texas always follows through. Always. Basically, the Rat claims to be a changed man and doesn't want to die, so he doesn't want to be sent to Texas and prosecuted."

I rolled my eyes at the irony. Over a period of more than six years the Rat had sent thousands of shipping containers filled with kidnapped Thai women into our country through the Long Beach port. One container had been partially damaged during the long voyage. Two of the large air holes had been crushed, cutting off most of the air. The thirty women suffered a slow, agonizing death. By the time the container reached Long Beach, the smell alone alerted port authorities. Something similar happened in Texas but on a smaller scale. Twelve women died in a smaller shipping container, but not from lack of air. That container simply got lost in the large stack of containers on the docks. The women died from dehydration.

"So," I said, "which agency brought you on board?"

"The U.S. attorney for the Central California district. Long Beach is under his jurisdiction. That attorney is a bulldog and heavily in favor of capital punishment. He's bucking his superiors because he doesn't want to grant this deal and have the Rat avoid prosecution for Texas. He wants justice, and so does the Texas AG. Those guys want me to give my testimony next week to help convince the top AG to not take the deal."

"Do you need me to testify also? Or maybe I should take your place since you're not exactly easy on the eyes."

"Good one, but no, you're not needed. In fact, I really shouldn't be talking about any of this. I'm actually going against a court order. But I absolutely had to tell you."

I nodded. "I imagine you told the U.S. attorney you didn't want witness protection. Right?"

"Of course." Slim took a sip of coffee and leaned back.

At that point, I heard my four-year-old son Simon shuffling down the stairs. Since I didn't want him to see Slim in his current state, I excused myself and scooped Simon up on the bottom step. I took him to my bedroom upstairs and turned on an episode of Paw Patrol.

When I got back to the kitchen, I remembered Slim said he had two pieces of news to share. "What's the other big news you have?"

Slim scraped his chair forward, clutching at his belly.

"That coffee doesn't seem to be helping," I said.

"Not at all." He pushed out a pained breath, then said, "So I came here for another reason, not just to tell you about the Rat." He swallowed. "I need your help, pal."

I waited.

He swallowed again. "With my latest client." He paused and emitted a slow breath. Clearly, his belly was in bad shape. He finally managed, "It's Henrietta Valenzuela, Chase."

"What?" I said, leaning forward. "The woman running for president?"

He nodded.

After Slim left *The Activity*, he started a private investigation agency. His primary clientele were members of congress. I imagined Henrietta Valenzuela was his highest profile client to date.

"She hired me to investigate her opponent." Slim paused and used his sleeve to wipe his sweaty forehead.

When he didn't continue after a few seconds, I stared at my friend. Right away I noticed his glazed eyes, which seemed to be looking right through me.

"You alright, pal?" I waved my hand in front of his face.

Slim didn't respond. Instead, he slipped off the chair and landed on all fours. He staggered to his feet, only to collapse onto his knees a moment later, all the while clutching his belly. When he started convulsing and clawing at his throat, I knew it was serious.

Figuring he may puke, I grabbed the garbage can from under the sink and placed it in front of his knees. Slim choked and sputtered, but he didn't puke. Instead, he gurgled up a foamy blood ball. It bubbled up and spilled over his bottom lip, then started dripping down his chin.

Before I knew it, Slim's eyes rolled back and the big man toppled forward; his face careening off the garbage can and smacking against the linoleum floor.

CHAPTER TWO

Corner of 14th and Ocean Ave.
Seal Beach, CA

THE EMPLOYEE STUDIED the license plate of the Chevy Caprice as it roared down the street.

He memorized the combination of letters and numbers and dialed a trusted associate with access to the DMV database. When his associate picked up, the employee recited the Caprice's license plate. He also mentioned the plate number of the woman's vehicle that had arrived minutes ago. Then he hung up. Nothing more needed to be said. The associate would text back the registered owners' names within minutes.

The employee climbed out of his grey Honda Civic, which was parked two blocks down from the house Hans Schlimmergaard had visited. He stretched, then straightened his white kitchen uniform and leaned against a palm tree. Above the lapel on the left side of the white jacket were the words, Hilton Hotels & Resorts.

He fished out a cigarette and lighter from his jacket pocket. He turned his back to the wind and covered his mouth while lighting the cigarette. The hand holding the lighter shook noticeably, but not from nerves, from anger. A few hours ago, the employee thought he'd planned the perfect undetected murder.

But it didn't go as planned. Not even close.

To calm his rage, the employee inhaled deeply on the cigarette, then slowly released the smoke through his nose. Hans Schlimmergaard should've died quietly in the emptiness of his hotel room. A maid should've found his dead body sometime mid-morning, whenever the room was scheduled to be cleaned. The cause of death would've likely been labeled a heart attack.

He took another deep drag, balling his fists and then releasing them. He couldn't believe Hans left his hotel room to visit someone so early in the morning. It would've been one thing if Hans visited his grandma or elderly aunt, but this man looked to be a friend or colleague. Which meant Hans might've told the man everything. And that meant adding another body to the count. Maybe two, though the woman was in the house only a minute before the man rushed out, so he had no time to tell her anything.

Killing wasn't a problem for the employee. The problem was his employer, who was already pissed to learn Hans had made it out of the hotel alive. His employer had specifically instructed minimal damage on this job. Hans's death was supposed to be under the radar. Zero attention. Now the employee would have to tell his employer he had another problem that needed cleaning.

Just then the cellphone in his pocket buzzed.

He took out the phone and read the names on the screen: Garrison Chase, Karla Dickerson.

CHAPTER THREE

Intensive Care Unit
Long Beach Medical Center

THINGS WEREN'T LOOKING good for Slim. I stood outside his small, private room in the ICU at Long Beach Medical. A large window overlooked his hospital bed. Slim's giant frame eclipsed the bed itself. Two different IV's loomed over the bed, dripping some sort of clear fluids into his veins. Slim had an oxygen mask over his mouth and nose.

My hands were sweaty, so I wiped them on my pants. Moments ago, Slim's physician told me Slim had a fifty percent chance of making it, which meant the doc obviously had no clue what was going to happen.

Leaning against the window, I stared at Slim and thought about his wife, Freda. She deserved a call right away. And I had every intention of calling her. But I wanted to wait a little longer in hopes of some positive information from the doc.

I felt a hand gently touch my left shoulder. Right away I knew it was Karla. She had an unmistakable, warm touch.

"Here you go," she said, stepping beside me. "I figured you needed this."

She handed me a cup of coffee from my favorite Italian coffee shop, Giuseppe's.

"It's like you're in my head."

She nodded toward his hospital bed. "How's he doing?"

Karla's sandy blonde hair didn't move when she nodded, which wasn't surprising since she kept it short and stylish. I always thought Karla looked like a more attractive version of Meg Ryan, when Meg was in her prime.

"Doc says it's tenuous. Touch and go for the next few hours."

She put her arm around me and gave a squeeze. "He obviously survived a brutal beating, so hopefully he'll survive this. If anyone can, it's Slim."

Karla and I had been dating for almost a year. She met Slim the last time he was at my place, which was six months ago.

"It's bad, Karla, real bad. Blood spilled out of his mouth. He collapsed and hasn't regained consciousness since."

"So what happened? What's the story?"

"Let's talk inside Slim's room." I opened the door for her.

She walked in and took a seat in an orange chair to the left of Slim's bed. "You sure we're allowed in here?"

"Yeah. I flashed my badge and told the nurses I needed to keep a protective eye on him."

Karla nodded. She knew the power of the FBI badge. We were both special agents with the FBI. We'd met on a crazy case a little over a year ago. Seeing each other wasn't controversial since Karla worked in the L.A. field office and I worked out of the Long Beach resident agency.

Before going into details about Slim, I wanted to know about Simon. Karla had rushed over to keep an eye on Simon while I followed the ambulance to the hospital. I'd also asked her to take Simon to daycare. Since Gina, my ex-wife, overreacted about most things, I hoped to keep Gina in the dark about Slim's collapse.

"So how'd it go at drop off?"

"Fine," she said. "How'd it go with Gina? That's the real question."

I shrugged. "My call went to voicemail. I told her I had to rush to the hospital to visit a friend, and that I'd get Simon to daycare."

She eyed me. "Chase, come on. Is she going to freak out when she learns I dropped him off?"

"It'll be fine," I said, though I wasn't so sure.

To avoid Karla's scrutiny, I launched into Slim's story. Since I had to maintain the classified status of the Rat's case, I only referred to the Rat as a warlord, and I didn't mention anything about the country he was from. I hoped those were broad enough details to not get me or Slim in trouble.

At the end of my story Karla stared straight ahead, digesting the details and repercussions and ramifications. About twenty seconds later, she said, "So he's beaten to discourage his testimony, then he spits up blood and collapses. Is that a result of the beating? Or another attempt on his life?"

"Good questions," I said. "I've been thinking about the same things since arriving at the hospital. Slim's collapse could be a reaction to the pain meds he's on, but it seemed too dramatic. I consulted with the doc and he agreed, though he hesitated to say anything definitive until a toxicology report is back. The thing is, I know this warlord and what he's capable of. My guess would be Slim was poisoned."

"How would that have happened?"

"This warlord has a criminal reach like no other. Perhaps it was something he recently ate, or maybe his pain meds were tampered with."

Karla walked over and reached for my left hip. She patted my service piece, a Glock 19M.

"What's going on?" I asked.

"Making sure you're carrying. This warlord guy has already gone to big lengths to silence Slim, maybe twice, so he may be sending someone to finish the job. And since you have a sordid history with this warlord as well, you could be next."

She had a point.

Karla gestured at my left sleeve. "Looks like you have blood on you, hopefully it's not yours."

I picked up my arm and looked at my sleeve. I had a blood spot, about the size of a softball, around where my elbow was. "Must've got that when I wrestled Slim to his side. He broke his nose when he hit the floor. It was pretty bloody in my kitchen by the time the paramedics arrived."

Karla pointed at my right leg. "And some on the bottom of your pants."

"Maybe I should change into some scrubs. I'm a mess."

"You are," she said, walking back to the chair. After taking a seat, she said, "So I take it you called Slim's wife."

I winced.

"You're kidding me," she said.

"I wanted more information on his condition, maybe something positive from the doc before calling Freda."

"Call her now, Chase. She needs to know."

Karla waited until I nodded. "Good. I'll give you some privacy." She left the hospital room, squeezing my arm on the way out.

I flipped open my phone. Yes, I was one of the few people left on earth that still used a flip phone. It was a recent purchase for me, if you can believe it. I tried for years to get by without a phone since I didn't want to be that person glancing at the thing all the time. I owned an old, thin Motorola Razr with zero bells and whistles.

Just as the phone started ringing in my ear, I ended the call because one of Slim's monitors distracted me. It sounded like Slim's heartbeat was starting to race.

A tap sounded on the window. I looked back. Karla nodded at the cell in my hand. I held up a finger and turned back to Slim. That was when I noticed his foot twitching.

Karla must've seen it, too, because she was in the room within seconds.

By the time I made it to Slim's bedside, my buddy's eyes were flickering open. The heart monitor seemed to be gathering steam, beeping faster and faster.

Slim blinked a few times. Within seconds his eyes found me. He stared for a moment, then his eyes darted around the room. His left hand came up. Figuring he was about to reach for his oxygen mask and pull it off, I intercepted his hand. I didn't want him off oxygen, not with his heart racing out of control.

Slim shook his head and fought off my hand, so I let go. Instead of reaching for his mask, however, he pointed across the room. Karla and I followed his finger.

He appeared to be pointing at a small cubby system to the right of the window. There were six holes of various sizes that held a patient's personal belongings. Slim's clothes, shoes, wallet, and cell were in the cubby holes. Karla hustled over and held up his clothes in one hand and his wallet and cell in the other. Slim pointed at the hand that held his wallet and cell, then he waved her over.

Slim motioned at the wallet as Karla approached the bed. Karla handed it to him. With a shaky hand, Slim opened the wallet and rifled through his cards. After a moment of searching, he found what he was looking for and flicked the business card in my direction.

I picked it up. It was a business card for some lawyer.

Slim wrestled with his oxygen mask. I helped him pull it down a little.

He swallowed.

I leaned forward.

He spoke in a quiet, raspy voice. "Call him. A pal of mine, my go between with the U.S. attorney. . ." He paused and gathered some strength. Then he continued in a whisper. "Tell him what happened." With a weak hand, he pulled me closer. "Testify in my place if I don't make it. Promise me, Chase."

Before I could respond, Slim's eyes went wide and his pupils morphed into big, black circles.

I wrestled the mask back on as his eyes turned glassy.

Then they clamped shut. After that, I heard that awful sound from the heartrate monitor. The one I've never actually heard in person, though I've heard it many times on TV shows and movies: the dreaded sound of a flat-lining heart.

I jammed my finger on the nurses' call button and yelled for help. Two nurses rushed into the room within ten seconds. When they realized the severity of Slim's condition, one of them barked at us to get out, which I was fine with.

We stepped outside the room. Karla watched the nurses try to save Slim's life through the window. I couldn't do that, so I paced the hallway, wringing my hands.

I rarely felt afraid. I mean, truly afraid. But I feared losing Slim. He was a decent, honorable man that saved my life on numerous occasions. Growing up, I didn't have a great fatherly figure to look up to. Slim was ten years older than me, so I didn't view him as a father figure exactly, more like an older brother that I looked up to and admired.

I was also afraid of calling Freda and telling her the love of her life passed away. Nobody wanted to call a wife and tell her she's now a widow and must raise three teenage boys by herself. But if Slim died, I couldn't let a doctor or hospital administrator call Freda and deliver that news. It had to be me.

I blew out a deep breath and prayed my friend wouldn't die.

CHAPTER FOUR

WHILE PACING THE ICU hallway, Slim's doctor brushed past me quickly. It was never good seeing a doctor rush into a hospital room like that.

"What's happening?" I yelled to Karla.

She turned from the window and walked my direction. "Honestly, I'm not sure. One of the nurses just closed the blinds on the window. From what I saw it didn't look good. The last thing I saw was the paddles coming out."

I ran my hand over my bald head and sighed. While I leaned against the wall, Karla started pacing.

Two, maybe three minutes later, Karla came over and touched my shoulder. "Listen, no point in both of us worrying and pacing this hallway. I'm going to swing by work and check-in, then I'll head over to your place and grab you a change of clothes."

"That's nice, Karla, but you don't have to."

"I know I don't have to, but I want to. It gives me something to do. That way I don't feel so useless." Before I could respond, she said, "You have to call Freda, right away."

I nodded, squeezed her hand, and watched her leave. Then I ducked into an empty ICU room and dialed Slim's home number. Five long rings later the answering machine picked up. I left a quick message for Freda. Told her it was an emergency and to call me back asap.

After that, I dug out the business card and called Jimmy Schuberman. He was Slim's lawyer friend. I needed to ask him some questions and update him on Slim's status. Unfortunately, that call went to voicemail, too. So I dialed my boss, Frank Lemming, to fill him in on my morning. But he didn't pick up either.

Frustrated, I snapped my cell shut. No-one answered their cell these days, which sort of begged the question why people even had them. The doc suddenly whisked by the door.

I hustled after him. "Doc, how's he doing? Did he make it?"

The doc turned and nodded, but he didn't stop walking. "Just barely. It's still touch and go, Agent Chase. The next few hours are crucial."

I matched his pace. "What exactly happened?"

"He coded."

"Right, I figured that. Anything else you can tell me?"

He stopped and faced me. ""Honestly, he's either on his way to recovery or on his way to further complications, which means most likely death."

Again with the useless information, though I refrained from making a sarcastic comment.

The doc must've sensed my frustration, so he elaborated. "Coding and then recovering tells me one of two things: Either his body rejected whatever's inside him and that was the worst of it and your colleague will recover in the next day or so. Or his body absorbed too much of whatever toxin's inside and coding was just the beginning of the end. Only time will tell. If his heart stops again, we probably won't be able to bring him back." He put his left hand on my shoulder. "I'm sorry. I wish I knew more or had better news." He paused. "Did you notify his next of kin?"

"I put in a call."

The doc nodded. "I'm heading to the lab to light a fire under those guys. I need to see his tox report to have an idea of what we're dealing with."

With that, he turned and left.

I walked to Slim's room to peek in on him, but the blinds were still closed, so I went back to the empty room. My thoughts quickly turned dark, thinking about Slim's death and what that would mean for Freda, and for his teenage sons.

To keep my mind off Slim's dire predicament, I thought about what he'd said right before collapsing in my kitchen. He'd mentioned that he really needed my help with his latest client: Henrietta Valenzuela.

What was that all about? I scratched at the stubble on my face.

The current president was on his way out after serving two terms. Primary season had just finished and there were now two candidates for the next president: Congresswoman Henrietta Valenzuela and a senator named Bradford Bollinger. All Slim said was that he was investigating Henrietta's opponent.

Why would he need my help?

As my mind contemplated some theories, a nurse appeared at the doorway and interrupted my thoughts.

"There's someone here to see you, Agent Chase."

"See me? Who?"

"A woman. She claims to be your ex-wife. She's been looking around the hospital for you. To be honest, she's making a bit of a scene."

I buried my face in my hands for a second, then looked up at the nurse. "You're kidding me, right? Please tell me you're kidding."

"I wish I were."

"I didn't hear anyone making a scene."

"Well," the nurse said, "she's not allowed in the ICU. She's outside the main doors. She's being argumentative, insisting on either speaking with you or the nurse manager."

I nodded. When wasn't Gina combative?

"Sorry about that," I said. "I'll take care of it."

"That would be appreciated."

She turned and left. I followed behind her, apologizing to the staff at the nurse's desk as I slipped out of the ICU.

Gina was in my face before the door closed. The first thing I noticed, as always with Gina, was a mouth full of gum. The woman chewed two packs of spearmint gum every day, easily.

"You're unbelievable," she said in between chews. "On so many different levels."

I didn't say anything. Sometimes it was best to stay quiet with Gina and let her get it out, sometimes it wasn't.

"Don't you do this," she said, breathing minty fire in my face. She flicked back her shoulder length jet black hair. "Don't you be silent and pretend to take the high road here. Don't give me that innocent face look."

My guess was that daycare had called Gina to let her know about Karla dropping off Simon. Gina's anger was somewhat understandable. I'd made a big deal about Gina's boyfriend never being alone with Simon. Of course, that situation was much different. Gina was dating my former therapist— court-appointed former therapist, that is. They started dating a little while after my mandatory treatment, but still, the whole thing was beyond unethical.

"Speak, Garrison." Her blue eyes narrowed to two dark slits.

I held my hands up. "What?" As soon I did it, I regretted it. I should've known better.

Gina pounced. She launched forward and poked me in the chest. "You're gonna stand there and pretend that nothing happened this morning? That whatever happened is no big deal? Is that so?"

A few people walking by stopped and looked. There was a nurses' station a little way down the hall. I saw two nurses lean forward and peer over the desk.

I probably should've answered Gina right away, but instead I waved my hand behind her and deflected. "Please, you're making a scene. People are watching. Let's go somewhere—"

"I don't care," she said, not letting me finish. "Everyone can listen. What I care about is hearing the truth from you." She rolled her eyes. "For once, just once, Garrison."

"Listen, you're right, I should've told you I had Karla drop off Simon at daycare. It's—"

She held up her hand. "Garrison, this isn't about that. Though you're the hypocrite of the year after how much you've drilled into me that Simon can't be alone with my boyfriend. I actually trust Karla with Simon more than you."

I ignored the jab. "Why are you so heated then?"

She pointed over my shoulder, toward the ICU. "Why you're here, Garrison."

"What do you mean?"

"Honestly?" She threw up her hands, waiting for me to speak.

I didn't respond.

"There it is," she said. "No surprise at all. You can't ever give it to me straight. Which I guess isn't surprising since you don't want me to know the truth. Right?"

"What are you talking about?"

She jabbed her finger over my shoulder. "His face, Garrison. His fricking face! You know I keep in contact with several people from our old neighborhood. I got a call from a girlfriend who witnessed your buddy being carted off in the ambulance. Even from across the street she could see how messed up his face was."

"Wait," I held up my left hand. "You think I beat Slim to a pulp? Is that what this is about?"

"Yes, Sherlock. But what really bothers me is it all happened while *my* son was in the house."

"Geez, Gina, we didn't fight. Slim was attacked a few days before coming to my house, maybe even a week ago. Those injuries to his face are old. You can ask the doc, for crying out loud. Slim collapsed in my kitchen. For all I know, he had a heart attack."

"See, I knew it. I knew you'd pretend it was no big deal."

Anger rose up in me like bile in my throat. I wanted to push it down, keep it at bay, but I couldn't. I stabbed my finger at her. "This is serious, Gina. The man's life is at stake, which has nothing to do with me."

She turned away, thought for a moment, then spun back. "Even if you didn't beat him, Garrison, what happened then? What's the story? I remember Slim, you know. I remember what you told me about him. I mean, who gets beat like that? Either someone who's in big trouble or someone with a checkered past. And both of you certainly have the latter. Honestly, I don't even care about his past or yours. Except for when it affects *my* son—"

"Stop it," I said loudly. "He's *our* son, not yours. And I'd never do anything to harm him or jeopardize his safety."

"I understand you're not trying to deliberately harm him, but you have a disastrous past, which is always going to follow you. I'm tired of Simon getting mixed up in your issues."

She had a point, which I hated to admit. Honestly, I didn't know how to respond to that comment.

Gina kept at it. "What's your perfectly good explanation for his messed-up face and heart attack? What's the truth? Go ahead, enlighten me."

I hesitated to answer. Even if I could tell her the truth about Slim and the Rat, should I? The truth was worse.

Gina stepped forward. "You just can't tell the truth. Can you?" She pointed at me. "Eventually I'll find out, Garrison. And if I discover you and your buddy are mixed up in something dangerous, that will be the end of our weekend arrangement. For good."

She spun and walked away, only to suddenly stop and turn around. "And you obviously forgot about the money you owe me, didn't you? You're something else."

Damn. This weekend was my son's fourth birthday party and I'd agreed to pay 200 bucks for the bounce house. I was supposed to give Gina the money this morning when she picked up Simon.

"I sort of did forget, Gina."

"Sort of forget? Well you can sort of forget about coming then."

"Please, Gina, don't do that."

She shook her head. "I don't want you there."

"Hear me out," I said, taking a deep breath. "I put the money in an envelope and left it on my bedside table, but I got a little distracted with the medical emergency. My place is on your way to work, why don't you swing by and grab the money. Here." I dug my house key from my pocket and held it out.

She snatched it. "I'll get the money because you promised to pay, but I never promised you could go. I'd rather you not be there. And I know my parents certainly don't want you there."

"I know it's on your weekend with him, but I just want to be there for the party."

She shook her head.

"Just think about it, Gina."

She walked away without saying a word.

I yelled after her. "Please, Gina. Come on."

"Fine," she shouted over her shoulder. "I'll think about it."

She opened the stairwell door and disappeared. As the door closed, I noticed three nurses standing in the hallway, slightly down from the door, staring right at me.

One of them had her hands on her hips.

CHAPTER FIVE

I SLINKED BACK into the ICU and hid in the empty room. I sat in an orange chair by the hospital bed. My thoughts ran rampant down a dark tunnel with no end in sight.

A good friend was on his deathbed, my ex-wife was once again irate with me, and I was most likely not welcome at my own son's birthday party.

Getting up, I tried to calm my mind by pacing the room, but it did nothing for my tanking thoughts.

What distracted me was my cell ringing. I looked at the screen: Freda.

Taking a deep breath, I answered the call and delivered the bad news. At first, Freda panicked when she heard about Slim, then she was in a hurry to end the conversation since she needed to book the soonest flight to the West Coast.

After the call, I left the room and headed to Slim's. The blinds on his window were open again. Slim was in the same position he was before his heart stopped: flat on his back with an oxygen mask on and two IVs attached to either arm.

So far nothing had changed. We were right back to where we were an hour ago. I tugged at the collar of my shirt. It felt like it was somehow choking me. The sterile, antiseptic smell of the hospital filled my nostrils and seemed to be getting stronger every second, which made me suddenly feel a little nauseous.

I had to get some fresh air.

I walked back to the nurse's desk and checked in with one of the nurses, told her I was stepping out for a bit and needed hospital security to keep an eye on Slim. I wanted better protection for Slim, but I couldn't just call the cops or the feds and demand protection. I first needed confirmation of foul play, then I needed to speak with Jimmy the lawyer to see how much I could reveal to authorities.

Once outside the hospital, I decided on a drive. I glanced at my watch: 9:30. It was past rush hour so the L.A. freeways would be relatively uncongested. Taking a drive without traffic always helped clear my head.

Within minutes, my green '86 Chevy Caprice hummed south down the 405 freeway. Before I was out of Long Beach, my cell chirped in my pocket. I dug it out. It was a text from Gina.

It read: *Thought about it. It's a no. Don't come.*

In a knee jerk reaction, I threw the phone across the car. The cell smashed against the passenger door and fell to the floorboard in pieces. I gripped the steering wheel and tried to dissipate my anger by squeezing, but it didn't help. So I floored the Caprice and rocketed south down the freeway.

I drove with no clear destination in mind. All I wanted was to get out of the city for a bit and see the ocean. That usually helped calm me down.

After merging onto the 5, I kept driving south, past San Juan Capistrano and San Clemente. I felt a little more tranquil once I was past San Clemente and the Pacific Ocean came into view.

As I drove along the sea stretch, I told myself I'd think positive thoughts. But telling myself and actually doing it were two separate concepts. I just couldn't stop thinking about losing my weekend visits with Simon.

I knew I'd be tapped as a witness against the Rat if Slim died. And I'd testify without hesitation. In fact, I'd do everything in my power to make sure justice was fully served against that man. However, testifying would then put my life directly in danger. And if Gina somehow discovered my life was in danger, she'd go straight to a custody judge and file a motion to have my weekend visits revoked, citing an unsafe environment at my house. But I highly doubted Gina would ever find out any details concerning the Rat. Not only was Slim's case classified, but Gina had no friends or relationships with people who knew Slim other than me.

That made me feel slightly better. Until, that is, my mind played devil's advocate.

I did need to provide a safe home for Simon; that was obviously super important. For my son's sake, should I reconsider testifying against the Rat if Slim didn't make it? Was that the wisest move? Or could I somehow feed my sense of justice and protect Simon, all at the same time?

As I thought about that situation, I realized I'd exited off the freeway and was navigating through a familiar neighborhood in Oceanside. I looked at my watch. I'd been driving for a little over an hour.

Two left hand turns later, I drove down a familiar street, then pulled into an even more familiar driveway. I parked on the right-hand side and shut off the engine. Looking up at the house, I shook my head.

What the hell was I doing here?

I was in front of my best friend's house, Mick Cranston. There were no cars in the driveway, so it appeared nobody was home. However, as I glanced at the house, I thought I saw the edge of the curtains in an upper bedroom window move slightly, but I wasn't positive.

Though the minivan wasn't in the driveway, it could be in the garage, which meant my best friend's wife may be home. If she was home, she probably wouldn't come running out to greet me. In fact, I bet she wouldn't even answer the door if I rang the bell.

We had a rocky relationship, and that was putting it mildly.

Mick and I had been a sniper-spotter team in the Marines years ago. We'd also worked together on a few black ops missions as operatives. About a year ago, I involved Mick in an intense case that injured him and threatened his family.

Mick's wife, Julie, didn't want anything to do with me. I hadn't talked to her in over a year, and I couldn't remember the last time I was at their house. Maybe two years now?

I drummed my fingers on the steering wheel, figuring my sub-conscience directed me here because it would be nice to get Mick's input on everything that had happened with Slim. Of course, it was plain stupid to be at Mick's house during the middle of the day. Like me, he was no longer in the operative business. He now worked down the road at Camp Pendleton as a sniper instructor. Mick's Jeep wasn't in the driveway, so he was obviously at work.

I looked at the house one more time and debated ringing the doorbell. A moment later, I decided that was a terrible and potentially super awkward idea if Julie was home, so I fired up the Caprice.

Before leaving the driveway, I thought that perhaps Jimmy Schuberman had called me back. The hospital may have called, too, since I'd asked one of the ICU nurses to call me if there were any changes in Slim's condition. Karla may be wondering where I was as well.

So I grabbed the pieces of my cell off the floorboard and tried my best to put it back together. There was a crack in the cell's screen, the back of the case had come off, and the battery had fallen out. At first, I wasn't convinced I'd broken the phone, but when I powered it up and nothing happened, I knew I'd broken it. I tossed the cell on the passenger seat and decided to head straight back to the hospital and check in on Slim.

It took me about seventy minutes to arrive at the Long Beach Medical parking lot. In total, I'd been gone from the hospital a little over two hours. Surely there would be some sort of update on Slim's condition. And hopefully a positive one.

Before exiting the Caprice, I swept up the cell and put it in my pocket. As I did, I felt the back of the case wasn't flush with the rest of the cell, so I flipped it over. Upon further inspection, I realized I hadn't put the cell together properly. When I took the back case off, and the battery easily dropped out, I quickly realized my mistake. I'd put the cell together with the battery in the wrong direction.

Scoffing at my stupidity, I put the battery in the right direction and powered up the phone. Within a minute, it beeped, alerting me to several missed calls and two voicemails. Frank, my boss, had made three of the calls and left one voicemail. Which wasn't surprising since I hadn't checked in with him today. The other voicemail was from Slim's doctor. He let me know the tox report was in and that things looked promising. He wanted me to check in with him at the hospital asap.

Finally, some good news.

Then I listened to Frank's voicemail:

"Chase, it's Frank. There's been . . ." He paused and cleared his throat.

"There's been an incident." My heart started beating faster as Frank continued: "I'm at your house . . ." He paused again.

My house? What the hell's he doing at my house?

"Just get over here," he continued. "It's not something I want to say over the phone or on voicemail. Just get to your house."

I swallowed.

The voicemail continued: "Please, just get to your house, Chase. Immediately."

Then he hung up.

CHAPTER SIX

12th and Ocean Ave.
Seal Beach, CA

WHEN I BURNED around the corner of twelfth street and saw the circus in front of my house, my heart paused. On the seven-minute ride to my place, I tried to convince myself that maybe it was a burglary or fire at my house. Maybe nobody was inside. Maybe nobody was harmed.

Deep down I knew better.

With all the vehicles around I couldn't park close to my house, so I wheeled the Caprice over to the side of the road, blocking someone's driveway, and hopped out. I left the keys in the vehicle, and maybe I even left it running. I wasn't sure.

As I ran to my place, my eyes didn't focus on the cop cars, news vans, or the ambulance out front. My eyes went straight to the street in front of my house where visitors typically park, searching desperately for Gina or Karla's vehicle.

Both were there, parked right in front of my house. One car in front of the other. My mind raced, even faster than my heart.

Where's Frank? Where's Frank?

My eyes flicked through the sea of officers and detectives. Frank was by my front porch. He was an easy man to spot in a crowd since he had the build and stature of a fire hydrant.

Frank spoke with a couple of plain clothes cops from the Long Beach City PD; I recognized one of them. I couldn't find Karla, though, or Gina in the crowd of people.

Were they both inside? Were they both . . .? I couldn't finish the thought.

As I approached the police line, I ducked under the yellow tape and didn't bother to pull out my badge. A uniformed officer chased after me, yelling for me to stop.

I picked up my pace.

The commotion brought Frank into the mix. He waved off the officer and intercepted me.

"What the hell's happening, Frank?" I jabbed my finger at my house. "Who's in there?"

Frank held up both hands, almost touching my chest. "Let's not make a scene."

I knew he meant well, and that he was just trying to calm me down, but I snapped at him anyway. "Now, Frank, tell me. Right now."

"There's several reporters around," he said. "We have a real situation here, Chase."

My blood boiled. "Really? So this isn't a pop-up booster for the local PD?"

He lowered his hands. "Fair enough. I'll tell you what's going on, but I also have something to show you. And I don't want to do it here, not out in the open, not with these reporters lurking."

I glanced around. Dammit, Frank was right. Two large cameras were trained on us.

Frank motioned toward a cruiser. "Let's talk in the backseat."

"How about my backyard?" I countered.

"Hell no. You can't go anywhere near your place. In fact, you're already too close. Let's go."

I reluctantly followed Frank to the cruiser, slipping into the passenger side of the backseat. Frank sat to my left.

I spoke quietly but forcefully. "Who's in there, Frank?"

He opened his mouth to tell me, then stopped himself and winced.

I held my breath.

"Gina," Frank managed to say. "It's Gina. She was murdered."

I collapsed into the seat, deflating. I put both hands over my face.

"I'm sorry, Chase. I really am."

Dropping my hands, I looked at Frank. "Karla's okay? She's safe?"

He nodded. "She found the body."

For a second, I felt relief, happy Karla was alive and well, but then Simon's face popped into my mind. I put my hands over my face again and shook my head, thinking about Gina. She and I had some serious problems, sure, but she was a decent mother. And Simon loved her a ton.

Frank touched my shoulder. "I hate to say this, but it actually gets worse."

I slowly looked to my left. Clearing my throat, I said, "How?"

"Before I get into this," Frank held up his hand. "Before you get mad, just remember, I'm only doing my job. If I have to go to bat for you, I need details. Preferably before they talk to you." Frank thumbed toward the cops on my front porch.

Now I was the one holding up my hand. "Wait. I'm a suspect? You guys think I'm involved? You gotta be kidding."

"You know as well as I do, everyone is a suspect in the beginning. Now tell me where've you been the last two, two and a half hours. Let's get that out in the open and make sure you have a solid alibi. Then you can tell me why your ex-wife's dead body is in your bedroom."

I sighed. All I wanted to do was race to Simon's daycare and grab my boy. Hug him and hold him and protect him and never let him go. However, my mind went into investigative mode since I immediately knew the situation didn't look good for me. I'd been driving alone the past two hours. I hadn't contacted another human during that time. The worst part: Gina and I had a public spat in which I left the hospital just five minutes or so after her.

Frank nudged my leg. "Listen, the longer you sit there silent, the more nervous I'm getting. Why would Gina be targeted?"

"Frank, my life just changed the moment you told me she was dead. I'm all Simon has now. He's my sole responsibility." I swallowed. "My mind's all over the place."

Frank nodded and gave me a few moments.

After maybe thirty seconds, I turned to Frank. "So my buddy, who's also my mentor from my days with *The Activity*, showed up at my place this morning with his face beaten to crap. He and our local U.S. attorney are working on a classified case together; that's what this is all about. The same person who's after my buddy now wants me. Gina wasn't being targeted; I was. That must be it. I don't want to say any more than that until I speak with the U.S. attorney. Do you know him by chance?"

Frank shook his head. "I don't, but Phil Hornsby does. I believe his name is Ethan Khang."

"Can you get me his number?"

He nodded. "Sure, but not this minute. You still haven't told me where you were."

"Things weren't going well at the hospital with my friend. On top of that, Gina showed up and we had a spat about some parent stuff, so I went for a drive to clear my mind and—"

"Wait," Frank interrupted, "Gina showed up at the hospital and you guys fought? Where? In public?"

I nodded. "It looks bad; I know."

Frank pulled out a handkerchief and dabbed at his forehead. "That's an understatement."

I continued. "I needed to cool down after our spat, so I drove south to Oceanside and ended up at Mick Cranston's. It wasn't planned, just happened."

Frank sat back. "Oh, good, thank goodness. Then Mick can put you an hour or so south in Oceanside. That works."

"Well," I said. "He can't. He wasn't there."

"What about his wife?"

I shook my head. "I didn't get out of the car, just sat in the driveway. Mick's car wasn't there, so I knew he wasn't home. I wasn't sure if Julie was home, and to be honest, I knew she wouldn't want to see me. You know about our past."

Frank nodded. "Did you stop for gas or grab a bite to eat somewhere? Use your credit card at all?"

I shook my head.

"How about a piss? Did you at least stop for a leak?"

"Nope. Didn't stop, didn't see anybody."

"Well, you had your cell on you, so that would've pinged off multiple towers. That will work."

I hung my head. "Actually, it won't."

"What? What do you mean?"

I sighed. "I was pissed at Gina and threw my phone against the passenger door. It broke into pieces and the battery came out, so it wouldn't have pinged off any tower."

"Great," Frank said, looking away. "This isn't good. Not at all."

"Why the worry? You know me, Frank, you know I wouldn't kill my ex-wife. I wasn't even in the same county when she was killed. We'll be able to confirm it somehow. Plus, I'm hoping the U.S. attorney's office will get talkative and shed some light on what's happening with my buddy. And—"

Frank held up his hand and stopped me. "You're being set-up here, that's the worry, Chase."

"How do you know I'm being set-up? Other than the fact that my ex-wife's dead body is in my house, which I guess is bad enough."

Frank pulled out his cell and fiddled with the screen. He slid the phone across the seat and said, "I'm sorry, it's a pretty grisly picture of Gina. GSW to the head, close range. We identified her from her driver's license in her purse. That's how bad it is. Normally I wouldn't show you this, but you have to see what you're up against. Keep the cell low, I don't want the detectives to know I'm showing it to you."

I slid the phone onto my left thigh. I reared back a little when I saw the picture. Honestly, I couldn't tell it was Gina. If Frank hadn't told me, I never would've guessed. The only way I knew it was a woman was the longer hair at the back of the skull, or at least what was left of the skull.

My eyes were also drawn to the gun on the floor beside her, sitting in a pool of blood. The set-up immediately became clear. Whoever killed Gina used one of my guns, my Desert Eagle, which I kept on the top shelf in my closet.

I leaned back and closed my eyes.

Frank cleared his throat. "Cops already know that's your Desert Eagle. And what about that envelope on the bedside table? Cops have questions about that, they find it a little suspicious."

I opened my eyes and looked at the picture again. Gina's body had crumpled to the floor, directly beside the bed and below the bedside table. On the table was the envelope of cash for the bounce house. After putting the cash in the envelope this morning, I'd written 'For Simon' on it.

"That's your handwriting, correct?"

"Yes, but it's innocuous." My eyes stayed focused on the picture. "The money was for Simon's birthday party this weekend. Gina was coming to my house to get it. It means nothing, it's no big deal." I ran my hand over my bald head. "She came into the house to get the money and took the bullet meant for me."

"You're positive?" Frank asked.

I thought about it, then nodded. "The killer was waiting in the bedroom for me. It could've been Karla if she arrived first. Geez. When I didn't show up, the killer shot Gina with my gun to frame me. That's my quick, professional opinion, anyway."

"Okay, I'll go talk with the detectives, explain you weren't even in the county the past two hours and see how they want to proceed. Sorry about all this. Should I mention to them anything about your buddy?"

I shook my head. "Not yet, I'm not even supposed to know. My buddy confided in me, against a court order, mind you. I'm waiting to hear back from his lawyer, so I can get some guidance on what to reveal. Ethan Khang could obviously help with that, too."

Frank nodded. "Hang tight. In the meantime, call my secretary. She'll get you Khang's number."

After Frank left, I called his secretary. She connected me directly to the U.S. attorney's office. However, the call went to Khang's voicemail, so I left Khang a message, telling him to call me back.

Then I looked out the window and searched for Karla. I wanted to flag her over and check-in on her. But I couldn't find her. I leaned back and closed my eyes. The picture of Gina's head filled my mind, so I quickly opened my eyes and stared straight ahead. Soon enough, I found myself gripping both kneecaps and breathing hard.

This was bad. Simon could never know exactly how Gina died. One day he'd find out his mother was murdered, I couldn't stop that from happening, but I didn't want him to know the gruesome extent of it: that his mom's head had been practically blown off. And that the bullet was undoubtedly meant for me.

I thought about my next steps. I had to catch the person responsible for murdering Gina, which was obviously one of the Rat's goons. I'd catch that person and help Slim bring down the Rat. Absolutely. Now that Gina was dead, I didn't have to worry about her discovering the danger I'd be in. However, I did have to make sure Simon was protected.

I figured my mom was the best person to take Simon for a little while. Of course, I'd pick up Simon from daycare today and had to be the one to deliver the bad news: that he'd never see his mother again.

That was too painful and stressful to focus on, so I thought about the cops instead. In their mind, I was the prime suspect. If they took me in and grilled me about Gina's death, I needed to give them a theory on what happened in my house so I wasn't a suspect. But I really couldn't talk about that until I consulted with Slim's lawyer or the U.S. attorney.

I exited the cruiser and leaned against the hood, checking my phone to make sure I hadn't missed any recent calls. When I looked up, my eyes quickly found Karla. She stood behind the two detectives speaking with Frank. I walked toward her, keeping a wide perimeter. As I got closer, Frank spotted me and waved at me to stop.

I focused on Karla and kept walking.

Frank hustled over and intercepted me before I could speak with her. He grabbed me by the shoulder. "Believe me, I know you want to speak with her, but you can't."

"What? Why, Frank?"

"Listen, she found the body in your house. You're a suspect, and the two of you are dating or seeing each other or whatever the hell your status is. It's not a good idea until you're off the suspect list. Got it?"

I shot a look at Karla. She mouthed, 'sorry.'

Looking back at Frank, I said, "Just ten seconds. I want to make sure she's okay."

"Not going to happen, Chase. I get it, trust me, but these guys," he thumbed over his left shoulder, "are hot for you as a suspect, one of them especially."

I glanced at the two plain clothes cops standing near my front porch. "The tall one, right? He's the one after me."

Frank nodded. "Detective Palmer."

"He's a detective now, huh? He was a sergeant a year ago."

"Great, so you know him?"

"I do. And he's not a fan of yours truly."

Frank pushed up his sleeves. "What happened?"

"I'll fill you in later. What do they want? A statement? Questioning?"

"Both. The taller one, Palmer, wanted to put you in the cruiser and take you to headquarters. But I negotiated some professional courtesy and told them I'd make sure you get there."

"Thanks, Frank."

"Don't thank me yet, we need to confirm your alibi. You should get a lawyer, just to cover your ass. This detective isn't objective, not about you, that's for sure."

"Frank, I was nowhere near my house when this happened. And I'm not being charged with anything, right?"

"I'll call a union rep for you then. At least have representation there."

I laughed. "The union? I'd rather work with a lawyer."

Frank sighed. "Where's your car?"

I motioned down the street.

"I'll meet you there. I'll let the detectives know we're leaving."

I headed to my car. Just before I reached the Caprice, I heard footsteps behind me.

Turning, I saw Detective Palmer hurrying my direction. He had the physique of a swimmer: tall, lean, and super square shoulders. His shoulders barely moved as he barreled my direction.

About a year ago Palmer and I had a run-in on the streets when he was working the beat. The encounter didn't go well, to say the least.

Palmer walked right up to me and leaned in until I could feel his hot breath on my cheek. I could tell he wanted to point a finger in my face, but he exercised control and kept his hands to himself. The man was plain looking, non-descript. The only thing about his face that jumped out at me were his ears. They were tiny and tucked close to his head. They simply didn't match his wide shoulders and big head. It looked like he'd had an ear transplant from a child.

Palmer said, "You better have one hell of an explanation, Gary. If not, your alibi better be airtight."

Obviously, he was still pissed. He knew I hated the name Gary. Gary was not the short form of Garrison, by the way. When people deliberately called me Gary, I wanted to massage their neck in a violent manner. But I took a cue from Palmer and practiced self-control.

To keep the mood light, I said, "Congratulations on the promotion to detective."

"When you get to the precinct," he said, ignoring the accolade, "I want you to write down everything that happened this morning starting from when you woke up. Got it? And I mean everything, Gary, even the exact time you took your first piss."

"Want me to include how many times I shook it?"

Palmer stepped back. His face turned a deep, pinkish hue. If he had a hat on, it would've popped off from all the pressure in his head.

He was about to say something, but he stopped himself and took a breath.

Okay, so he was more pissed at me than I imagined. It wasn't wise ticking off the man who was about to question you in a murder case, so I made a mental note to stop the smart aleck remarks.

"Got it, Detective Palmer," I said, climbing into the Caprice.

Palmer stepped in front of the door, preventing me from closing it.

Just then, Karla walked by and stopped in front of the car's hood. She mouthed that she was heading to her field office. I mouthed, 'glad you're okay.'

"Enough you two," Palmer said. "You two are to have zero contact until I get Agent Chase's full statement."

Karla shrugged and walked to her car.

Palmer leaned in and stared at me. "No games, you understand, Gary? I want to know exactly what happened this morning. And it better be the truth, the whole truth."

With that, he slammed my door shut and stomped off.

I leaned back and figured I was going to have a tough time telling the whole truth.

CHAPTER SEVEN

Long Beach Medical Center
Long Beach, CA

LONG BEACH MEDICAL Center was a sprawling, metropolis of a hospital. The employee sat in his parked car, staring at the behemoth building in front of him. He waited for his hospital contact, a former gang banger he knew who'd turned his life around but wasn't past taking a few extra bucks to feed his kids. The man worked IT at the hospital. The employee hoped to get a report from him that Hans was either dead or at the very least in grave shape.

A few minutes later, he saw his contact strolling through the parking lot toward him. The man looked like a regular office worker. The only thing that stood out was the neck tattoo that couldn't be totally hidden by his white-collared shirt.

The employee rolled down his window as the man neared. His contact didn't stop at the window. Instead, he walked past and stopped at the front of the car and bent down. He pretended to tie his shoe.

The contact said, "Not dead. Looks like he's going to recover. Two security guards are flanking his room." The man then grabbed the rolled up one-hundred-dollar bill that the employee left under the front bumper and continued on his way.

The employee blinked a few times. His hands grasped the sides of his bucket seats in an attempt to rip the cheap vinyl.

How had Hans survived?

The employee lit a cigarette, took a deep drag, then an even longer exhale. As he did, he thought about the implications of screwing up the Hans Schlimmergaard hit. The outcome would be unacceptable to his employer. And the consequences could be dire for the employee.

Obviously, he had to remedy the situation. He had to get out in front of it. And he knew just the man who could help fix the problem.

A few puffs later, the employee's mind drifted to Garrison Chase. It didn't go exactly as planned at the man's house either. The plan had been to take him out, but a woman arrived instead. Though it wasn't ideal, the employee figured the set-up was good enough to keep Garrison Chase occupied with the police for some time. Plus, he had one more card to play in that situation; a play that would put further heat on Garrison Chase.

He flicked the cigarette out the window and fired up his vehicle, knowing he had work to do.

If he didn't act now, he'd be dead by day's end.

CHAPTER EIGHT

400 W. Broadway
Long Beach City Police Dept.

"LISTEN, DETECTIVE PALMER," I said. "Instead of going around in circles about this, which I have a feeling is going to happen, let's stick to my alibi and confirm that first. Shall we?"

Palmer stood from his chair, then leaned over and placed his forearms on the table. "You've been on my side of the table many times, I get it, but you're not now. Let's be real clear what seat you're in. Got it?"

Palmer was simply gathering facts at this point. It wasn't like the detective was officially interrogating me since they hadn't charged me with any crime or read me my rights. But I wasn't about to be sarcastic or snarky with him over that fact.

The room we were in looked to be some sort of conference room. The air felt stale and smelled vaguely of coffee, though there was no coffee in sight. Perhaps some cops had a conference meeting in the room right before I arrived.

"I'm in charge here," Palmer continued. "And I decide what we talk about and when. Understood?"

We'd been butting heads for about five minutes. Palmer had learned about Slim collapsing in my kitchen. He wanted to know exactly what happened to my friend. I, too, would want to start at the beginning and set the context if I was questioning someone I thought was a potential murder suspect. The problem was that I couldn't talk about the Rat.

My strategy was to focus on establishing my alibi. That way I could officially get off the suspect list.

"Fair enough," I said. "However, here's the thing: my alibi will probably take some time to confirm, so it would be great if you guys could get working on it. Once that's underway, then I have no problems answering all your questions in detail."

"You're something else," Palmer said, straightening and stepping back. "You're beyond demanding. You know that, right?"

I shrugged. "I am divorced, so I may have heard that once or twice before."

Palmer muttered something under his breath, some curse word I was pretty sure. "What do you mean it's going to take time to confirm your alibi anyway? Elaborate and let's get this over with."

"Well, the thing is, I left the hospital and drove south to Oceanside and didn't stop. Nobody saw me; I had no contact with any people. And—"

Palmer cut me off. "If that's true, we can confirm your location through your cell. Your cell would've pinged off multiple towers on the way down and back. That won't take long to confirm at all. You know that."

"Therein lies the problem."

"Why? What's the problem?"

"As I was leaving the hospital, I stupidly threw my phone against the car door and it broke into pieces. The battery fell out, so it wouldn't have transmitted any signal." I dug out my phone and held it up so he could see the screen. "Even cracked the screen."

He threw up his hands. "You're kidding, right?"

"Nope, I'm not."

"That's a line of evidence that won't corroborate your alibi. I'm sure you understand that."

"Got it," I said, "just being honest, Detective. Like I said, confirming my alibi isn't going to be that easy. But we do have traffic cameras, right? And you know real life isn't like television shows where law enforcement can simply push a button and watch camera feeds from any road they want at any given timeframe. You're going to have to contact Caltrans and find out what feeds they have on the 5 and 405 freeways between Long Beach and Oceanside. Then you guys, or maybe Caltrans, will have to pull up that time-frame and watch thousands of cars passing by, trying to locate mine. Again, that will take time."

Palmer didn't say anything, so I knew I was making sense to him.

"See what I mean?" I said.

He blew out a breath. "Enough, okay? We'll work on your alibi as soon as you explain two things. First, what got you so heated that you broke your phone?"

I reluctantly answered. "Gina texted to say I wasn't welcome at my son's birthday party this weekend." No sense in glossing over the fact or being vague about it. They'd check my cell records, if they hadn't already.

Palmer pulled out a notebook and made a note, then said, "And the second thing." He opened a folder and pulled out a picture. Before he showed it to me, he said, "I understand this is your ex-wife. I'm not going to sugarcoat it, it was a traumatic crime scene, GSW to the back of the skull. Here's how she was found."

Palmer held out a picture at arm's length. He didn't hand over the photo. It was a full body shot of Gina. She was laying on her side in a pool of blood. The Desert Eagle was in the blood to the left of her head.

I quickly glanced at the phone, then got in front of it. "Before you ask, Detective, yes, that is my Desert Eagle. I keep it on the top shelf in my closet. It's out of reach for children, but it is easily visible when you open the closet doors. And, no, Detective, I did not kill my ex-wife with that gun."

To my surprise, Palmer took a different line of questioning. "Is it true you and your ex-wife had an altercation at the hospital this morning?"

"You heard about that?"

He nodded. "Frank told us you were at the hospital this morning, then went for a drive to clear your head. On our way back here, we called the ICU to confirm your presence at the hospital. The nurse was quick to point out the heated argument you had with the deceased." He motioned at the picture. "By the way, you don't look very surprised to see your ex-wife murdered and your own gun beside her body."

"Come on, Detective, I get that all this looks a little suspect. But please, do you really think I'd murder my ex-wife in my own home and then leave the gun at the scene to incriminate myself? This is a clearly a set-up. And a bad one at that."

"Maybe. Maybe not."

"You're kidding, I hope."

Palmer stared at me with dead eyes.

I pushed back from the table. "You actually think I may have done this?"

"I'm keeping an open mind to all theories."

"What's that mean?"

"Tell me your theory, Agent Chase." He used his chin to motion at the picture. "What happened in your bedroom? And why's there an envelope on the table with your son's name written on it?"

I exhaled slowly through my nose, then scraped my chair tight to the table and leaned forward. "After my friend collapsed, I rushed to the hospital. I owed Gina two hundred bucks for my son's birthday party this weekend and I left it right there on the bedside table. I was supposed to give it to her when she picked up my son this morning. But I was obviously distracted by the medical emergency in my kitchen and forgot all about it. Gina and I met up at the hospital, had a little spat, and I told her to drop by my house on her way to work and grab the money. Then she turned up dead on my bedroom floor."

I paused.

Palmer was busy scribbling in his notebook. He stopped, leaned back, and tapped the notebook a few times with his pen. "So your ex-wife goes to your bedroom to get the envelope of cash. She encounters the killer in your bedroom and takes a bullet to the back of the head. Then the killer exits your house, leaving the murder weapon behind."

"To set me up, obviously."

"That's one theory," Palmer said. He kept tapping his notebook with the pen.

I wanted to snatch the pen away and snap it in half. "Oh, so there's a more plausible theory, then? Enlighten me, Detective Palmer."

"Again," he said, leaning forward, "let me remind you, I'm asking the questions here."

I sighed.

He continued. "Your theory supposes a killer broke into your house and was targeting you. Gina, then, happened to be collateral damage in this story. This brings me to the most important question, why was somebody in your house trying to kill you, Agent Chase? Like you told me earlier, it has to do with your friend who collapsed, yet you won't elaborate on that situation. And you really need to elaborate."

I wanted to wipe the smug look off his face. At the same time, I totally understood where he was coming from. He was a decent detective asking the right questions.

"I do need to elaborate, Detective Palmer, and I will once I hear back from an attorney. I have a call in to my buddy's attorney as well as one into the local U.S. attorney. Once I hear back from either of those gentlemen, and get permission to elaborate, then I'll do so."

Palmer kept his head buried in his notebook and didn't respond.

"Why don't you call one of them, Detective? You're certainly welcome to do so. The U.S. attorney is Ethan Khang and my buddy's lawyer is Jimmy Schuberman. I'd be happy to provide either number."

He stood and cracked his knuckles, then started pacing. "I'm fifty-fifty with this story of yours. I—"

"Fifty-fifty? You're joking? You're saying it's equally as plausible that I killed my ex-wife as it is that I'm being set-up?"

"Try this theory out, Gary." He stopped pacing and walked toward me, stopping when he was about three feet from my face. "You clearly had a heated argument with your ex-wife, in public no less. Multiple witness can attest to that. From what witnesses overheard, it sounds like it had something to do with your son, and something to do about money. Then you're seen leaving the hospital right after her, and sometime soon after that you receive a text from her that enrages you. You head home and Gina shows up to get the money you owe her. The argument continues from there and escalates. If the argument was heated in public, it probably went red hot at your house. That's plausible, isn't it? Then perhaps you make the worst split-second mistake of your life and shoot your ex-wife and—"

"Please, I—"

"Let me finish," Palmer said, holding up his hand. "You're an investigator, hear me out. And like I said, this is just a theory."

I breathed slowly through my nose, then nodded for him to continue.

"Suddenly your ex-wife's dead body is in your bedroom and you're holding the murder weapon. So, what do you do now? You have almost zero options at that point. You can't get rid of the body in broad daylight, that's obvious. Circumstances are clearly pointing to you as the culprit, so you run with that. Make it look like you're being set-up, but a bad set-up, so that it ultimately points away from you. Like there's no way you would kill your ex-wife with your own gun and leave it at the scene. It's kind of brilliant if you think about it."

I stroked the stubble on my cheek. It was a decent theory actually.

He continued. "Or how about this: you kill your ex-wife out of rage. You drop the murder weapon beside her body since you're in total shock of what just happened. While you're standing over her body figuring out what to do, suddenly you hear someone at your door. You realize Karla's here. You freak out. You have no time to grab the gun, so you leave it behind and sneak out the back door as fast as you can."

He put his hands on his hips and stared at me.

Boy, that wasn't bad either.

"These aren't that farfetched, are they Agent Chase?"

"They're theories, detective, I'll give you that. They're remote possibilities. But they aren't the truth. Listen, if I did kill my ex-wife and I bailed out of there fast, I'd want my alibi confirmed right away, wouldn't I? I would've driven somewhere and stopped. Filled up my car with gas and used a credit card. Went into a convenience store and made sure my mug got on video. Something like that."

He took a seat in the chair across from me and leaned back. "At first that's what I thought, too. But here's the thing: the timeline is too tight. And you're an investigator, so you'd know that. You knew the timeline could potentially get you in trouble."

"What are you talking about?"

"Come on, Agent Chase, we don't have to wait for the coroner or medical examiner to tell us when Gina was killed. You know how this works. The coroner will probably put Gina's death within an hour, no sooner than that. I've never seen a ME pinpoint a death within thirty minutes. But Gina was seen leaving the hospital," he flipped back a page in his notebook, "around 9:30 a.m. And Karla found her body at," he glanced at his notes again, "10:15 a.m. And it takes ten minutes to get to your house from the hospital. So, if we assume Gina drove straight from the hospital to your house and figure it would've taken a bit for the argument to get super-heated, we're looking at a twenty-five to thirty-minute window for when Gina was murdered. That's a tight window, too tight of a window for you to get far enough away for a decent alibi, certainly not over an hour south in Oceanside. And you'd know that. Maybe that's why you've been preparing me for the difficulty in confirming your alibi."

He got up and walked around the conference table. He stopped at my right side and kneeled beside my chair. "Maybe you're lying about this little drive to clear your head. We certainly know you're capable of that. It wouldn't be the first time you lied to the police. Would it?"

I took the slowest, deepest breath I could. I had lied to Palmer a year ago during our run-in. To be honest, the accusation of lying didn't bother me that much.

What bothered me was the continuous assumption that I was involved in brutally killing my ex-wife.

"Maybe you weren't in Oceanside," Palmer continued. "Maybe, Agent Chase, just maybe, you were in your house staring at your dead ex-wife figuring out what to do."

He put his hand on my shoulder and leaned in. I could smell stale coffee on his breath. "How's that for a theory, Gary?"

As my blood pressure spiked, I looked him in the eye.

At that moment, all I wanted to do was slap my right hand against his cheek and bounce his face off the conference table.

CHAPTER NINE

E Burnett St.
Signal Hill, CA

"ARE YOU SURE you want to do this?" the employee's associate asked.

The employee didn't respond right away.

The man the employee had worked with for the past five years, a man he knew only by the name of Tanawat, shifted to the left in the passenger seat and stared at him. The man's hat was pulled down tightly, and he was slunk low in the seat.

Tanawat said, "Shock and awe isn't exactly your style. In fact, we've never done a job like this before."

"We haven't," the employee said, "but you have, correct?"

Tanawat pulled up his black and silver L.A. Kings hat. The employee could now see the man's dark brown eyes.

Tanawat narrowed his eyes and scowled. "Sure," he said. "This is definitely my style of job, but not yours. I know how cautious you are. I don't want you regretting anything. We've had a good relationship over the years with many successes to speak of."

"We have," the employee said, nodding. "You have a man you can get on this right away? Time is of the essence. I don't have time to do this delicately, to do this my way. I need a man to do this fast and effectively."

Tanawat laughed. "Man? You mean men. This isn't a one-person job, my friend. And, yes, of course I have men at my disposal. Probably could get this done in an hour and a half, maybe two hours tops. But that's going to cost you."

The employee winced. "How many men are we talking about?"

"Three. No more, no less. Two inside and one waiting outside in a getaway vehicle."

"Three men, you're sure?"

"Absolutely."

"Run me through the details," the employee said, "so we're on the same page."

Tanawat did.

After the employee heard the details, he had one concern. "Your men will stick to just the target and the guards, or at least try to, right?"

Tanawat shrugged. "Sure, they'll try. But this is basically a smash and grab job. Not to mention, in the day and out in the open. This isn't a finesse situation we're dealing with. And the guys I'm putting on this are blunt force guys. Discretion isn't in their vocabulary. They couldn't even pronounce the word. These guys will mow down anyone who gets in their way. I can't guarantee somebody doesn't try to be the hero."

"I understand."

Tanawat cleared his throat. "Last time I'll ask: you sure about this?"

"What's the cost?" the employee asked.

"Considering the exposure they'll face, and the incredible risk, double my usual rate. Plus, the cost of the getaway vehicle."

"Getaway vehicle? What?"

"We don't have time to steal a vehicle here, my friend. If you want this done now, we're going to have to use one of my vehicles. And burn it, of course, somewhere outside the city, maybe down at the docks. I have a 2016 Dodge Grand Caravan we could use. Sliding doors are good for this type of job, for a quick getaway. I'd say fifteen grand for the vehicle is fair."

The employee shook his head. "No way, not for a stinking minivan."

"Fine, ten then."

The employee shook his head again.

"If you want to slow this thing down and give me some more time, we can cut expenses and get a free vehicle. Steal something off the streets."

The employee thought about it. He needed the job done right away. "I'll agree to ten. I'll get you the money within an hour or so."

Tanawat nodded. "Consider the target," he looked at his watch, "taken out sometime mid-afternoon."

Then Tanawat left without saying another word.

CHAPTER TEN

400 W. Broadway
Long Beach City Police Dept.

I HELD THE stare with Palmer. Fortunately, I kept my hands in check and didn't do anything stupid.

Palmer was trying to get under my skin, make me say something I'd regret, and I wouldn't let that happen. I figured he was going hard at me because of our past, not necessarily because he thought I'd killed Gina. Truth be told, a year ago I really embarrassed him and his partner when I hand-cuffed him and left him in the backseat of his own cruiser. Though I felt I had to do that at the time, I was sure Palmer disagreed with me on that point.

At any rate, I was innocent. And I was positive my alibi would be confirmed soon. Plus, the timeline of Gina's death actually helped my case, so I had no cause for concern and no reason for getting upset. And for all I knew Ethan Khang could be pulling strings right now to yank this case from the local cops.

After a deep breath, I addressed Palmer. "Here's why your theories are bogus: I left the hospital at about 9:35 a.m. and drove straight south. That puts me in Oceanside around 10:45 a.m. Once we confirm my location around that time, my alibi vindicates me completely. Since Gina was killed sometime between 9:45 and 10:15, no way could I be the killer if I was in Oceanside at that time this morning. We can agree on that, right?"

Palmer didn't say anything.

I continued. "I'm sure traffic cameras will be your best bet to confirm my whereabouts. You could also try and call Julie Cranston." I motioned toward Palmer's notebook. "Jot this number down." I waited for him to pick up his pen. He didn't, but I recited the number anyway.

"Julie Cranston may have been home and saw me idling in the driveway. I'm not sure, but it's worth a shot. Then—"

"Enough," Palmer snapped. "You're a real control freak, aren't you? I'm investigating you and your story. You do realize you're not in charge of your own investigation, I hope."

I put up my hands. "Fair enough."

Palmer stared at me for a moment, then pushed back from the table.

As he walked to the conference door, I said, "My guess is you're not going to charge me since everything is circumstantial here, just a theory as you've mentioned, so I'm free to go. Right?"

He sighed. "Sit tight, Agent Chase. You're not going anywhere for the moment. Give me that number again, the one for Julie Cranston. I'll try her first."

I recited the number for Palmer.

Once he was gone, I leaned back and kept my mind active. I went over the steps I needed to take once I was free to go. After about ten minutes of thinking, I had a game plan. I'd head to the hospital and check in with the doc. After that, I would try Slim's lawyer again. I needed to speak with him to see what insights he had about the Rat. For all I knew, the government already had a task force investigating the Rat. Maybe they knew he was still running his organization from captivity. And if so, maybe they could shed some light into the Rat's known hired killers.

I stood and paced the room. Later in the day, I planned to pick up Simon. I'd have to get some of his things from Gina's house, then check in at a hotel or maybe head to my mother's place. I couldn't stay at Gina's since I knew her parents were there. And I couldn't stay at my house since it was a crime scene.

My thoughts stopped when the conference door suddenly wheeled open. I stopped pacing and looked up.

Palmer came into the room at a fast pace. He held up his cell. "Just got off the phone with Julie Cranston. Get this: she was home all morning, didn't leave the house, didn't see you or your car."

I shrugged. "Not surprising. I told you I didn't knock on the door, I didn't get out of my vehicle, and I wasn't there very long."

"Have a seat, Gary." Palmer motioned to a chair.

I didn't sit.

"Sit," Palmer commanded, pointing at the chair.

"Come on, Detective, I'm not a dog."

He stabbed at the chair. "We're going through everything again, Gary."

I reluctantly took a seat, then addressed Palmer. "They have a big house, by the way, so Julie could have been at the back of the house or in the backyard when I stopped by."

Palmer slid into the chair across the table from me. "It was nice you were so definitive on your timeframe for when you were at the Cranston home."

"What's that mean?"

He smirked. "You told me you were in Oceanside at the Cranston residence about ten forty-five. Isn't that correct?"

"Right. So what?"

"So Julie Cranston was adamant that she was cleaning the living room from 10:15 until approximately 11:15 this morning. And as I'm sure you know, the living room is at the front of the house. She says there's no way you could've stopped by at that time. No way. Her exact words."

CHAPTER ELEVEN

DETECTIVE PALMER STOOD directly across the table from me. His hands gripped the top of his chair. I could see his knuckles turning white. He leaned forward and glared at me.

"Don't play this off as no big deal," he said. "Please don't do that. I mean, a woman you know, your friend's wife no less, can't confirm your alibi. In fact, she's categorically rejecting your alibi. This is big, Agent Chase. We can't ignore this."

I cleared my throat. "When you spoke with her, Palmer, what did you tell her exactly?"

He held out his hands. "What do you mean what did I tell her? And what does that matter anyway?"

"I mean, did you tell her I was a potential suspect in a murder investigation and that you needed to confirm my alibi?"

He frowned. "Of course not."

"Right, because you're a good detective," I said, buttering him up. "That's information you would only share with fellow cops, especially being so early in your investigation. So, you kept it super vague, right?"

"What's your point?" Palmer put his hands on his hips.

"Julie's upset with me. Furious would probably be a better word. She wants nothing to do with me. When you called and asked if I had been at her house this morning, I guarantee she bristled as soon as she heard my name. I imagine she wanted nothing to do with me and whatever I was wrapped up in—"

Palmer interrupted. "You're saying she's lying?"

"Maybe, maybe not. Maybe she is lying, maybe she just got her times wrong. I don't know. What I do know is that I'd like you to reach out to Julie again and explain things in more detail. She deserves to know what's going on with me and that it's crucial I establish my alibi. If she knows the truth and still maintains there's no way I could've been there, then that's her prerogative. If that's the case, then maybe she's even more pissed at me than I realize."

"Why is everything so complicated with you?" He spun and walked to the corner of the room. "This alibi of yours keeps getting more and more difficult and controversial." He looked over his shoulder at me. "You realize that, right, Gary?"

I was at a loss for a quick comeback, so I said, "It's certainly less than ideal. I admit that."

As Palmer stewed in the corner thinking about what to do, the conference room door opened. A plainclothes cop peeked in and motioned at Palmer. The detective left the room without saying a word.

I sat back and thought about Julie Cranston. Naturally, I was frustrated with her, but if I was being honest, I wasn't surprised at her response to Palmer when he called. She wasn't the president of my fan club. Maybe I needed to call Mick and explain things to him, then he could speak to Julie about the severity of my situation and hopefully get her to rethink her statement to Palmer.

Thinking about that some more, I realized I probably couldn't get in touch with Mick until later in the day when he got off work. That was hours away. Surely there must be a better, quicker way to confirm my alibi.

After tapping my fingers on the table for a few moments, I pulled out the lawyer's card. I had to try the man again in hopes he'd pick up the phone this time. Palmer needed to know that the Rat was a big-time serious threat, that he was a man capable of just about anything, and with the resources to make it happen. Jimmy Schuberman may be my only ticket out of this mess. Or at the very least, maybe Jimmy had a direct line to Khang's office and could get quick clearance to declassify some details to the police.

Just as I started to dial the lawyer, the conference door opened. The detective hurried in. Palmer was tall and his knees barely bent, so he sort of shuffled quickly across the floor. He took a seat across from me and placed both forearms on the table.

"There's been a development," he said. "Significant one, I might add."

He paused and looked me in the eyes, but he didn't say a word.

Obviously, not good. His silence irritated me. "You want me to guess what happened, is that why you're not saying anything?"

He cleared his throat. "The development relates to the traffic cams. There are three cameras between Long Beach and the exit you claim you took off the 5. The first camera has you traveling southbound on the 405 at 9:44 a.m., but the other two cameras are down. The next working traffic cam is three miles south of the exit you claim you took in Oceanside."

"You're kidding me?"

Palmer shook his head. "I'm not. Apparently, Caltrans says that isn't out of the ordinary. When cameras go down, it's not like they jump at getting them fixed. Budget thing. Anyway, the first camera only puts you about nine minutes outside Long Beach, so—"

"So, it's a problem," I interrupted. "I get it, Palmer. According to your cockamamie theory, I could've circled back and taken side streets back to my house. Isn't that right?"

"It's possible. Which I'm sure you understand as an investigator. You know how important it is for a suspect to have an alibi, preferably an airtight one. In your case, perhaps you were originally headed south to Oceanside after the hospital, but then maybe you got that text, so you circled back to your house and encountered Gina there. You guys get heated again—"

"Right. And I shot my boy's mother in the head in some sort of cold-blooded rage."

He ignored the sarcastic comment. "Or you went straight back home from the hospital and met Gina there, killed her, then hopped in your vehicle and headed south, to give the appearance you had an alibi."

I pushed back from the table and stood. There were a couple of reasons why that wouldn't make sense, but I didn't have the time or stamina to keep arguing with Palmer. He'd counter any reasonable argument I made. I know I would if I were in his shoes.

I said, "Where are we at then, Detective? You going to press charges, name me as my ex-wife's killer? Let's cut to the chase. Give it to me straight."

"Come on, you know we have to consult the district attorney first, which takes some time, though I wouldn't be surprised if my boss is speaking with her now and going over the evidence."

I swept Jimmy Schuberman's card off the table and held it out so Palmer could read it. "Fine, then, let's get this moving. I'm calling my lawyer now. You or your boss or the DA can speak with my attorney from here on out. I've been more than cooperative with your questions, but that's over now."

Palmer rolled his eyes.

"This is a confidential call, so you'll have to leave." I waved him out.

After Palmer vacated the room, I stared at the card in my hand for a few moments.

Then I called Jimmy Schuberman.

CHAPTER TWELVE

I ONLY HEARD every third or fourth word from this lawyer guy, that was how fast he talked. He had a heavy Boston accent. The lawyer spent the first three minutes of our conversation chastising me for even alluding to the police about the classified situation Slim was a part of.

Anyway, he was still droning on in my right ear. It was like listening to an auctioneer for the first time. Honestly, my ear ached. If it could detach from my head and run off to a quiet place, I was convinced it would.

The only good thing about the lawyer's speech was he repeated himself a lot, so I was able to piece together his plan after the third go around.

The man finally paused, but only for a second.

"You hear me there, Chase?" he said. "Are you tracking with me?"

"I'm tracking, Jimmy."

"Good, good, good. Very good."

Four goods? This guy was something else. I envisioned the man on the other end of the cell sitting in a small lawyer's office with his feet up on the desk. One hand holding the cell and the other combing back his slick, dark hair.

"Alright, champ," he said. "Glad we can move forward on this one."

I cleared my throat. "We're definitely moving forward."

"Wicked," he said.

I assumed that was a good thing.

"So I'll get in touch with Khang," Jimmy continued. "Let him know what's going on, get permission from him for you to testify if Slim can't. That's okay, right? You're fine with that?"

"Like I said, I will, Jimmy."

"Good, good. In return, I'll handle this coppah, Chase. Put him on, champ. Hand the cell to him. I'll fix him up straight. I'll take the pissah outta him if he insists on questioning you any further, especially without me present."

"Gimme a second," I said.

As I walked to the door, I wondered if Jimmy Schuberman was drinking mid-day. I suddenly pictured him drinking Sam Adams in the backyard with his buddies, arguing over who was the all-time greatest Boston Bruins defenseman, then eventually getting into a fist fight over it.

I banged on the door. A few seconds later, the door opened, and Palmer walked in. I handed him my cell. "My lawyer. Sorry."

Palmer took the phone. Within moments, he pulled the phone away from his ear and motioned at me.

I shrugged.

Palmer tried to butt in and say a few words, but Jimmy wouldn't let him. I could hear the lawyer's voice pretty well, even though the cell was ten feet away.

About thirty seconds later, Palmer said, "I understand." But it was the only words he could get in before Jimmy cut him off and kept talking.

I sat and watched Palmer's face. Within minutes it went from a healthy pinkish color to a full-on deep red hue. Three times he managed to say 'but' before Jimmy interrupted him.

I could tell Jimmy was reading the detective the riot act. After about another two-minute conversation between the pair, Palmer pulled the phone completely away from his ear. "He wants to speak with you again."

Instead of walking around and handing over the cell, Palmer tossed it across the desk.

Before I had the phone to my ear, Jimmy started in.

"Walk out, Chase. Walk out now, don't look back."

He cut me off before giving me a chance to respond. "Walk out now."

Jimmy's command took me by surprise, so I didn't move or say anything right away.

"I don't hear you walking, champ."

I cleared my throat. "You sure, Jimmy?"

"Of course I'm sure," he shot back. "Get out now. They haven't read you any rights. No reason—none at all—to stay there. I'm ready to rip this coppah a new one."

"Sounds like you already did." I stood and walked toward the door.

Palmer didn't say anything as I moved past him.

I spoke softly into the cell. "What's my move here? Walk straight out of the room and building?"

"Darn tooting. Don't stop, don't you dare. And don't you look back either. If they decide to press charges, we'll deal with it later. Though that'll cost you, just for the record."

Did he just say, 'darn tooting'?

I stepped from the room without saying a word. Nobody chased after me, insisting I stay and answer more questions. In fact, nobody said a word to me as I weaved through headquarters.

So I stepped outside and headed straight to the hospital to check-in on Slim.

CHAPTER THIRTEEN

Chase Bank
Los Cerritos, CA

THE EMPLOYEE WAITED until the bank representative had drawn the curtain and left the vault, then he opened the safe deposit box.

Inside was close to fifty thousand dollars in two different bill denominations: hundreds and twenties. He took the stack of bills and loaded them into his small Northface Recon backpack.

Underneath the last stack of bills was the employee's passport. The only official piece of documentation he had left of his original identity. Everything he'd done in the past twenty years since joining the criminal ranks had been done under an assumed name, a bought name, which was all thanks to his uncle.

The employee opened the U.S. passport and read his name for the first time in many years.

Pham Van Lu.

Though his parents were foreign, Lu had been born and raised in America. His mother died in childbirth and his father was murdered in a gang shootout, so his uncle raised him. His uncle was a stand-up character who owned a convenience store in Little Saigon. The man sacrificed a lot for him, so when he found out Lu had entered a life in the criminal realm, his uncle disowned him for what he thought was a terrible decision.

Just before Lu moved out, his uncle presented him with a fake passport, driver's license, and social security card. It cost his uncle his life savings, approximately ten thousand dollars. Lu tried to refuse the identity and get his uncle's money back, but his uncle would have nothing of it. He said if Lu was going to choose a criminal life, that he had to protect the family's honor, along with its name. His uncle said that if Lu ever returned to a legitimate, non-criminal lifestyle, that he'd welcome him back to the family and call him by his proper name.

Lu peeled off ten thousand dollars in hundreds and placed the money in his wallet. He frequently carried ten grand in his wallet as an homage to his uncle, to remind him of the incredible sacrifice the man had made. Twice Lu had tried to pay back his uncle. Twice his uncle refused, saying the only way he'd take the money was if Lu could prove he earned it legitimately.

Just then, his cell beeped, alerting Lu to a text.

It was from Tanawat and read: *men in place, all I need is money*

They'd agreed to meet at a nearby park. Lu texted back: *be there in 10*

As Lu zipped up the backpack, he stared at the passport on the table, wondering if he should take it with him or leave it in the safe deposit box. After a moment of contemplation, he unzipped the pack and threw the passport in with the money.

As he left the building and walked to the park, he pulled out his phone and dialed the Long Beach police station.

CHAPTER FOURTEEN

E Willow Ave.
Long Beach Medical Center

SEEING THROUGH THE hospital room window that Slim was awake, I flashed my badge to the hospital guards and entered the room.

My buddy raised his right arm and pointed a shaky finger at me.

"It wasn't you," he said with a hoarse voice. "Was it?"

"Was what?"

"Your damn coffee. You tainted it, didn't you?"

Slim smiled.

I took a seat and scraped the chair to the left side of his bed. "Yup, it was me. Been meaning to get rid of you for a while. I also hired those men to give you that facial."

He dropped his arm. "Figures."

"How you feeling? Because you're certainly not looking better. At least your busted nose distracts from that ugly nodule on your forehead."

Slim slowly raised his middle finger, then motioned at a Styrofoam cup of water on the table to my right. I grabbed the ice water and let Slim take a sip from the straw.

He cleared his throat. "Aside from my throbbing nose, I feel like everything inside me wants out, by whichever route is quickest."

"That would be via your butt, I imagine." I held up my hands. "If you're asking me to help with the bedpan, pal, forget it. We're not that close. I'll call a nurse."

He grabbed his stomach and laughed.

"Sorry," I said. "I shouldn't make you laugh."

He waved me off, telling me it was alright.

"Seriously, buddy, how are you doing?"

Slim shifted onto his side. "Honestly, it feels like my insides are rotting. Though whatever they gave me sure perked me up, at least my mind. Everything was pretty foggy about twenty minutes ago, now I'm ready to solve America's problems."

I leaned back in the chair. "I checked in with your doc before coming here. I imagine he brought you up to speed on what they found."

Slim nodded. "Yup, he confirmed it was poison. Oleander to be precise. Which is a rare poison. Weird, huh?"

"Totally," I said. "Poisoned by a flower. Who'd have guessed? Maybe the Rat wasn't responsible after all. Maybe it was your gardener. Have you not been treating him well?"

"Funny guy, you are."

"You probably haven't been sniffing highly toxic flowers lately, so how'd the Rat get oleander into your system?"

"Well, from what the doc told me, I had high levels of the toxin inside me. And since the poison acts quickly in your system, I must've ingested it this morning. It couldn't have been something I ate last night, otherwise I would've died in my sleep. This morning the only thing I ate and drank before coming to your place was room service breakfast, which included a coffee. My guess is a hotel worker tainted the breakfast or coffee. There's also the possibility that my pain meds were tampered with since I took two pills this morning as well."

"Either way, this screams of the Rat's MO."

"I agree," Slim said. "Doc said oleander is a cardiac glycoside toxin. It affects the electrolyte balance in your heart muscle. Basically, oleander would've eventually stopped my heart if they hadn't pinpointed it as the culprit. Which the doctor tells me you were somewhat responsible for."

I furrowed my brow. "I was?"

"Oleander isn't something that's screened for on a standard test. So when the first tox report came back negative, the doc ordered a more detailed one since you were adamant that foul play was involved. Oleander popped up on the more detailed screen, and the doc acted quickly to counteract its effects."

"So, basically," I said, grinning, "I saved your life."

"Sure, and now you only need to save me two more times for us to be even."

We joked and made small talk for another minute. Eventually I turned the conversation serious. "Freda was pretty freaked out when I told her about you, which is understandable. Buddy, it was touch and go for a while. Edge of life teetering type stuff."

He nodded. "I heard. The Rat underestimated me again, though. We have to get this guy, Chase, we have to." He jabbed his right pointer finger at me. The movements made him wince.

I nodded. "We will."

He struggled to sit up a little.

"Take it easy, pal," I said.

Slim didn't listen to me. He put himself into a more upright position. "I'm not sure I'll be able to testify, so—"

I cut him off. "I'll take your place if need be. Don't worry. I've already brought it up to your lawyer, who's a real piece of work, by the way. He's going to ask Ethan Khang if that's okay."

"Good." Slim collapsed into a prone position. "Really good to hear."

"Enough exercise for you. Just take it easy." I put the ice water in front of him again.

Slim pulled from the straw, then said, "You know, the Rat wants me dead, that's unequivocal, so his men will probably be coming after you if they find out you're taking my place. You obviously have to be super careful."

I sighed. "They already have, unfortunately."

Slim's eyes went wide. "What? What happened?"

I hesitated. Slim's face was pale underneath all the cuts, and his breathing was becoming shallower. I didn't want to stress him out any more than need be. "Maybe I should come back later, once you've rested and calmed down a little. I don't want you getting upset."

"Just tell me, Chase. Now I have to know, absolutely. Tell me what happened. Tell me everything."

So I did. Starting with what happened after Slim smacked his face off the kitchen floor to Gina being killed at my house and ending with me being named the prime suspect.

During my story, Slim rested with his head back, listening intently. My story took the better part of ten minutes.

When I finished, Slim blew out a deep breath. "I'm so sorry, buddy. About Gina, about Simon, about everything. I should've never come to your house." He placed his right hand over his face. "Stupid move. We should've met at a neutral place."

The Rat had underestimated Slim's ability to survive, but Slim had underestimated the Rat's deviousness. Slim knew that, so there was no point in mentioning it. Instead, I said, "You couldn't have known, pal, you can't beat yourself up over that. You're already beat up enough."

Slim shook his head with his face buried in his palms.

I steered the conversation away, to something more positive and productive. "Listen, if we can tie the Rat—his men, that is—to your beating and poisoning and Gina's murder, sometime in the next few days before the Rat's hearing, then we'll have even more ammunition for Ethan Khang."

Slim nodded.

I continued. "We need direct proof that the Rat is still criminally active. That his claims of being a changed man are a blatant lie, that sort of thing. If we can find Gina's murderer and whoever poisoned you, and tie them back to the Rat—"

"Man, you keep saying 'we'. I feel so useless being in this bed."

I waved my hand. "Forget about it. Karla and I will work on this; we're a good team."

"I'll tell you everything I know. That's about all I'm good for."

I thought about it, then motioned at his face. "Why don't you start with how the Rat's goons got the one up on a big, talented guy like yourself."

"Sure." Slim took another pull of water. "You remember my property, right?"

I nodded.

"About four months ago," he continued, "I built my dream shed, a man cave, on the back quarter of the land. Half of the structure stored my hunting, fishing, and work-out gear. The other half was a home office and bathroom. Anyway, I was working late one night, just billing and paperwork stuff, when all of a sudden, a stun grenade came blasting through my office window. I didn't stand a chance."

I rubbed my hand over my head. "Pal, that means the Rat knows where you live."

"I know, back to that in a second. When I came to, I was on the other side of the man cave where I kept my workout equipment. My hands were tied over my head. The rope used for my hands was looped over the thick ceiling beam that held my punching bag. My feet were tied, too. There were two average sized guys in there with me. Both had dark masks on and neither spoke English. When they spoke, it sounded like Chinese or some other similar dialect. They used me as a punching bag for a while, then transitioned into whipping my face with these long, flexible strips of bamboo. At least I think it was bamboo. It was a strange choice of weapon, but it was effective in terms of pain and damage to the face. The men spoke the same two English words over and over: you stop, you stop."

"Sounds like the Rat," I said.

"Agreed. Anyway, Freda found me strung up early that morning and took me to the hospital. She and the boys have been hotel hopping the past week. I told her it would all be over once I'd finished testifying, which I hope to be the case. Or I guess I should say you testifying, since I probably won't be able to."

"We're going to end this, pal. We must. For ourselves, but more importantly, for our families."

Instead of agreeing with me, Slim leaned his head back and sighed.

"That's quite the sigh," I said. "What's going on in that head of yours?"

He didn't look at me. "Just bringing you into this. I'm sorry, man. That was never my intention. And now you're neck deep in this stuff. And—"

"Listen," I interrupted, "this man is responsible for the murders of innocent women in agonizing fashion. It's incredibly important that justice is served. Justice in its entirety. I couldn't sleep if the Rat got away with anything, or if he got off easy. Don't worry about bringing me into this, or my family. Tomorrow my mom's going to take Simon somewhere safe until this is all over."

Slim nodded but still didn't look at me.

Silence ensued for thirty seconds or so. Slim had both hands on his head. It seemed like he had more stuff on his mind.

"Something else going on?" I asked.

He met my gaze. "The main thing I wanted to tell you this morning was about the Rat. But, like I said, I also showed up because I needed your help."

"Right, with Henrietta and whatever's happening there."

"Now it's super bad timing for you, which is all my fault, so forget about it. You need to establish your alibi and shake off the cops, investigate the Rat, get justice for Gina's murder."

"Tell me what's going on."

He shook his head.

"Slim, you're one of my closest buddies, just spit it out."

"Fine," he said. He tried to sit up, but he appeared to be losing strength, so he buzzed the bed to a more upright position. "As I mentioned in your kitchen, before things went blank for me, Henrietta hired me to see if I could dig up any dirt on her opponent."

"The blind senator from California. What's his full name? I can never remember."

"Barrington Bradford Bollinger III. At least I think it's the third, maybe the fourth. Who freaking knows? He insists on being called Bradford to downplay his pompous ass sounding name, though I'm not sure that's any better." Slim laughed, then quickly clutched his belly.

After a breath, he continued. "Anyway, Bradford's currently holding rallies around L.A. and Orange County. To make a long story short, I think I've discovered something controversial about Mr. Bollinger. Something that could alter the presidential election. I wanted you to come with me and watch this guy. Confirm my suspicions before I put it into a report for Henrietta. She's obviously a huge client, our biggest one yet."

I leaned forward. "Confirm what?"

He winced. "That's the thing. I don't want to tell you."

"What? What do you mean?"

"I mean, I need complete independent, third party verification of my finding. Considering the serious nature of the finding. But if I tell you . . ."

I nodded. "I'd be looking for it."

"Right. I don't want to be wrong on this, buddy. It's huge. It would break my career if I'm wrong."

"You basically want to see if my observation skills pick up the same thing you did. Before you go making a complete arse of yourself to Henrietta."

"Exactly. If I tell you anything, you'll zero in on that detail. Maybe see something that's not really there. And I don't want that."

I stroked my stubbled cheek. "Gotta admit, this sounds intriguing, especially since we're dealing with candidates in the upcoming election. But this just isn't my thing. Spying and watching people are far beyond what I want to be doing with my limited time on earth. And, as you said, the timing is bad. And that's a gross understatement."

Slim nodded. "I know. That's why I hesitated to say anything."

"Anyone else on your list to help?"

"Not yet, but I have some time to think of someone. Gives me something to do while cooped up in this bed." He looked up at the ceiling. "I'll probably make some calls later when I come up with a short list."

A moment later, I heard him whisper to himself, 'Who do I trust, though?', 'Who do I trust?'

I blew out a breath. "Maybe I can help, Slim. Not promising anything since I don't know when I'd fit this in."

He perked up. "Totally get it, pal. And not to sell this further or create more pressure, but I'll pay you. And it'll be a lot. My daily rate these days is twenty-five hundred."

"Really?"

He nodded. "I'll make it worth your while, if you make the time. Find the time, that is."

I changed the subject since I didn't want to get his hopes up any further. "So what did the doc say about your condition? What's your length of recovery? What are we talking about here? A couple of days? A week? More?"

Slim opened his mouth to respond, but he never got any words out.

The thwap-thwap of a silencer stopped him in his tracks.

CHAPTER FIFTEEN

I HEARD TWO bodies thump to the floor. Figuring the security guards had just been taken out, I flung my chair back and dropped to my knees. Just as I did, the large window shattered to my left. Shards of glass blew into the room in a flurry, raining over my body.

Three bullets tore into the wall above Slim. Fortunately, they missed Slim's head by a few inches. To save my buddy, I placed both hands on the edge of his bed and tried to push it out of the way. The brake was on, so the bed didn't budge. My adrenaline spiked at that moment, though, and I heaved the bed over with all my might, sending Slim's giant body crashing to the ground.

He howled on impact, but his cry was drowned out by the metal bedrail smashing against the hard floor. I scrambled to my left, toward the wall underneath the blown-out window.

Staying crouched, I jammed my back against the wall. My left shoulder was pinned against the side of the cubby system. The blinds on the large window had been blown clear off the wall. They laid in front of me in a tangled mess, along with the IV tower and heartrate monitor that had toppled when I overturned the bed.

Before I could unholster my piece, a man's hand jutted through the broken window, about a foot above my head.

The hand grasped a pistol with a silencer attached. It coughed twice in the direction of Slim's bed. Instinctively, I grabbed the gun, smothering my left hand over the silencer and burning my palm in the process.

The gunman was on the other side of the wall, standing in the hallway. Suddenly he leaned forward and reached into the room with his free hand, grabbing at my head. Fortunately, I had no hair to grab onto. The man adjusted, however, and started clobbering the top of my head with his fist.

But I didn't let go of the gun. Instead of fighting off the hits, I reached up and used my right hand to grasp the gun's stock. In one quick motion I snapped the gunman's wrist downward with as much force as possible.

A yelp came from the other side of the wall.

The wrist broke like a popsicle stick, and the gun easily slid free into my left hand. While holding the gunman's wrist with my right hand, I brought the gun up to fire a shot over my head. But the gunman's free hand knocked the gun away before I could pull the trigger.

Then the hospital room door kicked open. A barrage of bullets hissed into the room, hitting the underside of Slim's bed.

A second gunman.

Immediately I knew I was in trouble. Any second I expected to see someone in the doorframe opening fire on me.

I reacted to the situation by lunging back and grabbing the man on the other side of the wall under the armpit and shoulder. I heaved and scraped the man over the windowsill with all my might. He let out a deep, guttural scream during the process.

As I pulled him to the floor, I saw there were two jagged shards of glass still attached to the base of the window, which now had blood dripping from them and explained the screaming. Apparently, I'd gutted the man from stern to belly as I raked him over the window ledge.

A second intruder, a short, stocky man with a balaclava on, stepped into the doorway. My eyes ballooned as his gun arm swung my direction.

With no time to unholster my gun, I pulled the bloody gunman on top of me. Which was a lifesaving move since the second gunman hesitated on pulling the trigger.

Warm blood pooled on my chest as the gunman's heart pumped what remaining blood it had left in it all over my sternum.

The second gunman side-stepped to his right, to get a better shooting angle. To block the angle, I grabbed the man on my chest by the throat and moved his head to my left. His eyes were saucers behind the mask, but they shut after a second. Then the man went limp in my arms.

The second gunman realized his partner was likely dead, so he pulled the trigger and tried to shoot me through the body. The bullet tore through the right shoulder of the gunman on top of me, missing my left shoulder by inches.

With the human shield on top of me, I held the gunman's head and upper body away from me with my left hand. Then I unholstered my sidearm with my right hand and jammed the service piece into the gunman's ripped open chest. I fired three shots through the body at the second gunman.

Two shots missed. One hit, grazing the right side of the man's upper chest. No surprise I missed. Flesh and bone easily misdirected shots.

The man I'd shot dropped to his knees; his gun hitting the floor with a dull thud. He clamped both hands over his right nipple. I may have blown the nipple clear off; I wasn't sure.

I could have—and maybe I should have—shot him again. But I wanted this guy alive in order to interrogate him, so I let go of the dead man and charged the man I'd just shot. On my second step, however, my right foot slipped on the oil slick of blood covering the floor. I flopped onto my back and dropped the gun.

The second gunman was on his knees searching for his gun, but there were wires and tubes and a tangled mess on the floor. Somewhere amidst the mess were both our guns.

The gunman quickly gave up on the search and launched at me. I snatched the long IV pole off the ground and caught the man by the throat with the metal pole. Pinning his throat to the ground, I applied pressure until I felt his trachea crumbling.

Saliva and blood bubbled from the small mouth hole in the intruder's mask. Realizing I may kill the intruder, I eased back a little.

Which was a mistake.

The man still had enough strength in him to jam his left knee into my groin. Hard. The guttural pain flooded my body, which caused me to loosen my grip on the pole some more. The intruder used the moment to flip me forward in some sort of quick, judo-type move.

I crashed onto my back, landing on something hard. Excruciating pain shot from my balls to my back. What took over me, however, was rage. I flipped over, got to my knees, still struggling to catch my breath. I looked up just in time to catch a silver flash in my periphery.

Clang! Something flush and cold connected squarely with my right cheekbone. Immediately I toppled to my left. My left forearm caught the weight of my body and stopped me from collapsing to the ground.

For a second, I couldn't see. Just blackness, no stars. I shook my head.

Moments later, my vision came to, right in time to see a bedpan arcing toward me. I caught it mid-swing with my right hand.

The realization that I'd just been clocked with a bedpan took my rage to a new level. I overpowered the bedpan from the intruder. Flipping it around, I grabbed it by the edges and lunged at the gunman, trapping his face in the large opening and smothering him backward until he hit the ground.

I held the bedpan over his face for a few moments. Then I started bashing his face with the pan. The edges of the bedpan connected with the polished floor.

Clang. Clang. Clang.

I'd smartened up, too. This time I kept my lower body close to the intruder's thighs, so I didn't get groined. Fortunately, a gasp from the hallway snapped me from my violent rage.

I looked up. I could see some panic in the hallway through the blown-out window. Two people were running fast away from Slim's room. What caught my attention was a nurse. She stood frozen outside the room; her fingertips covering her open mouth.

"Get hel—"

I took a judo chop across the throat.

Gagging and sputtering, I collapsed to the right, bracing myself with my right forearm against the floor. I massaged my throat with my left hand. My eyes watered and I gasped for air.

The gunman was clearly trained in martial arts.

After blinking a few times, I saw the gunman on his belly crawling toward his gun. I got to him just before he grasped it. I picked the man up and jammed him against the wall, wedging my right forearm under his chin and holding him firmly in place.

Leaning all my weight on my forearm, I planned to choke him out. Not relent until he slithered to the ground. But I guess I was too close to see the man's left arm grabbing the green oxygen bottle mounted on the wall. Because the heavy metal cylinder suddenly connected with the right side of my head, just above my ear.

The blow landed with a dull thud against my skull. I fell to the ground. The blow wasn't that hard, so I managed to bring the gunman to the floor with me. I wrestled him until I gained a top position.

Then I grabbed him by the scruff of the neck and back of his pants and rammed his head into one of the cubby holes that held Slim's belongings. I drove my left knee repeatedly into his gut. By the third knee to the stomach, I realized the cubby hole was too big since the man's head rattled around the hole. I pulled his head out, slid him back a few feet, then jammed his head into a smaller hole, one about the size of his head.

The man howled as his ears scraped into the small hole. The yelp didn't stop me from unloading my knee into his gut, however. After the fourth knee, the man had stopped squirming and went limp. I stepped back in anticipation of kicking his side.

But I stopped myself. With his head wedged in so tight, there was a chance I could break his neck and kill him. So I let the man be and grabbed my gun off the floor.

Keeping it trained on the gunman, I yelled to my buddy.

"Slim, you okay?"

No response.

"Slim!"

Nothing.

I shuffled backward until Slim's body came into view. He was face down on the floor. The upper left side of his gown was soaked in blood.

I yelled as loud as I could. "Doctor!"

CHAPTER SIXTEEN

N Kinglsey Dr.
East Hollywood, CA

LU SAT ON a brown leather couch in his apartment. His cell was on his knee. He blinked twice and looked at the screen for the third time.

Tanawat had texted moments ago. It read: *job went sideways, my man dead, another in custody*

Lu's heart started beating faster; his diaphragm pushed his chest up, causing his breathing to escalate. A minute, maybe two minutes later, Lu made his first movement: wiping sweat from his forehead.

How could they have screwed up so badly?

But before he could contemplate an answer, his mind went into flight mode. Picking up his tablet, Lu began searching for the soonest flight leaving LAX for Hong Kong. Within eight minutes, he found a direct flight leaving LAX at 6 pm, which was in about three hours. The only available spot was business class and cost over six grand.

Lu knew his employer well. They'd worked successfully together for years. He knew his first mistake with Hans Schlimmergaard would be overlooked. But a second mistake would not.

No way.

Certainly not such a massive mistake. *Who knows what this man in custody might divulge to the cops?*

Lu's life was worth more than six grand, so he reserved the business class ticket.

Twenty minutes later, Lu stood at the base of a queen bed in his small, one-bedroom apartment. Sprawled over the bed was every personal item Lu owned. The only items left in the apartment were some sparse furnishings and ordinary dishes and cooking equipment.

In one corner of the bed was a pile of shoes and clothes. To the left of that were a few handguns and two knives. In the middle of the bed were five burner cell phones that he'd used over the past six months. Below that was a small suitcase, one small enough to be carried on a plane. To the right of the suitcase was a small pile of personal documents and personal identification.

Aside from the original fake documents his uncle had provided him, Lu had three more sets of fake identification. Over his years in the criminal realm he'd worked for four different bosses. Each boss knew him by a different name, and no boss knew his real identity.

When he boarded the plane this evening, he'd officially assume his original name. Now was the time to destroy all evidence of his former selves.

Lu pocketed his passport, then scooped up the remaining documents and identification and took them to his small veranda. He piled the material in the middle of his grill, which was a small hibachi-style BBQ. After dousing everything with lighter fluid, Lu lit the pile and stepped back.

While his criminal life went up in flames, Lu grabbed his burner phones from the bedroom. He went back to the veranda and pulled out the SIM cards from each phone, then threw them on top of the flames. After wiping down each phone, he tossed the phones in a garbage bag. He planned on getting rid of every personal item, including the guns and knives.

He didn't plan to get rid of his current phone, however, in case he still needed it today. He glanced at his watch: 2:45 p.m.

Lu figured his real identity was the only thing that would keep him alive. His uncle's wisdom had paid off. Pham Van Lu had no criminal record at all.

Nobody he'd worked with knew him by that name. He figured he could disappear and hide in plain sight, so to speak.

From Hong Kong, Lu would travel to some remote location in Southeast Asia and make a new life. He had ample money in two offshore accounts, so he could live a quiet, crime free life. Maybe he could even convince his uncle to come live with him. Hopefully he wouldn't have to look over his shoulder for the rest of his life.

Hopefully.

CHAPTER SEVENTEEN

E Willow Ave.
Long Beach Medical Center

MY LEFT HAND was wrapped in ice while my other hand held a cold compress against the right side of my face. I was sitting upright on a bed wearing only a hospital gown. A nurse had just finished taking my blood pressure.

When she pulled the stethoscope from her ears, I asked, "So my buddy Hans is alright?"

She put her hands on her hips. "Alright? Your definition of alright and mine are worlds apart, Agent Chase."

Fair enough. I tried again. "Hans is going to live?"

She nodded. "We think so. He was shot in the upper left quadrant of his back; the bullet went clear through and exited out his clavicle. He also has a hip pointer from when he fell out of bed. The bullet wound isn't life threatening. He also seems to be responding well to the drugs we've given him for the poisoning. That is one tough man."

"You're telling me."

I blew out a breath and leaned back in the hospital bed. I was in a room across and down the hall from Slim's former room. I wasn't sure where Slim was currently being worked on.

The nurse blew out a breath, as forceful as mine. "I think I need a hospital bed, too. And a couple of valiums. I've seen dead bodies before, certainly in my line of work I have, but never like that."

She shuddered.

She wasn't the nurse I'd seen standing outside Slim's room when I was bashing the bedpan off the intruder's head, but she was a first responder and did witness the carnality.

I smiled at her. "Here, why don't you take this bed. Maybe I should check your pulse and BP? Hand me your stethoscope." I put down the compress and wiggled the fingers of my good hand.

She retreated backward, pointing at my bad hand. "About eight more minutes of ice on that hand. You sure you don't need an Ativan? You just had a man bleed out on your chest."

I shook my head. "I'll be okay. Unfortunately, that's not the first time it's happened. What about you? You sure you're going to be okay? Like you said, that was a pretty awful scene. Maybe one of the worst I've seen. And I've been in war before."

She winked. "We nurses are a resilient bunch. I'll recover just fine."

With that, she left the room.

As the door swung open and closed, I heard chaos in the hallway. The local cops were already here, and I wondered if the feds were, too. Now that I was directly involved, our agency would get involved somehow. The FBI typically works well with local law enforcement, but when something big and dramatic like this happens it can get ugly if one party wants to take over and not share any information.

I checked my watch: 3:15 p.m. Simon was due to be picked up in less than two hours, but I was in for a busy afternoon. When an agent was involved in a shooting and/or a death, a criminal and internal investigation was standard operating procedure. Soon I'd be on paid leave pending the outcome of both investigations.

I thought about the investigations. I wasn't too worried, but maybe I should be. After all, that nurse did witness me losing my cool with the intruder. It was a good thing the intruder was wearing a mask. That way it was clear to her who the bad guy actually was. At least I hoped it was clear.

Frank swept into the room and interrupted my thoughts.

"You okay? You look terrible."

He didn't wait for me to answer.

"Well, at least you look better than those two." He thumbed over his shoulder towards Slim's hospital room. "One dead, the other seriously injured."

"Is he critical?"

Frank shook his head. "Serious, not critical, he'll make it. Which means we may get some information from him." He walked up to my bedside. "What the hell, Chase? This is going to require some serious explanation, not to mention some serious paperwork. You're okay, though, right? That was pretty shocking in there. I mean, there were gut parts on the floor. You really raked him over the glass pieces?"

I nodded. "Gutted him. Adam's apple to belly button."

Frank swallowed. "Seriously, you okay?"

I shrugged. "I'll survive. Not sure what else to say."

He pulled a chair up to my bed. "Compartmentalizing it, like I thought you would." He shook his head. "Anyway, tell me what happened."

I filled him in on what happened in the hospital room.

At the end of my story, he said, "You know what I have to do, don't you?"

I nodded. "My badge and Glock are there." I pointed toward the table on the other side of my bed.

"It's only a temporary thing, Chase, I hope you know that."

"It's S.O.P. I get it."

Frank took my badge and service piece. "You need to decompress after what you just went through. That was brutal in the hospital room. No other way to put it. And you need time off with your son, anyway. Big changes coming up for you, Chase."

Before I could respond, my cell rang. I looked at the number and quickly answered. "Hello, Mr. Khang."

"Hello, Agent Chase. We need to talk, obviously. A serious one on one conversation." The man's tone was calm and measured, obviously the straight to business type. "Are you alone?" he asked.

I cleared my throat. "In a second I will be." I pulled the phone away and told Frank to leave, mouthing 'sorry' as he stormed off.

"We're alone now, sir," I said.

Then Ethan Khang laid into me, in the same measured, professional tone. "Word has trickled down to me that someone can't keep their mouth shut, Agent Chase. It's in the wind that my U.S. attorney's office is engaged in a top secret classified mission with a civilian. Since Hans has been poisoned and shot, I can't imagine it's him blabbing his mouth, though he was the initial leak to you, of course."

"I—"

"I can overlook Hans's mistake. I imagine he may have been on his deathbed and revealed information to you so that you'd testify in his place. I get that, I guess. But you, it's inexcusable, Agent Chase, that you'd even mention anything to anybody about a top secret, classified case. Surely you know to never bring it up. For heaven's sake, how many black ops missions have you been on?"

"Well—"

"You know why I don't know how many missions you've been on? Because they're black ops. Black ops, Agent Chase! Classified. They don't exist. They didn't HAPPEN."

Khang's tone had turned downright angry. While he tried to calm himself, I also pulled the phone away and took a breath.

The lawyer was right, of course. I shouldn't have said anything to Frank or Karla. The downright stupid move, however, was mentioning anything to Palmer.

A moment later, Khang was back on the line. His tone was more civilized. I put the phone to my ear.

"You know why I didn't call you earlier?" he asked.

He didn't wait for an answer.

"Because I was pissed, Agent Chase. My office got a call from the Long Beach PD inquiring about a classified case that for all intents and purposes doesn't exist. I needed time to calm down before calling you back. In hind-sight, I guess I needed more time."

"Understood, sir. I had a lapse in judgment. The cops are going after me for my ex-wife's murder. Which I'm clearly being set-up by the—"

"Whoa, Agent Chase," Khang interrupted. "No names, no nicknames, no reference to gender, nothing like that. Got it? I'm on a secure line but I can't speak for you."

"But I need to somehow speak about the, uh . . ."

Khang filled in. "Potential person of interest in potential custody." Silence for a moment, then he continued. "It's a bit wordy, admittedly, but it'll have to do."

I rolled my eyes at the lawyer speech, then said, "The potential person of interest is still potentially active, even though the potential person is in potential custody." I sighed. "No way, I can't talk like this, sir."

"You're right," Khang said. "That was even more painful to listen to."

"Listen, Mr. Khang, I'm using my cell, so it's secure."

The lawyer hummed and hawed for a few seconds. "Okay, let's go with simply 'suspect.' And by the way, the suspect you're referring to can't possibly be potentially active."

"What? How can you say that? How could you even know that?"

Khang didn't respond right away.

I realized my questions came out rather heated, so I said, "Respectfully, sir."

He sighed. "I'm not sure how much you know, Agent Chase, but we've been watching the suspect for months. Plus, we've had the suspect in custody for two weeks, in prison solitary. The suspect is only out of his cell for one hour a day to get exercise. He hasn't come in contact with another inmate, let alone seen one."

"Surely," I said, "you can't be serious." I wanted to call the man naïve, but I refrained since he was one of the most powerful attorneys in California. "You know the person we're dealing with, sir, and the reach this person has."

"No need for the lecture, Agent Chase. Understood. Which is why we're treating the suspect as such. Serial killers have had more latitude in prisons than this suspect. Now—"

"But the suspect could have someone on the inside that's feeding intel and commands to the outside world, a guard or someone like that."

"Already thought about and addressed. We brought in a few top federal guards from Ohio because of that very fact, with the sole job of watching the suspect."

"Sir, with all due respect, you can't underestimate this suspect."

"Agent Chase, with all due respect, stop it. I'm sure Hans told you that

I'm relentless for this suspect's throat. I want justice in its highest form. On top of that, what Hans didn't tell you, because he didn't know, is that this case is deeply personal to me. If I thought there was a chance the suspect was connecting with the outside world, I'd investigate and intervene. Believe me."

"You honestly think there's no chance the suspect is involved with what happened to Hans and my ex-wife? Seriously?"

Khang paused, then said, "No, there's always a chance. I just think it's highly unlikely given the measures we have in place. You and Hans have certainly worked on other cases that could explain why someone or some group is targeting you two. Right?"

I kept the pressure on. "So it's purely coincidental that Hans was beaten, poisoned, almost gunned down in broad daylight, that my ex-wife was murdered in my house hours after Hans visited, all this just days before Hans testifies against this suspect? Coincidental, sir?"

Khang ignored the question. "Agent Chase, we've been watching the suspect for months in an attempt to confirm his identity. Trust me, the suspect doesn't have anywhere near the reach of previous years. Nor the wealth. The suspect is indigent, and that's putting it mildly. To boot, the suspect claims to be a peaceful, changed man. A man of the Word, from what I understand."

"You can't be that naïve," I said, immediately regretting it. But I couldn't help myself. "You aren't buying the suspect's act, really? You can't be. You're the guy sending him to the chair."

"Who knows, Agent Chase? The suspect seems contrite. People can change."

"Not this person," I shot back.

"Just because the suspect is no longer violent or criminal doesn't mean the suspect gets to avoid paying the penalty for his past actions. I believe in retributive justice, Agent Chase, not restorative. That's why I'm going after the suspect. That's why I'm lobbying to have him sent to Texas to pay for his crimes."

I got up from the bed and stood. "This suspect is still just as evil and vile as before, Mr. Khang. Don't be convinced otherwise."

"You're being quite myopic, Agent Chase."

"What?" I squeezed the phone. "What are you saying?"

"You don't know what myopic means?"

"No, I'm perfectly aware of the meaning."

"Then you know you're too close. You need distance to see things clearly."

I laughed. "Says the man trying to put this suspect to death, a man who just told me he has a deep, personal interest in the case. What did you mean by that, anyway?"

Khang didn't respond right away. After a few moments, he said, "I was born and raised in America, Agent Chase, but my parents and every generation before them were born and raised in Thailand. My given name is actually Khemkhaeng. When my parents moved here in their early forties, they Americanized and changed our family name to Khang. Then when I came along, they picked a nice, easy sounding American first name: Ethan. The suspect in question is a national disgrace and a shameful embarrassment to my ancestors. And I intend to make it right for the Thai people, even though they'll probably never get the full truth. It's that simple and straightforward."

"Understood," I said. "But you still didn't answer my question."

"What question?"

"You think everything that's happened to Hans and me is coincidental? That it's not the work of the suspect you have in custody. Really? That's your stance?"

"Like I said, given the measures we have in place, I find it very hard to believe, extremely hard to believe, that he's communicating outside of his concrete bunker."

"Well, sir, I have an extremely hard time believing he's not."

"I guess we're at an impasse then, Agent Chase."

"I guess so. Perhaps the federal investigation into what happened here at the hospital will reveal otherwise."

Khang cleared his throat. "There's not going to be a federal investigation into the crimes committed at the hospital. No way. The feds are not interfering. I'm making sure of that. The local cops have full investigative authority on this one. I'll be making calls right after this conversation ends to make sure that's the case."

I blew a breath into the phone.

Before I could say anything, Khang tried to justify his actions. "We just have a few days before the AG makes his decision, Agent Chase. Nothing can interfere or derail that. I don't want anybody mentioning our suspect. There are too many people who know about our suspect already. Hopefully, the attorney general decides to prosecute the suspect in California first, followed by Texas, all in a private trial. Eventually, then, our suspect will meet his fate. Justice will be served. The end."

I didn't say anything for a moment. There didn't seem to be a chance the feds would take over the hospital investigation, so I changed the subject. "Long Beach is hot for me as a suspect in Gina's murder, so I need some help—"

"Tell me, Agent Chase," Khang interrupted. "Did you kill your ex-wife?"

"Of course not."

"Then you'll be fine. You're a big boy, you're smart, you have nothing to worry about."

"It's my understanding, sir, you may need my testimony. Isn't that right?"

A pause, then Khang cleared his throat. "It is, Agent Chase, since Hans won't be healthy enough to testify, especially after what just happened."

"You need my help, yet you don't seem willing to offer yours. Plus, for all you know, I could be in custody soon if I don't clear any charges that may come my way."

"We'll cross that road if it comes to it."

"What does that mean?"

He cleared his throat. "It means that if you're still in trouble immediately prior to meeting with the AG, my office will intervene. But only as a last resort. Only if absolutely need be. Got it?"

"I do, but I need more, sir."

"More what? More assurances? In writing?"

"No, I want something else. A few things actually. First, I want to look the suspect in the eyes prior to sentencing. Hear and see everything for myself, of what you're telling me about the suspect. Second, if the feds are not taking over these hospital murders and attempted murder of my buddy, I want to be at least kept in the loop on the investigation—"

"No way," Khang said, scoffing. "Especially as it relates to your first request. You're going to be a witness for me, Agent Chase. You can't be interacting with the suspect you're testifying against. It's impossible. I won't let that happen."

I figured that. "Fine, then I'll need Agent Dickerson to do it for—"

"Uh-uh, Agent Chase, not going to happen."

"She already knows you have a controversial suspect in custody. She's already broadly in the loop. You have to approve her meeting the suspect or I'm out. And she needs to be kept apprised of the investigation into Hans's attempted murder. You need something from me; I need something from you. Tit for tat. That's the deal. It's that simple and straightforward. Oh, and I need federal protection for Hans in this hospital."

After a moment of silence, Khang said, "I'll make sure Hans is adequately protected, but not by the feds, it has to be the local PD. That's non-negotiable, Agent Chase. As for Karla meeting the suspect, I would need to run this by my superior for approval. And I'm not sure I'll get it."

"Then I'm not sure about testifying," I said. "Guess we're at an impasse."

A pause, then, "Fine. I'll see what I can do."

"Where's the suspect now?"

"Nope," Khang said quickly. "Not over the phone. I'll text you the details after this call, then immediately delete the text. Understood?"

"Understood," I said.

"Also, so you know, Hans' lawyer is going to shadow you to the police station. He's on his way to the hospital to see Hans. I've told him to meet up with you. The local cops are going to be all over you for a statement about what happened in the hospital room, so Schuberman is going to help you with that. He's on my dime. I've hired him as an outside contractor."

"Thank you, sir, that's—"

"Wait, this is for me, not you. Let's make that clear. He's there to make sure you don't say a word about our suspect. Not a word. Understood? If you don't stay quiet about our classified case, he'll report back to me. And there are consequences for that."

"Great, sir, thanks for all your support. And thanks for sending such a colorful character with incredible lawyerly skills."

"You can thank your buddy for that. Schuberman knows what's going on, so he's the default. I'm not bringing in another attorney on this. Nobody else finds out about this or breathes a word. I don't want you tying today's hospital fiasco or your ex-wife's murder to our suspect. That's final. Once the AG has decided on the course of action, then my position can be re-negotiated if you're still in legal jeopardy and have proof our suspect has been active. But I just don't see that being the case, not at all. We're not dealing with the same suspect you used to know."

Before I could argue or say anything else, Khang said, "Good luck with everything."

And hung up.

CHAPTER EIGHTEEN

Tom Bradley International Terminal
LAX Airport

LU QUICKLY STUFFED his feet into his shoes, grabbed his wheeled carry-on luggage, and strode away from airport security. On the outside, he was the picture of calm, but he was in turmoil on the inside.

During his Uber trip to the airport, he kept his head turned so he could look out the back window. He wasn't positive, but he thought he'd spotted a tail, so he got out and requested another Uber. Eventually he made his way to the airport after a circuitous route with three different Uber drivers. He didn't notice any unusual vehicles tailing him again, but he couldn't shake the uneasy feeling.

As he walked into the secured section of the Tom Bradley International Terminal at LAX, he used his shirt sleeve to wipe his brow. He was through security, now all he had to do was kill two hours until his flight left the country.

Lu found a seat in the far corner of a busy food court. His back was to a wall, but his eyes were straight forward, searching for anyone unusual. He figured the uneasiness he felt was simply paranoia for botching the Hans job twice.

Lu planned on spending the next two hours moving from gate to gate, never in one place more than five or six minutes. He'd arrive at his gate just before boarding. Since he was flying business class, he'd be among the first to board. He knew he wouldn't relax until he was sitting in his comfy chair on the plane.

He took out his cell. Earlier, right after Tanawat texted that the job went south, Lu pulled out the SIM card in his phone. He wanted to reach out to Tanawat to figure out what went wrong, but Lu wasn't going to risk it. Cells were easily traced. For all he knew, one of Tanawat's men was currently spilling the beans. Not that Lu could be connected to Tanawat's men. But if one of the men gave up Tanawat, then Lu could be traced back to Tanawat.

Before sticking in the SIM card and turning on the phone, Lu set the timer on his watch. He wanted to make one final call with the cell, but he wouldn't talk longer than three minutes.

After reinserting the SIM and dialing his uncle, Lu waited. Five long rings later, voicemail picked up. He stabbed the END call button and removed the SIM.

He'd try one more time, right before boarding.

CHAPTER NINETEEN

Intensive Care Unit
Long Beach Medical Center

THE COPS WERE taking forever to question me.

By now, I'd at least expected the cops to sweep in and tell me they were taking me to headquarters for questioning. But so far, the only person I'd seen was the nurse.

I had a solid welt on my face from the bedpan and 2nd degree burns on my palm, but nothing that would require a stay in the hospital.

During my hospital room stay, I'd received a text from Khang. Apparently, the Rat was being held in San Quentin. Karla needed to be there promptly at 8 pm tomorrow. He also made it clear that I was forbidden to escort Karla into the prison or even be on the prison property.

Karla had texted as well. She'd been keeping her distance because of Gina's investigation, but when she heard about what happened at the hospital, she said she was heading over. And that she had a change of clothes for me.

Jimmy Schuberman had yet to make an appearance. Glancing at my watch, which read 4 pm, I knew time was tight. I'd have to either blow off the cops and leave at 4:30 to pick up my son—which would get me in further hot water with the authorities—or I'd have to find an alternate source for pick up.

Like Karla. Maybe I should reroute her to Simon's daycare?

Just as I was about to dial her number, there was a quick knock on the door.

"Come in," I said.

The door opened to reveal a smiling man in a dark blue suit.

"Hey, champ," he said. "How you doing?"

Jimmy Schuberman.

The lawyer walked over and extended his hand. "Jimmy Schuberman, Esquire."

"Esquire?" I said, grinning. "I didn't know attorneys actually used that term." I shook his hand. "Garrison Chase."

He winked and gave me the finger gun. "You'll notice, Gar, I use a lot of terms West Coast folks don't know. It's my East Coast charm."

His smile grew. Both sides of his face wrinkled all the way up until they met the wrinkles from his forehead. By the way Jimmy Schuberman talked and carried himself on the phone, I figured he was younger, like in his thirties or early forties. But this guy was mid-fifties, for sure. He looked like he'd spent a lot of time lying out on the beach, or perhaps under some lights.

"How's Slim, Jimmy? Do you refer to him as Slim?"

He nodded fast. "All his college buddies do. Slim's stable and alert. He's a tough son of a gun, ain't he, Gar?" Jimmy slugged me on the shoulder.

"Listen," I said. "I know you're pals with Slim, but even my buddies like Slim don't call me Gar or Gary. Okay?"

"Sorry, champ. So . . ."

"No more champ, either."

He dropped the smile.

Honestly, I felt a little squirmy in his presence, which was how most lawyers made me feel. After a moment, I tried to shake off my apprehension and appear less dickish. After all, I needed the man's help.

"I usually let the first one slide, Jimmy, but if people keep calling me Gar or Gary or even champ, well . . ." I held my hands up and mimicked a choking; but all in good fun since I had smile on my face.

"Got it." Jimmy laughed and threw his head back, which caused a chunky strand of his dark hair to break free from its shelled casing. He tried to comb back the chunk with his right hand. "Good one, Chase. It's alright to call you that, right?"

"Perfect," I said.

"Good, good, good." While he quickly surveyed the room, he used his left hand to try and fix his hair, but he couldn't tame the strand back into place.

"You know," I said, "you could use the bathroom to fix your hair."

"Ah, stupid hair, what a pissah." He waved me off. "Nothing but trouble hair is. Consider yourself lucky."

He thought that was funny.

When I didn't laugh, he carried on anyway. "In the office I wear a hat to keep this mop held back. Never know what to do in public."

"Let me guess, you wear a Boston Bruins cap?"

He tilted his head like a puppy dog. "How'd you know?"

I shrugged. Jimmy was somewhat how I'd pictured him when he was on the phone, though he was older and leaner than I thought. I figured Jimmy was six foot and about one hundred and eighty pounds, give or take a few. His hair and face reminded me of a well-tanned Robert De Niro from the Cape Fear movie, minus the menacing demeanor and mole on the right side of his upper cheek, of course.

Jimmy wore a fashionably tailored dark blue suit with no tie. Simple white shirt underneath with the top two buttons undone. It appeared to me he shaved his chest. From my current distance, the shaved hair on his chest looked like squashed ants. The lawyer was fidgety and no doubt uncomfortable in the suit. He'd be more at home if he was wearing track pants and a hockey jersey.

"Tell me what went down in the hospital room," Jimmy said, adjusting the crotch of his tight suit pants. "They'd taken the body out by the time I got a look at the room, obviously, but the amount of blood and mess in there. Jeepers, Chase. What the H-E double hockey sticks?"

It took me a moment to realize he meant 'hell.' "What's with you, anyway?"

"What do you mean?"

"I mean, I've never met anyone who says 'darn tooting' and 'jeepers' and spells out 'hell'. What gives?"

Jimmy collapsed into one of those hard and uncomfortable square lounge chairs you find in hospital rooms. He kicked back. "I have a potty mouth, Chase. It's pretty bad, even for East Coast standards. When we moved here, I noticed west coasters were somewhat offended by my mouth. Plus, my wife had enough of it and wanted me to stop. I figured I should since I wasn't coming off as a very professional lawyer.

"Anyway, starting in January, we did the swear jar thing. A buck for every bad word. I swear, Chase—no pun intended—it worked. For January and February, I was averaging about ten bucks a day. And my wife got to use that money for anything she wanted. No questions asked. She bought more jams and jellies for her face and skin and hair than I knew even existed." He whistled. "By April, I'd straightened up completely. And now my wife thinks the expressions I use are sort of endearing."

"That's debatable," I said.

Jimmy pointed at me. "I'll grow on you, believe me. I still say the word 'pissah'. That's an East Coast thing that I simply can't drop. Part of my DNA." He cleared his throat. "Alright, now tell me what went down in Slim's room."

"Do I have to?"

"Nope, I guess you don't since I'm not your lawyer. You do know why I'm here, though, right?"

"Khang filled me in. Listen," I checked my watch, "I have childcare issues soon. What's the deal with the cops? Are they coming here and taking me or are we meeting them at the station?"

Jimmy sat up. "I told them we'd meet them at the station after you and I conferenced a little."

"We don't need to conference, Jimmy. At least not about what happened here. I know how to give and take statements. Though I may need your help . . ."

I stopped myself, wondering if I should get Jimmy to help with my alibi. The cop's suspicion surrounding my involvement in Gina's death was a thorn in my side. And now that the cops weren't going to learn about the Rat, I knew things would get trickier for me, legally speaking.

"Need your help with what?" Jimmy prodded.

If the situation was different, I'd handle the cops on my own. But I needed the cops off my back quickly, so I said, "I need your help with my other problem."

"What other problem?"

I sighed. "My ex-wife's murder, Jimmy. My alibi. Remember? Maybe you can get the cops off my back on that one."

He collapsed back. "Right, right, right."

"Okay, fine, I guess not. That's certainly not the posture of someone wanting to help. I thought you and Hans were buddies. You can't help a buddy's buddy out?"

He held out his hands. "It's not that, Chase. Believe me. It's Khang. He wants minimal involvement from me on this one. He has me on retainer. I know as a fact he wouldn't be happy to learn I'm working with you on your ex-wife's murder."

I knew I'd have to speak Jimmy's language to convince him, so I said, "Nice set of balls you have on you. I mean, jeepers, you're an independent lawyer who doesn't report to the U.S. attorney for the Central California district. Isn't that right? I mean, you're not a federal or state employee. Grow a pair, pal."

Jimmy stood, but he didn't bite. "My hands are tied."

"What if I hire you as my lawyer? Put you on retainer. Don't tell me you can't be on retainer for two clients. Don't tell me you're going to pass up a client in need, who's a friend of a friend."

Jimmy walked over and slugged my shoulder. "You couldn't afford me."

"Try me."

"Honestly, 10 grand, and that's my buddy's buddy price. Normally, it'd be 15."

I tried not to flinch. I definitely couldn't afford him. Maybe I did have to rethink things.

"Told you," he said. "Federal employees are not my usual paying client."

"I'll consider it. Now hang tight, I'll be back in a few minutes."

"Where you going?"

"Like I said earlier, I have some childcare issues to arrange. When I'm back, we'll head over to the station together."

Jimmy shrugged and took a seat, whipped out his cellphone.

I stepped into the hallway to call Karla, hoping she could swing by and pick up Simon. Unfortunately, the call went to voicemail. I didn't leave a message. Instead, I walked to the ICU breakroom to get a cup of crappy coffee. I needed an afternoon caffeine fix.

As I poured a cup, I performed a quick mental calculation of my limited savings. Even if I could afford Jimmy or another lawyer, I was innocent after all. I couldn't imagine using my savings to pay a lawyer to prove what I already knew. Talk about a waste.

I'd only hire Jimmy if I absolutely had to.

When I returned to my hospital room, I was surprised to see Karla sitting on the edge of the bed. Jimmy was still in the chair.

"There's the man of the hour," Jimmy said. "We were just talking about you." He held out his hands, palms toward me. "Nothing but good things."

I turned to Karla. "How are you doing?"

"Sorry I didn't answer your call," she said. "I was just around the corner when you rang."

"No prob. You doing alright?"

She waved me off. "Forget me. What about you? Jimmy just gave me some quick details about what happened in Slim's room. Crazy. Are you okay?"

I nodded. "Well, it was definitely physical and bloody in there, but I'll manage."

Karla touched my face, then checked out my hand.

Before she got more handsy, I asked, "You alright with picking up Simon from daycare?"

"Sure," she said. "No problem."

"Great, I'll call daycare and let them know you're coming." Then I turned to Jimmy. "How long do you think we'll be at the station? Since I'm not saying much, it shouldn't be too long. Maybe two hours tops?"

"Tops," he said, winking.

I glanced at Karla. "You okay with keeping Simon until 7ish? He doesn't know about his mom yet. I'll tell him this evening."

She nodded. "You going to be okay?" She put her arm around my waist and squeezed.

"Wait," Jimmy said. "Are you two . . .?"

I glared at him. "Jeepers, pal, drop it."

Jimmy held up his palms again, obviously a trait of his.

Karla furrowed her brow at my expression.

"Never mind," I said.

While Karla walked back to the bed and began another conversation with Jimmy, I headed to the corner of the room and dialed my son's daycare.

They picked up on the third ring. Brenda introduced herself.

"Brenda, it's Garrison Chase. Just wanted you to know that Karla Dickerson will be picking Simon up around five."

"Oh," she said. "Well, that's strange."

"What do you mean? What's strange? She dropped him off this morning."

"No, it's strange you don't know."

I swallowed. "Don't know what? What's going on?"

"That Simon was picked up early today."

"Picked up early?"

I said it loud enough that Karla and Jimmy immediately stopped talking and looked my way. I swallowed a second time since I felt a tennis ball in my throat. My heart thumped on the inside of my chest.

"Who picked him up early?"

"His grandparents did, about an hour ago, Mr. Chase."

"What?" I snapped.

"They're on the approved list, sir. Your ex-wife put them on it."

"The Diekelman's?" I asked.

"Uh-huh."

"Did they say anything?"

"Well . . ."

I prodded her when she didn't continue. "Well what, Brenda?"

"They did appear upset, Mr. Chase, especially Mr. Diekelman. And they said they'd be picking up and dropping Simon off for the foreseeable future."

I muttered, "Over my dead body."

"What was that, sir?"

"Nothing, Brenda, thanks." I hung up.

Karla was to my immediate left. I hadn't noticed her walk over. "What's going on?"

"I have to go. Now." I blinked a few times. "I mean, right now."

"Where?" Karla asked.

"We'll talk in your car," I said.

Jimmy stepped toward me as I rushed toward the door. "Chase, you can't leave. You're needed at police headquarters."

Before opening the door, I stopped and addressed Jimmy. "You're a lawyer, you're convincing, at least I hope you are. Plus, I'm a federal agent. Surely that buys me some leeway, right?"

He shrugged. "Maybe, maybe not. It certainly won't go over well. And you're already in hot water because of your ex-wife's murder."

Gina's parents lived in Oregon, but they were down for the week to visit and celebrate Simon's birthday. Surely Dan and Helen Diekelman knew their daughter was dead, maybe even murdered, by now. And those two loathed me. Had they told Simon about his mother? Perhaps they'd poisoned Simon against me already. How much have they told my son in the past hour?

Suddenly my breathing became shallower.

Jimmy put his hand on my shoulder and snapped me out of it. "I'm not sure what's going on, Chase, but you can't leave. Not now."

"You're hired, Jimmy." I looked him in the eye. "You're my official lawyer now. Get me out of this mess, both messes, in fact. We'll work out the retainer later. Tell the cops I'll be in for questioning in the morning. Smooth things over."

"Chase, you can't—"

I didn't hear the rest of his sentence because I was already out of the room with Karla hot on my heels.

CHAPTER TWENTY

Park Ave.
Belmont Shore, CA

KARLA AND I sat out front of my ex-wife's house in Karla's blue Ford 500. I was in the passenger seat incessantly tapping my left foot, itching to charge through the front door and grab my son. Karla had shifted in the driver's seat and was holding her arm across my chest, effectively holding me back.

"I know you're pissed, beyond pissed, I get it. But Simon's in there, Chase. For his sake, it's best this is handled calmly and diplomatically."

I shot her a look. "Then I'm not the man for the job. Certainly not."

"You can be." She pulled her arm away and rested her hand on my left knee. "Just give yourself a minute to calm down."

I practiced slow and steady breathing, which made me feel like I was in my former therapist's office. Which didn't help considering my ex-wife had been dating my former therapist. I suddenly wondered if Dr. Frances Julian was inside Gina's house. Maybe right now he was comforting my son.

I felt Karla's warm hand on top of my fist. "Your hand's shaking, Chase. Why don't you step outside the car and get some fresh air?"

So I did. And it helped. A little.

Karla came around and stood beside me. We both leaned against the side of her car. My head was craned toward Gina's house. Most of the lights were on, but the California shutters on the windows were closed.

"I think I'm ready," I said.

Karla gently held me back. "Kids Simon's age start forming their first memories around this time. I know my first memory was around four years old."

I nodded. "Been thinking the same thing."

She grabbed my hand and squeezed it. "At his age, it's gonna be hard for him to understand his mom's never coming back. You don't want to make it extra hard on him by yanking him from his home in a fit of anger."

I squeezed her hand back. "You're right, you're absolutely right. I don't want that to be his first lasting memory. I'll keep it together."

Shaking out my fists, I continued. "Though, Karla, if I'm being honest, right now I'm picturing bouncing Dan Diekelman's face down every step of Gina's front porch. And he's the somewhat normal one of the couple. Probably not the one behind this. I won't tell you where my mind's going with Helen."

"What do you mean 'normal one of the couple'?"

"Never mind," I said. "I should get Simon. I'm ready."

She smiled. "Sounds like you need another minute."

I thought about it. "Maybe I do."

"What's Helen like?" Karla prodded me. "Tell me about her."

I took a deep breath. "Well, she definitely wears the pants in the relationship. She runs their multi-million-dollar farming operation in Oregon. She has the business acumen but Dan's the true genius, at least scientifically speaking. He has his PhD in plant sciences from UC-Davis. They're both seriously into all the new food movements: organic, grass fed, gluten free, non-GMO, if it's trendy, they're into it. They run a massive organic potato operation just outside of Portland."

"Dan tends to stay in the background then?"

"Definitely." I nodded. "She's the vocal, opinionated, ultra-liberal one. She hates the fact that I carry a gun and have fought in two wars. I mean, hates it. She'll be over the top now that her daughter's been killed by a gun, not to mention that I get sole custody of her grandson."

Karla's eyes got big. "Sounds like this is going to be fun."

"Yeah, real fun."

"You want me to come with you?"

"No, you should hang back."

"Got it."

"Here it goes." I took off across Gina's lawn, climbed the porch steps, and rapped on the front door.

Keeping my arms straight at my side, I rolled my shoulders to stay loose. A moment later, I could see Helen Diekelman striding toward the front door. The door itself was solid wood with no window, but it was part of a French door set so there were two narrow, tall windowpanes on either side of the door.

Helen didn't make eye contact with me. And instead of opening the door, she simply turned the small blinds closed on the French windows. I could hear her steps walking away.

"Aw, come on, Helen. Let's not do this."

I rang the doorbell twice and waited.

Nothing, though I did hear voices coming from the back of Gina's house.

What I wanted to do was kick down the door, but I refrained and hurried down the front steps, then made my way around the side of the house. There was no open window to look into. I even tried the back door into the kitchen, but it was locked, and so was the sliding door into the living room.

By the time I circled the house and arrived back at the front door, I was irritated. With a flat palm, I pounded twice on the front door. I didn't hear footsteps, though I did hear a car door open.

When I looked back, I saw Karla hurrying over.

I held up my hand. "I'm fine, Karla."

"I know, I just think it's best I'm here."

"You're probably right." Then I pounded twice more. "Come on, Helen, I know where your daughter keeps a hidden key."

Some moments of silence ensued, then the blinds on the left window opened.

I was startled to see Helen Diekelman standing less than a foot away from the window.

"My daughter," she seethed in a low tone, "was murdered in your house." She leaned closer. Her bright green eyes barely visible beneath the scowl. She pressed her finger against the glass. "Get off my daughter's porch, you murderer."

I took a step closer to the window. "I had nothing to do with it, Helen, nothing."

Karla stepped out from behind me and stood to my left.

I continued. "I understand you're upset, I'm sorry for your loss, so sorry, but you have to believe me, I had nothing to do with it."

Helen scoffed. "You're a suspect, aren't you? That's what I heard. And I don't have to believe anything you say, Gary. Don't tell me what to believe."

She knew how much I hated that name, but I kept my cool. "I'm devastated over this, Helen, just like you."

"How can you say that? Unbelievable. You and my daughter were not on good terms, don't you dare say that or pretend that to be the case."

"Fair enough. I'm devastated for Simon; that's what I meant. Never in a million years would I want him to lose his mother."

She shook her head and stayed silent. I could tell she was seething underneath her silence. When she was mad, she reminded me of Gina. They shared a similar angry face, along with the same green eyes, thick, dark hair, and aquiline nose. Helen had that sallow look of a woman in her sixties, though. The skin on her face sagging after years of gravity pulling it down.

Helen finally spoke. "Like I said, off my daughter's porch, Gary. Now."

I tilted my head. "You know I'm not leaving, not without Simon, Helen."

She shook her head.

"I'm his father. I'm the sole guardian now. I—"

"Exactly." She pressed her finger against the glass again. "There's your motive. There's your wretched motive."

I stepped forward until I was now about a foot away from the glass. "Oh, please, quit that."

Karla chimed in. "Mrs. Diekelman, Garrison has custody rights. You can't do this, legally speaking."

Helen didn't look at Karla, just glared at me. "I'm not even going to ask who that is. I'm calling the police."

"Fine," I said. "Go right ahead. I'm getting the key and coming in."

While Helen scurried away, I grabbed Gina's hidden key from the bushes to the right of the front door.

After putting the key in the lock, I glanced back at Karla. "This is okay, right?"

She nodded. "At this point, you've been calm and reasonable. Now go get your boy. I'll be right behind you."

I opened the door and walked in. When I made it to the kitchen, I saw Helen with the phone pressed to her ear.

"You seriously calling the police, Helen?"

She pulled the cell away. "I'm calling my lawyer first. No way is this right when your ex-wife was killed in your house and you're a suspect. No way." She stabbed her finger at me.

I ignored her and walked through the kitchen to the living room.

Dan Diekelman was sitting on the couch facing me, crouched forward watching Simon. My son was on the floor pushing around a large transport truck. Simon turned when he heard my footsteps.

For a moment, the smile on his face transported me away from the awkwardness of the moment and the craziness of the day.

"Daddy," he said, running toward me.

I scooped him up and squeezed him. "Hey pal, how you doing?" I pulled him back to get a good look at his face. He beamed. Clearly, he hadn't been told about Gina. Perhaps the Diekelman's hadn't said a word about it, or perhaps they just said mommy wouldn't be home tonight.

While I hugged Simon against my shoulder, I glanced at Dan. The man ran his fingers through his silver hair and sighed. His eyes were bloodshot. The skin below his lower lids was bulging and swollen. I imagined if someone poked the skin tears would gush from his eyes.

I mouthed, 'so sorry.'

He quickly waved me off, like it was too emotional and hard to even be in my presence.

Karla was already heading back through the kitchen, so I followed her. I turned to the right and headed straight to the front door, not looking to my left at Helen. I could hear Helen in a heated conversation with her lawyer. The woman stopped talking as soon as she saw me.

Next thing I knew I felt fists pounding into my upper back as I walked toward the front door.

"Let him go, let him go, Gary. NOW!"

Karla turned and I immediately handed Simon to her, then shooed her out. Karla covered Simon's face and rushed out the front door, quickly closing the door behind her.

I stood and let Helen wail on my back. Let her get it all out. I didn't want to say anything and escalate her emotions. The last thing I needed was Helen screaming louder so that Simon could hear outside.

When I thought she was finished hitting me, I turned around. Dan had his right arm around his wife's waist, pulling her back into the kitchen. With his left arm he waved me off, even quicker and more forceful than last time.

I didn't need to be told. As I slipped out the front door, I heard Helen yelling, "This isn't over, Gary. My lawyer will be in contact tomorrow. This isn't right. It's not RIGHT!"

Karla fiddled with the car seat straps as I approached her vehicle. She heard me coming and looked back, making an 'ouch' face. I tried not to look dejected because Simon was watching me over Karla's shoulder.

He beamed at me for a moment, then made a cute, serious face. "Why's gammy upset, Dad?"

Karla finished with the straps and backed away. I moved in and kissed my son on the forehead, then tickled his belly.

"Never mind about that, pal. Grandma is upset your leaving with me. She wanted more time with you . . ." I stopped tickling him because he was laughing pretty hard at this point.

I looked him in the eye. "Everybody wants to spend time with you cuz you're a super awesome dude." I messed his hair, then climbed into the passenger seat.

"You okay?" Karla asked.

I shook my head, then leaned it back on the seat rest. Didn't say anything or want to say anything. I needed a few moments to process everything. Karla knew I didn't like to talk right after a tense situation, so she respected my silence and fired up the Ford.

I was awash in various emotions, which was unchartered water for me. Normally I was very dude-ish and could compartmentalize my emotions. But I didn't know how I was supposed to feel at the moment.

Part of me was joyous, exuberant may have been a better word to describe it. Here I had sole custody and responsibility for my only son. I no longer had to fight with my ex-wife over anything as it relates to Simon. But I was also a little scared to be the sole provider, caretaker, rule maker, shaper of his psyche. What if I messed this kid up? Surely, I'd mess him up at some point, at least accidentally, right?

I found myself gripping my thighs. I was also crushed for Simon. Devastated to tell him he'd never see his mom again. Questions raced through my mind, which stressed me out. What exactly do I tell him? How do I handle it?

Don't get me wrong, I wasn't feeling bad for myself for having to broach the awkward conversation with Simon. My dread was for Simon no longer having a mother, for him missing out on that special relationship. To be honest, I was a bit of a momma's boy growing up, probably because I had a hardened, non-responsive father. Anyway, I loved my mother to bits, and still do, even though she drives me bonkers sometimes.

Thinking about Simon missing out on the mother-son relationship was overwhelming.

"I know you're deep in thought, Chase," Karla said. "But any idea where you want me to go? Simon really wants to know, too."

I tuned in and realized Simon had been repeating himself for the past minute. "Where are we going, Daddy? What are we doing? Where are we going?"

"Somewhere exciting," I said, turning to face my son. "Dad's got an awesome plan."

CHAPTER TWENTY-ONE

Tom Bradley International Terminal
LAX Airport

LU BREEZED PAST his gate and glanced at the electronic board. His plane would be boarding in less than fifteen minutes. He figured it was time to call his uncle.

He walked to the next gate and chose a seat with no passengers nearby. After re-inserting the SIM card, he waited for the cell to power up. As he did, he noticed boarding lines were starting to form at his gate. Soon he'd be on the plane and could finally breathe a sigh of relief.

Just before turning his attention to his phone, Lu glanced at a tall Asian man leaning against a glass window to the right of the check-in area. What got Lu's attention were the man's eyes; they immediately looked away when Lu looked at him.

Perhaps it was an innocent, bypassing look, Lu thought.

To re-check, Lu looked away for about forty-five seconds, then suddenly flicked his eyes in the direction of the man. Sure enough, the man's eyes were back on him. Again, the man quickly looked away.

Lu didn't know if paranoia had gotten the best of him or if the man was truly watching him. But he did need to find out.

So he quickly stood and walked away from the boarding gate with the intention of finding the nearest restroom. He didn't look back until he reached the restroom opening. Before ducking into the bathroom, he glanced over his shoulder.

Unfortunately, there were lots of people walking, so Lu's glance didn't reveal much. The only thing he gathered was that the tall Asian man wasn't immediately following behind him.

Lu kept going into the restroom and chose a stall at the farthest end of the bathroom. Once seated, he shook his head. His nerves had certainly gotten the best of him.

After a few deep breaths, he dialed his uncle. Again, voicemail picked up, but this time Lu left a message.

"Uncle," Lu said in his native tongue, "it's your disgraced nephew calling, for maybe the last time in a while. I wanted to thank you for your sacrifice. Thank you for what you did for me. I'm forever grateful for what—"

"CLEANING," a voice suddenly yelled, interrupting his message. "We're closing for cleaning."

Lu looked under the stall. A few pairs of feet exited the bathroom. He also saw a wheeled cleaning cart roll into the bathroom.

He finished the voicemail, telling his uncle that he'd be out of touch for some time, but would reconnect when he could. After hanging up, Lu figured he may as well pee since he was sitting on a toilet and about to board a plane. When he finished, he realized he was the last patron in the bathroom, aside from the whistling worker.

"You almost finished down there?" the worker asked. "We're closing."

Lu didn't respond. Instead, he glanced under the stall again. The worker had a mop in hand and was mopping his direction. The worker had pushed the cart closer to Lu's end. What caught Lu's attention, however, was another pair of feet standing by the door.

The worker moved closer to Lu's stall and said, "Who were you talking to?"

Lu's eyes widened. What shocked him wasn't the question itself. It was the fact that the worker asked it in Lu's native tongue.

After sitting still for seconds, though it felt like a minute, Lu snapped out of it and looked under the stall for the third time. The worker headed straight to his stall, pushing the cart alongside him. The other pair of feet was still by the door.

Breathing heavily, Lu looked around the stall for something that could be used as a weapon, but there was nothing. He quickly took the SIM card from his cell and threaded it into the front crotch part of his cotton briefs. He left the tiny card tucked all the way in and under his balls. Then he rebuttoned his pants and buckled his belt.

When the man's feet stopped in front of his stall, Lu flushed the toilet. Suddenly the man kicked open the stall door, busting the latch with little problem.

Immediately Lu recognized the man, but he didn't react as the man stepped into the stall. No cowering or covering or turning away. He'd face his demise head on.

The man stated again in Lu's native tongue: "Who were you talking to?"

Lu calmly said, "You'll never know." He held up the cell. "I just flushed the SIM card down the toilet. Kill me now if you have a gun because I'll never come with you. I know who you are."

The man smiled, showing off his yellowed, crooked teeth. His front right tooth was missing, which provided definitive confirmation of the man's identity. He was indeed the man nicknamed, 'Ke Tra Tan'—the Torturer.

The Torturer spoke. "Let me guess, the call was to your uncle." The Torturer then recited the address of his uncle's store. "That's right, Pham Van Lu, we know exactly who you are, too. You underestimated our mutual employer."

Lu did his best to hide his surprise.

How long had his employer known?

The Torturer continued. "You will come with us." He motioned to the man at the door.

Lu heard footsteps, followed by the movement of the cart. Moments later, the cart appeared behind the Torturer. The cart was open in the middle and large enough to hold a man.

The tall Asian man stepped into view, right behind the cart. He reached into the cart, pushed aside some garbage bags, and pulled out a hotshot, otherwise known as a cattle prod; the Torturer's known choice of weapon.

Smiling, the Torturer took the prod and clicked it on. An eerie hum echoed throughout the bathroom.

Lu fought off the first two jabs with his hands. The third jab of the cattle prod, however, connected with his chest. The last thing he remembered before everything went dark was pain.

Excruciating pain.

CHAPTER TWENTY-TWO

Target Department Store
Long Beach, CA

I NEVER THOUGHT an 'awesome plan' of mine would include a trip to Target. Not in a million years.

Back in the day, Gina and I would argue incessantly over the department store. She'd spend hundreds of dollars there every two weeks. And every two weeks I'd try to stop her from going, telling her we didn't need another new rug for the front door since we'd just purchased one three months ago.

I lost every one of the arguments, for the record.

Simon needed some things, however, so here we were at Target. Currently, we were in the toys section. I promised Simon he could pick out two toys, but nothing that made loud noises.

Since Simon was preoccupied picking out his toys, it gave Karla and me time to discuss tomorrow's plan. She was down with questioning the Rat at San Quentin, really excited about it actually.

Simon chose a Chewbacca stuffed toy that fortunately didn't make any sounds and a Millennium Falcon Lego set. My son was obsessed with Star

Wars, in particular Chewbacca. I could do a decent impression of the Wookie, and I would often do that for Simon's amusement. We'd also picked out some new clothes for him, a bathing suit, a pair of pajamas, and a new Star Wars toothbrush and toothpaste set. I'd also purchased a compact GPS tracking system for kids. Even though I felt Simon would be safe with my mother, I wanted to know his exact whereabouts at all times.

When we finished at Target, we grabbed a quick bite to eat, then Karla dropped us off at a Holiday Inn Express in Long Beach. We could have stayed at Karla's place for the night, but Karla and I agreed it would be best if I had some alone time with Simon to tell him about his mom. Also, I'd promised Simon we'd swim in the hotel pool. Once I mentioned that, there was no turning back.

Karla planned on taking care of Simon in the morning while I went to the station and gave my statement. Then I'd drop Simon off at my mother's house and head north to San Quentin with Karla.

After swimming in the pool for an hour—which really wasn't swimming at all, more like tossing Simon into the water over and over until my arms ached—we went back to the room and got ready for bed. I put a Paw Patrol episode on the television and tucked in tightly next to my son.

Simon had one arm clasping Chewie while the other arm was hooked around my neck. I cradled Simon's body tight to my right side. Every minute or so he glanced over and smiled at me, telling me what a great night he had. He also kept asking me about my face and what had happened.

For the third time, I said, "Dad had an accident, but I'm okay."

He followed up. "Does it hurt, Dad? It must hurt."

I cleared my throat. "At first I was like, 'Arrrrrrrrrr.' I did the best Wookie yell I could muster. "But now it doesn't hurt, not at all." I purred like I thought a Wookie would.

Simon grinned ear to ear. "I love you, Daddy." He squeezed his arm and brought me closer, then kissed my bruised and swollen cheek.

After that, he turned and watched TV.

I was euphoric; I really was. It sounds cliché, but a warm feeling enveloped me. Considering all the chaos that happened to me today, it was a strange moment. But I embraced the feeling and basked in it for a while.

I probably should've been thinking about how to tell Simon about his mom, how to get money to pay Jimmy, about my testimony against the Rat, all those sorts of things. But I didn't think about any of them. My mind stayed in the moment.

In the end, I decided I wouldn't tell Simon about his mother tonight. I couldn't. We both had a fabulous father/son evening. I wasn't about to ruin the day and the memory.

As I lay there, though, my mind flipped. Maybe I should tell him about his mom. Maybe I was being selfish. Super selfish, in fact. Was I?

I blew out a breath, which caused Simon to perk up.

"Dad," he said. "Where's Mom? When am I going to see Mom again?"

I kept stroking his hair and smiled. I didn't want to tell him the truth, but I also didn't want to lie to him either.

"When Dad? When?"

I cleared my throat. "Let's talk about it in the morning, son." I tried distracting him. "How about one more episode of Paw Patrol, then lights out?"

He nodded feverishly.

We watched another episode, pointing out our favorite dog every time the pup came on screen. After lights went out, I lightly scratched Simon's back until he just about fell asleep.

Right before closing his eyes for the night, Simon looked up at me.

"Dad, I love you, but I miss Mom. I miss her a lot."

I cradled him, holding him just tight enough so that he wouldn't squirm away. "I know, son, I know. I'm sorry."

As Simon drifted off to sleep, I stared at the ceiling and thought about Simon losing his mother. I thought about him in his teenage years asking me a bunch of questions about her. 'What was she like, Dad?' 'Show me some pictures.' Why did you guys break up, Dad?' 'Did you guys break up because of me?'

All the questions he'd have over the years. All the emotions he'd go through, some I could help with, some I couldn't. All these thoughts rifled through my mind.

But the thought—the one that took me over the edge—was Simon telling his wife one day that his mother was murdered in his father's house, and what it was like growing up in the aftermath. I envisioned Simon breaking down and being vulnerable with his wife, telling her how hard it had been. I pictured his wife holding him and crying, too.

My pillow caught the cold tears rolling down my cheeks. I'd only cried a few times in my life. And the times I did cry, I fought back the tears with as much muster as I could since I was embarrassed someone might see me.

Not this time. I didn't fight it. I didn't even try. I'd heard the expression before, but to me it was only an expression. It didn't really mean anything to me. I didn't even think it was possible. But it was.

That night, I cried myself to sleep.

And I wasn't embarrassed at all. Not one bit.

I was simply devasted for my son.

DAY TWO

CHAPTER TWENTY-THREE

Holiday Inn Express
Long Beach, CA

SIMON BRUSHED HIS teeth in the bathroom while I lounged on the king-sized bed. We'd just returned from a very limited 'continental' style breakfast the hotel offered.

I laid on the bed and prepared to tell him about his mom when he finished with his teeth. Karla would be at the hotel in about an hour, so this gave Simon some time to process the news.

Simon popped his head out of the bathroom. "Going poop, Dad."

"Got it, buddy." I gave him the thumbs up, then grabbed my cell and turned it on. When I'd arrived at the hotel yesterday, I turned it off so I could focus on my son and not be distracted. It was something I frequently did at the end of a long day, or when Simon visited me on the weekends. I told Karla to call the hotel room if she had to get a hold of me.

To my surprise, the cell lit up when it powered on. Seeing all the numbers in the queue caused me to sit up and turn sideways on the bed.

There were three different phone numbers, but fifteen calls in total. Wow,

I'd missed fifteen calls in the last twelve hours? That had never happened before. I was positive the most calls I'd ever had in a twenty-four-hour period was like three.

My palms were sweaty as I scrolled through the different numbers. About a third of the numbers were Frank's cell. The other third were Jimmy Schuberman's phone number. And the third number in the queue was unrecognizable to me, though it was a local Long Beach area code.

What on earth? Was I in that much trouble for not going to the police station yesterday afternoon? I was so deep in thought I didn't notice Simon sitting beside me. He shook my knee.

"All done, Dad," he said. "You alright? You look funny."

I smiled it off. "Fine, buddy. Dad needs to make a call or two. Why don't you work on the Lego set? I'll help you after I'm finished with my calls."

Simon shrugged. "Sure."

I set him up with the Lego set on the small table near the hotel door, then went back and sat on the edge of the bed.

Should I call Frank or Jimmy or try the unknown number? After some thinking, I knew I wasn't going to call the unknown number and get sucked into a conversation and/or situation I wasn't prepared for. And I didn't want to call Frank either. He'd lay into me for not going to the station and putting my statement on record.

So, I called my lawyer.

Jimmy picked up on the second ring. "Geez, Louise, Chase. Are you kidding me? Where have you been? Jeepers. You're close to making me swear again, Chase."

While he paused and took a breath, I said, "I take it you didn't smooth things over with the police, Jimmy."

"Don't even start, champ. And, yes, I'm going to call you champ. After all the stress you've put me through overnight, I've earned the right to call you champ. In fact, I'm liable to start calling you G—"

"Don't you dare," I interjected. "I can't believe everybody is so worked up over me postponing my statement. I mean, really—"

"Wait," Jimmy said. "Have you not spoken with Frank or Detective Palmer? I know both have been trying to reach you."

"Nope, Jimmy, you're the first person I've called this morning. Figured since I was paying you so much, I should start with you."

"First of all, Chase, you haven't paid me a dime yet, for the record. Second, your troubles have nothing to do with your statement. We're beyond that."

"Then what the hell's going on?"

Jimmy took a big breath. "Yesterday afternoon cops got a call from an anonymous source. The man said he was your neighbor, but he didn't want to identify himself for fear of retaliation."

"What? You're kidding? I hope you're kidding."

"I'm not. The neighbor said he saw you climbing over your back fence around 10 am. He thought that was a little strange but didn't think twice about it until the cops rolled in a half hour later."

I hung my head. The ultimate set-up continued. I gripped the phone tight in my right hand while my other made a fist. I looked over and saw Simon staring at me with an inquisitive look on his face. I released my fist and waved to him that everything was fine.

"I need you at the station, Chase. Pronto. We've got to deal with this straightaway and head on. It's not good. The DA is filing charges as soon as she gets in this morning. Get down to the station asap. I can meet in thirty."

I didn't respond. My mind switched gears into investigative mode. I was in serious trouble. I needed a solid plan.

"Chase, can you meet in thirty?"

Looking at Simon, I said, "I need an hour, Jimmy, maybe less."

"Fine. I'll tell the cops you'll be there in forty-five."

After Jimmy hung up, I called Karla and told her to get to the hotel as soon as possible. She informed me she was already on her way. Apparently, Frank had called her this morning looking for me. My boss filled her in on the latest development with my alibi.

When I hung up, Simon asked again, "You sure everything's okay, Dad?"

I didn't respond right away since my mind was focused on clearing my alibi. I needed to call Mick and let him know what was going on. If Julie did see me in the driveway, he was obviously the best person to convince her to come clean. Or maybe Mick had a security system at his place; maybe one of those doorbell cameras. Perhaps the camera picked up my car pulling into their driveway.

"Dad!" Simon repeated.

"Sorry, pal," I said, walking over and ruffing up his hair. "Everything's fine. Karla will be here soon, and we'll take you over to grandmas."

He turned back to his Lego set. I used the opportunity to call Mick. When voicemail picked up, I ducked into the bathroom and left my buddy a long-winded message.

Since I was a sweaty mess, I hopped into the shower. By the time I toweled off and changed, Karla was knocking on the hotel door. When I let her in, she immediately hugged Simon and engaged with him for a minute or so.

"Pack up your Lego set," I told Simon. "We're off to grandmas."

As Simon swept his Legos into the box, Karla gently rubbed my back with her right hand.

We loaded up our limited stuff into Karla's vehicle and drove in relative silence to my mom's house. Karla waited in the car while I spoke with Mom and informed her of Gina's death and the repercussions that followed. It was painful saying goodbye to my son and leaving him behind, but I knew he would be in safe hands with my mother.

I ended up being at Mom's much longer than I thought. So when I got back to the vehicle, Karla had a coffee waiting for me.

"Sorry," I said. "I guess you got tired of waiting."

"No prob. I know your mother. And I know you can't stand the terrible coffee in hotels."

"You're the best." I reached into my wallet and pulled out a small, flat GPS tracker along with the folded instruction manual.

As I was unfolding the paper, Karla said, "A GPS tracker, huh? I saw you throw that into the cart at Target. Not a bad idea."

"I'm taking no chances here." I held up the tiny tracker. "There were two of these in the system I bought. They're super flat and meant to be put in a kid's shoe, but it also fits easily in a wallet. Anyway, I just put one in Simon's shoe. You know I bought him those Steph Curry Under Armour shoes for Christmas. It's all the kid wears, only takes them off for bed."

"I know," Karla said. "I helped him put them on yesterday morning. I hope the smell of those shoes doesn't ruin the signal."

I laughed. "Good one. Now I just have to figure out how to set up the GPS. It's supposed to be a piece of cake. Apparently, you track the signal through your cell. Some app, I guess, makes it easy.

She frowned. "You know the app will need to be downloaded onto your phone, right?" She paused and kept staring at me. When I didn't respond, she continued. "From the internet, Chase."

I suddenly realized my stupidity. "And I don't have an internet plan for my cell."

Karla patted my knee. "I was wondering how long it'd take you to figure that out. You know, we could set it up on my phone."

I thought about it. "I'm fine with that, if you are."

She nodded. "Why don't you drive to the police station and I'll download the app and set it up on my phone. I think that'll be best. You're not exactly tech savvy."

"Probably wise," I said.

After switching seats, I looked at my watch. "We need to double-time it to the station."

I dropped the gearshift in drive and zoomed off. When we reached the Long Beach police station, I pointed across the parking lot. Jimmy was pacing back and forth in front of the station doors.

It'd been about an hour and a half since I spoke with Jimmy.

"How can I help you out of this mess?" Karla asked, looking up from her cell.

I turned to my right. "I'm going to have Jimmy help me out of this mess. After all, the guy's going to suck up my savings and then some. If I can't shake these charges quickly, I'll need you to head to San Quentin by yourself. You okay with that?"

"Sure," she said. "If you're not out in two hours, I'll need to get on the road since it's a six or seven-hour drive. You're going to be fine, right?"

I shrugged. "Well, I didn't murder my ex-wife, so I should be. I just have to prove it. Except I'm limited on what I can reveal."

"You'll figure it out, you always do."

She squeezed my hand as I exited the vehicle. As she hopped over the gear shift and into the driver's seat, I leaned in and motioned at her cell. "Is it all set-up?"

"Yup, I'm tracking your son as we speak."

"You okay with checking on his whereabouts every so often?"

"You know I am."

After she drove off, Jimmy rushed over. "Forty-five minutes, maybe an

114

hour, talk about bull crap. Coppahs are pissed, pal. We have to get in there now."

Jimmy grabbed my arm and ushered me into the station. Palmer waited just to the left of the front desk. When he saw Jimmy and me, he came directly over.

Stepping in front of me, he said, "Garrison Chase, you're under arrest—"

"Really, Detective?" Jimmy stepped in front of him. "You're going to do this now? Here? Is that necessary?"

Although Jimmy was between us, I could feel the anger radiating off Palmer. For him, this was the ultimate payback. Obviously, this was also about how I humiliated him a year ago.

Palmer ignored Jimmy's comments. He looked at me over Jimmy's shoulder. "You're under arrest for the murder of Gina Diekelman, Garrison Chase. You have the right to remain silent ..."

I tuned out, positive Detective Palmer's rendition of Miranda would be spot on.

CHAPTER TWENTY-FOUR

Little Saigon
Orange County, CA

LU LAY ON his bare back in a dark, cold, putrid smelling cell. The air was thick and damp with moisture. The distinct kind of moisture that comes from being fairly deep underground in a warm city. Lu knew exactly where he was, unfortunately.

A thin crack of light emitted from under the steel door of the holding cell. Lu didn't know how long he'd been there, but he did know it was somewhere between eight and twelve hours. That was his best guess, anyway. His eyesight had become fully accustomed to the nearly non-existent lighting. The basic size and shape of the room was detectable to Lu, but the details were not.

Which was probably a good thing.

The six by ten foot holding cell was filled with the awful smell of old urine and feces. Twice Lu had relieved himself and added to the odor. Now, clad in just his underwear, he rested on his back to conserve energy.

Lu had been to his employer's underground chamber once before, about a year ago. The one and only time he came face to face with his employer.

The chamber, its smell, feel, and layout was seared into Lu's memory. The underground structure was shaped in a 'V'. Three rooms were on either side of the two long corridors, six rooms in total. Four of those rooms were holding cells and two of the rooms were storage rooms. Places where the Torturer kept the clothes and personal belongings of his victims.

The stairwell landing was situated directly at the point of the V. When you arrived at the bottom of the stairs, you could go left or right down either corridor. Or you could go straight through the door in front of you.

And directly into a chilling chamber. The middle V shaped area used to be an underground wine grotto. Now the only things in the cavernous room were six large meat hooks embedded into the three massive ceiling beams that spanned across the room.

The man known as the Torturer always brought his victims through the chamber first, paraded them around the room, then took them to the holding cell. That way the victims had time to reflect on what was about to occur to them. From what Lu understood, his employer was all about compliance, not necessarily about torture for torture's sake.

Many victims would often comply with whatever was asked of them by simply seeing the room and the dangling meat hooks. The more stubborn victims would then be tortured until they complied or died. Whichever came first.

While lying on the floor, Lu heard his first sound in some time: footsteps. He listened intently, concluding after a few moments that there was only one set of footsteps coming his way. Either the Torturer or his tall sidekick was coming for him.

Sure enough, two shadows suddenly blocked the small ray of light from under the door. Only one man was standing on the other side of the door.

Lu shifted onto his side, then slowly and quietly drew the deepest breath he could.

The lock on the other side of the door rattled, then the handle engaged with a clunky metallic clang. The heavy door swung open silently and effortlessly, like the hinges had just been greased.

The feet belonged to the tall sidekick. Lu recognized them from the bathroom.

Since just his left eye was open and looking along the ground, Lu couldn't see much. He waited and held his breath and thought of his plan. His heart thumped so hard Lu felt like his ribs were about to crack. Pressure inside him was building. He was ready to explode.

Finally, the man stepped into the holding cell. The first step was too far away from Lu, and so was the second. But as the man's third step hit the ground, as the heel touched the dirty floor, Lu's right leg reacted by exploding forward.

He kicked at the foot, simultaneously pushing his hands against the ground for power and leverage.

The man howled on impact as his ankle crumpled and the man's leg swept out from under him. The man fell back, landing on his tailbone with a dull thud. Then he flopped onto his back.

As Lu scrambled to his feet, the tall man struggled to sit up. Lu lunged toward the man and swung his right hand in a sideways chopping motion at his neck. Lu connected flush with the side of his palm against the man's Adam's Apple.

The man fell back again, gagging and sputtering and unable to breathe. Moaning and holding his neck with both hands. Lu figured he crushed the man's larynx.

Wasting no time, Lu leapt over him and exited the room, heaving the door shut as soon as he cleared the threshold. Then he latched the deadbolt and closed the padlock, sealing the man in. After that, his head swung left and right to get a bearing on his location. It only took him a second to locate the storage room. He dashed to his right and charged into the room, flicking on the light switch.

Once inside, he doubled over and finally took a deep breath. Seconds later, he tip-toed back to the open door and listened for sounds. The man he'd locked in shouted and pounded on the door.

Lu had to hurry. He assumed the Torturer was nearby.

He opened the drawers on a dusty, metal desk in the far-left corner of the room. The third drawer, on the bottom right, held his belongings: his passport, plane ticket, wallet, and phone, which had the battery taken out.

Grabbing the phone and battery with one hand, Lu reached into the front of his underwear and retrieved the SIM card. He snapped it into place, put the battery in and cover back on, then frantically pushed the power button.

He wanted to give his uncle a quick warning call, just in case the Torturer had plans to harm the man.

As the phone powered up, he dressed and headed to the stairwell. While hurrying down the corridor, Lu wondered if he could get a signal since he was underground. Once the phone finally turned on, Lu was relieved to see one bar of reception. Just as he started dialing his uncle, however, the phone cut out. No signal. Lu watched the screen and saw the reception bar flickering on and off every few seconds.

He'd have to wait until he got above ground to make the call. Unfortunately, just before reaching the stairwell door, Lu heard footsteps coming down the stairs. He quickly backpedaled to the storage room.

Looking around, his heart sank.

He had nowhere to go. Nowhere to escape to.

Lu eased the door shut to the storage room, then put the cell back in the drawer. Lu figured the only thing he could do was hide. Perhaps jump out and surprise the Torturer.

Whatever he encountered, Lu was prepared to go down with a massive fight. And if he didn't win the fight, hopefully he'd be killed.

Because that was much better than being slowly tortured to death.

CHAPTER TWENTY-FIVE

400 W. Broadway
Long Beach City Police Dept.

"ONE MORE TIME," Detective Palmer said, leaning forward in his chair. "So I'm crystal clear on exactly where you were, Agent Chase, at 10 am yesterday morning."

My lawyer leaned forward and interrupted. "Nope. No way. Not a third time, Detective. My client has already been clear. Very clear, in fact. He told you yesterday, and he told you ten minutes ago. The story hasn't changed. And for the love of Pete, you guys have it on tape." While locking eyes with Palmer, Jimmy pointed at the video camera in the corner of the room. "I know whatcha trying to do here."

Palmer rolled his eyes. "And that is?"

Jimmy held up his hands. "Trip my client up, of course. Have him repeatedly tell a story until you can pounce on him for some minor discrepancy." My lawyer snorted, and really didn't seem embarrassed by it either. "Something ridiculous, too, like change the tense of one of his sentences."

I looked away while Palmer and Jimmy kept at it.

To keep my mind off things, I glanced around. We were in a non-descript holding room with boring beige walls. One wall contained a large one-way window. The only other items on the walls were a fire extinguisher and a light switch. The room couldn't be any less memorable. The temperature inside was beyond chilly, probably on purpose. Every few minutes the air conditioner kicked on or off. It rattled and purred and pumped cold air across my bald head. I looked at the ceiling and focused on my alibi, thinking if there was any other way to prove I was on my way to Oceanside around 10 am.

A minute or two later, however, Jimmy nudged my ribs and pulled me into their conversation. He pointed at a pad of paper and pen on the table.

"My client," Jimmy said, "will give his final statement in writing. Actually, he'll give two written statements. One concerning his whereabouts yesterday, and the other about the hospital room incident involving Hans Schlimmergaard. When he's finished with those statements, that's the end of it. If you keep badgering him, he *will* exercise his right to remain silent."

Palmer glared at Jimmy, then pushed back from the table in a show of disapproval.

Jimmy motioned at me to get writing.

My statements took some time to complete. While writing, Palmer and Jimmy argued back and forth. Jimmy, of course, made the case that I'd been set-up by the perpetrator of Gina's murder, and that the perp later posed as the fake neighbor who provided a false testimony of seeing me hopping my fence at 10 am. He used the hospital incident as proof that someone was after me. Palmer kept asking the same two questions over and over: who was after me and why. Since Jimmy was forbidden from mentioning the Rat, my lawyer kept things vague, simply mentioning that I'd been on many classified missions and had multiple foreign enemies.

Which was pretty much the truth.

Anyway, the two had basically reached an impasse and were no longer talking. When I finished the statements, I pushed the pad of paper towards Palmer's chair. Palmer had been pacing and working off his anger.

While Palmer read what I'd written, I put myself in the detective's shoes. From his perspective, he now has two independent sources that directly contradict my written and recorded statement. Even though one source was anonymous, the other was known and had a relationship with me. Palmer had enough circumstantial evidence to feel confident I was either Gina's killer or somehow involved.

What I wanted Palmer to do was recanvas my neighborhood and try to locate the anonymous source (which he wouldn't find, of course). I also wanted him to visit Oceanside and re-interview Julie Cranston. The problem: Palmer wasn't going to do either, at least not anytime soon.

Jimmy was thinking along the same lines. When Palmer finished reading my statement and looked up, my lawyer told the detective exactly what he needed to do: find the anonymous source and check-in with the Cranstons again.

Palmer sighed. "Boy, you both are a pair, aren't you? Let me remind you, gentlemen: I'm the detective in this case. Neither of you get to tell me what to do. I don't have to pursue anything you tell me. For the record."

Jimmy was about to point at Palmer and lay into him, but I intercepted his hand as it went up.

I tried to calm the tension. "I'm sure Detective Palmer will recanvas the neighborhood and follow up with the Cranstons. He's a good detective, Jimmy. He's thorough." I eyed Palmer.

Palmer put his hands on his hips and shook his head at us, then left the room without saying a word. I was sure he was going to speak with his superior or the DA or both, who I imagined were watching everything through the one-way window.

I turned to Jimmy as soon as the door shut. "What I need you to do is pay a visit to the Cranstons." I tore off a piece of paper from the pad and wrote down their address, then handed it to Jimmy. "The cops aren't going to jump on this. They obviously think I'm guilty. I called Mick this morning but haven't heard back. I was there yesterday morning at the time Gina was murdered. You need to let Mick and/or Julie know the stakes, what I'm being charged with, etc. If Julie really didn't see me parked in their driveway, then check for a security camera on their property. Perhaps the camera picked up my vehicle, which may be even better because it could be time-stamped."

Jimmy nodded along. "Got it. This is good, Chase. You really were there, right? At the time of the murder that is. Wait, I shouldn't ask that." He shook his head.

"Is this your first criminal case, Jimmy?"

He gave a nervous laugh but didn't answer the question.

Once Jimmy left to visit the Cranston home, I collapsed into my chair. As I stared at the ceiling again, I wondered if I was ever going to get out of this mess.

CHAPTER TWENTY-SIX

Little Saigon
Orange County, CA

LU TIP-TOED TO the far corner of the storage room. Aside from the desk, there were three large, wooden wine storage racks along one wall in the room. The wine racks were empty and easily moveable.

As quietly as he could, Lu scraped out each wine rack so that it was approximately a foot away from the wall. Then he slipped behind the last of the three racks, side-stepping until he was in position, around the middle of the rack.

He focused on calming his body and nerves. Typically, he wasn't nervous with confrontation, but in this case, he had no gun or weapon of any sort. Plus, he was dealing with a professional.

Lu slowed his breathing to once every ten seconds or so. As he did, he listened to the footsteps in the corridor, which clearly were getting louder and approaching the storage room.

A moment later, the door swung open. The Torturer, he assumed, didn't step into the room right away. Three agonizing seconds passed, then Lu heard the man step in.

The Torturer didn't say anything.

All Lu heard was a click, followed by the eerie electric hum from a cattle prod.

Next, Lu heard feet shuffling to his left. Following that, he heard a wine rack scrape across the dirty concrete floor.

The next sound was metal on wood, quickly followed by the scraping sound of the rack against the floor again. Lu imagined the man used the cattle prod to push the wine rack back in place along the wall.

Against his will, Lu's breathing picked up. Now every breath came in five second intervals. Soon it hit a three second interval.

Much too fast and too loud, Lu thought.

He closed his eyes and tried to calm his sympathetic nervous system.

The same scraping sound happened again, followed by some brief seconds of silence. Lu knew the man was checking behind the racks during that time. The distinctive sound of metal on wood happened as the cattle prod pushed the rack back in place.

His rack was next.

Lu's breathing wouldn't slow. He couldn't control it. By this point, Lu wasn't about to fight it. Instead, he went with it, allowing his diaphragm to pick up pace. He'd use it to his advantage. Hopefully it would build up a ton of adrenaline in his system so he could collapse the wine rack on top of the man in one powerful motion.

Lu heard a step in his direction and knew the man was right in front of his wine rack.

Then Lu made his first move. He placed his palms flat against the backside of the wine rack, about two thirds of the way up. His second move was to shuffle one step to his right, as quietly as he could. Since his wine rack was already a foot from the wall, Lu feared the man may lead with the cattle prod and jam it into the open space to Lu's left.

But the man didn't lead with the cattle prod. Instead, Lu saw four fingers curl around the edge of the wine rack to his left. As soon as he saw that, he exploded, grunting as he pushed the wine rack forward with every muscle in his body.

It toppled over and pinned the Torturer underneath, but only the top left part of the rack covered the man. Lu scrambled on his stomach to the area where the man was pinned, hoping his body weight would keep the rack in place.

The Torturer groaned and then heaved as he tried to escape the crushing pressure on top of him. The rack undulated like a rolling wave.

Lu slowly got to his knees, keeping his palms flat on the backside of the rack in order to keep his balance. When the rack stopped moving, he hopped onto his feet and started jumping in place as hard as he could, bringing his knees up high and exploding downward with his feet.

Wood cracked and splintered. The Torturer had the round wine holes smashing into his face and body. Lu had the luxury of jumping on the flat backside of the rack.

Unfortunately, though, holes started opening on the backside of the rack. Every time a new hole widened, Lu would adjust left or right and keep jumping. He had to keep the pressure on until he felt no movement underneath him.

He started losing his edge on the seventh jump. The explosive downward power he previously had started to wane. Lu's breathing was nearing hyperventilation status, too. By the eighth and ninth jump, Lu was only bringing his knees up a little.

On his tenth jump, all the wood underneath his two feet fractured and collapsed downward in a heap. As Lu sank to the floor through the broken wood, the cattle prod suddenly jerked up through the hole. It missed Lu's privates by inches, digging into his belly like a plunging knife, sucking all the remaining air from him.

Then Lu felt, just for a millisecond, the most excruciating pain of his life.

CHAPTER TWENTY-SEVEN

400 W. Broadway
Long Beach City Police Dept.

I SPENT MOST of my two and a half hours in the holding room thinking about Jimmy Schuberman. If you can believe it. And, no, I wasn't thinking about the guy because he was growing on me. Far from it. Both my current legal and parental situation were stressing me out. Every time I thought about either situation, I'd feel my blood pressure skyrocket. So, I kept my mind off those situations by thinking about how to pay Jimmy for his services.

Since I knew I'd be beyond bitter if I had to use my savings to pay the lawyer, I entertained the idea of helping Slim out with his PI work. Just for a day or so to pocket some money and pay off Jimmy. It would also stoke out Slim. My buddy definitely needed something positive in his life after being beaten, poisoned, and now shot.

Plus, Frank had put me on admin leave until the criminal and internal investigation of the hospital incident had concluded. That meant I couldn't go to work and use those resources to hunt down the Rat's goons. I'd have to rely on Karla for help there, which she was already doing on her own. Since I was still in custody, I'd given her the go ahead to leave for San Quentin without me.

By the time I'd cemented my plan to do some PI work for Slim, Detective Palmer breezed into the room and brought me back to reality. He had a few sheets of stapled paper in his hand, which I figured was the DA's official written statement of the charges against me.

He slid the paper in front of me. "You might want your lawyer to check this over. Where'd he run off to, by the way?"

I didn't answer the question. Instead, I started reading the formal charges.

Less than a minute later, the holding room door opened, and Jimmy Schuberman waltzed in, grinning ear to ear.

He pointed at the papers on the table. "Tear that paperwork up. Toss it right in the pissah, will you."

Before Palmer or I could say anything, Jimmy thumbed over his shoulder. "I brought a witness to corroborate my client's alibi." He nodded his head and gave a giddy smile. "Yup, I did. I certainly did. Julie Cranston's here in the waiting area, waiting to speak to you, Detective. To give her official statement, or I guess I should say correct her initial statement she gave you."

He pointed at me. "Totally vindicates my client."

Jimmy sauntered my direction and held his right hand up, waiting for a high-five. Typically, I never high-fived another guy. Just felt weird and college-fratish and totally unnecessary. But in this case, I ignored my self-imposed rule and slapped my lawyer's hand. Hard.

Then I settled back in my chair and gave a deep sigh. I knew Julie Cranston would come through.

Jimmy turned and addressed Palmer, in a condescending way, like a true lawyer. He waved Palmer out of the room, flapping his hand upward, essentially shoeing the man away. "Go speak to her, Detective Palmer. Hear what she has to say, in particular what she saw."

Palmer closed the door a little too forcefully on his way out.

"What happened?" I asked Jimmy as he turned back.

He scraped a chair up to the table. "As soon as I told her what was happening, that Gina was murdered and you were being framed, Julie broke down and came clean. She feels awful, Chase, truly awful. She saw you from the upper bedroom window when you pulled into the driveway."

I remembered thinking I saw the blinds move.

"Listen," Jimmy continued. "I guess you two have history, she didn't go into details. Anyway, when Palmer initially contacted her, she didn't want her husband to get wrapped up into whatever your problem was, so she lied. Like I said, she feels terrible. So terrible she insisted on coming straight to the station with me to clear everything up. Julie even looked at her watch when you arrived at their house, by the way, which puts you in Oceanside at exactly 10:44 a.m."

I gave another deep sigh. Thank you, Julie Cranston.

Jimmy proceeded to give me every single detail that happened during the two and a half hours he was away. The man was a talker, to say the least. I tuned out for some of the conversation, thinking about what my next course of action would be, which I decided would be visiting Slim in the hospital.

So," Jimmy said. "When she's finished giving her statement, you're free to go. And I guess my services won't be needed anymore. I think we're at about twelve billing hours now."

"Twelve hours?" I said. "Really?"

Jimmy ignored the comment and tapped his fingers on the table. "Since you haven't actually given me the retainer fee, I'll bill you on an hourly basis."

I didn't want to ask, but I did anyway. "And what do you charge per hour?"

"Four hundred usually, but I'll give you the twenty-five percent bro discount, so three hundred."

"Three hundred bucks an hour? Highway robbery, Jimmy."

He slapped me on the back, which I hoped he never did again, otherwise I may have to break his wrist.

"Just think," Jimmy said, "you're free to go soon, Chase. And you can't put a price on freedom, can you? No siree. Now sit tight; I'll go check on where things stand."

Jimmy was gone about nine minutes. I spent the time deliberately not thinking about him. When he opened the holding room door, he was all smiles. "You're free to go, Chase, free as a bird." He sang the last part.

I walked over and shook his hand. "Thanks, Jimmy."

"See," he said, "lawyers aren't all bad, right? Though you didn't say it outright, I kind of picked up on a vibe that you weren't a big fan."

I reluctantly nodded.

As I walked away, Jimmy said, "My office will send a bill."

I held my left thumb up over my head. On my way out of the station, I looked around for Julie Cranston, but I didn't see her. I imagined she was still speaking with Palmer or the DA or both. I'd have to call and thank her later.

Once outside, it took a few minutes to find and hail a cab. Locating yellow cabs in the city were harder these days since Uber was taking over. Since I didn't have an internet plan on my cell, I couldn't use UBER services. I increasingly felt like a fossil in our current age.

When I arrived at Slim's hospital room, two Long Beach uniformed officers flanking the door grilled me. Since Frank took my badge, they weren't willing to take my word for me being a federal agent. One of them escorted me into the room and checked with Slim before allowing me to speak.

When the cop left, I looked at Slim. "At least they're thorough, and slightly better than hospital security."

Slim motioned at my hip. "Where's your piece? That's the kind of security I want."

"Paid leave, pal. No badge or gun. You doing okay? How's the shoulder?"

He shrugged it off. "I've had worse. Believe or not, my hip's more painful than my shoulder."

Before I had a chance to make a smart aleck remark, he said, "You just missed Freda, by the way."

I sniffed the air and smiled. "I thought I smelled something good, like perfume, certainly not your stinky arse. Where'd your lovely wife go?"

"Back to the hotel for a few hours of sleep. She hasn't slept in close to twenty-four hours."

"How's she holding up?"

"You know her, she's a trooper, she's just really glad I'm alive. And she really wants this to be over, naturally."

We made small talk for another minute or so, then I brought Slim up to speed on my time in custody and how Julie finally corroborated my alibi. I also told him about Karla heading up to San Quentin, which brought our conversation back to the Rat.

"Our man is relentless, isn't he?" I said. "I mean, sending two goons in broad daylight like that to take us out. He's getting desperate, beyond desperate. We both have to stay safe the next few days."

Slim nodded. "Those two met the wrong dudes, though, didn't they? Geez, Chase, the way you gutted that man was like old times. Was that your intention? Did you see the shard of glass sticking up like that?"

"Wait" I said, furrowing my brow. "Did you see that? I thought you were shot by that point."

"I was. I didn't see it. A nurse told me about it, probably to decompress and get it off her mind."

"Got it. Anyway, I had one hand focused on the man's gun while my other hand tried to pull the dude into the room. That's all I could think about at the time. I didn't see the glass sticking up like that. Didn't even know it happened until I saw all the blood."

We looked at each other for a moment. I knew Slim was thinking along the same lines as me. That we were lucky to be trained in combat, but more importantly, lucky to be alive.

I pointed at him. "Saved your life again, pal. We're close to being even."

Slim held up his good arm and pinched his fingers. "Close, but not quite there."

I took a seat by his bed and switched gears. "So, I also wanted to chat about your offer."

Slim looked puzzled.

I cleared my throat. "To do some PI work for this presidential candidate of yours."

Slim narrowed his eyes. "You're kidding, right? I thought you were opposed to my line of work?"

"I was. But I'm on paid leave and can't use my office's resources, and Karla's away for the day and evening. Plus, I had to hire your lawyer buddy and now have to pay the man. You know how much he charges?"

"Wait," Slim said. "Is he not giving you the bro discount?"

I laughed. "Twenty-five percent discount on a lot, is still a lot."

"Jimmy's a bit of a loon," Slim said, "but he's a decent lawyer and knows his stuff. And he came through and got you off."

"I guess, though I told him exactly what to do. Anyway, it doesn't matter now." I cleared my throat. "Before I change my mind, tell me all about this Bradford character and where he is right now."

Slim motioned at the cubby holes along the wall. "Grab that file over there, in the top left cubby."

I retrieved the thick file folder. "Where'd you get this?"

"I'd left it in my hotel room. Freda swung by there last night and grabbed it, along with a few other things."

Taking my seat again, I held up the huge folder. "Man, this is a dossier."

"It's everything I have on the senator," Slim responded.

I started flipping through the pages, stopping when I found a photo of the senator. He was somewhat of a handsome man, especially for his age, which I pegged at about seventy. I guessed he was about six foot, give or take an inch. He had wavy steel grey hair and wore dark sunglasses. In fact, every picture I'd ever seen of the man he wore the same dark glasses, which wasn't surprising since he was blind. My eyes gravitated to his cleft chin.

I pointed at the photo and held it up for Slim's benefit. "Look at that thing. It's a butt chin."

Slim laughed. "I know, you could slot a quarter in there and I bet it wouldn't fall out."

Now I was the one laughing.

Slim continued. "That dossier is everything I could dig up on the California senator. There's not too much about the man himself, at least not his past. Most of those documents in there are his travel itinerary, summaries of bills he's authored or co-authored, voting record, philanthropic awards he's won, charitable donations, all stuff like that."

I nodded as I flipped through the documents. "What do you know about the man? What salient points should I be aware of?"

"Right," Slim said, thinking about it for a moment. "He comes from money, though he never likes to talk about that or really admit it. His parents and grandparents and a couple generations prior to that were large landowners in L.A. and Orange County. They were initially farmers, mainly into fruit crops, but you know what happened there."

"Land became highly valuable, I imagine, and they sold everything for a pretty penny."

"Exactly. Barrington Bradford Bollinger III wanted nothing to do with his silver spoon upbringing, so when he turned eighteen, he enlisted and was shipped off to Vietnam. There's debate over how much combat action he saw over there, but the most salient point you need to be aware of is the fact that he spent five years as a POW.

"When he was freed from captivity and returned to America, he was highly outspoken against the war. Though he was tortured, he believed America did far greater damage to the Vietnamese people in the long run. He even married a Vietnamese woman and adopted two orphaned babies from the country. The man never did go to college. He went into local government in his late-twenties, then worked for the California legislature a number of years until eventually running and winning one of the two California senate seats in Congress."

I whistled. "A blind man who lost his vision as a POW climbs the political ladder without a college degree and then runs for the most powerful job in the world. That's quite a convincing story."

"It is," Slim said, "which is why Henrietta probably hired me to get one up on the man. Although, she's a formidable candidate herself, not to mention she could be the first female president in history. Still, she really wants to find something on this guy."

"And you think you've found something?"

He grinned. "Maybe."

"Not even a hint, right?"

Slim shook his head.

Just then, my cell buzzed. I quickly checked it and saw that Mom was calling. I'd have to call her back in a second. No doubt she was calling to ask if she could feed Simon ice cream for lunch. She was a typical grandma.

"So tell me," I said. "How am I going to get close to this guy to watch him and follow him around? I mean, he's campaigning in his own state, so I imagine the crowds will be huge. Plus, he probably has a Secret Service detail forming a huge entourage around him."

"Here's the thing," Slim said. "His platform is all about avoiding government waste, so he refuses to use any government resources on himself. He wants money and services to be used on those who truly need help. As a result, he donates his salary as a senator to a charitable organization. He refuses any compensation for travel. He refuses a Secret Service detail. Currently, the man travels with just his German Shepherd and a personal security guard he's employed for twenty years."

"That seems crazy."

Slim nodded. "I agree. However, every time Bradford is asked about it, he's adamant that's how he wants it to be. He wants to be a man of the people. He wants to be approachable. That kind of thing. Which will all have to change if he becomes president."

"It will, for sure. Where's Barrington Bradford Bollinger—who we should really call triple B, by the way—going to be the next couple of days?"

Slim pointed at the file. "Everything's in there. Details about times and locations of his campaign events, even his rental address, which was the hardest thing for me to find out, by the way. He's renting an ocean view place for a couple of weeks while he campaigns throughout Southern California. I want you to watch him at that location, too, until he calls it lights out around midnight. He's active at night."

"Really?"

"Really. It's important. Trust me."

"Okay." My cell buzzed. It was Mom again. "I need to take this."

"Sure," Slim said.

"What's up, Mom?"

"Gary, this is bad." She took a big breath.

Mom was the only person who could call me Gary and not irk me. "What's going on, Mom?"

"A lawyer and the Diekelman's just showed up at my house. Well, I guess it was just the lawyer and Helen who showed up. I think I saw Dan waiting in the car. Or maybe it was somebody else."

"Mom, focus, what did they want?"

"Helen wanted Simon. The lawyer wanted you. He has papers for you. He even flapped them around in my face. He was a real pushy bugger. And he was using all sorts of legal jumbalese, Gary. Talking about a court order or an emergency order or maybe he said the word injunction. Perhaps it was a combination of all three. I'm not sure. All I know is they were dead set on taking Simon from you."

I started breathing rapidly into the phone. "Mom, you didn't give them Simon, did you?"

"Heck, no, dear. Helen was furious, spewing awful things about you being a suspect in Gina's murder. She was out of control. I didn't like her when I met her at your wedding, and I certainly don't like her now. I wouldn't under any circumstance give my grandson to that person. Over my dead, wrinkled body, hon."

I breathed a sigh of relief. Mom was great. "So where are you now?"

"Driving around, illegally talking to you on my cell. I grabbed some of Simon's things and hopped in the car as soon as they left."

"Good. I'm at the hospital, Mom. Swing by and pick me up as soon as you can. I'll figure something out."

"Be there in five minutes or so."

I hung up and motioned bye to Slim.

"Everything okay?"

I looked over my shoulder as I exited the room.

"Probably not."

CHAPTER TWENTY-EIGHT

Sea Cove Dr.
Rancho Palos Verdes

I'D CHECKED MY son and mother into the Great Wolf Lodge in Anaheim, CA. The place was a sprawling hotel with an indoor water park. The only vacant rooms in the entire hotel were suites. I booked them in for two nights, and when I got the bill, I about lost my lunch. They charged Jimmy Schuberman type rates at the place.

Speaking of Jimmy, I'd called him to see if he had any child custody experience. He didn't, but he told me he still wanted to help. He planned to consult with a couple of his colleagues about what the Diekelman's were trying to do.

I chose Great Wolf Lodge for my family because the place was public and swarming with people. Plus, it would keep my son occupied for the next two days. I didn't want him to burden Mom with repeated questions about Gina, so I hoped by distracting Simon he'd temporarily forget that he hadn't seen his mother in a while. After testifying against the Rat, I planned on sitting him down and telling him about his mother.

I'd also chosen the Anaheim location because Bradford had a campaign event at the Anaheim Convention Center in the late afternoon. I'd rolled over there a couple of hours ago to see what I could find out about triple B. It was somewhat enlightening.

Currently, I was parked one house down the street from the senator's rental estate, doing some reconnaissance. To be honest, I was sort of grateful for the temporary PI job. It kept me on the move, which provided a measure of safety. Plus, it would be hard for the Rat's men to follow me and/or anticipate my moves since I didn't even know where I would be next. So far, I'd been planning my moves hour by hour.

Keeping focused on the senator also kept my mind busy. That way I wouldn't dwell and worry too much about my upcoming testimony against the Rat or the potential custody battle I wasn't prepared to engage in.

I'd taken a taxi from the hotel to pick up my Caprice. I sat in the back seat of my vehicle since it had tinted windows and I didn't want to be spotted by any nosy, rich neighbors. On my lap were my cell and the senator's dossier. While watching the house, I planned to make a couple of calls.

My first was to Slim. I wanted to ask him something about the senator. Nothing major, just something odd I came across.

On the fourth ring, Slim picked up.

I asked, "How you doing? Better yet?"

"I'm not dead," he said. "Can't complain then, I guess."

"You rarely do. Listen, I'm calling because I just finished visiting a campaign event for our senator. What a circus. I can't tell you how many thousands of people were packed into that place. The senator has a cult following, like that other guy who ran in the last two elections. What's his name? Bernie . . ."

"Sanders," Slim finished. "You're right, they share many of the same philosophies, that's for sure."

"The crowd was super young, and they spontaneously broke out into chanting 'Brad-ford' at least on five separate occasions. It was nuts."

"Young kids are super passionate, that's for sure. Who knows if they'll turn up to vote, though? How close did you get to the senator?"

"Fairly close, I'd say. What caught my attention wasn't him, though, it was his dog."

Slim laughed. "Ha! My boy Ranger. That's the German Shepherd's name. Pretty skittish, am I right?"

"Absolutely. It doesn't make sense to have a seeing eye dog who's skittish and standoffish like that. The dog seemed afraid of crowds. I mean, really afraid. It looked as if he'd scamper off if somebody stormed the stage or a shot rang out."

"Actually, the dog freezes and then pees when he gets nervous."

"What?"

"Yup, dog's a pisser. Get that boy nervous and it's Niagara Falls. I've seen it happen at least three times in the past month."

"What's the story with Mr. Tinkles? It's an odd service dog choice."

"Wait, the senator didn't mention 'ole Ranger in his speech tonight? He typically talks about his sidekick and how the dog is sort of a metaphor for the disenfranchised citizens in our nation."

"Nope, he didn't say a word about Ranger."

Slim cleared his throat. "Well, Ranger was trained as one of the bomb sniffing dogs for the war in Afghanistan, but the dog and his trainer were captured by the Taliban. A few weeks later, a team found the dead body of the trainer along with the dog standing by his master's body. The dog was traumatized, as if he'd been tortured or severely beaten over the two-week period. The dog was emaciated and had several cuts on his body. Anyway, after that incident, Ranger couldn't do his job anymore. He was eventually shipped back to the states where he became even more of a nervous nelly. It got so bad they were going to put the dog down, but when the story went viral, Bradford stepped in and saved the dog. The senator promised to rehabilitate Ranger and give him a good home. He wanted the dog service-worthy again, but when that didn't happen, the senator started using Ranger as his seeing eye dog.

"If you want my opinion, it's all part of the senator's story to make him look good; to appear sympathetic and gain votes. I know people would disagree with me—in fact, even Freda does on that point—but that's my take on the matter."

"You don't think there's a possibility he's actually a good person who's an animal lover?"

"You just keep watching him, pal, and report back to me in a day. Now, anything else unusual?"

I thought about it for a moment. "Nope. Just wanted to know what was up with the scaredy-cat dog. I'll let you know if I come across anything. Stay safe."

"You too."

With that behind me, I turned my full attention to the senator's rental house. During my conversation with Slim, I'd kept my eyes on the place, but I hadn't seen anything unusual. In fact, nothing had happened since I arrived an hour ago. Nobody came in or out.

However, the fact that Slim wanted me here until midnight meant something. I knew my buddy well. He wouldn't waste my time—or his money—if he didn't think there was a good chance that I'd learned something about the senator.

In the senator's dossier, Slim had included a schematic of the ocean-view property in Rancho Palos Verdes. On Seacove Drive where I currently parked, the north side of the house faced the street. It was gated all the way across. The east, west, and south sides had a tall, thick, green hedge running the entire length of the property. The south side also had a beautiful view of the ocean and butted up against a nature preserve. Beyond the preserve was a steep, jagged cliff. The only thing after that was the expansive Pacific Ocean stretching for as far as the eye could see.

The entry and exit points of the home were, therefore, the north and south sides, of which I was only watching the north. Later, if nothing happened from my current vantage, I'd have to enter the park and check out the south facing part of the property.

Looking at my watch, I decided to contact Karla. It was about a half hour before she was scheduled to interview the Rat. Since I didn't know her exact whereabouts, and if she was able to take a call, I tried texting. Aside from making and receiving calls, it was the only other thing my Motorola Razr could do.

I had only texted a few times in my life, so I was slow and amateurish at it.

I pecked out a text to Karla. It read: *Where you at?*

So poetic.

I followed that up with: *Did you make it safely?*

Karla's return text read: *Wow! A text from my boyfriend. Welcome to the 21st century. This relationship may actually go somewhere after all. JK!!*

JK? I ran my hand over my bald head. What does that mean?

As if Karla read my mind, she replied: *JK is just kidding*. Then she sent me a happy face.

As I fiddled with the keyboard and wondered how she did that, she sent another text: *Drive mostly traffic free. About to enter the prison. Gotta run. I'll call after the interview. Other news to share as well. Big development with Slim's case. Just spoke with LBPD.*

After reading it, I quickly fired back—though quickly was an overstatement: *What kind of development? Don't leave me hanging!*

A moment later, she replied: *Guy who didn't die in hospital room struck a deal with DA. Gave up important information. Cops are checking out lead now.*

I pecked out: *What kind of lead?*

She sent back: *No cell use in prison. Will call after and fill u in.*

I didn't push it. Karla needed to focus on interviewing the Rat. I sat back and wondered what type of information the gunman had given up. For a few minutes, my mind spun with wild ideas. Then I figured I should stop wasting my mental energy on it and wait an hour or so to find out.

Turning my attention to the dossier, I flipped through the documents and read the articles and newspaper clippings I found most interesting about the senator. Every ten seconds or so, I'd look up and scan the front of the property for any signs of movement. From my vantage point, I couldn't see any lights on inside the house. Then again, the senator was blind and didn't need lights, so that didn't mean anything.

After about forty-five minutes, I stopped reading and thought about what I'd discovered. There were some fascinating things about the man. The most interesting fact was that the man was a prisoner in the Hanoi Hilton, an infamous torture place I'd heard about before; a place that housed hundreds of American POWs during the Vietnam war. Apparently, the prison had an infirmary where POWs were taken if they were near death and needed to be nursed back to life. At one point in his five-year stint in the Hanoi Hilton, Bradford ended up in the infirmary. He tells the story of a gentle, caring nurse who, indeed, nursed him back to health. Well, somewhat of health, I guess. It's not like the Viet Cong wanted the POWs in tip top shape.

Anyway, after the war Bradford traveled back to Vietnam, sought out the woman who cared for him, and eventually married her. And he took two orphan girls back to the states and raised them there.

The man had an unbelievable back story, ripe for being a political rock star.

As far as his politics were concerned, the man voted extremely liberal, so liberal some of his foes accused him of being a socialist. His greatest enemies, though, went so far as to say he was a closet communist. At any rate, suffice to say, he was on the far-left end of the political spectrum.

Bradford was the chair of the Senate Committee on Small Business and Entrepreneurship. The senator routinely lobbied and championed in favor of small businesses whenever he could. One newspaper article quoted him as saying that small businesses are the life blood of the American economy. He decried the giant corporations that tried to monopolize certain sectors.

I ran my hand over my bald head. Now it made total sense to me why Henrietta Valenzuela was willing to pay Slim to dig up dirt on this guy. Barrington Bradford Bollinger III was a formidable opponent, without a doubt. Apparently, he was also a star high school swimmer. So good, in fact, he was offered swim scholarships to a few Ivy League schools. However, he turned them down and chose Vietnam instead.

Since my eyes were tired from reading in limited lighting, and my body ached a little from sitting, I decided to stretch my legs. I exited the vehicle and walked toward the nature preserve, figuring it would be good to check out the other side of the property and see if there was any activity inside or outside the house.

Once inside the preserve, which was basically just undeveloped, woodsy land, I headed east toward the rental place. A rough trail snaked through the preserve, looping at one end. When I reached the house, I paced across the property to get a feel for the backside. There was not much to see since the back and side hedges were at least eight feet tall. Behind the hedge was a red brick wall close to seven feet high.

At the southeast corner of the property, a brick pillar extended a foot or so higher than the rest of the wall. It was purely decorative, with a cornice on top and all. To break up the monotony of the wall, every other brick on the pillar jutted out a few inches. Fortunately, this provided me with a mini ledge to climb. When I reached the top of the brick wall, I noticed an equally tall hedge on the other side of the brick wall. I leaned against the cornice at the top of the pillar and focused my eyes on a narrow slit through the row of hedges.

All I could see was the outline of the house. No details were evident due to the moonless night. The only thing I could see in the large sprawling back-yard was a long, narrow lap pool. I could see the lap pool because there were two small lights underneath the water at either end of the pool.

And somebody was swimming in the pool.

To get a better look, I climbed over the brick wall and eased myself onto the lawn.

Clearly trespassing, but not caring, I side-stepped to the north until I found a decent sized opening in the hedges. I kept my body behind one of the hedges and slowly leaned my head into the gap.

A dog paced back and forth following the swimmer from end to end. It was a German Shepherd, so I assumed it was Ranger. There was also a large man, who I figured was the senator's bodyguard because of the man's size, sitting in a lounge chair. He appeared to be cleaning something, maybe a gun. It was hard for me to see details because of the distance, not to mention non-existent ambient lighting.

I focused my attention on the person in the pool. At first, I assumed it was the senator. After all, this was his rental place, not to mention his dog and bodyguard were back there with him. Plus, the figure in the pool had a man's physique and the senator was a known swimmer. But the longer I watched the figure swimming the front crawl, the more doubts I had. For one, the man in the pool wore a swimmer's cap and goggles.

Why would a blind man need goggles?

I kept watching. The swimmer was clearly skilled. As he approached the wall, he turned underwater and kick-flipped off the wall, then headed back the opposite direction. Never once using his hands to touch the wall.

Could a blind man kick-flip like that? If a blind person was swimming in a lap pool, wouldn't they keep their arms extended and stop when their hands hit the wall? Or did blind swimmers, ones as skilled as the senator, simply count their strokes and flip accordingly?

Since I didn't know the answer, I kept watching. About thirteen minutes later, the man stopped swimming and exited the pool. He didn't exactly hop out of the pool like a young person, so right away I knew the man was older. He also appeared to be the approximate size and age of the senator.

Unfortunately, it was too dark, and the man was too far away for me to have one hundred percent certainty it was Bradford. However, I was about ninety percent sure.

I watched the man turn to his left and walk directly toward a chaise lounge chair. Ranger trotted close behind the man. To my surprise, I witnessed the man reach the chair and immediately scoop up a towel and start drying himself off. None of his movements mimicked a blind man. This man's movement were decisive and precise, as if he could see just fine.

Wait, was this even the senator? If it was, could he see?

As I continued staring and thinking, I was startled by a ring. It took a second to realize it was my cell ringing in my back pocket.

Damn.

Scrambling to get it out of my pocket, I fumbled with the buttons until I got the stupid thing to shut off.

When I looked up, I was relieved the swimmer and bodyguard weren't looking my way, or the dog for that matter. I planned to continue my reconnaissance, but the big bodyguard got up from his chair and started walking the perimeter of the property. Since I didn't want to push it, I back tracked to the corner of the property and climbed over the brick wall, quickly walking back to my vehicle.

Along the way, my mind kept replaying what I saw.

When I got back to my car, I had more questions than I did answers, so I distracted myself by checking my phone. Karla had called. I fired up the Caprice and called her back.

She picked up on the second ring. "You screening my calls?"

"There's only a few numbers I actually answer, Karla, and you're definitely one of them."

"Good to hear," she said. "What's going on? Why didn't you pick up earlier?"

"I was a little preoccupied when you called. I was doing some surveilling."

"Who were you surveilling? The senator?"

"I think so. Maybe."

"What do you mean maybe?"

I spent the next few minutes relaying the details of what I'd been doing and what I thought I'd seen.

Karla listened without interjecting. At the end of my story, she said,

"You're saying there's a possibility that one of the candidates for president, a man who claims to be blind, could be faking it?"

"Could be. Maybe. That's the thing, I'm about ninety percent sure it was the senator, but not one hundred percent. The way he moved didn't exactly strike me as a blind man, but there could be an explanation. Perhaps he counted off steps from the lounge chair to the edge of the pool, and maybe he counted strokes while swimming so he knew where the wall was."

"Possibly," Karla said.

I thought for a moment. "Or perhaps the senator can see and he's been duping the American people all along. Maybe that's what Slim discovered; what he wanted me to confirm."

"Wow," Karla said. "The latter's a bombshell if it's true."

I nodded as I thought about the implications. "It is. And if I confirm it, and Slim reports back to Henrietta, the election is over. She wins. Wouldn't she?"

"Most likely. Not only does Bradford lose the presidential election in one of the biggest scandals in American politics, his political career is over for good."

"If it's true," I added.

"Right," Karla said. "If it's true."

We didn't speak for a few seconds, both processing the enormity of the situation.

I broke the silence. "I'm dying to know how your meeting with the Rat went, but I'm also dying to know about the lead you mentioned. Tell me that first. You said the cops got the gunman to talk?"

"Yup. The man you didn't kill has a healthy criminal record. He was obviously facing life in prison for killing the security guards. The DA and the man's lawyer struck a deal, however, to avoid the death penalty, not that it means much in California. The career criminal gave up his boss, the man who hired him to take down the guards and Slim. That person was a man named Tanawat, who the cops picked up. Turned out Tanawat was hired by somebody else, of course, and he wouldn't give up anybody. The man wouldn't even talk with authorities. But the cops surprised Tanawat before he could destroy his burner phone. There was an incriminating text on there to another individual. The cops were able to trace that phone to a location."

"That is progress," I said. "Nice. What happened?"

"Not sure. That's the last update I got from the cops. They moved in on the location a couple of hours ago, but I haven't heard anything since. Probably will have to wait until the morning."

"Probably, now that it's pretty late. This could be big, though. We could finally catch a break and get our direct link back to the Rat."

Karla didn't respond.

I said, "Right? This is a big break, Karla."

"Maybe," she responded.

"Maybe? What's going on?"

"It totally could," she said. "You're right. It's a possibility. I just don't want you getting your hopes up. Maybe Anurat is involved, maybe not."

"Anurat? You're using his real name? Not you, too." I pulled the phone away and pushed out a breath, then put the phone back. "Don't tell me you're drinking the Kool-Aid as well. You think the Rat is innocent? He got to you, didn't he? Sold you some grand story I bet."

"I'm not drinking any Kool-Aid," she shot back.

I kept at it, though. "He must be good, a smooth talker, a real actor. I mean, you and Khang are two smart people. Really smart, actually. That he could get one up on both of you is—"

"Enough, Chase," she interjected. "I just spent an hour with him dissecting his every word and body movement. And I'm a decent read of people, aren't I?"

She was, so I acknowledged it. "You are."

"Then just calm down and hear me out."

Fair enough. "Sorry, go on."

Karla took a second. I could hear her breathing through her nose.

"Okay, where to start? He was beyond frail, Chase. I mean, he's emaciated, so thin he could've slipped through the slats in the chair he was sitting in. Apparently he's been diagnosed with stomach cancer—"

"Ha!" I scoffed. "Apparently is right." I couldn't help my sarcasm. "The man probably paid a doctor for a fake diagnosis, Karla."

"You done?" she said.

I composed myself. "Again, sorry, go on."

"He converted from Buddhism to Christianity a couple of years back. Said he contemplated suicide because of the atrocities he committed in the past, but Christianity helped him forgive himself."

Buddhism? That man was never a Buddhist. However, I refrained from making a comment out loud.

Karla continued. "Any time I asked him a question, he would respond by quoting Scripture."

"Deflecting," I added. "As expected. Surely you picked up on that. Didn't you?"

She ignored the question. "Honestly, he seemed repentant. He seemed like a changed man. Before you say anything, Chase, I get it. I certainly do. I understand it could all be an act. You don't need to say it."

"Oh, it's an act alright."

Karla sighed. "Listen, you asked me to meet this guy and get my opinion. Do you want it or not?"

"I do."

"Good, then listen."

"You're right," I said. "What's your direct take on him? Give it to me straight."

She cleared her throat. "That he's broken and not the man he used to be. That he may very well have changed. There's also a possibility he's faking it all. But I'm leaning toward a changed man. He doesn't want to die. He wants to make amends for his sins. That's what he kept saying."

She waited for my opinion. I wanted to blast her take on the Rat, but I refrained and took a few seconds to calm my thumping heart.

"Okay," I said, "thanks for being honest. You're certainly entitled to that opinion."

"Plus, Chase," she continued, "the prison and guards run a super tight, minimal personnel operation over there. It would be near impossible for him to be communicating outside the prison walls. He—"

"Now that I can't understand, Karla. You sound exactly like Khang, for crying out loud. You know how it works. You're smarter than that. The Rat has reach and money unheard of, easily making him capable of paying somebody off or of threatening a guard's family. There are several ways for him to get messages out. Come on, Karla. Think."

As soon as I said it, I regretted it.

"You know what?" she said. "Forget it. You're hot over this, and now I'm bothered. Really bothered, in fact. Let's drop it, or maybe talk about it later in person if you can act a little more sensible. I feel like we're just going to get more heated over the phone. If we're going to keep this conversation going, we should do it face to face."

I quickly responded. "I agree."

"Good," she said.

A few seconds of awkward silence ensued. Karla broke it. "Stay at my place tonight. I know you can't go back to your house yet. I'll be there early morning. That will give us time to calm down and maybe talk about it civilly."

"Sounds good, Karla."

We said an awkward goodbye, then I headed to Karla's place.

During the drive, I was mad at myself for not being more objective and open-minded. For some reason, I couldn't open myself up to another opinion. Probably because I felt like the Rat was winning so far. Considering what type of man he was, that irked me to the core. It appeared to me he had the U.S. attorney on his side, and now possibly my girlfriend.

After some fast driving, I calmed a little, which meant my thoughts were slightly more rational. Perhaps the Rat didn't have anybody on his side. Perhaps I was being emotional and overreacting, which wasn't hard for me to do when it came to the Rat. Perhaps Ethan Khang and Karla were simply more objective and better able to weigh an alternate opinion.

When I got to Karla's house, it was close to midnight. She only had one bedroom, and the couch in her living room was a short two-seater, so I reluctantly crawled into her bed, hoping she didn't get home and curl up on the tiny couch because she was still mad at me.

As I lay there, I promised I'd apologize to Karla in the morning. I fell asleep and didn't wake until I heard the bedroom door creak open. I couldn't see because it was pitch black in the room. The only light came from the alarm clock that read: 4:05.

I could hear, though, very well, in fact. The sounds I heard were of buttons being undone and clothes slipping to the floor. I'm not sure there's a sexier sound than that.

Next thing I knew, I felt the cool sheet lift off my body as Karla slid across the bed toward me. As she snuggled in, I could smell her hair and feel her warm, lithe body touching mine. The moment was electric. I could hear her heart beating fast and I was positive she could hear mine.

She didn't say a word.

But I did. I whispered, "I'm sorry."

She quickly put her pointer finger against my lips, then kissed me behind the ear. After that, she planted a couple of soft ones on my lips. The taste was erotic. Her lips were slightly wet and sensuous. She placed another kiss on my lips, a harder one. Her tongue moved in and teased me for one second.

Then she slipped on top of me; her warm body fitting neatly into the grooves of mine.

Her lips touched my chest and proceeded down my body in a slow, deliberate manner.

Oh my.

The final thought I had before my mind went blank was: *We needed to argue more often.*

CHAPTER TWENTY-NINE

Little Saigon
Orange County, CA

TWELVE, SIXTEEN, MAYBE eighteen hours ago, Lu experienced the most excruciating pain of his life when a charged cattle prod rammed into his stomach.

That previous pain paled in comparison to what he was currently experiencing. He'd take repeated shocks with a cattle prod over the slow, agonizing pain of being tortured.

Lu was strung up in the former wine grotto turned torture chamber, hanging by a rope on one of the meat hooks embedded into the ceiling beam. His compressed body was folded at the stomach. To keep him in that tight, bowed position, his hands were bound to his ankles and the rope was looped over the meat hook.

He dangled and swung and quietly moaned in pain. His limbs were grotesquely swollen and turning a darker shade of purple with each passing hour. Just breathing was laborious.

Making matters worse was the fact that The Torturer slit his belly. Not a super deep cut, but just deep enough for Lu to slowly bleed out. Earlier he'd felt the blood dripping down the sides of his hips. Now that entire area was numb.

Since he was bent forward and pressing his belly to his thighs, the pressure on the wound most likely kept him alive a little longer. If the ropes were suddenly cut loose, he'd drop to the ground and his intestines would spill out.

Ke Tra Tan knew exactly what he was doing.

Once he'd strung up Lu, the Torturer left the chamber without so much as a word. Nobody was around, so there was no point in yelling or shouting. Even if Lu did try to speak or shout out, he couldn't make noise for more than a second or two anyway. The pain from moving his diaphragm and stomach was too much to bear.

Knowing how he'd die, and that it wouldn't be for another day, was mentally torturous. Almost as bad as the physical pain itself.

Distracting him from the ominous thoughts was the sound of distant footsteps, followed by some muffled talking in the corridor. Next, Lu heard the chamber's door open.

Moments later, a hand smacked across his face.

"Open your eyes, Pham Van Lu," a voice said.

Moving meant agonizing pain for Lu. Even opening his eyelids was a painful chore, but he did it anyway. Unfortunately, he couldn't see much. He could, however, feel the presence of a person to his right. It was dark in the chamber and Lu had his eyes closed for who knows how long. He needed time for his eyes to adjust.

The person leaned in and spoke into his right ear. "You forced our hand with this."

It was the Torturer.

He continued. "We didn't intend for you to die on this hook; we just wanted you to experience it for a while, a consequence for screwing up the Hans job and trying to flee the country. You knew you were in this for life, Lu. You can't leave our organization; you know way too much. You sealed your agonizing fate with this."

The Torturer held a tiny object up to his face.

Lu blinked a few times. His vision came around just enough to see that it was the SIM card to his phone.

He waved the card. "You've jeopardized everything with this. The cops traced your location. They were here a few hours ago, poking around. Fortunately, they didn't find anything because we're hidden underground. But the entire operation hangs in the balance now. You've brought scrutiny and jeopardy to everything our employer has been trying to accomplish."

Another smack to the face. Lu heard something behind him. It sounded like a whimper or squeal. He couldn't be sure which sound it was. He wondered if another person hung on a hook.

"I'm sure if you could talk," the Torturer continued, "you'd beg for this." He held a switchblade up to his face, about a foot in front. The six-inch blade suddenly popped up. "I'm sure if you could, you'd plunged this into your own heart instead of enduring twelve more hours of hell. You sealed your agonizing fate by making terrible decisions. That was your choice, Pham Van Lu, and your mistake."

As the Torturer started walking away, he heard movement in the chamber. It sounded like footsteps. Multiple footsteps. Who else was here? How many people?

Lu would never know since the door was behind him.

As the Torturer faded from his periphery, Lu caught a final glimpse of the blade in the man's right hand. He did agree with the Torturer on one thing:

He'd gladly plunge the switchblade into his heart if he had the chance.

DAY THREE

CHAPTER THIRTY

Irvine Spectrum
Irvine, CA

KARLA DROPPED ME off at the Irvine Spectrum just before 11 a.m. A rally for the senator was being held there. She planned to follow up on the lead from the gunman who'd spilled the beans to the police. We were both anxious to hear what happened at the location the cops had traced the cell to.

I was at the Irvine Spectrum to surveil the senator and determine if the man was indeed faking his blindness. This was the second campaign stop for me this morning. I hadn't learned anything new about the senator at the first stop, or seen anything unusual about his movements, so I decided to do something different at the Spectrum. I thought the Spectrum would be the ideal place to enact my plan because the venue was much smaller than most of the other stops on the campaign trail, so it would be easier to get close to the senator, not to mention fewer cameras around to record my antics. From what I understood, the Spectrum rally was for Bradford's most committed followers.

The Irvine Spectrum was a large, outdoor shopping mall. The rally was being held in the middle of the shopping center, in a decent sized area that held about a thousand people. I was currently in the middle of the frenzied crowd, milling about with the other crazies and chanting 'Bradford.' The senator had just finished a twenty-minute speech and was now coming off the stage and mingling with the crowd.

At the first stop, I'd picked up some campaign items so I would blend in nicely with the crowd. I wore a bright red t-shirt. On the back of the shirt it read, 'Bradford!' The front contained a line from a Bob Dylan song, 'I feel a change comin' on.' I also held a stupid pro Bradford election sign in my left hand.

As the senator weaved through the crowd and headed my direction, I walked toward him. I wanted to meet him head on. My hope was to look like a desperate supporter who wanted to get close enough to the senator to yell an encouraging word. Since the senator was apparently blind, there wasn't much handshaking or high fiving going on.

Deep down what I wanted to do was waltz up to the man and punch him in the face. See if the senator flinched or ducked or in any way saw the punch coming at him. In my mind, that was the quickest and easiest way to see if somebody was faking their blindness. However, I couldn't do that for fear of repercussions. Like jail, for instance.

As I approached the senator, I picked up my pace, making sure to have a large, excited smile on my face.

"Senator! Senator!" I yelled, waving my right hand to get his attention.

Even though the man was supposedly blind, I'd noticed at the first rally this morning that a few supporters would still wave to get his attention. Though not many, some would even stick out their hand for a handshake.

When I was within ten feet of the man, I pretended to be one of these crazy fans. And I timed my antics to make sure the senator's bodyguard was looking the opposite direction.

I thrust my right hand out for a shake, yelling, "Senator! Over here! Senator!"

When I was a few feet away, I faked like I'd tripped. Dropping the sign to my left side, I stumbled toward the senator with my right hand outstretched. My right palm was flat and aimed directly at Bradford's face.

The senator didn't flinch. Not a trace of movement.

Just before connecting with the senator's face, I brought my right arm down. Instead of hitting his face, my right hand grasped the senator's shoulder, spinning the man to his right and almost knocking him over.

The crowd gasped. The chanting momentarily stopped.

The last thing I saw, before the senator's bodyguard smothered me with his body, was Ranger scampering off into the stunned crowd.

I went into the turtle position and took a few body blows, nothing serious or harmful.

While on the ground, I yelled, "My bad, my bad. I tripped. I tripped."

"Get him to his feet," I heard a gruff voice say. "And get him the hell out of here."

As the senator's bodyguard yanked me to my feet, I grabbed the election sign on the ground to my left. Once on my feet, I thrust it into the air and screamed, 'Bradford.'

The crowd erupted. Cheering, clapping, whistling. The Bradford chant instantly started again.

Not sure the bodyguard bought my act, though. He and another security guard, who appeared to work for the mall, flanked either side of me and ushered me away.

The senator's bodyguard, who was on my left, said, "You got your fifteen minutes of fame, buddy, but it cost you. I don't wanna see your face at another one of these events again."

I just kept smiling and thrusting the sign straight above my head, which kept the crowd frenzy going.

When we made it out of the crowd, the senator's bodyguard dropped off and another mall security guy took over. The mall security guards weren't too bent out of shape over the incident; they simply escorted me to the parking lot area without talking.

They took me to the mall's south entrance. One of the burly guards put his hand on my shoulder. "It's best you stay away from the Spectrum today."

"Sure, fellas," I said. "No problem."

When they were out of sight, I took off the red shirt and put it in the nearest garbage bin, along with the election sign. I texted Karla that I was ready to be picked up. She texted back that she was on her way.

Close to ten minutes later, she rolled up in her blue Ford 500.

"You look dejected," she said as I climbed in.

I didn't feel like reliving my moment with the senator, so I said, "Not getting anywhere. Tell me you have better news."

She pulled from the curb. "I did get an update from the cops. The cell they were tracing pinged at a location in Little Saigon, at a restaurant. The cops followed up and searched the location but couldn't find who they were looking for, not even the cell. A couple of hours later the cell went dark. I thought since we were close to Garden Grove we could swing by and check out the location. Who knows how thorough the cops were?"

"Good idea."

"I'll head there now. I also tried to dig up some information on the senator."

"What'd you find?"

Karla navigated out of the parking lot. "Not much, certainly nothing about the senator's personal life. It's like his past doesn't exist. I did learn something interesting, in a general sense."

"What was that?"

She glanced over. "Have you ever heard of blindsimming or a blindsimmer?"

"Um, no. Never heard that term."

"It's pretty rare, so not surprising. I came across it on Google when I was searching ways to detect if a person is faking blindness. Anyway, a blindsimmer is a person who pretends to be blind."

"And why would anyone do that?"

"Who knows? But apparently, it's a real thing; a mental condition, of course. Though from what I've gathered, it's not officially recognized. Certain people have this overwhelming desire to be blind. So much so, they sometimes take drastic measures."

"Like poke their eyes out, drastic like that?"

She batted her hand at me. "Heck, no, Chase. I mean they wear blindfolds around their house or purchase glasses to obscure their vision in public."

"Right, that makes more sense." I laughed at myself. "You think the senator is a blindsimmer?"

"Who knows? Possibly. What I find interesting is in that folder." She gestured to a manila folder on the seat between us. "Check out the pictures of glasses I found that they sell to people who suffer from this condition."

While Karla punched the gas and entered the Garden Grove freeway, I picked up the folder and rifled through the pictures. There were four different glasses. Immediately the third pair of glasses jumped out at me.

I held up the picture.

Before I could say anything, Karla chimed in, clearly excited. "Isn't that crazy?" she said. "Don't they look identical to the senator's?"

I nodded. "They do." My mind began processing the information.

Karla interrupted my thoughts a moment later. "Maybe the senator can see. Maybe everything that has happened to you and Slim isn't related to the Rat. Maybe it's about the senator."

I opened my mouth to argue, but Karla held up her hand. "Hear me out, Chase. Maybe Slim found out the senator was a phony, and maybe the senator caught wind that Slim knew his secret. The senator freaked out and hired some people to beat Slim to keep him quiet. But, of course, that didn't work, and the senator stepped up his game."

"It's a theory. I'll give you that. And I imagine the senator would go to great lengths to keep this information on the down low because it's career wrecking, not to mention a national scandal. But we're talking about poisoning Slim, murdering my ex-wife, gunning down guards in broad daylight at a hospital. Come on, that's not the MO of a career politician like Bradford."

She sighed. "I know. It's a big discovery if he is faking his blindness, but the lengths to cover it up are too extreme."

"But they are in line with what the Rat is capable of," I added.

She quickly responded. "Or was capable of."

I refrained from commenting because I felt like that may lead to another heated argument, which I wasn't in the mood for—even though it turned out nicely for me last time.

Instead, for the remainder of the ten-minute ride, we discussed various ways to find out for sure if Bradford was faking. I had every intention of going back to Palos Verdes tonight to see if the swimmer came out again.

The restaurant in Little Saigon was closed and deserted. Abandoned may have been a better term. The sign in the window said CLOSED, though according to the business hours sign it should be open.

There was nothing unusual or memorable about this particular restaurant. The front of the business was all windows, so I peered in and saw a typical set up: to my right was a check in desk and cash register, behind that several booths with large comfortable chairs lined either wall, and further back from that was a door that led to a back room. The only thing in English inside or outside the building were the huge neon letters above the store that read, RESTAURANT. Everything else was in Vietnamese, I assumed, since we were in Little Saigon.

"Let's check around back," I said to Karla.

The first thing I noticed was the back door into the building. It was clearly new and recently painted. You could tell because it was a different beige color, brighter and fresher, than the walls of the building that butted up against it. There was no window on the door, but there was quite the security system. It appeared you needed a card to swipe and a code to enter on a keypad for the door to be opened.

"That's strange," I said.

"Excessive," Karla said, stepping beside me.

I banged on the door once, then again. The knocks came as a dull thudding sound. "And the door is probably two or three inches of thick steel."

As Karla and I continued to make notes of the door's unusualness, we were surprised to see it suddenly open a crack, then swing open about three feet.

When the woman's eyes on the other side of the door met mine, she immediately tried closing the door. I stubbed my foot into the door jamb and stopped it from closing. The short Asian woman rushed away; her long, dark hair bouncing behind her.

She kept saying, "Leaving, leaving, leaving."

Karla rushed in to confront her. The woman grabbed a small box off a desk that appeared to contain a few personal items, then she headed for the front of the restaurant. Karla went after her.

I stayed back and surveyed the back office, which was a tiny room that contained a desk and chair and a few open lockers that I imagined workers kept their lunch and personal belongings in. One door led to the front of the restaurant and the other door led into another room.

I opened that door and stepped into an old kitchen. The large, square kitchen contained all the typical commercial restaurant equipment. Everything was stainless steel and had a layer of dust on top of it.

In the back corner of the kitchen, where the walk-in cooler and some steel storage shelves were located, was the backside of the roll-up door. On the floor directly in front of the door was a hinged piece of thick plywood. The plywood sat flush with the floor and had an inch gap around the outside, which made it easy for me to pull up.

About eight steps descended at an angle. I took them down. The steps stopped at the bottom of an underground storage area, which ran directly underneath the cooler; an area approximately six foot by twelve. The floor was covered with a piece of thin commercial rug. There were a few random boxes of kitchen utensils, nothing else down there.

Since the floor didn't feel one hundred per cent solid to me, I jumped up and down hard. Sure enough, there was some give in the floor. Plus, my jumping made a loud banging noise.

Immediately I thought it could be a false floor. Working quickly, I grabbed the boxes on the floor and took them up the stairs, leaving them on the main kitchen floor. Once the storage area was empty, I peeled back the carpet, starting on the wall farthest from the stairs. It came up easily since it wasn't glued or tacked down. There was definitely a false floor underneath.

"You okay? What's going on?"

Karla was at the top of the stairs with her hands out.

"What do you mean?" I said.

"I heard loud banging."

"Sorry, that was me jumping on this floor. It's a false bottom."

"You're kidding?" Karla raced down the stairs to help me.

"I'm not. Cops probably peeked in this storage area but didn't come down."

As Karla grabbed one end of the carpet and helped me roll it up, I asked, "What happened with the woman?"

"Not much. She barely spoke English. Once I flashed my badge, she was even more insistent on leaving. I was going to grill her, but then I heard the bangs and thought maybe something fell on you or somebody was at the back door. So I left her. I'm sure she's long gone by now."

"Probably just a restaurant worker and wouldn't know much. Was that your take?"

She nodded.

With the carpet out of the way, we turned our attention to the floor, which was split down the middle. One side had an inlaid handle. It reminded me of those outdoor storms doors that houses in tornado alley had, except these doors were half inch steel, not wood.

I used the handle and propped one side of the floor up about a foot or so. Karla swept in and helped me push it fully open. Immediately we felt a rush of damp, musty air.

Looking down, we saw a few steps, followed by a small, square landing area. We stepped down onto the landing area and I flipped a light switch on the wall.

A single bulb, midway down the next set of stairs, flickered on after a few tries. The yellow, cascading light barely reached where Karla and I stood. The light dimly illuminated about twenty steps or so, which descended at a rather steep angle. The light at the other end stopped at another landing area. I couldn't see beyond that.

And I couldn't hear any sounds coming from below.

I looked at Karla and shrugged. "Here goes nothing."

"Or everything," she was quick to reply. Karla pulled out her Glock 17M and handed it to me. "You take it if you're going first."

We proceeded down the steps, not fast, but not slowly either. Karla was one step behind me. I wanted to get to the bottom quickly and find out what we were dealing with, but I also didn't want to make a lot of noise and announce our presence. Who knows what was waiting for us at the bottom?

Fortunately, the stairs were solid, three-inch thick pieces of wood, so they didn't creak or groan. They felt sturdy and well-built. The stairwell was clearly constructed years ago when contractors used the best materials they could. The walls to my left and right were still open construction. Every sixteen inches was an open stud with a thin piece of insulation wedged in between the studs. No finish carpentry at all.

More than likely, whatever was underground was simply storage. Nobody felt the need to make this underground area attractive.

When we reached the bottom landing area, I stood still and listened for about a minute. Which also allowed my eyes to adjust to the relative darkness in front of me. Feeling like we were alone, I finally got a good look around. Directly in front was a large, thick wooden door. Two hallways jutted off on either side of the door at a forty-five-degree angle. I saw another light switch on the wall, but I hesitated to flick it on.

Karla agreed. She shook her head as I motioned my eyes toward it.

I wanted to ensure we were alone before turning on any more lights.

We whispered, agreeing to first investigate the hallway on our right. But before going down there, I motioned at the door in front of us. I wanted a quick peek into the room.

The door was unlocked, so I gingerly pushed it open about six inches, then leaned in and placed my eye to the opening. A musty smell overwhelmed my senses, but only for a second as I suddenly found myself holding my breath.

My eyes widened as they locked onto the folded over body swinging gently on a meat hook in the center of the room.

CHAPTER THIRTY-ONE

I JAMMED THE Glock behind my belt, then bashed open the door with my palms and raced toward the body.

Behind me, I heard Karla gasp as she spotted the man. Just as I reached his naked body, Karla flicked on the lights. I didn't waste a second to assess the situation or see who it was. I immediately grabbed the man underneath his tailbone and curled his whole body upward to relieve the pressure on his hands and feet.

As Karla raced over to help, I looked up at the man's hands and feet tied together. His wrists and hands and ankles were swollen to double their normal size. Everything was black and blue and grotesquely deformed. I think I heard the man whimper, which meant he was alive, but I couldn't be sure. All I wanted at the moment was to get the body down.

When Karla reached us, I motioned at the thick rope above me. I'd lifted the body high enough to create some slack in the line. Karla jumped up and swiped her arm sideways. It took her three attempts to unloop the rope from the hook.

The full weight of the body dropped into my arms. I slowly bent down, cradling the body, then I eased the man onto the dusty, cold concrete floor. Immediately Karla went to work, checking for a pulse, for a breath, for any signs of life.

She pulled the man's head back and delivered a few breaths.

His eyes fluttered open, then quickly shut again.

I looked at Karla. "He's breathing, but we need water, a blanket, an ambulance. We need it now."

She nodded and pulled out her cell. A moment later, she said, "Can't get a decent signal. One bar, but it keeps going in and out. I'll go upstairs and call 911."

I whipped out my pocketknife, a Kershaw Blur Folding Knife, and cut the man's hands and ankles free. On the ground, below where the man had been dangling, I noticed blood droppings. I took a few seconds to assess his condition, to see where the blood had dropped from.

The man had an abdominal wound. Since he was compressed and folded over, though, I couldn't get a look at the size or condition of the wound. All I could see was dried blood streaking down his bare hips and sides of his butt.

I checked his breathing; it'd stopped. His pulse was gone, too, so I began CPR. A minute later, after delivering the man some breaths, I checked his pulse. His heart pumped again. I put my hand over his mouth and felt him breathing, too.

Next thing I knew, Karla swept in beside me. "Ambulance is on its way. Should we open him up and then—"

"No way. Pretty sure he has a nasty abdominal wound that could be fused shut because of his position. Since all the blood is dried, that's my thought. We shouldn't move him."

Karla gave the man the once over, then nodded. "Right. He may bleed out if we peel him back."

I motioned toward the hallways. "Why don't you check the rooms. Maybe there's water or a blanket, something like that."

Karla was out of the room before I knew it.

When I looked back, the man's eyes began flickering.

"You're going to make it," I said, waving my hand in front of his eyes.

The man didn't respond, not that I expected him to. All he did was blink twice and lick his lips once. His eyes had finally focused and were now staring right back at me. I had a feeling that we'd gotten to him just in time.

The man opened his mouth, but no words came out.

I waited.

He coughed, then winced from coughing. After that, he managed to whisper something. He did it again. And again. That was when I realized he was whispering my name.

What?

He choked out in a dry voice, "I'm sorry."

That caught me off guard. I didn't know how to respond. Why was this guy apologizing?

Before I could figure out what to say, Karla was at my side. "No blanket," she said. "But I did find some water." She handed me a plastic Crystal Springs water bottle.

Desperate for water, the man had already parted his lips and tilted his head back as far as he could. I sprinkled some water into his mouth, then gave him a little more. He coughed most of it up. I repeated the procedure, this time with just a few drops of water.

Karla stood and backpedaled to the door. "I'm going upstairs to direct the paramedics."

The man on the ground shook his head at me, very slowly, and whispered, "No ambulance, no cops."

I leaned over him. "You're getting both, don't you worry."

He swallowed. "Sorry." He winced in between breaths. Then he said sorry again, though it seemed more to himself than me.

The man was delusional or feverish or both. I asked him questions anyway. "How do you know my name? Did the Rat hire you? Is that how?"

The man blinked twice, then managed in between labored breaths, "Rat? Who's the Rat?"

I scowled. "The man who hired you. Anurat Wu, the infamous Thai warlord."

He slowly shook his head.

"Don't play coy," I said, glaring at the man. After a few seconds of looking him in the eye, I realized that he may not be playing coy since he looked genuinely confused.

He motioned for some water with his lips. I gave him some.

Then he said in a croaky voice, "I'm Vietnamese, not Thai." He swallowed and took a second to get his breath. "I was hired to take out Hans." He licked his lips. "You and the woman, the one at your house, were collateral

damage." He cleared his throat. "Not hired by this rat man. My employer . .
."

He motioned for more water, so I obliged.

After he swallowed, he coughed out, "is a woman."

CHAPTER THIRTY-TWO

LU KNEW HIS body was shutting down. For good. It was only a matter of minutes. He only hoped he'd die before the ambulance and police arrived. He didn't want the paramedics and doctors to perform life-saving measures. If he lived, he'd spend the rest of his life rotting in a federal prison.

No way, he thought.

Lu was ready to die now, prepared to face whatever the afterlife held. Ready to pay for his sins, atone for them in the afterlife if he had a chance. Before he died, however, he needed Garrison Chase's help. He wanted to do one good thing before leaving the earth.

Water splashed onto his face.

"What do you mean a woman?" Garrison Chase said. "What woman? Who?"

Lu motioned with his lips toward the left hallway. "My wallet," he said. "In the desk." He licked his lips to get some moisture in his mouth. "Room with wine racks."

"No," Chase said. "Tell me about your employer."

Lu gently shook his head. "Wallet, before I talk, it's important." He swallowed. "Bottom right-hand drawer, not sure it's still there."

Chase reluctantly left. Lu knew the man was desperate for information, desperate to learn what was going on. And Lu was prepared to tell him, at least as much he knew. However, Lu feared the man would be disappointed by what little he knew of his employer. He needed Garrison Chase to give his word, to promise. He hoped Chase was a man of integrity and would follow through.

Minutes later—though Lu wasn't sure how many—Garrison Chase returned.

Lu breathed a sigh of relief to see the wallet in Chase's hand. He motioned for Chase to open it.

Chase shook his head. "I already saw it contains thousands of dollars. What's this all about?"

"Promise me." Lu swallowed. "Get the money to my uncle."

Chase narrowed his eyes, thought for a few seconds, then said, "Why?"

Lu shook his head. "Never mind, promise."

Chase sighed. "Who's your uncle? Where does he live?"

"Say it, say you promise."

Chase sighed again. "I promise. If you tell me who the woman is."

Lu waited and looked Chase in the eye. The man didn't flinch or blink.

Lu said, "Uncle owns convenience store." He took a breath. "Five miles from here. Corner of Brea and Hallsworth. Same family name as mine."

He waited until Chase nodded, then continued. "Tell him this: I fell on the wrong side, but I crossed back over. I always intended to."

"What does that mean?"

"Never mind, just tell him." Lu coughed twice. "Give me your word."

"I promise," Chase said.

Lu cleared his throat, shaking his head in the process. "Swear on your name."

"I swear on the Chase name I'll do it. If you give me information."

Lu hardened his eyes. "In my culture, your family name is your everything."

Chase nodded. "Understood."

Immediately Lu felt a wave of relief over him. Typically, he didn't trust the white man. But there was something about this man, Garrison Chase, something about him he believed he could trust. It was in his eyes. Maybe Lu was being overly optimistic, maybe not.

Lu motioned for water. Chase poured a little into his mouth.

Then he said, "Mama H. That's her name, my employer."

As suspected, Garrison Chase spat, "What? Mama H? Come on. Who the hell's that? I need a real name."

Lu shook his head. "All I know. Don't know her given name."

"No, no, no." Chase kept shaking his head. "I need more than that."

Lu took a breath. It felt like one of his last. His body was letting go. A sense of calm and peace enveloped him. It was hard to focus, hard to speak.

He managed, "Mama H. . . she's the key. Find her. Take her down."

"Come on," Chase said. "Is this for real? Is Mama H even real?"

Lu nodded. "Met her once. Tell my uncle I helped you, did something good in the end."

"More," Chase shouted. "I need more."

Lu swallowed. "My cell, in same room. Her contact info on cell."

Garrison Chase pushed himself off the ground and headed toward the door. Lu knew his cell wasn't there. And if it was, the SIM card wouldn't be in it.

But Lu wanted to die alone, not die looking into the face of Garrison Chase.

After the man left the room, Lu took his final breath, then closed his eyes.

CHAPTER THIRTY-THREE

I OPENED EVERY drawer in the stupid desk. Twice. There was no cell phone.

Slamming the final drawer shut, I put my hands on my hips and took a deep breath. I felt like I'd been had by the man in the other room.

Mama H? Come on. Was that really his employer? Was that really the name the woman went by?

I glanced at everything I'd found in the desk: the wallet, a passport, and a plane ticket to Hong Kong. I opened the passport and read the name, Pham Van Lu.

Was that even the guy's real name?

Hearing Karla coming down the stairs snapped me from my anger. I stuffed the wallet filled with money in my back pocket and left everything else on the desk. I met Karla at the bottom of the stairs. She had a blanket tucked under her arm.

"Paramedics just arrived," she said. "What are you doing?"

I thumbed over my shoulder. "Some of his personal things are in there. Apparently, his name is Pham Van Lu. And he claims he doesn't work for the Rat."

"He told you that?"

I nodded. "He doesn't know the man, at least that's what he said. We had a short conversation. I'll tell you about it later."

We hurried to the room where Lu was. Karla rushed over to put the blanket on the man. When she reached the body, however, she paused and dropped the blanket.

"What's wrong?" I asked.

"Doesn't appear to be moving or breathing." She bent down and checked for a pulse. About ten seconds later, she said, "Dammit, he's gone."

But she gave mouth to mouth anyway, for about two minutes. That was when a paramedic rushed into the room and took over from Karla.

During that time, I'd taken a seat on the cold floor with my head hung between my knees.

Karla walked over. "Doesn't look good. Sorry, Chase."

A minute later, the paramedic looked over at us and confirmed. "Sorry, too far gone."

I nodded. We watched the paramedic drape the blanket over the dead, naked body of Pham Van Lu.

"Ever heard of a woman named Mama H?" I asked.

She scowled. "Mama H. No, never."

I motioned at the body. "He's Vietnamese, by the way, not Thai. He said he works for a woman named Mama H. She gave the orders to take out Slim. Like I said, he told me he'd never heard of the Rat."

Karla wracked her mind and didn't say anything.

Cop sirens interrupted our silence about twenty seconds later.

Karla looked down at me. "I'll go meet them and update them on what happened."

I nodded and stood. Soon cops would be swarming in this underground chamber, so I wanted to get a good look at the room I was in.

It only took a few observations to realize this room was once a wine grotto, for the restaurant, I assumed. Now it appeared to be converted into a torture chamber. Why else would there be six large meat hooks embedded into the wooden beams that spanned the room?

This Mama H, if she existed, brought her victims down here for some excruciating punishment.

I inspected the area directly below the hooks. Underneath two of the hooks there appeared to be small smatterings of blood, but the spots were so dry and old it was hard to tell for sure if it was blood.

The only other discovery I found that piqued my curiosity was a wet stain in the front left corner of the room. The stain started about two feet off the floor and continued downward into a round puddle on the floor. I inspected the area around the liquid. Since the floor was pretty dusty, I could see that there had been a person or maybe two standing in the corner. Getting down on my knees, I sniffed the middle of the spot where it was wet.

Right away I knew it was pee. No surprise there. Again, not sure what that meant, or if it was significant in any way. It did mean somebody was down here recently, or it simply could've been urine from Pham Van Lu. Maybe he was held in this room before being put on the hook, and he relieved himself in this particular corner.

However, I doubted the pee was Pham Van Lu's since there were holding cells down here with heavy-duty locks on them. I'd seen two on my way to the room that held Pham Van Lu's personal belongings. A cell would be the likely place to hold the man before hanging him up to die.

Also, the urine spot was still wet. Surely Pham Van Lu must've been hanging on the hook for a while, long enough for a pee spot to dry. I ran my hand over my head. Then again, it was damp down here so maybe a urine spot took a long time to dry.

My inspection ended when I heard voices and footsteps coming down the stairwell. Two uniformed officers were the first police to arrive. They swept into the room and conferenced with the paramedics. They paid no attention to me.

Karla was at my side by that point. When the officers finally came over to us, she flashed her badge and did most of the talking. Eventually the entire police task force that had been assigned to the hospital murders had joined us underground, including Detective Palmer.

I kept my distance.

After about an hour, Karla and I were escorted to the Long Beach cop shop to make an official statement. Long Beach PD took the case from Garden Grove PD since this was all related to Slim's poisoning and attempted murder at the hospital.

The cops spared me and didn't send Palmer in to question me. Karla and I gave statements in separate rooms, all standard operating procedure stuff.

Naturally, it took far too long. In fact, I spent the afternoon with the local cops, telling them everything I could. Well, almost everything.

Yes, I took the wallet filled with ten grand in cash from the crime scene and didn't tell anyone about it, including Karla. Sure, I was fully aware that I'd stepped across an ethical line. It was a fuzzy line in my opinion, and it was a step I was willing to take. After all, I did promise a dying man. And I was a man of my word.

If the tip about Mama H panned out, I'd follow through and get the money to the guy's uncle. I didn't trust the local cops to get the job done right. The stakes were too high to entrust this situation to somebody else.

I'd made it through questioning and statements before Karla, so I was outside the police station waiting for her. She'd texted that she'd be out soon. Flipping open my cell, I was about to call my mother and check-in with her, but a kid about twenty years old screeched to a stop beside me on a pedal bike.

He looked at me, all smiles. "Are you Garrison Chase?"

I looked at him skeptically, eventually nodding.

He took off his backpack and unzipped it. Before I knew what was happening, I held a rather large envelope in my right hand.

"You've been served." That's all the kid said. He pedaled off before I had a chance to respond or process what had happened.

I tore open the envelope with a little too much vigor and read quickly. After a moment, I dropped the documents to my side.

The Diekelmans, the damn Diekelmans, were fighting for sole custody of Simon.

CHAPTER THIRTY-FOUR

Park Ave.
Belmont Shore, CA

I WAS HOT—beyond pissed at the Diekelmans.

Karla tried to convince me not to confront my ex in-laws, but I didn't take her advice. She'd driven me back to her house to get my vehicle, then I headed to Gina's in my Chevy Caprice to 'dialogue' with the couple about their wishful thinking.

Meanwhile, Jimmy Schuberman was conferencing with another lawyer to see if the two had any chance at making a case for custody of Simon.

Currently, I sat in my car in front of Gina's house trying to calm down.

A few minutes later, I barged up Gina's front steps and pounded on the door.

A distraught Dan Diekelman answered the door and stepped outside.

"What the hell's going on, Dan? Filing for sole custody? You have to be kidding. I had nothing to do with your daughter's murder. I've been cleared of any wrongdoing."

He held up his hands. "It's Helen, Chase, she's furious and slightly out of control. You know I can't stop her when she's emotional. She's acting alone on this one. I love my grandson, but I'm certainly too old to raise another child."

I wanted to punch the man and toughen him up and demand he reason with his wife. But Dan Diekelman always took a backseat to his wife. Plus, he already looked beaten up.

Instead, I said, "Fine, Dan, I'll talk with Helen then."

As I stepped toward the door, Dan shuffled in front of me. "She's not here, Chase."

"Out of my way, Dan. I know she's inside."

Dan was about to object again, but when I moved closer to the door, he stepped aside. "Suit yourself," he said. "Go ahead and check. I'm telling the truth; she's not here."

I brushed past Dan and wheeled open the door.

"Helen," I shouted as I entered the foyer. "We need to talk."

I waited about a minute. When there was no response, and no sounds of movement in the house, I rushed in and checked every room on every floor.

Dan was right; Helen was nowhere to be found.

Dan had waited outside, sitting on a porch step.

"Where is she?" I asked when I got outside.

He shrugged. "I honestly don't know. Like I said, Chase, we don't see eye to eye on this. She doesn't want to be around me. I haven't seen her all day."

I backpedaled to my car. "Let her know when you do see her that we need to talk."

"Sure," he said. "You two do need to talk, but both of you need to calm down first. Maybe you guys should chat in a day or two."

As I fired up the Caprice, I couldn't help but think that Dan was probably right.

I drove to downtown Belmont Shore, which was a small town just east of Long Beach. By the time I made it to the downtown area, I'd calmed down. I was sort of glad that Helen wasn't at the house. Who knows what I might've said to her?

There was a string of trendy restaurants in Belmont Shore. Karla and I had planned on meeting for dinner to discuss our next steps. We'd agreed on a loud, busy, Mediterranean place we were both familiar with. We needed the noise since we didn't want people overhearing our conversation.

Karla had arrived before me. The first thing she said as I sat down at our quaint outdoor table was, "How'd it go?"

"Don't worry, I didn't do anything stupid. Helen wasn't there. Dan said it's all her idea. Jimmy's looking into whether there's any merit for them gaining custody."

"Maybe Helen is doing this just to piss you off," Karla said.

"If so, it's obviously working."

Karla held my hand. "Maybe she'll back off once she comes to her senses. Even if she doesn't, no way they're taking Simon from you. They can't. No way."

The waitress came and I ordered a double IPA, along with a shot of Bulleit bourbon. Karla ordered a glass of Pinot Grigio.

"Let's talk about the case," I said. "I have to get my mind off the Diekelmans."

She nodded. "What else did Pham Van Lu say when you were alone with him?"

I thought about it for a moment. "Aside from telling me he was hired to take out Slim and that his employer was a woman, he said I was collateral damage, so was Gina."

"Did he elaborate on that?"

"Nope. The only other thing he said concerned his uncle."

"His uncle?"

I paused. Karla would lay into me for taking money from the crime scene. But she deserved to know everything. So I came clean. "He asked me to give his uncle some money. If I agreed, he'd provide information about his employer. The man had a bunch of cash in his wallet, in a desk in that storage room."

"Okay," Karla said, eyeing me. "Do you still have the money and the wallet?"

I reluctantly nodded.

After some awkward silence, she said, "So you took a wallet with money in it from a crime scene. A wallet from a murder victim, who's also a murderer himself." She looked away, then back to me. "How much money?"

Fortunately, the waitress dropped off our drinks and interrupted us.

Karla asked again, however, the second the waitress left. "How much money, Chase? Come on, tell me."

"Ten grand," I said.

Karla downed half her glass of wine. When she finished swallowing, she said calmly, "You have to give the wallet and money to the LBPD. The sooner the better."

"I promised the guy, Karla. And he gave up some information. Not sure if the man was well-intentioned and telling the truth or feeding me some line. I want to wait and see how the Mama H lead pans out."

She held up her hands. "I'll say this one more time, and then that's it, I'm not going to get pushy or start an argument over this. You need to report what happened and turn in the wallet with the money. It's unethical, Chase."

I nodded, then downed my bourbon and blew out a breath.

There was some awkward silence. Fortunately, my cell buzzed in my pocket. I dug it out. "Didn't hear it ring, it's a voicemail."

After I listened to the message, Karla asked, "Who was it?"

"Slim. He wants me to stop by the hospital when I can. Says there's been a development."

"What kind of development?"

"He didn't say."

"We have work to do, Chase. Leads to follow up on. People to call."

"Absolutely."

"Where should we start?"

I thought about it, then leaned forward. "Pham Van Lu said Mama H was the key. So we have to figure out if she's real, and if so, who she is. Since I'm on paid leave and don't really have access to our databases, I think you should investigate this Mama H alias. You could also check our databases for who owns the restaurant business and/or the building. They could be different people."

Karla tapped her nails on the table. "Sounds good. I like it."

We ordered food, then spent the next fifteen minutes discussing who we could enlist to help. We both had numerous contacts in the agency that may have heard of a criminal using the alias Mama H.

When our dinner arrived, we took a break from talking and focused on eating. Midway through our meal Karla broke the silence. "So I have sort of a wild theory about everything that I wanted to run by you."

I pushed my plate back. "Fire away. I spit-balled a couple of wild ideas in my mind this afternoon, too. Hit me with yours."

Karla leaned in. "So we've been focusing on the Rat so far, but now this Mama H character pops up. What if the H stands for . . ." She paused. "Henrietta. Henrietta Valenzuela."

I shifted forward in my chair. "Funny thing, I thought about the same person."

"Really?"

"Yup, but it's crazy. I mean, she hired Slim to investigate Bradford, her competition. She wouldn't hire Slim and then try to kill him, not to mention frame me. Why and what for?"

"Right, I'm not saying Henrietta is directly involved in all this, but what if Bradford is?"

"What do you mean?"

Karla looked around, then back to me. "What if Bradford knew Henrietta hired Slim to investigate him. What if the senator is indeed faking his blindness and found out that Slim knew that, so the senator hires Pham Van Lu to take out Slim, but the senator does so under the guise of a fictional person named Mama H? The senator does have a connection with Vietnam after all, and Pham Van Lu was Vietnamese. Anyway, it's all done to point back and implicate Henrietta, which rids Bradford of his competition, or at least casts huge doubts on Henrietta and her involvement. You're simply collateral damage in all this. The senator assumes that Slim told you about the fake blindness, so then you had to be dealt with."

"Boy," I said, "you're really convinced the Rat is innocent, aren't you?"

She waved me off. "It's a theory, just think about it. It's a huge double win for the senator. He gets rid of Slim who was about to blow the whistle on his phoniness. And it gives him a clear path to the White House."

I thought about it for a second. "It explains motives, Karla, but the means are what I have a problem with. Those are some incredible lengths to go to: poisoning, murder, broad daylight shootings. And for a United States senator?"

Karla nodded. "I know, and I agree. Torture's actually the biggest problem for me. Why would the senator not just put a bullet in Pham Van Lu? Why torture the man?"

"Exactly. Plus, the senator wouldn't and couldn't have known that we'd find the hitman in the torture chamber and that he'd mention Mama H in his dying words."

"Is there a better theory?"

I nodded. "I think so."

"What'd you got?"

"This is all about layers, Karla, which you just hinted at."

"Go on," she said.

"Any criminal with a brain uses layers in their criminal activity. You don't go out and directly hire somebody to kill a person. You hire somebody who will then go out and hire somebody else to kill that person."

"Sure," Karla said. "Absolutely."

"That way you're always one layer removed. That way the actual killers won't truly know who they're working for and therefore can't implicate their ultimate boss. That's exactly what Pham Van Lu did. He hired this Tanawat person, who in turned hired the thugs to mow down Slim in the hospital. The cops caught a break with getting Tanawat's cell before he could get rid of it."

"So what are you saying?"

"I'm saying our best theory is still the Rat."

Karla was about to interject.

"Hear me out," I said, holding out my hand. "The Rat is behind all this, but he's using a layer. He's using Mama H to do all his dirty work. Maybe she's real, maybe not. It really doesn't matter; she's simply another layer in all this. Hired hands like Tanawat and Pham Van Lu have no idea who's ultimately behind their hiring. They think it's this Mama H character, but they don't know who's really calling the shots. It's what most mastermind criminals do."

"You could be right. Was the Rat ever known for hiring Vietnamese hit men? Was that standard operating procedure for him?"

"Honestly, I don't know. I do know, however, that the Rat uses these means. Torture and poisoning and broad daylight shootings are within his specialty, for sure. And he also has the motive. He doesn't want Slim or I to testify against him."

"Maybe," Karla said.

"What do you mean maybe?"

"The Rat's motive is in question for me. He's not seeking freedom from charges; he's trying to avoid dying. What you're saying is that he's going to these great lengths just to avoid the death penalty, to avoid being extradited to Texas."

"Some people are terrified of dying, Karla, so it's not all that out of the question."

"I agree. I'm just not one hundred percent convinced, that's all. There's holes in the theory."

"Fair enough; I'm not one hundred percent either."

"Like I said earlier, we have work to do."

I nodded. "We need more research into Mama H, to figure out if she's real."

"I'll get to work on that. What are you going to do?"

"I need to close the loop with the senator, go back to his place and see if the swimmer makes another appearance. See if it's really Bradford, and if he's faking his blindness. Then I'll check in with Slim and find out about his new development. Then I can turn my full attention to this Mama H character and pursue leads with you tomorrow."

Karla glanced at her watch. "We better get out of here then."

"Right. We've spent enough time theorizing. We need facts and answers."

We left the restaurant and went separate ways, agreeing to meet around midnight at Karla's house.

CHAPTER THIRTY-FIVE

Sea Cove Dr.
Rancho Palos Verdes

I PARKED FARTHER down the street from the senator's rental than last time. I wasn't taking any chances of being spotted. While sitting in my Caprice, I dialed Karla.

She picked up on the third ring. "What's up?"

"I'm at the senator's place waiting for it to get dark. I had a thought about the underground crime scene in Little Saigon."

"Fire away."

"Do you know any of the local techs working the scene?"

"Ummm. I do remember seeing someone underground who I'm vaguely familiar with."

"Think you can contact him or her?"

"Him. Why? What's up?"

"I know the crime techs swept for fingerprints because I watched them do it. And I know they'll be checking the dried blood spots in the chamber.

They'll be able to get a DNA profile from that. Just wondering if they'll check the urine I spotted in the far corner of the room. It was still wet, so it was relatively recent. I'm not sure what sort of DNA profile they can get from urine, but maybe that leads somewhere. Just a thought."

"It could, you're right. Urine's not ideal for a definitive profile, from what I understand, but it's worth a shot. It could be from Pham Van Lu, you realize. They may have been holding him in there before stringing him up."

"I do. I'm a little skeptical on that because a couple of the rooms underground were holding cells with dead bolts on the door, so it would seem wiser to keep him in one of those rooms."

"Right," Karla said. "And there wasn't a lock on the wooden door into the wine grotto, at least not a good sized one that I can remember. I'll call Long Beach and see if the tech I know is still working. I'm working on something else, too, but I need more time. I'll ring back in an hour or less."

After hanging up, I watched the house for signs of activity while waiting for Karla to call back. Ten minutes later, a black Tesla with tinted windows passed me on the right. Slim's dossier had mentioned the senator owned a black Tesla. Sure enough, the automatic gate slowly wheeled across the rental's driveway. The car zoomed through and disappeared into a below ground parking garage. I wondered how many people in this neighborhood even knew the senator was temporarily living in their neighborhood.

About forty minutes after speaking with Karla, she rang back.

"Tell me some good news," I said. "Was the tech in?"

"Actually, he was. The man loves to log overtime. He'd spent most of the day with the fingerprints, ultimately getting no hits in any database. He's waiting on results from the two dried blood stains, including a DNA ancestry test. In the morning, he said he'd look at the urine sample and get back to me. He wasn't that hopeful, though."

"Why not?"

"He said you can get a DNA profile from urine, but it's not very good. The best samples are from blood, tissue, and hair roots. He said he'll send me his report on the urine, probably later in the morning. He'll get back to me whenever he hears back on the blood, too."

"Okay, what else did you find out? Anything about Mama H?"

She sighed. "No immediate hits on that alias in our main database. But I have some other databases to check. It's going to take some time."

"Got it," I said.

"You know, while waiting on database results, I entertained another wild theory."

"Oh boy."

"Hear me out, Chase, because what I'm about to say is crazy. And it doesn't necessarily mean the person is involved. There's a big hole in the theory. I'd thought about it earlier, but I wanted to do some more research before telling you."

"Go ahead, I'm all ears."

"Don't get mad," she said.

"Fire away, don't worry."

"Did you know your mother-in-law—ex, that is—has a criminal record?"

I laughed. "Wait, you think she's Mama H because her name is Helen?"

"See, I knew you'd think I was crazy."

"Karla, why would you even suspect her? It's a little crazy, for sure."

"You're right. It's just that Helen's demeanor when she found out about Gina was odd. She was pissed and not mourning. It seems like a mother would mourn first, then feel anger later."

"Maybe," I said. "But denial is the first stage of grief, right?"

"Listen, it's not like I suspected her straight away or anything. But when I learned the hit man was Vietnamese, not Thai, I started to entertain Helen as a suspect because I know Portland really well. And I know Portland has a huge Vietnamese population, like the fourth largest population of Vietnamese in America."

"Pretty coincidental, Karla."

"Granted," she said. "After learning she has a criminal record, though, I got more suspicious. It's just a wild theory, Chase."

"Wild is right. What did she get arrested for? Some hippy sit-in somewhere? I bet she tied herself to an old, historic tree some developer was going to cut down. Right?"

"Much worse than that."

I cleared my throat. "Really?"

"Absolutely. The Diekelman's own more than just their organic potato operation. They own a number of other produce companies in the area. They employ close to a thousand people, many of whom are seasonal, migrant workers.

"Anyway, Helen is the head of Human Resources for Diekelman, Incorporated. To make a long story short, she hired and rehired illegal immigrants and paid a pretty price for doing so."

"Wow," I said. "Definitely didn't know that. That's surprising."

"Legally speaking," Karla continued, "it's a misdemeanor for companies when they're caught hiring illegal immigrants. But that's not the case when you rehire illegals you know are illegals. Which is what the Diekelmans did. The worst part for Helen is that a few of these illegal Vietnamese workers she hired, over a period of approximately three years, were convicted of various crimes like . . ." I heard her flipping through some paper. "Kidnap and extortion, grand larceny, drug possession with the intent to sell, and one for murder. Helen hired some bad individuals, Chase, to say the least. And she did it more than once."

"How come I never heard of this?"

"Because they're wealthy. Really wealthy."

"Stupid rich," I said. "That's what Gina used to say about her parents. But what does them being rich have to do with anything?"

"Because they own the county newspaper, that's why you and most other people have never heard of these stories."

"Catch and kill," I quickly responded. "Except in these cases, they didn't have to pay anybody. They just killed these stories from the start. Made sure they never saw the light of day."

"And Helen pled guilty so there was no public trial. It's clear she was trying to save her company's reputation. In the end, her punishment was monetary, hefty fines to the county, that sort of thing. It's not like she spent any jail time."

"When was this?"

"About three years ago."

"It's almost unbelievable."

"I know it's crazy," Karla responded, "but it's worth considering. We know the hired killer, Pham Van Lu, was at your place to take you out, but Gina unexpectedly rushed into your bedroom and took the bullet. What if Helen wanted you out of the picture for good and hired the Vietnamese man to kill you, but the whole thing went sideways when he mistakenly killed Gina. Maybe Helen never wanted you to have even weekend custody of Simon."

"Maybe she does have a crazy motive to get rid of me, Karla, but not Slim. Why was he targeted?"

A moment of pause on the other end. "I know, that's the big hole. Maybe she knew Slim was your mentor and somewhat responsible for training you. It's a stretch."

"It is. But I appreciate you looking into everything. I mean, Helen Diekelman certainly doesn't have a strong custody case against me now."

"I know, that's the other unspoken reason for why I was looking into her past."

"You're the best."

"You're not so bad yourself."

"Listen," I said, changing the subject. "It's dark enough for me to spy on the senator, so I'm heading out. I'll touch base soon."

After hanging up, I left the Caprice and headed into the nature preserve. I headed straight to the southeast corner of the property, climbing up the pillar and peering into the backyard. Nobody was in the pool. In fact, nobody was in the backyard at all.

So I climbed back down and settled into some foliage a few feet away. While waiting and hoping for an appearance by the swimmer, I felt elated knowing the Diekelmans had a shady past. I did worry, however, that they had a ton of money and could hire a powerful attorney to fight me in court.

To keep my mind off that, I spent the time thinking about the theories Karla and I had entertained. I focused on basic investigative theory: motive, means, and opportunity.

Keeping those three things in mind, I evaluated the potential suspects: Helen Diekelman, Henrietta Valenzuela/Senator Bradford, and the Rat. After about an hour, I came back to my original conclusion that the Rat clearly had the best means and motive for setting everything in motion. Sure, his opportunity was somewhat in question since he was in a maximum-security prison, but I felt like his criminal tentacles reached broad and far, so being in prison wouldn't be that big of a problem for him.

My butt was sore and my knees were stiff from sitting. Just as I repositioned, I saw a light flicker on in the backyard. I climbed the corner pillar and confirmed the pool's lights had turned on.

And saw that the swimmer was back in the water.

Like last night, the German Shepherd paced from one end of the pool to the other, following the man. Unlike last night, however, the bodyguard was on the move, sweeping the western edge of the property. I ducked down and waited until I heard the bodyguard passing my corner. Then I climbed over the wall and side-stepped along the eastern edge of the property, keeping my eyes trained on the bodyguard's back. The man was not a vigilant security guard. He walked the perimeter looking down at his cell the entire time. In his defense, he probably never suspected a trespasser would be in the backyard.

About midway down the property, I stopped walking, settled in, and watched the swimmer. Every few seconds I glanced at the bodyguard to track his whereabouts. All I could hear was the rhythmic splash of the swimmer's strokes. There was a brief moment of silence when the man went underwater during his kick-flip off the wall.

I passed the time by counting the swimmer's arm strokes. To my surprise, the man had identical strokes from end to end, which meant the swimmer could indeed be blind. All he had to do was count his strokes, and when he hit the magic number, flip, feel the wall with his feet, then push off in the opposite direction.

The man stopped swimming after thirty minutes. When he climbed onto the pool deck, and pulled off his cap and goggles, I immediately confirmed it was the senator. Since I was much closer to the pool than last night, I had no problem identifying the spry, seventy-year-old man.

My heart picked up its pace as I watched Bradford head to the lounge chair and grab his towel. Like last night, the man showed no signs of hesitation with his movements. It appeared he knew exactly where the chair and towel were located. That didn't prove anything, however.

But after toweling off, the senator sat on the lounge chair, turned slightly to his left, then reached over and picked his watch cleanly off a small table between the chairs.

What? How the hell did he do that?

In shock, I watched Bradford strap on his watch and then actually look at it. Following that, he reached to the table and picked up his wedding ring. No patting around the table for it. He picked it up without so much as a fumble, like he could see exactly where it was located. No way could a blind man do that.

My breathing suddenly fell in rhythm with my rapidly beating heart. This guy can see. He can see!

No doubt in my mind.

CHAPTER THIRTY-SIX

THE DECEPTION SHOCKED me to the core. So much so, I stood frozen in place. All I could think about was confronting the man. It probably wasn't the best idea to expose myself since I was trespassing, but nothing was going to stop me from getting to the bottom of things.

So, after the bodyguard made his next pass, I stepped from the shadows and quickly rushed in behind the big man. As I did, I jammed both thumbs on either side of his neck, right into the pocket between the clavicle bones; into a spot called the jugular or suprasternal notch. The bodyguard instantly dropped his phone, then collapsed to his knees. I used one hand to cover his mouth, stifling the man's cry. I used my other arm to wrap around his neck and squeeze the carotid artery until the man went limp and fell unconscious.

Wasting no time, I unholstered his sidearm, pulled out the magazine and pocketed it. Then I racked the round from the chamber and returned the gun to his holster.

I approached the senator with my hands in the air. Ranger saw me first. Instead of barking or charging, the dog whimpered and cowered behind the lounge chair. I walked onto the pool deck and headed straight toward the senator. When he looked over at me, I saw his eyes widen. Something a blind man would never do, could never do.

"STOP!" the senator shouted, holding out his hands. He shouted for his bodyguard.

As I walked, I slowly spun and lifted up my shirt. "He's incapacitated, senator, but don't worry, I'm not here to harm you. I'm not armed. I just want answers."

The senator reached for his dark glasses with a shaky hand. They were also on the small table between the chairs.

"Save it, Bradford," I said. "Please do me that favor. I know you can see. That much I just witnessed."

"You don't understand, you don't understand." His chest rose with each breath. "You can't understand. You couldn't possibly."

As I approached, I pointed. "Then make me, sir."

I sat on the lounge chair to the left of the senator.

Bradford leaned in and stared at me. "Wait . . .you're the man . . . at the . . . . what the . . ." The senator stumbled with his words. Which, for the record, was the first time I witnessed him speak ineloquently.

I shook my head. "You're a fake. A phony. A liar. You can see so well you even recognize me. Don't you, Bradford?"

When he didn't respond, I said, "How'd you recognize me anyway? You were wearing those glasses when I barged into you at the Spectrum. Don't they obscure your eyesight? Or can you see fine while wearing them?"

Again, the senator didn't respond.

"Bradford," I said. "I hope you're not silent because you're thinking about how to keep up this charade. It's over; your ruse is up. You need to come clean and stop lying."

"Okay, okay." He held up his hands, then sighed. "The glasses definitely obscure my eyesight. I have to wear them in public, otherwise I'd be found out rather quickly. It's fairly difficult maintaining blindness when you can actually see. You can screw up in so many ways. Maybe cringe or put my hands out at someone coming toward me like you did. Or perhaps something innocuous like shake a person's hand I see extended, you know, an instinctual type thing, a habit. You wouldn't believe how many people extend their hand to me even though they know I'm blind."

"Or think you're blind," I corrected.

He hung his head. "Sure."

"So how'd you know it was me at the Spectrum if you had your glasses on?"

"After rallies, I watch tapes of the events. It's all part of a standard security review. But I also do it to listen to my speeches and see what the crowd reacts to, see what's working, that sort of thing. Anyway, I watched the security video of the Irvine Spectrum rally and saw you fake stumbling into me. That's how I recognized you."

"And you still don't know who I am? With all the resources you have at your disposal."

"I've been busy in case you haven't noticed. I am running a campaign for president after all."

"Don't get saucy, senator. *Was* running a campaign. Don't forget the proper tense. We'll be inaugurating our first female president in a few short months. That's certainly clear now."

Before he could whine or protest, I continued. "Are you a . . ." I took a moment to recall the term Karla used. "A blindsimmer? You have some sort of mental condition, is that what you're going to tell me? Make some lame excuse like that?"

He slowly shook his head. "No, not at all, though I have heard of that term and did get the glasses recommendation from a blindsimming website."

"What's your excuse then if you don't have a mental condition? Why fake blindness when you can see perfectly fine? Because right now, from my vantage, it seems pretty clear this all has to do with gaining a political advantage."

"No, no, no," he said. "It isn't, and I can't see perfectly fine, for the record. Who are you, by the way?"

"All you need to know is that I work for the feds."

The senator closed his eyes and shook his head, muttering, "Damn, damn, damn." He suddenly opened his eyes and looked at me. "Are the feds investigating me?"

"Not that I know of. I was hired by my buddy, a private investigator named Hans Schlimmergaard. And he was hired by your opponent."

The senator collapsed into the lounge chair and threw his towel over his head.

I let him stew for about thirty seconds, then said, "Start talking, Bradford. You need to tell me why you've been lying about your vision."

He pulled the towel away, sat up and pleaded. "I was totally blind when I left Vietnam; that's the truth. You have to believe me. I was in enemy territory when I got caught in an Agent Orange fly-by from some friendly aircraft. The Viet Cong picked me up right away since I was blinded near instantly. I became a POW for five years, and I couldn't see for decades. But now with contacts in, which I only really wear swimming, I can see about 20/100. Without contacts, I'm still considered legally blind at 20/200."

"You're saying your vision came back on its own then?"

He cleared his throat. "No, not at all. After decades of total darkness, I started dabbling in some controversial medical practices. I'd come across this cutting-edge medical research startup; a company that was testing their product and service on animals. They were injecting cord blood into blind rats' eyeballs with a super tiny gauge syringe, and also supplementing the procedure with a new drug they'd developed. The whole idea was to re-stimulate optical nerves and promote new cell growth, that sort of thing. Eventually I bank-rolled the company and insisted on being a human guinea pig for them, which I did for about a year with no results. Then I cut ties with the company, and the company subsequently went under. But six months after stopping treatment, I started coming out of my black fog. It was slow, painfully slow, in fact. Another six months later, however, I started to vaguely see shapes. To my surprise, my vision progressed to around 20/200 another year and a half later. And then with corrective lenses I was able to achieve 20/100 vision and see relatively decently."

I frowned. "That's quite a remarkable story, sir. Really remarkable, actually."

"It is, you're right."

"Why not capitalize on that then? Why not tell the world? Why not invest in that company? Make a fortune and make other people's dreams come true."

He nodded. "That's exactly my plan. Exactly. But I—we, I should say—screwed up."

"How so?"

"I was ecstatic to let the CEO of the company know about my progress. He was ecstatic, too. But the problem was our initial rush into the human trial phase before we got approval. The company was nowhere near entering the human trial phase when I intervened and gave them money and insisted

I be tested. Do you know how long it takes for a new drug, combined with a new surgical procedure, to be approved and adopted by all the medical governing boards in this country?"

I figured it was a rhetorical question, but I answered anyway. "Years, I imagine."

"Could be a decade," he responded. "Anyway, after news of my progress, the company went back into business. They started filing all the proper paperwork again, including patents, IRB approvals, that sort of thing. And this time they were going to do everything by the book. If the National Institute of Health or the FDA found out the company was previously involved in human experimentation without approval, who knows how much scrutiny they'd receive moving forward? That scrutiny could certainly affect approval, or at least prolong the already long, arduous process for approval. Everyone, including myself, thought it best to keep my progress quiet, on the down low, until the time was right."

I scoffed.

"What?" the senator said.

"Probably best for your political career, too, right?"

He pointed his finger at me. "This isn't about that. Please, you have to believe me. This is about giving people sight, in the quickest possible way. It's what's best for the greatest good. It wasn't even my decision to keep quiet anyway; it's what the company thought was best."

"Do you really believe that, senator? Are you buying that line? If you came forward with the truth, wouldn't the FDA step in and fast-track the drug and procedure?"

"Astute observation," he said, nodding. "Initially I thought that as well. However, from what I learned it would actually slow down approval from a medical governing board. It seems counter-intuitive, but it's the truth."

"How so? What do you mean?"

"Generally speaking, if a governing board found out that human experimentation had been done with a new drug or procedure prior to approval, they'd actually be extra cautious about moving forward. They'd first want to thoroughly study and monitor the subjects involved to ensure there were no side effects. Typically, new drugs go through all these pre-human trials, and then when they reach the human experimentation phase, the drug is finally administered. Following that, side effects are carefully documented and tracked for quite some time. In my particular case, I was the only human being tested, so it wasn't a representative sample. Therefore, the data points would be limited and nothing would've been fast-tracked. Before another round of human experimentation would be approved, governing boards would wait to monitor me to ensure there were no detrimental side effects from the procedure or drug. The irony is that my coming forward could postpone approval by probably 2-3 years, that's what the company experts say, anyway."

I thought about that for a second. It sort of made sense.

Before we could carry on our conversation, I saw movement in the corner of my eye. Looking left, I saw the bodyguard had staggered to his feet, and he was reaching into his holster.

The senator yelled out and waved his man off, but the bodyguard didn't listen. He lumbered toward me, pointing his gun in my general direction.

"Put the gun down," Bradford shouted.

As the bodyguard got closer, I could see the pissed look on the man's face. I debated what to do. Since I didn't particularly want to deal with the bodyguard, I decided my visit was up.

"Don't worry, Bradford," I said, reaching into my pocket. I handed the magazine to the senator. "There's no bullets in the gun. Your man is too disoriented to realize that."

I brushed past the senator and headed toward the northwest corner of the property.

"Please," Bradford called after me. "We need to work this out."

I looked over my shoulder as I kept walking. "I've heard enough, senator."

"You can't say anything," he shouted after me. "Please. I need more time before going public. Don't ruin this for me, for all the others."

I climbed over the brick wall and wondered what the hell I was going to do with this newfound information.

CHAPTER THIRTY-SEVEN

I ROCKETED EAST down Palos Verdes Drive in the Caprice, eventually weaving my way onto the Seaside Freeway and connecting with the 710. I headed north on the 710 toward the hospital, anxious to tell Slim everything, though I figured he already had a sneaky suspicion that the senator had been faking his blindness.

I wondered exactly how much Slim knew. I also wondered how to proceed with the senator. If the man was telling the truth, I didn't want to get in the way of prolonging approval for a life-altering drug and procedure. But on the other hand, the man was clearly duping the American people by faking his blindness. It wouldn't surprise me if he just lied about this medical company to keep me from exposing the deception.

Minutes later, after weighing all the pros and cons, I exited off the freeway onto E Willow Avenue and pulled into a hospital parking spot. I still didn't know what to do, so I called Karla. I couldn't wait to tell her about the senator, and to get her input on the situation. However, I'd have to wait. My call went to voicemail after three rings. I didn't bother leaving a message. I'd try her again after my hospital visit.

As I exited the Caprice, a vehicle driving slowly on Willow caught my attention. It was a black Tesla with tinted windows. When I looked over, the electric car zipped away.

To be honest, I wasn't too surprised at the tail. I imagine the senator was paranoid about what I was going to do next, so he ordered his bodyguard to follow my every movement. Heck, knowing what I know now, maybe it was even the senator himself doing the driving.

I shook it off and headed into the hospital. A nurse let me into Slim's unit. After checking in with the two uniformed officers guarding Slim's room, I was allowed in. Slim was sitting up in his bed watching a Die Hard movie, which looked to be the original one.

"It's about time," he said, flipping off the TV.

"I was hoping you'd be asleep so I could twist your nipples and wake you up."

That was Slim's MO for waking me during my training days, when I had to get up super early and run ten miles with him barking at me to pick up the pace.

He grinned. "Payback for all those years."

I took a seat and got down to business. "The senator, geez, this guy, Slim. Unbelievable. Wait till I tell you what I learned. Also, I found the man who killed Gina, and tried to kill you."

"Really?" Slim buzzed his bed to a more upright position. "You've been busy. This is exciting." His eyes lit up. "Start with the senator."

"He's a phony. He's been faking, buddy. The man can see. He can see fine with his contacts in."

"I knew it." Slim tilted his head back, looked at the ceiling, then closed his eyes. He brought one fist up in a triumphant shake, then repeated himself. "I knew it. I knew it. I just didn't know for sure. Couldn't get final confirmation."

"Oh, it's for sure alright."

Slim looked at me. "How'd you find out? What happened. When did it happen? Do you have proof? Did you figure out why he's faking. Tell me everything."

So I did. I scraped the chair closer to his bedside and relayed everything I'd seen and come across with the senator since following him.

When I finished, Slim whistled and shook his fist again. "Man, I'm actually going to write you a check with a smile on my face, which is unusual for me, not sure I've ever done that before. This is big, Chase. I know you know that; I just had to say it."

I nodded.

"This senator is something else," Slim continued. "So he's faking his blindness until the company that cured him gets IRB approval to start the human trial phase, then he'll reveal to the public that he's gained his vision back. Is that the gist of his explanation?"

"Basically. We didn't talk about the exact timing of his reveal, whether that would come once they received approval to begin human trials, or if he'd go through the first human trial and then reveal he's cured. He pleaded for me to keep quiet about things until the time is right."

"I'm sure he did. Everything makes sense now. Did he tell you about the millions in federal grant money the company received, at the behest of the senate committee he chairs?"

"What?" I said, frowning. "No, he didn't. He certainly didn't."

He pointed at me. "He gave you the partial truth, but not the full truth."

"Apparently so, bring me up to speed on what I don't know."

"It all started when I looked into the senator's charitable giving. One of his charities was this start-up medical company. I did some research and learned from their investor news that a significant infusion of capital into their company came from a federal grant they won; a grant that was at the recommendation of the Senate Committee on Small Business and Entrepreneurship. A committee that—"

"The senator chairs," I said, finishing his sentence. "He's been using his power and influence, and government money, to promote a company for his own personal medical benefit."

Slim nodded. "And another reason why he wants to keep his ties to this company, not to mention his sight, under wraps. Though according to him it's until the time is right." Slim scoffed.

"And here I sort of felt sorry for the senator, thinking that maybe in his zeal to regain sight he'd made a bad judgement call, insisting on being a guinea pig before approval and all."

"And it gets worse."

"What do you mean?"

"This leads to the new development I just uncovered." Slim motioned at a file on his lap. "I started looking into other grants that were recommended by the senator's committee during Bradford's tenure. Then I cross-checked the grants with charities that the senator had donated to. There was one other match: a charity by the name of Second Chances. But there was nothing on the web about this particular charity. Nada. Zilch. Like the organization never existed. Seemed to cease existing about five years ago. Luckily, though, the charity was tied to a federal grant, so I found out which agency awarded the grant, then filed a Freedom of Information Act request with that agency to see what details I could learn. I hadn't heard anything back from this agency for quite a while. So, I refiled my request. And then again for a third time after more time went by without a word from the agency."

Holding up the file, he said, "This finally arrived at my office, on the morning I was flying out here. One of my employees got it to Freda before she flew out."

He handed me the file.

I opened it and was immediately struck by all the black. Line after line was redacted. Flipping through, every page was filled with redacted marks.

I looked up. "This is useless, it's so redacted I can't even put one piece of information together."

"Tell me about it. It shouldn't be redacted at all. This isn't national security stuff, buddy; this is a benign federal grant to a charitable organization. Why would one piece of information in there be redacted? There's about thirty-five pages there, and if you read all of what you can, you still have no clue what the organization is about, or who's involved. All my team and I could gather is that it appears to be a woman's charity that works with Vietnamese immigrants."

"So weird," I said, "that it would be redacted. Something's obviously going on."

"Plus, get this: hours ago I called the agency to inquire about the information and why it was redacted. What was going on. Why the need for redaction and secrecy, that sort of thing. You know what I discovered?"

Slim didn't wait for me to answer. "It shouldn't have been redacted at all! The woman I was speaking with was surprised as I was when she confirmed the redaction. As far as she knew, she'd never seen redacted paperwork for any similar federal grant. She kept apologizing and saying she didn't know how it happened. The real problem is that you're holding a copy, of course."

I finished the thought. "The woman couldn't even correct the situation and send you an unredacted copy because the originals were compromised."

Slim nodded. "Now that I know for sure the senator would fake his own blindness, and abuse government resources for his own benefit, who knows what's he into with this organization? He clearly has no ethical compass guiding him. He could've hired someone inside that federal agency to redact the paperwork. That's my guess, anyway."

"Why would he go to these lengths? What's up with this charitable organization? What's your best guess?"

Slim pointed at me. "My guess is it's a sham organization he created himself that doesn't exist in reality, only on paper somewhere. He steers his committee to drop large sums of money to this organization through a federal grant; money he ultimately uses for his own political gain, for his campaign, et cetera. Who knows? Did you know he's outspending Henrietta by a margin of two to one?"

I shook my head. "I didn't."

"Some journalists have questioned the senator on where and how he's raising all this money. You know what he says? He says it's from his supercharged base and from his family inheritance. But the problem with that is his base is comprised of eighteen to twenty-two-year old kids. Millions of them. And that demographic is the worst for raising money. Everyone who's run a national campaign agrees on that."

I kicked back in the hospital chair, trying to wrap my mind around another new development. After a moment, though, my mind played devil's advocate. I didn't want us to get too far ahead of ourselves.

"You know, buddy," I said. "It could be a legitimate charity, or once was. And the senator was a legitimate champion of the charity, maybe even using —or abusing, I should say—his position on the senate committee to get the charity a grant. I mean, a Vietnamese charity makes complete sense for him. After all, he did marry a woman from there and adopt orphans from that country. Perhaps later on the senator or the committee or both found out it was corrupt in some way. Then the government forced the charity out of business, redacted the paperwork, so as to not embarrass themselves for giving a corrupt charity millions of dollars. A basic coverup. Which is a possibility, right?"

Slim thought about it. "Maybe, could be. The senator may not be funneling money through this particular charity, but him faking blindness, and funneling money to the medical company for his own gain, makes me question everything about the senator."

"And it should," I said. "It's bad."

We both kept thinking. Another thing that didn't sit well with me was the fact that the senator was from old money, from a super wealthy land-owning family. For him to siphon money illegally for his own gain, whether personal or political, made me a little suspicious of Slim's theory.

But I didn't get a chance to bring up my concern.

Slim said, "Tell me about the man who's been trying to kill me. Pardon the pun, but I'm dying to know."

"My pleasure." I leaned forward and told Slim everything I knew about Pham Van Lu. Where Karla and I discovered his tortured, hanging body, and what he said to me concerning Mama H.

When I finished the story, Slim eyed me. "You think the hitman was telling the truth about this Mama H character?"

"My gut says yes. I think the Rat is using Mama H, whoever she is, as a layer between him and Pham Van Lu."

"Makes sense," Slim said. "The Rat was probably furious at Pham Van Lu for screwing up the hit on me."

"And multiple times at that," I added.

"Right. So he used Mama H to torture the man in the most heinous way. Definitely something the Rat would do." Slim took a sip of water. "What does Karla think of all this?"

"Actually, she and Ethan Khang are somewhat skeptical of the Rat's involvement in all this."

He perked up. "You're kidding? How so? Why?"

I told Slim about my conversation with Ethan Khang, followed by Karla's take on the Rat after she visited the man in San Quentin.

Slim rolled his eyes when I finished. "A changed man, come on. You're not buying that, are you, buddy? That the Rat isn't involved, really?"

"No, I'm with you, I think the Rat is responsible for everything. But I also want to keep an open mind, which I'm not very good at when it comes to that man."

We sat in silence for a few moments.

Slim broke it. "What would an alternate theory be?"

I thought about the theory Karla had told me over dinner. There was slightly more credibility to her theory now that the senator was involved in finance violations.

Motioning at his battered face, I said, "Maybe Pham Van Lu was hired by the senator. Maybe Bradford has been trying to take you down. He discovers a few months ago that you're looking into his questionable charitable giving. Then he figures you may have uncovered his fake blindness on top of that. So he stops at nothing to get rid of you. He hires Pham Van Lu through—"

"Mama H," Slim said. "To take me out. Then you're targeted because the senator figured I told you everything." He looked up at the ceiling, then back to me. "It's a possible theory, I'll give you that. Those are pretty incredible lengths for a United States senator to go to, however."

I nodded. "I agree. The Rat is our most plausible suspect, for sure."

"Still, I'll keep the heat on the senator and his charitable giving. We have to figure out why the FOIA request was redacted. I'll have my team pull out all the stops to see what they can uncover about Second Chances, even trolling the dark web for information."

"I don't even want to know what that is."

He laughed. "Probably not."

I stood to leave. "I'm wondering what to do about the senator. My thought is to loop Ethan Khang into all this. What do you think?"

"Probably a good idea. I think we're beyond Henrietta at this point. We need Khang and his protection if we're going to make accusations against someone like the senator. He's the top federal lawyer in our area, so we need his counsel on how to proceed. Accusing a presidential candidate for faking his blindness along with potentially engaging in criminal finance charges is huge."

"Okay," I said, moving toward the door. "We have a plan. You'll find out as much as you can about Second Chances and I'll speak with Khang in the morning." I held up my cell. "Call or text as soon as you hear back from your team."

"Text? You're texting these days? Are you finally coming into the twenty-first century, pal?"

I turned and walked out without saying a word.

As the door was shutting, Slim yelled, "It's like I don't even know who you are anymore, Chase."

I flipped open my phone and tapped out a text to Slim while walking down the hospital hallway. I went with an old but classic comeback: *Up Yours*

I heard him laugh as I rounded a corner to exit the unit. Then I drove straight back to Karla's house, excited to tell her about the new developments. Since the hospital was only ten minutes from Karla's place, I didn't bother calling her to tell her I was on my way.

When I arrived at her house, I was surprised to see that her car wasn't parked out front or anywhere on the street. She had a fenced property with no garage, so she always parked out front. I shrugged it off and used my key to enter the front door. After a quick scan of her house to make sure she wasn't there, I called her cell.

Straight to voicemail this time. No three rings. Honestly, I didn't know what that meant. My guess was her battery had died.

I didn't start feeling anxious until an hour passed and Karla still wasn't home. She hadn't called me back from her cell or work number either. I tried her office number but that eventually went to voicemail, too.

After considering where she could be, and working myself up, I decided to stop worrying about the situation. I was fairly positive she had a good explanation for why she wasn't calling me back. She could be down in her field office's basement, in the records area, digging through some information after coming across a lead. From what I understood, the basement at her field office received horrible cell reception.

I called Jimmy next. Since it was pretty late, I wasn't surprised my call went to voicemail. I left him a message, asking him to set up an appointment for us at Ethan Khang's office in the morning. I didn't elaborate on what it was about, only that it was super important.

Since I wanted a decent sleep and had a big day ahead, I went to the kitchen and brewed some chamomile tea. I hated the taste but wanted the relaxation. After finishing the tea, I crawled into Karla's bed and sent one last text to her. I had a pleasant but selfish thought that if Karla did come home late, perhaps she'd slip into bed and provide a sexy apology for not calling back sooner.

Sometime in the next hour I fell asleep with the cell on my chest, waiting for a return text or call.

DAY FOUR

CHAPTER THIRTY-EIGHT

KARLA NEVER CALLED. She didn't text either.

I woke a little after five a.m. to an empty bed. First thing I did was touch the sheets where she should've laid.

The spot was cold.

I performed a quick search of the house. After finding no sign of Karla, I plopped onto her couch and immediately knew something was wrong.

I felt it deep in my body.

Even if Karla came across a lead and decided to work at her field office all night, she would've contacted me somehow. If her cell was dead or she had no reception in the basement archives, she'd come up from the dungeon and use her office phone to call me.

At some point in the night. Without a doubt.

I brewed a cup of coffee to calm my nerves and get my mind working. While the grounds steeped in the French Press, I quickly put yesterday's clothes on and splashed some water on my face.

Grabbing a mug of coffee, I jammed out Karla's front door. I had a list of three places in my head to visit: Karla's field office, my resident agency, and our favorite coffee shop. While walking to my car, I tried Karla's cell one last time. It rang in my ear.

But I heard another ringing in my other ear, which stopped right after my call to Karla went to voicemail.

I quickly dialed her number again. Sure enough, a few seconds after the first ring in my ear I heard another one twenty feet to my right.

Pulling the cell away, I followed the ringing sound, stopping in front of some bushes on the other side of Karla's fence. Right away I could see that something happened to the bushes. Like someone had crashed into them.

I parted the bushes and stuck my head in, immediately spotting Karla's large iPhone at the base of the fence. I also saw blood on the fence, around the height of Karla's head. My right hand shook as I picked up her cell. I stuffed it into my pocket and pulled back from the bushes, took a few steps to my left and assessed the scene.

Clearly, Karla had crashed into the bushes, probably after being thrown back. I imagined she was hit first on the head and started bleeding before going into the bushes. I was skeptical that banging her head on the flat fence boards would make her head bleed so quickly.

I could be wrong.

Karla always kept her cell in her back pocket, but the cell was so big and her pockets small that it easily could've fallen out when she was thrown into the bushes. Or maybe she ditched it in an effort to leave evidence of her abduction.

This was bad, beyond bad.

I breathed deeply through my nose and looked closer at the scene. I noticed a three-foot stretch of grass before the sidewalk. Angling across the grass were some scuff marks. My guess was Karla was pulled from the bushes and dragged to a vehicle. There was another car parked out front of Karla's that I'd never seen before, which didn't necessarily mean anything, but it was odd since the rear passenger tire was flat. There was a carjack still under the frame, just in front of the flat tire, but the tire hadn't been changed.

Odd. It could mean nothing, just that the owner hadn't gotten around to finishing the tire change. Or it could mean everything. Like maybe somebody was waiting there for Karla. Maybe they jumped out and surprised her and wrestled her into the bushes.

I noted the license plate, with the intention of running the plate through the system at work.

I pulled out Karla's cell as I crossed the street and hopped into my car.

Since I used her cell often, I knew her passcode. Nothing unusual popped up once I accessed her phone. All the calls and texts in the last twelve hours were from me. Her email was linked to her phone, so I checked that, too. There was a quick email from her crime tech contact regarding the blood stains, stating the profile and ancestry test concluded the blood spots in the chamber were from different females, both of Southeast Asian origin.

Sitting in the driver's seat, I ran both hands over my bald head. What did that mean? After a few moments of wild thoughts, my mind turned back to Karla.

Where was she?

I sipped some coffee to settle my nerves, then turned my mind proactive, debating what to do next.

It seemed fruitless to drive around looking for her since the evidence clearly pointed to an abduction, but I decided to do it anyway. Before I drove off, though, I made two important phone calls. The first was to the local PD, informing them of Karla's situation and that she was a missing person under suspicious circumstances. My next call was to Phil Hornsby, Karla's direct supervisor and the assistant director in charge of her field office. I requested Phil pull out all the stops, like put a trace on her credit card and bank accounts, issue an APB for Karla and her car, anything that could possibly help us locate her. Phil agreed and got to work immediately.

Then I drove to Giuseppe's, our favorite coffee shop, and saw no sign of Karla's car. After that, I drove to my resident agency. Naturally, Karla wasn't there. Not many people were in the building since it was early, so I was able to sneak into my office and quickly run the license plate without being noticed. I had a name and address that needed looking into.

My next stop was at our favorite breakfast place. Of course, she wasn't there. I felt a little silly trying these spots given the circumstances and evidence, but I had to do something.

While sitting in the car outside the restaurant, I figured my next move would be checking in with the local hospitals. Although unlikely, I thought there could be a small chance that Karla was in an emergency room some-where having her head stitched up. And she hadn't called me because she'd dropped her phone after hitting her head.

Just as I dropped the gear shift in drive, my phone buzzed and alerted me to a text from Slim. It read: *East Coast team confirmed Second Chances is a charity for Vietnamese women. Women are brought to America on a work-visa thing, they're given jobs at nail salons. Still no reason for the redaction, though. Let's chat at the hospital, come when you can.*

Nail salon?

I shut off the car and leaned back; my mind spinning. I wasn't sure how long I sat in the driver's seat with my head tilted back, maybe five minutes. But at the end of the five minutes, a theory started forming in my mind. I seemed to recall a nail salon being located next door to the Vietnamese restaurant. And I also remembered an out of place door in the restaurant's kitchen on the shared wall between the two businesses. I couldn't be sure of either, though.

My mind drew out the connections. Perhaps the nail salon was connected to the restaurant, which was connected to the torture chamber. Since the dried blood spots in the torture chamber were from females of Southeast Asian origin, perhaps the Vietnamese women from the nail salon were being trafficked through the Second Chances charity.

Pieces of the puzzle were there; I just didn't know for sure if it was all related. I needed proof. So I fired up the Caprice and drove back to the crime scene in Little Saigon.

During the drive, I put my cell on speaker and called Jimmy Schuberman.

My lawyer picked up on the second ring and was as chipper as usual.

"Chase, Chase, Chase, my favorite client. Good to hear from you. And I've got good news. Real good news."

By how fast he spoke, I figured he'd already had at least three cups of coffee this morning. "Great," I said. "I certainly need it."

"Whoa, my friend, so glum sounding. Not to worry, this should lift you spirits." He paused.

"What is it, Jimmy?"

"Well, after collaborating with a colleague, it appears the Diekelmans have a slim chance of gaining custody."

I sighed in relief. "My odds get better, too, Jimmy, in light of what I learned about Helen."

"Really? And what's that?"

I filled Jimmy in on Helen Diekelman's criminal record.

He must've said, 'You're kidding?' seven times during my story. And 'jeepers' three times.

"I'll file a motion to have this immediately dismissed," he said. "In fact, no, I won't. I'll contact the Diekelman's lawyer and tell him what we know, which should force them to drop everything right away. Yup, yup, yup. That's what I'll do."

At least something was going my way.

"You're still on my dime, right?" I asked.

"Last time I checked."

"Okay, something's happened to Karla, and I need your help."

"Wait, what? What happened?"

I blew out a breath. "She's been abducted."

"Abducted? Really? No, no, no, not Karla."

Jimmy asked a bunch of questions, and I answered them as best I could.

Then I read off the name of the owner and the address of the vehicle I'd tracked at my resident agency. "I need you to scope out that address and see if you spot anything unusual. Then I need you to check the emergency rooms of two hospitals and inquire about Karla. You'll need to come up with some cover story for who you are and why you're asking." The two hospitals were in the direction that Jimmy would be headed, so it would be quicker for him to check out those hospitals.

I read off the names of the hospitals. My plan was to check Long Beach Memorial myself, once I was finished in Little Saigon.

"Got it, Jimmy?"

"Absolutely," he responded. "This is some real detective, undercover spy work stuff. I'm in. All the way. You can count on me. I only met Karla once, but she seemed like a sweet person."

I hung up the phone before Jimmy could say goodbye, then I pulled off of the Garden Grove freeway and headed directly to the restaurant with the torture chamber.

CHAPTER THIRTY-NINE

Little Saigon
Orange County, CA

AS SOON AS I pulled in front of the Vietnamese restaurant, I knew my theory had merit.

A nail salon was right next door to the restaurant.

I zoomed around the back of the businesses and parked. The back door to the restaurant had yellow police tape stretched across it, but I banged on the door anyway. Of course, I didn't expect anyone to be in the restaurant, but I held out hope.

My hopes were dashed a few minutes later when nobody opened the door.

Frustrated, I stepped back and surveyed the buildings. There was no back door into the nail salon, further confirming my suspicion that the restaurant and nail salon were likely one larger business sometime in the past, or somehow connected.

When I was in the restaurant's kitchen two days ago, I thought the door on the shared wall between the businesses opened to a shallow pantry or something like that, so I didn't give it a second thought.

Now I did.

I hustled to the front of the building, stopping and peering into the restaurant's front window. Police tape stretched from one edge of the window, across the door, and stopped at the window's other edge. After a few moments, it was clear to me nobody was inside, so I proceeded next door to the nail salon.

Though I couldn't see anyone inside, I banged on the glass door anyway. Fortunately, an Asian woman emerged from a back room and headed to the front.

When she saw me, however, she waved me away. "Closed, mister, come back in one hour. We'll be open then."

I smiled but shook my head. "I don't have an hour. Please." I motioned at the door.

"One hour," the woman said, shaking her head and turning around.

Pulling out Pham Van Lu's wallet, I yelled, "Money, I have money."

The woman stopped and turned back.

I fished out a hundred-dollar bill and slapped it against the glass door. "Please," I said.

As the woman approached the front door, I grinned. "Just need a gift card, this is my girlfriend's favorite salon. She'll be over the moon. Her birthday's today."

The woman still hesitated to open the door, so I pulled out another one-hundred-dollar bill. "How about a two-hundred-dollar gift card? I'll do two hundred if you get me the gift card now."

"Okay, mister." She finally smiled. "Can't pass up two hundred dollars, can I?" She opened the door.

I stepped in and handed over the bills.

While the woman went behind the cash register and began writing out a receipt for the gift card, I pretended like I was innocently looking around. The door to the restaurant wasn't in the main part of the nail salon. The door to the back room, however, where the woman had rushed out from, was partially open. I heard some voices coming from inside the room.

I hustled toward the door, yelling over my shoulder, "Going to use the bathroom while you finish that."

"No, mister," the woman shouted after me.

I knocked quickly on the door and pushed it open before hearing a response.

Three women were in the room, and all three shrieked when I stepped inside. There were bunkbeds in one corner of the room and a microwave and hotplate in the other. The women were clearly living in the room.

As soon as I saw the door into the restaurant, which was to the left of the bunkbeds, I stepped out of the room and apologized profusely.

I knew it.

The women writing up my gift card came running back, shaking her finger at me. "No, mister, no, you can't do that."

I held up my hands. "My mistake, my mistake. Thought it was the bathroom."

The woman thrust the gift card into my hand, then put her hands on her hips. "You need to leave."

"Okay, okay, sorry. Can I ask a couple of questions before I leave?"

"You need to leave," she repeated herself; this time pointing at the front door.

I pulled out a hundred-dollar bill. "I have more money. I'll pay you."

Hearing that, the three women in the back room suddenly emerged and fell in behind the woman.

"I don't know," the woman said, looking skeptically at me.

"Easy questions," I said. "You women are Vietnamese, right?" I looked over my shoulder at the three women. They nodded very slowly. "See, easy questions. An easy one hundred." I handed the lady the bill.

I was about to ask another question, but the lady shook her head, then used her lips to point at the wallet in my hand.

"One hundred dollar per question," she said with a big smile.

The woman was obviously the business manager of the salon.

"Fine," I said, pulling out another bill. "Do you women work for a charity called 'Second Chances?'"

I focused my attention on the three women behind the manager. Instead of nodding, their eyes grew. The manager quickly turned around. I couldn't see her face, but I was positive the woman gave her workers a keep quiet look.

When nobody said anything, I rephrased. "You've at least heard of the charity, right?"

Again, silence. The manager narrowed her eyes at me. After a moment, she motioned at my wallet again. "That's a two-hundred-dollar question, mister."

I reluctantly peeled off another bill and handed it to her.

"Sure," she said. "Most of the women who work here were brought over from Vietnam by Second Chances. But that was some years ago."

I held out another hundred. "And do you work, or use to work, for a woman named Mama H? Or know of a woman named Mama H?"

The manager's eyes swelled. Before she could say anything, the three women retreated into the back room.

I hit a nerve. Clearly. The women were scared just at the mention of Mama H's name, which told me a lot.

"Out." The manager pointed at the front door. "Out, mister, now." She waved her right hand upward in a dismissive manner.

I fished out a few more bills and thrust them toward her. "Do you know a Mama H? Please. Can you tell me about her?"

She shook her head. "Out, or I'll call the police."

"Ma'am, I am law enforcement."

She wriggled her fingers. "Show me your badge then."

Ignoring her request, I walked into the back room, pulling out even more money as I stepped in front of the locked door into the restaurant. "Can you open this for me? There's five hundred dollars in it for you?" I addressed the question to the three scared women crammed together on the lower bunkbed.

"You're not police," the manager said from behind me. "You wouldn't need to bribe us. You need to leave now, mister. I'm calling the police."

I stood in front of the door, thinking about Mama H. She was tied to this women's charity, and she was obviously a scary force to be reckoned with. My guess was Mama H tortured these nail salon workers if the women got out of line, just like she did with Pham Van Lu. Mama H was likely trafficking these women through a charitable guise.

The manager tapped me on the shoulder. "Like I said, mister, I'm calling the police."

I didn't think the manager would. She wouldn't want the police snooping around. The woman tapped my shoulder again and demanded I get out.

But I ignored her and turned my thoughts to Karla. What if Karla was abducted because she was looking into Mama H. Mama H then, or one of her associates, could've brought Karla to the torture chamber. They could've brought Karla in through the nail salon. That way she'd avoid disturbing the police tape next door. It was sort of ingenious since the cops were probably finished processing the crime scene and wouldn't be back soon.

I looked at the woman. "Open the door or I'm kicking it down."

"No way," she said, storming off. "Police it is."

She was bluffing. Even if she wasn't, I wouldn't leave the building without first checking for Karla.

So I kicked down the door. It took three big boots. The women had huddled even closer together on the bunk bed as I destroyed the door's lock and part of the door frame.

With the door now open, I rushed into the restaurant's kitchen and down into the storage area. Fortunately, the hinged door to the false floor was open, so I flew down the steps.

Reaching the bottom, I flicked on the lights, then burst through the large wooden door.

Empty.

I proceeded to check all six rooms, including the holding cells in the different hallways.

Empty. Nobody was there.

I ran up the stairs just in case the manager was serious and had called the cops. Although, if she had, I think I could talk my way out of it, even without my badge.

When I returned to the salon, the three women were frantically pulling pictures off a corkboard on the wall opposite the bunkbeds. I quickly studied the contents of the corkboard. On it were various documents, a number of pictures, and quite a few newspaper clippings.

"Stop," I yelled at them.

The women cowered for a second, then rushed out of the room in single file. I walked over and grabbed the pictures they'd already taken down. Since there were still items on the corkboard, I pulled out Karla's iPhone to take a picture. As I did, the manager rushed into the room, yelling at me and swatting at the phone.

I held her off with one hand and managed to click a few pictures.

One of the pictures or newspaper clippings could identify Mama H.

"Police, police," she screamed, making her way to the corkboard. She ripped the remaining pictures off the corkboard. "They're on their way." Then she shredded the two newspaper clippings I'd taken a picture of into tiny pieces.

"Give them my regards," I said, exiting the back room while still clutching the pictures.

As I passed the cash register, I left a few hundred on the till to pay for the busted door.

CHAPTER FORTY

E Willow Ave.
Long Beach Medical Center

AFTER CHECKING THE ER for Karla and coming up empty, I barged into Slim's hospital room and collapsed into the chair beside his bed.

"What's going on?" Slim asked, pushing a food tray aside. "That's quite the entrance."

"It's Karla, Slim. They got her. Mama H does. She's gone, and I have no idea where."

"Dammit," he said. "You sure it's this Mama H person?"

Looking at the ceiling, I said, "Yup, she's real. Just confirmed it. Karla never showed up at her house last night or called. Mama H or her goons picked Karla up in front of her place sometime in the night."

"How do you know?"

I held up Karla's cell. "Found this in Karla's bushes this morning. There was blood on the fence behind the bushes and signs of her being dragged off. Prior to the abduction, Karla was at her field office running the Mama H alias through various databases."

He slammed his good fist on the bed. "You inform the cops?"

I nodded. "And I have her boss pulling out the stops."

"Okay," Slim said, eyeing me. "How'd you confirm Mama H is real?"

"When you texted and said the charity helps Vietnamese women get nail salon jobs in America, I went back to the restaurant crime scene because I remembered a nail salon being close by. It was right next door."

"Really," Slim said, using his good arm to help him sit upright.

"Yeah, and the two business were connected by a door between a shared wall. I managed to get inside the salon to confirm that, and I also spoke with the women who worked there. They were, of course, Vietnamese, and they were brought here by Second Chances."

"Wow," Slim said. "And the torture chamber was underneath these businesses."

"Right. And female blood of Southeast Asian origin was found underneath a couple of the meat hooks down there. Plus, at least three women were living on the premises in a tiny back-room."

"This screams of human trafficking," Slim said.

"Exactly, which is right up the Rat's alley. My guess is the Rat's now using Mama H to traffic these women into the country through Second Chances. Mama H is probably the head of the organization, or intimately tied to them somehow. Slim, at the sheer mention of Mama H's name, the women went running."

"You're kidding?"

"They were terrified to talk about her; I could see it in their eyes. They wouldn't acknowledge Mama H, not even when I dangled a few hundred dollars in front of them. And I offered them five hundred bucks to open the door between the businesses. They didn't even consider doing it."

Slim buried his face in his palm. "And now this woman has Karla. I'm sorry, Chase."

Since I didn't want to dwell on that, I steered the conversation elsewhere. "I'm trying to figure out the senator's connection to all this. Is he involved? Or is his tie to Second Chances just coincidental?"

Slim thought for a moment. "You're right, that's tricky."

"I mean, it's not surprising that he'd be involved with a Vietnamese charity. After all, he has deep ties to Vietnam, so helping women from there was something he'd be passionate about."

"Right, it's just whether he knew the organization was a front for trafficking women."

I pointed at Slim. "Somebody knew it was a front, whether it was the senator or not, I'm not sure. But that must be why your FOIA document about the grant came up redacted, and why the web is scrubbed of information about the charity. I know the senator is sleazy for faking blindness, and for steering government money for his own gain, but my guess wouldn't be he didn't know it was a front. Or once he found out, he cut all ties."

"I agree," Slim said. "The Rat found a new way to get women into the country, and he's using Mama H to do the dirty work while he's incarcerated. We have to find out her identity and whereabouts."

I nodded. "This might help." I leaned to my right and pulled out the pictures from the nail salon from my back pocket.

"What's that?" Slim asked.

Just then, my cell buzzed. It was a text from Jimmy telling me he'd scheduled a meeting with Ethan Khang at 10 am this morning.

"Who's that?" Slim asked.

"Jimmy, last night I asked him to schedule a meeting with Khang this morning so I could tell him about the senator." I looked at my watch. "We have a meeting in an hour. I wonder if I should cancel since that could wait. Karla's the priority now."

"No way," Slim said, shaking his head. "Khang knows the Rat well. That man's been gunning for the Rat for a while. Khang could know something about Mama H or other known associates of the Rat who could lead us to Mama H, or maybe he's heard of Second Chances. You need to ask him everything he knows about the Rat."

I thought about it. "You're right, I do."

Slim motioned at the pictures in my hand. "What are those about?"

"The women at the nail salon were frantically pulling these down from a corkboard; it was clear they were trying to get rid of evidence."

"Mama H may be in those pictures."

"Right," I said, plopping the pictures on his lap. "I went through them. Nobody or nothing popped out at me, which isn't surprising. Have a look."

While Slim rifled through the pictures, I held up Karla's cell. "I also took a picture of other items on the corkboard. There were a couple of newspaper clippings on the board. However, the pictures I took are a little fuzzy since the manager of the salon was shaking my arm. I sent the pictures to a tech in the L.A. field office, someone who Karla works closely with. Hopefully he can clean up the pictures so we can get a better look at the newspaper clippings."

"Good," Slim said. "We might catch a break."

"And hopefully fast," I added.

As I opened the hospital room door, I turned. "Before I leave, anything else you can tell me about Second Chances?"

"There's not much out there, buddy. For all intents and purposes, the charity doesn't exist anymore. When it did, they focused on poor, struggling, downtrodden Vietnamese women. The women were brought to America for a second chance at a new life. That was the basic gist. Geez, the sheer irony. Anyway, they were given nail technician jobs in various salons all throughout L.A. county. Thousands of women were brought here to work in these salons. Like I said in the text, it was a work-visa thing."

I nodded.

"I'll get my team to re-troll the dark web, looking for connections between Second Chances and the alias Mama H."

"Sounds good, I'll keep you updated on what I find out."

Before I left the room, Slim was already on the phone making a call to his team.

CHAPTER FORTY-ONE

N Spring Street
Los Angeles, CA

I WAITED FOR Jimmy Schuberman in a parking structure across the street from the U.S. attorney's office for the Central District of California.

While waiting, I pulled out Karla's cell phone and opened the app that tracked my son. Within moments I confirmed his location at the hotel. After a quick sigh of relief, I looked at the picture I'd taken of the corkboard in the nail salon. Using my fingers, I zoomed in and out on one particular newspaper clipping. Unfortunately, I couldn't make out any details. I could see that the picture was of two individuals and that there was a caption below the shot. Hopefully, Karla's tech colleague could sharpen the image and text. I'd told him to send any progress on the picture to Karla's email.

When I looked up from the phone, I saw the black Tesla rolling down Spring Street. The bodyguard, or the senator, or both, were still tracking my movements. They'd be sweating now, knowing I'd just parked in the U.S. attorney's lot.

Since I'd been watching the Tesla out the driver's window, I didn't notice

Jimmy approaching. He slipped into the passenger seat. "Shoot, shoot, shoot," he said, smoothing his coiffed hair. "Wanted to have better news for you about Karla. Wish I did. Sorry, Chase."

I let out a slow breath. "Nothing at all, huh?"

"Nope. She wasn't treated at the two hospitals I visited. I then checked the apartment address you gave me, which was on the east side of Compton, by the way, and certainly not a safe neighborhood. But I didn't see anything suspicious like a body being brought in or taken out of the place. Plus, the apartment had the blinds open on the front window. Not sure that would happen if you abducted someone and kept them at your place. I'd button my house up tight."

"Thanks for checking, anyway."

As we left the car, I motioned at his wrinkled blue suit. "How many days in a row have you worn that thing?"

"What? I have like five blue suits. See the faint grey pin stripes on this baby." He held out his sleeve, then tugged at his collar. "And this is a fresh, starched shirt and new yellow tie. Faint grey pin stripes on the tie, too." He got all serious and pulled out his tie for me to check.

"Jimmy, I'm busting your balls."

"Ahhh." He winked. "Got it. Now tell me what this is all about, you didn't say much on your voicemail." He wiggled his fingers. "Let me hear it."

I glanced at my watch: 9:55 a.m. "I'm about to lay everything out for Khang. I'm certainly not doing it twice."

"Suit yourself," he said, laughing and gesturing at his suit.

"That's the last stupid joke from you. Every cornball joke from here on out subtracts a hundred bucks from your bill."

He shrugged. "You're going to need some discounts, pal, that's for sure."

About ten minutes after entering the government building, Khang's secretary—or maybe it was his legal aide, who knows? —ushered us into his office.

The office was a stereotypical federal lawyer's office. On one taupish colored wall were two pictures: the current president and the current attorney general. Another wall contained bookshelves to the ceiling. Every shelf contained lawyerly books with the most boring, dark colored spines ever. It didn't invite reading, it scared you from it.

Khang sat in a comfortable black leather chair in front of a dark stained wooden desk with tons of paper on it, skewed every which way. The desk was wide enough that three large, dark red leather chairs sat beside each other with about a foot of space in between them.

After handshakes and hellos, Jimmy and I sat in the two chairs to Khang's right. Khang had a plain, light grey shirt on with the sleeves rolled up. He had the look in his eye that he'd already been hard at work for hours. The man's hair surprised me. You'd think as a federal lawyer he'd keep his hair clean cropped and combed nicely. Instead, the man's thick black hair flowed nicely back from his forehead, tucked behind his ears, and fell in a wavy line just above his shoulders. I imagined he constantly ran his fingers through his hair to keep it from flopping in his eyes.

He leaned forward and eyed me.

Khang had smooth, taut skin except for a few deep crinkles around his eyes. Honestly, the guy could be in his low thirties or early fifties or anywhere in between.

"This better be good. Jimmy here," Khang pointed at my lawyer, "is quite the persistent one and insisted I clear my ten o'clock. He said it was important. You have one hour, Mr. Chase."

I shifted forward in the chair. "Originally, sir, I asked Jimmy to schedule this meeting to get your input on a situation with a U.S. senator, which I'll get into later, but first I have a more pressing issue." I held out my hands. "Now I understand your position concerning Anurat Wu, and that you think he can't be active. But I think he's still active and involved in human trafficking."

I paused to see if Khang had any objections. He didn't interrupt, so I continued. "It's my professional opinion he's using a Vietnamese women's charity to traffic women into our country. He's using a woman with the criminal alias Mama H to aid him in this endeavor. That woman was directly implicated by her hired hitman. Mama H ordered the hit on Hans Schlimmergaard and also tried to frame me for Gina's murder."

Khang placed his arms on his desk. "This is a lot to take in, Agent Chase."

"Understood," I said.

After a moment of processing, he said, "So this woman is doing the dirty work for the Rat, who's ultimately pulling the strings in the background." He tapped his fingers on the desk. "Which means he's somehow getting communication outside of prison. That's what you're saying, right?"

"I am. Sir, I can't explain how he's communicating, but the methods employed by Mama H scream of the Rat's handy work."

"How so?"

I told him about the torture chamber, including finding the hitman strung up. I also told him that female blood of Southeast Asian origin was found at the scene below the meat hooks.

By this point, Khang had collapsed into his grandiose leather chair. He was silent, with a contemplative look on his face.

I broke the silence. "Sir, have you heard of the criminal alias Mama H? Or in the evidence you've seen concerning the Rat, have you come across anything about a women's charity named Second Chances?"

Khang tucked his flowing black locks behind his ears. "I don't recall either."

"Do you know in the past whether the Rat was involved in trafficking Vietnamese women along with Thai women?"

He took a moment, but ultimately shook his head.

I kept at it. "Do you have a file on the Rat? Something maybe you could go through to double check. With all due respect, time is of the essence. I discovered this morning . . ." I cleared my throat. "That my colleague, another FBI agent, has been abducted, and it's most likely the work of this Mama H."

Khang got out of his chair and walked to a filing cabinet.

A few minutes ago, Jimmy had started pacing the length of the office, adding to the overall tension in the room.

Khang pulled out a file from the cabinet. He plopped it onto his desk and opened it. There were maybe forty of fifty pages of material in the file.

He handed me half the stack. "This is unorthodox, Agent Chase, letting you see the classified file, but an agent's life is at stake. And you already know about Anurat anyway."

Khang and I started rifling through the documents. I separated the documents into two stacks. One stack I put pictures, the other stack I put text documents. Khang did the same. We went through everything. I read every printed word in my stack of papers and studied every picture. During that time, Jimmy went to the bathroom twice. Apparently, the man was a nervous pee-er.

"Anything?" Khang asked after about forty-five minutes of reading.

I pushed back the paperwork. Rubbing my eyes, I shook my head. "You?"

"Nothing." He leaned back in his chair. "But I do have a question."

"Shoot," I said.

"How did you come across this women's organization in the first place? You said the hitman implicated Mama H. Did the hitman also tell you about Second Chances?"

I shook my head. "Hans discovered Second Chances through a FOIA request, actually. Which is a perfect lead-in to the original reason I had Jimmy schedule this meeting." I looked at my watch. "My hour's nearly up. You're definitely going to want to clear your next meeting after what I'm about to tell you."

He narrowed his eyes.

"Sir," I continued, "it has to do with the two presidential candidates running in the next election."

He wiggled his fingers. "More, Agent Chase."

Jimmy began pacing again. I motioned at him. "Jimmy, have a seat, you're making me nervous."

I waited for Jimmy to sit, then said, "Hans was hired by Henrietta Valenzuela to dig up dirt on Senator Bradford. To make a long story short, Hans learned that Bradford is somehow involved with this same Vietnamese women's charity, Second Chances. We're not sure his exact role. What he knows or doesn't know about the charity. But given the man's character, we're not so sure he's innocent in all this."

Khang tilted forward in his chair. "What do you mean by that. What about his character?"

"Hans discovered, which I later confirmed, that Senator Bradford is faking his blindness. The man used his government position to funnel money into this charity of his, and he also steered money to the medical company he used to help him regain his sight."

Khang didn't say a word, and neither did Jimmy. For the record, it was the first time I'd witnessed my lawyer speechless.

To my surprise, Khang was the first to speak. He pushed a button on his intercom and told his secretary to clear his schedule for the foreseeable future. Then he looked at me and asked for all the details.

So I told Khang and Jimmy everything I knew about Barrington Bradford Bollinger III.

Khang reasoned out loud after hearing the facts. "So Hans is hired to dig up dirt on the senator, in which he discovers the senator is involved in a criminal charity. And it turns out the charity is potentially run by the very criminal he's scheduled to testify against."

I nodded.

Khang scowled. "That's quite a coincidence, Agent Chase, especially if the senator is ultimately innocent and doesn't know a thing about the true nature of Second Chances."

"Agreed, sir. I don't like coincidences, not at all. It's just hard for me to reason that a United States senator would be privy to torture, hired killings, poisoning, and the like."

"Sure," Khang said. "Understood. It's hard for me to buy coincidences, too. In fact, as a prosecutor, my job is to find links and to dispel coincidences."

Before I could respond, Khang's office intercom crackled on.

"Mr. Khang. Um, the uh, the senator from California is here." The secretary then lowered her voice to a whisper. "The one, sir, running in the presidential election. And he has his dog with him."

CHAPTER FORTY-TWO

KHANG, JIMMY, AND I were speechless, shooting quick glances at each other.

Khang hadn't responded to his secretary, so she crackled in again. "Should I send him in, sir? He wants to meet with you, asap."

Khang snapped out of it and pressed the intercom button. "Give me two minutes."

The U.S. attorney started gathering together the documents concerning the Rat. I handed him my stack of papers. After closing the file and putting it back in the file cabinet, he glared at me.

I held up my hands, still at a loss for words.

Jimmy broke the silence. He gave a nervous laugh. "Well, this should be interesting."

Khang narrowed his eyes at me. "What's our play, Agent Chase?"

"Me?" I said. "You're the powerful attorney, sir. I'll take my lead from you."

"I may be the attorney," Khang shot back, "but he's probably coming after you, pissed that you came here and told me everything."

"That, sir," I said, "I could care less about. Whether or not he has a valid reason for faking his blindness, he's still lying and duping the American people. Plus, there's his dubious involvement in a criminal charity. We have the upper hand. I think we say nothing and let him do all the talking."

Khang nodded and pressed the intercom button. "Send him in."

Moments later, the California senator stepped into the office with his German Shepherd, Ranger, tight to his side.

He didn't say anything upon entry. Instead, he commanded Ranger to sit, which took him repeating himself and offering the dog two treats from his suit jacket pocket. The senator's suit was similar to Jimmy's, but his was clearly high-quality wool without a wrinkle in sight. Of course, the senator kept up the ruse and sported his dark glasses.

Finally, the man looked up and addressed us. "Everything I'm about to say, gentlemen, is off the record until we reach an agreement."

Khang nodded.

I didn't. An agreement? On what?

If the senator was surprised to see me or Jimmy, he didn't show it. Then again, he wore those blindsimming glasses, so perhaps he was currently unaware of our presence.

Khang closed the office door and offered the senator the other red leather chair, which he took; the dog laying at his feet as the senator settled in.

Bradford lifted his glasses for a second, then turned in my direction. "Agent Chase, I take it you filled in Mr. Khang and your personal lawyer on everything?"

Now I was the one trying not to show surprise at the senator knowing who I was and that I had a lawyer. The man had done some research last night.

I cleared my throat. "Everyone in this room is in the know, Bradford." I wasn't about to afford him the senator title. He didn't deserve that respect.

As Bradford reached for his glasses, he said, "This is the first time I've ever done this." He squinted after taking off the dark glasses. Three long blinks later, he focused in and looked around the room, meeting each one of our eyes.

I watched Jimmy and Khang's expressions. They were both taken aback.

"Yes, I can see," Bradford said. "What Mr. Chase told you is true about my vision. Hopefully he also expounded on why." He held up his right hand. "Not that I'm saying it makes it totally right, certainly not. I've had relatively decent sight while wearing contacts for about two years now. My only defense is that I kept up the blind ruse because I wanted to make a real difference. I wanted other blind people to experience the miracle of sight. And I didn't want to prolong the process for medical approval. Also, I had political ambition. Certainly, I did. And I think that made it easier for me to keep up the ruse. I believed wholeheartedly that I could make this great country even greater, especially if I made the White House my residence. Total honesty here, I thought that being blind made me more likeable and sympathetic to the voters and gained me an advantage. It was terribly misguided. I, I . . ."

He struggled to find the words, then stopped trying and lowered his head slightly.

Honestly, I wasn't sure if Bradford was acting or baring his soul. As I studied his demeanor, I felt Karla's cell buzz in my pocket. The senator sighed a couple of times, then continued pleading his case about his involvement with the medical start-up. He'd already told me everything, so he focused his attention on Jimmy and Khang.

I used the moment to glance at the cell. It was an email from Karla's tech colleague. The email contained a small picture, which took me a moment to zoom in on with my two fingers. Upon closer look, I realized it was actually a picture of a newspaper photo; one of the clippings I'd asked him to sharpen if he could.

The caption for the picture was, 'Second Chances Organization Wins Humanitarian Award.'

It was dated over six years ago. There was some man in the picture handing a plaque to a woman. A woman I sort of recognized. Someone I felt like I'd seen recently, but just couldn't place from where. I stared at the picture a moment longer, then my eyes flicked down to the picture's caption, where it described who was whom. Not only was the woman named, but she was also described as the head of Second Chances.

My eyes swelled.

"You okay, Chase?" It was Khang's voice.

I noticed the three men were staring at me. I blinked twice, then swallowed. "I'm fine, sorry. Go on."

I took two deep, silent breaths. I needed to speak with Khang as soon as possible, so I focused on what Bradford was saying in order to find the best moment to break in.

"So," the senator was saying, "I have important information to provide that goes beyond me faking blindness. Before I go on the record about that I need two things, two assurances: One, nothing leaves this room. Nothing at all. I want no new players in on the information you gentlemen already know and the new information you're about to know."

There was no objection, so Bradford continued. "Second, I want immunity, plain and simple. I—"

"I need to know what's going on," Khang interjected. "Just for the record since we are talking about the record. I couldn't even start the immunity talks until I get a better sense of what you're hinting at, sir. Which is obviously criminal otherwise you wouldn't want immunity. And, at the very least, in an immunity case I would need to inform and get permission from the California AG, sir."

Before Bradford could reply, Khang leaned forward in his chair and kept at it. "Plus, we also know more than we're letting on, sir. More about you than just faking your blindness. For instance, your propensity to steer government money in your favor. So if you're trying to pin that on someone else or get immunity from your involvement in dubious charities, forget it." He leaned back and shot a smug look at the senator. "For the record."

Ethan Khang wasn't a man to be played.

"I've certainly made my mistakes, Mr. Khang," the senator said. "But what I'm offering is information about a person who is engaged in far more nefarious activities than I. Far more."

"So you are here to shift the blame to save your hide?"

"Mr. Khang, I'm very certain your government—our government, I should say—would want the information I have."

Wait, what was he doing? I had to interject before he carried on.

Standing up, I hustled over to the bathroom door. I apologized for the interruption and motioned at Khang to join me. I steered him into the bathroom, whispering in his ear as I closed the door:

"You're not going to believe this."

CHAPTER FORTY-THREE

I OPENED KARLA'S cell. The picture was still on the screen. I thrust it toward Khang.

"A tech from the L.A. field office just sent this. Do you know who that is?"

Khang pulled the phone close and studied the picture. I watched his eyes flick from the picture to the words below it. He ran his fingers through his wavy, black hair.

"Wait," he said. "That's . . . "

While he stuttered, I turned on the sink faucet to hopefully drown out our voices.

I turned back and whispered, "His wife. It's Bradford's wife! She runs, or ran, Second Chances. That's what the caption says."

"Wait," Khang repeated himself. "Does that mean she's Mama H?"

"Maybe," I said. "Maybe not. His wife's name is Bian Bollinger, not sure what her maiden name is."

Khang asked, "Who's he referring to then? Who's into more nefarious activities than him?"

I found it hard to believe that Bradford was referring to his wife, and that the man was about to turn on her. I quickly thought about other suspects. Henrietta Valenzuela came to mind.

Grabbing Khang's shoulder, I brought him closer. "Listen, this guy knows his political hopes are toast now that we've caught him faking blindness. He's probably desperate and willing to do anything. Maybe he's going to implicate his opponent, Henrietta, in all this."

"Maybe," Khang said. "Or maybe he's so desperate he's going to turn on his wife."

"You could be right. I don't know. He's definitely serving up somebody. Nothing about this man surprises me."

Khang nodded. His eyes looked wild as his mind raced.

Just then, a light knock on the bathroom door interrupted us.

I cracked the door. Jimmy pushed his way in.

"What's going on, guys? It's getting awkward out there."

Khang didn't answer.

I didn't either. I shot a look at Jimmy. "What's awkward is three guys in this tiny bathroom." Turning to Khang, I continued. "How do we handle this from a legal perspective?"

"Well," Khang said, "since we're not sure who he's talking about or what's exactly going on, we need to keep him talking. However, he's not a stupid man. He's here to make a deal, so . . ." Khang closed the toilet seat and sat on it.

"So what?" I prodded.

"He's probably not going to give us anything in detail. If he doesn't, we should lay out exactly what we know about his involvement with Second Chances, and his wife's. Then see how he responds. We can go from there."

"So wing it, is that what you're saying?" I said.

Khang shrugged. "If he plays coy, then yes."

"His wife?" Jimmy asked. "What's going on here, gents? What's this pow-wow about?"

Again, we both ignored Jimmy.

Khang exited the bathroom. I was right behind him. Jimmy stayed back. I shot him a look.

"Gotta go again," he said. "Way too much coffee this morning. Don't start without me."

Khang didn't wait. "How do you want to proceed, Senator? I can't make any deals with such broad strokes and language about supposed nefarious activities by an unknown person. Certainly you're aware of that. You have to give me something, sir."

"I'm fully aware of your position and needs, Mr. Khang. Time is very much of the essence here, though. That's why I'm here in person. If time wasn't an important factor, I would've handled all this through my lawyer. Trust me."

"What's the time factor?" Khang asked. "What's the rush? We need to make sure we do this right."

"Fair question," the senator responded. "My part of the bargain is to physically deliver this person to you. Like I said, this is a person of incredible interest and importance to the American government. And the person is on the verge of fleeing the country, within hours, in fact. If we don't act soon, the person will be gone by sunset. I want your word, Mr. Khang, that until this person is in custody, everything stays between the four of us in this room. In fact, we have to move rather quickly, so we don't have time for you to call up the chain to the California AG, like you said you had to."

While the senator paused for a breath, Khang went for the jugular. "Where's your wife headed, Bradford? Where's she fleeing to? That's who you're referring to, right? Can't believe you're desperate enough to turn on your own wife."

The senator's face remained stone-like. For a second, I thought Khang was wrong by implicating the senator's wife, but then Bradford's Adam's apple betrayed him. It bobbed up and down in a painfully slow manner.

He recovered nicely, though. "Well played, Mr. Khang. You know more than I anticipated. You know all about my wife then?"

Khang nodded. "We certainly do."

Bradford's shoulders sagged, then he cleared his throat. "That doesn't change all that much. You'll still need her before she flees to a country with no extradition treaty. If indeed you know all about my wife, as you say you do, then you know you absolutely can't let her leave. This is a national security crisis."

Khang frowned. "Not sure I share your theatrics here, Senator, or your sense of imminence. Or that this is a national security crisis."

"It isn't?" Bradford held up his hands. "If you know all about my wife, what else could it be?"

"It's certainly nefarious and horrible, I'll give you that. But finance fraud and trafficking Vietnamese women, including torturing them, wouldn't be considered a national security issue, would it, Senator? What am I missing?"

"Torturing women?" Bradford said. "Wait, what on earth are you talking about?"

Khang leaned forward. "What are *you* talking about?"

I looked at both men.

Clearly, there was much more to this than anyone in the room realized.

CHAPTER FORTY-FOUR

THE SENATOR APPEARED genuinely shocked. In fact, so much so, that he couldn't speak.

So Khang did. "I'm talking about your wife running this charitable organization called Second Chances. An organization that you've directed millions of dollars to via federal grants by abusing your position as chair of the Small Business and Entrepreneurship Senate Committee. I'll just assume you've been using that money for your campaign or personal benefit. Because certainly this isn't a true charitable organization that intends to help these poor Vietnamese workers. After all, we assume the women have been tortured by somebody named Mama H."

The senator coughed. "What?" He swallowed. "What did you say?"

Khang blasted on. "We'll assume your wife hired Mama H to keep these women in line. Or perhaps she's Mama H herself? I—"

Bradford held up both hands. "Stop. Please. Mama H?" He looked up to the ceiling, then put both hands over his face. "She's worse than I thought."

The senator suddenly reached into his pocket with a shaky hand. He pulled out a yellow pill bottle. The pills rattled around as he pried off the top. "I have pretty bad anxiety. Always have since being tortured all those years ago. I need an anti-anxiety pill, and some water, if you have it."

Khang directed him to the bathroom.

The senator went in without closing the door. He turned on the water and kept it on. The three of us sat there staring at each another with wide eyes. What we knew about his wife, he didn't appear to know. And what he was prepared to tell us about his wife, we didn't appear to know.

No-one in the room said a word. We simply listened to the senator splashing water on his face in the bathroom. A minute later, he emerged looking pale.

After taking a seat, he addressed Khang. "Tell me what you know about the torture of the women. I had no idea that was going on with the charity. No idea. I promise."

Khang motioned to me. "I'll let Agent Chase tell that part."

I gave a fairly succinct version of the events. "My friend and former colleague had been hired by your political opponent to dig up dirt on you. He was also targeted by a hitman, narrowly escaping death a few times. We now assume he was targeted because he was looking into your wife's charity. Anyway, we eventually discovered the hired killer through a GPS phone trace. He was in a wine grotto underneath a restaurant/nail salon in Little Saigon. The man was folded up with his hands and feet tied together, dangling by a meat hook. I got to him right before he died. He told me he was responsible for trying to kill my buddy, and that he was hired by a woman named Mama H."

"Unbelievable," the senator said. "I can't believe she's active like that again." A moment later, he looked away. "I guess I shouldn't be. Now that I know what I know." When he looked back at me, he was beyond pale, almost grayish-green looking. "I'm sorry. So sorry. I had no idea."

Khang said, "Tell us what you do know about your wife, Senator."

Bradford took a deep breath to compose himself. "Nobody but my wife and I know this, but she wasn't my care-giver in Vietnam during my tenure in the Hanoi Hilton. She wasn't my nurse. Far from it. Bian was one of the guards, one of the many responsible for torturing us POWs. There were actually quite a few female torturers at the Hanoi Hilton, but she was the most notorious woman on staff. Eventually she earned the nickname, Mama Hanoi or Mama H. The torture method you described, Agent Chase, was common practice at the Hanoi Hilton, a common method my wife used. I had no clue she was employing that method with the women in her charity. No clue about that, or that she was trafficking women."

I looked at the senator. "If she wasn't your caregiver, how'd you two end up together?"

He searched for the words. "What's that term they use for sympathizing with your captor?"

Jimmy said his first words. "Stockholm syndrome."

"Right," said the senator. "It was a bit of that. On both of our ends, I imagine. My western worldview eventually wore off on her, too. But not until many years later. I was in captivity for five years. They tortured me hard for the first four years. The final year they basically stopped torturing me since they were unable to break me. By the end of that year, however, I'd developed a strange psychological alliance with Bian. I'd become somewhat of a communist sympathizer, which surprised me and delighted her."

Bradford winced and held his stomach. A moment later, he continued. "Anyway, those views still pervade my political platform, as I'm sure you know. And Bian changed, too, in that time we were together. Near the very end of my stay, she did act as my caregiver. To make a long story short, we bonded near the end of the war and after it. We both were disillusioned by American involvement in Vietnam and by the brutality of the north Vietnamese soldiers versus their southern counterparts. By the end of the war, we both questioned everything. It's like us being together helped us make sense of what went on during those years of war, of what we endured. That's the best I can describe it. Though now everything I thought I knew about Bian is in question."

I prodded him. "What did you find out, Bradford?"

"The simple truth" he continued, "is that I gave up my inheritance when I enlisted with the Marines. My family was outraged at my decision and disowned me and wrote me out of the family will. Bian and my adopted girls were my new family when I returned from war. Eventually my political career started taking off and so did her charity. We had little money as a new family, so we used the proceeds from her success with the charity to build our personal and political life. In the end, I abused my political position to launder money through the charity."

The senator looked away for a moment. "That's the immunity I need, immunity from being prosecuted over campaign finance fraud."

"Bradford," I said. "You said everything about her is in question. What did you exactly mean by that?"

He nodded. "Right, you told me what you know about my wife, which I didn't know. Now, unfortunately, I need to tell you what you don't know." Bradford eyed Khang. "I know we can't draw up documents right now about immunity, so I need your word. Are you a man of your word, Mr. Khang?"

Khang didn't answer directly. Instead, he met the senator's gaze. "If you give me something valuable, something that is clearly nationally security related, I don't see a problem with striking a deal. Now tell me what you know, Senator, because I'm still confused as to how all this is a national security threat."

The senator looked around the room, meeting each one of our eyes.

"Gentlemen," he said, "My wife . . . He swallowed. "I still can't believe it. I just found this out late last night. I honestly had no clue."

He paused, then said, "My wife is a foreign spy. She's an operative with the TC2."

CHAPTER FORTY-FIVE

I COLLAPSED INTO the chair.

Jimmy and Khang looked at the senator, then at me, then at each other. Jimmy broke the silence. "What the hell's the TC2?"

Khang shook his head, obviously he didn't know either.

So I informed them. "It's a Vietnamese intelligence organization. I can't pronounce the Vietnamese name, but it basically translates as the General Department of Military Intelligence."

Bradford added, "TC2 is short for *Tổng cục Tình báo* in Vietnamese." The senator hung his head. His dog stood and licked his right temple, whined a little.

"I'll stick with TC2," Jimmy said. "That's certainly easier to pronounce."

"This is crazy," I blurted. "TC2 reports directly to the Communist Party of Vietnam and the president of Vietnam."

The senator kept looking at the floor. "I had no idea she's been working for them. No idea."

I thought about the depth of the conspiracy. We could've had a first lady who was an actual spy for a foreign, communist government. No wonder Bian went to such lengths to cover everything up. My mind suddenly focused on Karla. Bian likely knew Karla had been investigating everything. The senator's wife must have Karla, or at least know where she is.

Khang said his first words. "How and when did you find this out, Senator?"

I intervened. "Time is of the essence. We need to capture your wife, Bradford, asap. You can explain more on our way to get her. Where is she?"

The senator didn't move or respond.

"Look at me, Bradford," I said.

A moment later, the senator looked up. The grayish skin was gone; he looked green now.

"Another agent," I said, "a woman by the name of Karla Dickerson has been abducted. We've been working together on identifying Mama H. Her life hangs in the balance. Did your wife take her?"

"I'm not sure. Possibly. Now that I know she's been torturing and trafficking women, it's certainly not out of the question. I can't believe I'm saying that. We've shared the same bed for forty years and now I feel like I don't even know her. Anything is possible with her."

"We have to go," I said.

The senator eased out of his chair and stood. "Agent Chase is right. We have to move. My wife is already out to sea, probably in international waters by now."

"Out to sea?" Khang questioned.

Bradford nodded. "In our yacht. I also own a fast fishing boat that I keep at the L.A. yacht club. We can intercept her with that. I'll explain everything on the way." He looked around. "Wondering how to get there quickly. My bodyguard dropped me off. I'll call and see how far away he is. Though we can't all fit in my Tesla."

"My SUV is big enough," Jimmy said. "And it's just across the street."

"Let's take that," I said. "Rather not deal with your bodyguard, Bradford."

"Sure," the senator said, nodding.

Khang pulled me aside and whispered into my ear. "We need backup, don't we?"

"Definitely," I said. "I'll contact Frank on the way, and also call the Coast Guard."

Khang looked at the senator. "Let's get a move on then."

He held up his finger. "Give me a second, feeling very queasy."

Bradford rushed into the bathroom; his dog trotting close behind.

I used the moment to call Frank. Unfortunately, my boss didn't answer. When voicemail picked up, I told Frank to call me back immediately.

After the call, I banged on the bathroom door. "Senator, let's go."

I heard him throw up. "One minute," he said. "Gimme one minute."

Standing by the bathroom door, my mind reeled from what we'd uncovered, and if we were going to get to Karla in time. And if she was even . . . I stopped my thoughts from going there.

Instead, I walked over to Khang. "You think he's being honest about what he discovered and when? After all, he has been lying about his vision."

Khang looked away for a moment, then back to me. "I do think he's telling the truth, especially since he's giving up his wife. I mean, he could be out to sea with her right now, heading to Vietnam, which has no extradition treaty. He didn't have to come here to try and strike a deal."

I thought about it.

"What about you?" Khang prodded. "What do you think?"

I shrugged. "Not sure yet. He did seem genuinely shocked over the whole Mama H thing and sickened over everything in general."

Before I could say anything else, the senator and his dog came out of the bathroom, interrupting our conversation. Bradford was about to say something, then stopped himself and charged back into the bathroom.

We listened to him throw up again.

This time, he emerged from the bathroom wiping his mouth with a handkerchief. "Sorry you had to hear that. Time to go."

Once outside the building, Jimmy led us to his SUV. We all piled in, including the dog. Jimmy took the driver's seat. The senator sat behind him in a captain's chair. Ranger took position between the second-row captain's chairs. I sat in the passenger seat with Khang directly behind me.

As Jimmy punched the yacht club into the SUV's GPS system, I received a text from my boss, Frank Lemming.

It read: *In meeting. What's up?*

I texted back: *How fast can you get to LA yacht club? Super important. An emergency. Also, Coast Guard may call you.*

Frank replied: *45-60 min. What's this about?*

I replied: *No time. Will explain when you get there.*

He texted: *Roger.*

Next, I pulled out Karla's phone and used its internet capabilities to locate the nearest Coast Guard station to the yacht club.

"What exactly are you doing, Agent Chase? Who are you contacting?" Bradford motioned at the cell in my hand. "I told you gentlemen not to involve anyone else."

"Bradford, if you think we're heading out to international waters without backup, you have another—"

"Fine, fine," Bradford said, holding up his hands. "I get it."

I called the Coast Guard number I'd found, letting them know I was a special agent with the FBI and that I needed their fastest boat in the fleet. I told the person on the other end that it was an emergency and a matter of national security. I gave her my badge number and my boss's direct line if she needed confirmation and authorization. She told me she'd have someone call me back as soon as possible.

"Okay," I said, turning to Bradford. "Now tell us what went down. How and when you found out about your wife."

Bradford petted Ranger a few times, calming the dog down. "Bian's been my top political advisor all these years. She's run all my campaigns. Five years ago she had eyes on the presidency for me. She had more vision and desire for the position than I did. Which, I guess, all makes perfect sense now, because that was about the same time she connected with her former government. It was also the same time she started phasing out her involvement with Second Chances. I'm sure the TC2 saw an opportunity they couldn't pass up. I mean, having one of their operatives infiltrate the American government as a first lady would be the ultimate spy accomplishment, wouldn't it?

"Anyway, a few months back, word got out about all the campaign money I had coming in. News stories were speculating about it, and to be perfectly honest, so was I. Bian instructed me to tell reporters it was from my supporters, and that I was also supplementing my campaign with my own personal money, from my vast family fortune. Except, of course, I had no fortune. And I knew that all the money couldn't have been from my young supporters. When I asked Bian where all the money was coming from, she told me not to worry about it. And I listened to her, though I was skeptical. Since I was busy enough with campaigning, I decided not to worry about the financial side of things."

By this point, I'd turned all the way around in my seat. "So what happened? What changed?"

The senator pointed at me. "You happened."

"What?" I said.

"Last night when you discovered I was faking, I assumed everything was about to unravel. I called Bian and let her know that my ruse was up. That you'd been hired by Hans Schlimmergaard to investigate me, and that your buddy was employed by Henrietta. Naturally, Bian was incredibly upset, but she told me not to worry. She knew that you and Hans were on to me, and that she had it handled. When I pressed her on what that meant, she said there were things that needed to be done that I shouldn't know about. Things I needed to be protected from. She told me she was rushing home and that we'd figure everything out."

He looked at Khang. "But I was spiraling after that conversation, really bad. I had to know what she meant. It only took a few minutes to search on Google and learn about the attempt on Hans' life in the hospital. Gentlemen, I couldn't live with myself if I was inadvertently involved in attempted murder. I wanted to know exactly what Bian had been up to, so I started going through her home files, and the files on her personal computer. And found some evidence . . ."

He paused.

Khang prodded him. "Evidence of her hiring the hitman?"

The senator shook his head. "Nothing of that sort. I discovered where all the millions of dollars were coming from to aid my campaign. So much money flooded into our offshore accounts over the past nine months. I traced the cash back to two individuals. One person worked for the Communist Party of Vietnam and the other for Military Intelligence."

Jimmy twisted the rearview mirror so he could see Bradford. "You're saying the communist Vietnamese government has been supporting your campaign for president?"

"That's exactly what I'm saying," Bradford replied. "Exactly what has happened. And without my knowledge."

"Makes sense," I said. "When the TC2 saw an opportunity to have an operative inside the White House—are you kidding me? —like you said, Bradford, that's spy nirvana. They'd contribute whatever it'd take to see that happen."

Khang nodded. "Absolutely." He turned to Bradford. "Obviously you confronted your wife, and obviously it didn't go well since she's fleeing the country."

"What happened there?" I asked.

"I didn't sleep last night," Bradford said. "Not a wink. She admitted right away she'd been recruited as a TC2 agent. She didn't try to hide that truth. Apparently, they approached her during the peak of my political rise and told her they'd finance all my campaigns, including a White House run, and they'd donate as much as it would take to get me into the Oval Office."

I scoffed. "But for a price. For traitorous actions in return. They'd require any American intelligence info that she could glean from you. Right?"

The senator reluctantly nodded. "I promise you I didn't know. Bian never confided a thing to me since she knew I wouldn't go along. Which she was damn right about. From her perspective, this was all about the presidency, at any cost."

Jimmy turned in disgust. "And I'm sure last night she fed you the classic, 'end justifies the means' BS. Didn't she?"

Khang kept the conversation from devolving. "How'd it end with your wife?"

Bradford looked out the window. "She couldn't figure a way out of the mess, like she thought she could. And I certainly couldn't either. We both realized the White House would never happen. We also knew that if all the facts became known, we'd face some considerable prison time. So Bian wanted us to flee and take refuge in Vietnam, start a new life there."

The senator looked over at Khang, then back to me. "She apologized profusely for lying, insisting that she fed the TC2 mostly benign intelligence, little bits and pieces of what she'd heard from me over the past five years. She begged for me to escape with her. I said I needed a little time to think about it, wrap my mind around everything. She understood, but she wanted out of the country asap. She took our yacht this morning out to international waters and moored it there. Said she'd wait until sunset tonight for my decision."

The senator sighed. "You guys know the rest, and obviously the decision I've made since I'm giving her up. Country first. Always."

Nobody said a word for about a minute. It was a lot to digest.

I spoke first. "What about the Rat, Bradford? Has your wife been working with the Rat to traffick these women into America?"

Bradford frowned. "Who's the Rat? No idea who you're talking about, Agent Chase."

I studied his eyes to see if he was telling the truth or not. Bradford didn't flinch or look away. "Anurat Wu," I continued. "One of the most notorious human traffickers in our country's history. I imagine your wife and the Rat were in cahoots somehow."

Bradford shrugged. "Maybe, I don't know. I mean, I had no idea she was treating these women like this. Maybe she was working with this person. Like I said, years ago she phased herself out of the charity so she could focus on my campaigns."

And treason, I thought. But I didn't get a chance to say it aloud since a buzz in my pocket distracted me. It was from Karla's phone. I dug it out and saw that an email had come through from the Long Beach PD; it was an attachment of the crime scene report from Karla's contact.

I double-clicked on the pdf and breezed through the findings, stopping at the part where the report evaluated the urine sample in the torture chamber. The technician writing the report speculated over the sample in a lengthy paragraph, stating it was an unusual DNA profile.

Khang interrupted my reading. "We're almost at the yacht club, Senator, what's our game plan on the boat?"

"Exactly what I've been thinking about, too," he said. "We'll board the boat and head straight to sea." He looked at his watch. "We really have no time to spare. Bian gave me her coordinates, which should take us about five hours to get there, depending on how fast we push the fishing boat. When we get close, you guys will need to stay hidden. Obviously, she's just expecting me and the dog, so she can't spot you."

The senator glanced at me. "It was the Coast Guard you called for backup, right?"

I nodded.

"That's fine; we just can't have the Coast Guard come charging in either. We don't want to tip our hand in any way. She's on a sophisticated yacht with high-tech radar, so the Coast Guard has to keep their distance. Otherwise, we'll spook her. That yacht can outrun my fishing boat and a Coast Guard cutter."

I thought about it, eventually agreeing with Bradford on that point.

He continued. "The boat is a twenty-nine-foot Striper with twin outboard 250 horsepower motors. The wheelhouse isn't huge, but three men can tuck themselves out of sight in the front part. You guys hide there, and after I board the yacht, I'll take Bian inside the yacht's galley or upper wheelhouse. Then you three can sneak on the stern and surprise her. Once we secure Bian, we'll call in the Coast Guard. How's that?"

He specifically looked at me.

"Definitely have some questions," I said. "I'm a visual guy, so I want to see the fishing boat's layout and the yacht's layout. Even if you need to make a sketch of the yacht from memory. Anything will help."

"Got it," Bradford said.

I continued. "My biggest concern is firearms and weapons. Not just that we're currently unarmed, but what weapons your wife could possess. It's great to plan on sneaking up and surprising someone, but it's far too optimistic thinking. It's best to plan for the worst and assume there'll be a confrontation. Will she be alone on the boat?"

He shook his head. "This is a large yacht, gentlemen. She'll have a Vietnamese worker, who's a captain, on the boat with her."

"Do you know that boat inside and out, Bradford?" I asked.

"Sure, why?"

"Because Karla could be on that boat, and who knows what shape she's in. We have to find her fast."

"Agreed," Bradford said. "I know all the nooks and crannies."

"Anyone else on board?" I asked. "Any other workers?"

He shook his head.

"Will your wife or the captain be armed?"

"Armed," Bradford said, "but not carrying. Like my fishing boat, we keep a pistol onboard the yacht. In the glovebox inside the wheelhouse."

"So we will have access to a firearm?" I said. "You have one on the Striper?"

"Absolutely, Agent Chase. It's all yours."

That made me feel more comfortable with the plan. I'd have to evaluate the set-up once onboard the Striper, though.

I used the final five minutes of our drive to study the findings on the DNA profile from the urine sample. By the end of five minutes, I was admittedly torn and confused over what I read. The implications in the report could be huge. However, the tech admitted in the report that more research needed to be done.

We arrived at the yacht club and parked near the fishing boat. When I climbed from the SUV, my eyes locked onto a nearby parked car.

Everyone took off in the opposite direction from where I was standing, toward Bradford's boat slip. I hustled over to the car since I couldn't read the license plate.

Jimmy called out to me. "Chase, where you going? Come on, this way. Let's go."

When I was close enough to read the license plate, I stopped and hung my head.

Moments later, Jimmy was at my side saying, "You okay? What's going on?"

I motioned at the car in front of me. "It's Karla's."

CHAPTER FORTY-SIX

International Waters
200 miles NW of Long Beach, CA

BIAN BOLLINGER SAT on the edge of a small tub in the saloon's head, staring at Karla Dickerson. The federal agent was tied by her hands and feet and dangled about a foot off the floor on a chrome hook. The hook was supposed to be used for hanging a bathrobe. Karla's body was folded at the waist. The back of her legs touched the wall and her tailbone slowly swung like a pendulum.

Karla moaned every time her tailbone scraped or bounced off the wall.

From Bian's experience, she knew Karla had about an hour or less before she slipped into unconsciousness.

She spoke softly to Karla. "I'm sorry it had to go down like this."

Karla groaned, then swallowed. "Sorry? Please." She let out a dry, hacking cough, then spoke weakly. "You torture innocent women all the time. Spare me the sympathy."

"That's a common misconception," Bian replied calmly.

Karla scoffed. "Really?"

"Only five women from my charity have experienced what you're experiencing now, Agent Dickerson. Contrary to what you said, it's not all the time. And for the record, they chose that path for themselves. They weren't innocent, and I didn't actively torture them. They made bad choices and paid the consequence."

Karla shook her head with her eyes closed. "You keep telling yourself that in an effort to believe it?"

Bian kneeled beside her and whispered into her ear. "Those women had nothing, came from nothing. Something a privileged, white woman like yourself can't possibly fathom. I paid for their travel to America, gave them a job, a place to stay, food for their belly, a new life, and most importantly: hope. Hope, Agent Dickerson, there's nothing better than that. In return, the women promised to work for me for five years. That was it; that was the deal. They had to pay off their debt, plain and simple."

She paused and stroked Karla's hair.

Karla, still with her eyes closed, turned and spit into Bian's face.

Bian smiled. She didn't bother wiping the spit away or stop stroking Karla's hair. "The women knew the consequences, Agent Dickerson. Each woman was given a tour of the wine grotto after they were hired. They were told if they reneged on the deal, if they left to pursue other work or a new life, before their five years were up, they'd be brought to the chamber as a consequence."

Bian thought about it for a second. "About every year one woman would renege and pay the price. Considering the thousands of women who didn't, I believe that was an effective deterrent. Wouldn't you say?"

Karla started humming.

Bian knew the woman wouldn't respond, or even listen to her, but she spoke anyway. "I can't expect a weak American like yourself to understand. Women like you have no idea what it takes to keep others in line and keep them accountable."

"Enough," Karla said, clearing her throat. "Just let me die." Her voice was but a whisper now. "Much better than listening to you."

Bian stood. "You won't die like this; don't you worry, that's not the plan." She moved toward the head door. Before she closed it, Bian laughed.

"If you just *hang* in a little longer, you'll soon find out what is."

CHAPTER FORTY-SEVEN

L.A. Yacht Club
San Pedro, CA

"ARE YOU SURE it's her car?" Jimmy asked.

As soon as he said it, he corrected himself. "Sorry, of course you'd know that. Dumb question. Dumb, dumb, dumb."

Ignoring Jimmy, I walked over and tried the doors. They were locked. I peered in and immediately saw blood on the back seat.

Jimmy saw it, too. "No," he said, sitting on the back bumper. "I'm sorry, Chase, so sorry."

I kicked the front tire, then motioned to my lawyer. "Karla's obviously on that yacht, and hopefully still alive. There's not that much blood back there. We have to move, Jimmy."

He followed behind me as I walked quickly toward the Striper. The Coast Guard called back along the way. I listened to the woman's explanation of what was happening; my hand gripped the cell tighter the more she talked. When she finished, I said, "Fine. I'll have someone waiting at the slip." Then I stabbed the End Call button.

Jimmy asked, "Are they helping?"

"Yes, but they're out on a training exercise. They're heading back to assist right now. They're about forty-five minutes out, however."

When we reached the fishing boat, I jumped aboard and addressed Bradford. "Do we have any time to spare?"

He looked at his watch and shook his head. "I can maybe get forty knots per hour out of this boat, but we have two-hundred plus miles to cover. Why? What's going on?"

I looked at Khang. "Coast Guard is approximately forty-five minutes out."

"That's cutting it too close, gentlemen," Bradford said.

I kept my eyes on Khang and thumbed over my shoulder. "Karla's vehicle is parked back there."

Khang mouthed, 'I'm sorry.'

"She's on that boat," I said, turning back to Bradford. "I agree, we can't wait. Somebody needs to hang back and wait for the Coast Guard and Frank."

Jimmy volunteered. "Listen, I'll hang back and help direct them. Fill everyone in, too. I do terrible on small boats like this, especially out in the open water. Can't imagine how many times I'll puke if I stay aboard this thing. I'm already feeling queasy, and we're tied up still."

Khang held up his cell. "Jimmy can track our location through GPS."

"And I'll give you the yacht's coordinates," Bradford added. "Plus, you can call us and track us on my satellite phone." Bradford opened the glovebox and pulled out a sat phone. "Here, call this number." He read off a phone number to Jimmy.

Jimmy punched the digits into his cell and called the sat phone. Seconds later, it began ringing.

"Got it," Jimmy said.

Khang glanced at me. "What do you think?"

I hesitated to answer. While I mulled over the plan, Bradford reached into the glovebox and pulled out a pistol.

"This should make you feel better, Agent Chase. This was a gift from my wife, years ago. Naturally, she gave me a Soviet made gun, which now makes sense."

Bradford handed me a classic Russian made semi-automatic pistol.

"A Makarov," I said. "A beautiful weapon."

I inspected the gun in my hand. It was a medium-size, straight-blowback-action handgun. It was a simple design with limited parts, but incredibly accurate. Soviet military and police had been using it forever. I'd heard it was extremely well-balanced and wanted to see for myself.

"Careful," the senator said as I aimed the gun at the boat's hull. "It's loaded."

It was. I could tell by the weight of the pistol. I quickly pulled out the magazine and noted it was full. Holding a loaded gun provided a sense of relief.

I pulled Khang to the stern. "How are you feeling about this?"

He bobbed his head side to side. "Just you and I on a boat with a seventy-year-old man. And you have a gun. So . . ."

Khang was right. However, it wasn't us I was concerned about. I looked over at Jimmy, who was already climbing out of the Striper. I needed a word with the man.

"The engines need to warm for at least five minutes," Bradford said. He called Ranger to his side. The dog trotted over and dropped at his feet.

While I joined Jimmy on the dock, I motioned at the dog and addressed the senator. "He never leaves your side, does he?"

"Nope," Bradford said.

"Never?"

"Never, Agent Chase. He goes everywhere with me."

I nodded, then steered Jimmy down the dock about ten feet and stopped. "I have concerns about leaving you here alone."

"Concerns about what?"

"I don't fully trust Bradford." I motioned over my shoulder.

Jimmy leaned closer. "Why? Whatcha think's going on?"

"Honestly, I don't know, but I'm a cautious man, very cautious. And you need to be as well."

He frowned. "I'll be alone here. Plus, your boss will be here in a half hour or so. Cautious about what?"

I thought for a moment, then said, "Just keep your wits about you. You know, don't talk to strangers, that sort of thing." I reached into my pocket, pulled out the Kershaw folding knife and handed it to Jimmy.

"You're over-reacting," he said.

"Maybe. Maybe not. Just take this and be on alert. Agent Lemming will meet you at that Coast Guard slip in about thirty minutes." I pointed toward a large, open slip toward the other end of the docks.

"It's the middle of the day, Chase. I'll be fine."

"Listen," I said, curling his fingers around the knife, "always plan for the worst, Jimmy. Always."

He nodded.

"Good, now take these as well."

I handed him Pham Van Lu's wallet but kept mine in my back pocket. I also gave him Karla's cell. Then I went through a detailed plan of what to say to the Coast Guard and how to specifically track the Striper.

Being overly cautious, I went through the plan with Jimmy again, then made him repeat it back to me. By the time I finished, the engines were good and warm.

I boarded the Striper and left Jimmy dockside.

Khang had been sitting in the captain's chair, familiarizing himself with the cockpit while Jimmy and I had been talking. Bradford was in the passenger seat with Ranger tight to his feet. He motioned at the helm. "I'll take over once we're out of the harbor and away from the public eye."

As Khang navigated out of port, I examined the fishing boat. There was not much to it, just a basic wheelhouse and a holding/storage area underneath the stern's floor. Inside that hatched area were a few life jackets and two large ice chests, for fish or ice or a combination of the two. Nothing else was down there.

The gunwales on both sides of the boat contained some fishing poles and paddles. Mounted on the port side of the gunwale was a gaffing hook for fish. The wheelhouse itself was small, but big enough to protect us from the waves and a strong headwind. It was also deep enough for Khang and me to stow away without being seen.

After my inspection, I asked Bradford to sketch an outline of the yacht, making sure to include a rough floor plan of the different levels. During that time, I asked him a number of questions about the yacht. Once we were out of the harbor and slapping our way through the waves, I knew we wouldn't be able to communicate well without shouting.

When we reached the outskirts of the harbor, Khang and Bradford switched seats. Before Bradford engaged the throttle, Khang asked him,

"What are you going to do after all this, Senator? After we secure your wife, that is. What's your plan from there?"

Bradford frowned. "My plans immediately after or bigger picture stuff?"

I interjected. "I'd like to know both actually."

The senator looked across the water for a moment. "Well, immediately after I have plans for my lawyer to meet me at your office." He motioned at Khang. "The whole point of having limited people involved in all this is to keep the situation under wraps. As I'm sure you gentlemen can imagine, I don't want everything to become public. In fact, I'll have to insist on it."

I walked to the stern, shaking my head.

"Hear me out," Bradford said. "My hope is that the government won't want everything public either. I can't imagine they'd want the general public to know a communist spy had infiltrated their government for the last five years."

He was right, unfortunately. I shot back, "Or that she almost became the first lady."

"Exactly," Bradford said. "My proposal to your boss, Mr. Khang, is to give up everything I have on my wife for immunity. Obviously, I'll withdraw from the election and disappear. We'll have to work on some cover story. Maybe I withdraw from the election because Bian is killed and I'm devastated over it. Or she becomes deathly sick and goes back to Vietnam to see family before dying. Something like that, anyway."

"And where would you disappear to?" I asked.

"Honestly, I'm not sure. Everything has happened so quickly I haven't had time to think about it. Maybe Cuba, or some other communist country. Although, there are only five of those countries left. I've espoused extreme socialist philosophy—borderline communism—for years now. I was not just brainwashed about it by my wife. I believe in it whole heartedly. I'd like to live in a place like that and truly live out the philosophy, test out its viability, so to speak. If Cuba won't take me, maybe I'll go to some socialist country in Scandinavia."

Sighing, I looked out over the water. As Khang and Bradford carried on, I tried to breathe and cool down. I knew Bradford would probably get everything he asked for. As a former government operative, I'd been involved in a few state conspiracies. It's amazing what our government will do to keep a secret under wraps. I had a feeling Bradford would be able to write his own ticket for giving up his communist spy of a wife.

Soon enough, Bradford engaged the throttle and brought the Striper up to cruising speed, somewhere between forty to forty-five miles per hour. Though the Striper had a deep V hull, and cut through the ocean waves pretty well, it was still exhausting slapping up and down on the water.

For the first half hour, Khang and I had tried our best to examine the yacht's floor plans and come up with a decent surprise attack plan. I felt mildly confident with what we'd planned. Again, my confidence was bolstered by the Makarov behind my belt.

At about the hour mark, we stopped trying to talk and simply huddled close together. With each passing hour I grew more concerned about Karla and if we'd get to her on time. I tried not to entertain the idea that she may already be dead, but by the four-hour point my mind had gone there. And stayed there.

So it was a relief, an hour later, when Bradford finally pulled back on the throttle.

He pointed to the horizon.

I looked up and couldn't see anything. At least not at first. After squinting, however, I noted a small dot on the horizon.

"My wife's yacht," Bradford said. "It's time, gentlemen."

Bradford motioned Ranger to the stern. Khang and I crouched into the open space underneath the cockpit and passenger seat. Once we were settled in, Bradford leaned over and addressed us.

"We'll be at her stern in about fifteen minutes or so. After I tie up, give it another fifteen minutes before you board. I'll have her occupied by then."

Khang didn't say anything. I simply nodded.

Sure enough, about fifteen minutes later the Striper slowed to a crawl, eventually easing to an idle. Moments later, the senator exchanged a quick round of pleasantries with a man's voice, obviously the yacht's captain.

The voice said, "She's in the saloon waiting for you, sir. She's happy you're here. Let me help you and Ranger disembark."

Before Bradford left for the bow, he dropped his left hand below the cockpit. He flashed his fingers and thumb three times, reminding us to wait fifteen minutes.

I waited ten. At that point, it was as long as I could take.

I motioned Khang out and proceeded to the Striper's bow; the Makarov stretched out in front of me. We carefully hopped onto the yacht's lower platform, which was roughly level with the water. There were two staircases on the stern, one on each side of the ship. I led Khang to the port staircase. On that side of the stern, another boat, a Boston Whaler, was moored to the lower platform.

Moving quickly, I motioned Khang to follow me as I crept up the staircase.

Before the top, I crouched and peered over the final step.

The aft of the second deck was all saloon, just like Bradford had drawn out. The social area was floor to ceiling windows on three sides. The saloon stretched from port to starboard with only narrow walkways on either side. The side of the saloon facing us was wide open. There were glass doors on that side that opened from one end to the other. The doors folded at the saloon's corners like an accordion.

My eyes locked onto the senator behind the wet bar. The man was busy fixing himself a cocktail. His wife was walking toward a door on the left side of the saloon. A sign on the door read, Head.

While Bian went into the bathroom, I backtracked down the stairs and looked at Khang. "Now is a perfect time to go; they're both in the saloon, and Bian just went into the bathroom. No sign of the captain. Why don't you head to the bridge and surprise him."

Khang nodded.

I looked at the Makarov, wondering if I should give it to Khang. After all, Bian didn't have a weapon, and Bradford told us a gun was stored in the wheelhouse, which was where Khang was headed.

As if reading my mind, Khang motioned at the gun. "You keep that. I'm not sure I'd do well with it, never fired a handgun before. And you have two people to deal with, so you need it."

"Let's go then," I said.

I crept up the final two steps, then headed across the stern's deck toward the open doors. Bradford saw me straight away. He gave a weird smile.

Before I could process that, a man stepped out from behind the folded doors on the starboard side.

I stopped.

In the man's left hand was a cattle prod, but my eyes gravitated to his right hand, which held an assault weapon, a classic AK-47, otherwise known as a Kalashnikov.

What the hell?

I aimed the Makarov at the man, who I assumed was the captain. In turn, the man smiled—flashing some crooked, yellow teeth—and aimed back. The man was of Asian descent. His skin was deeply tanned and leathery, like he'd been working on this boat in the blazing sun for months on end.

He was barefoot and looked like a well-armed street bum.

I glanced at the senator, who was still smiling.

Right away I knew I'd been played.

The armed street bum proceeded toward me with his finger curled snugly around the Kalashnikov's trigger. I had no idea if he was about to drop Khang and me, but I wasn't going to wait around and find out.

I aimed center chest and pulled three times. Bang. Bang. Bang.

The man kept coming. When he didn't drop to the ground, or stop his advance, I knew Bradford had filled the gun with blanks.

I kept pulling the trigger anyway, unloading the blanks in the man's direction. When the mag was spent, I threw the gun at the advancing man, hitting him center chest.

Khang, who was to my right, turned and made one step toward the stairs.

The Kalashnikov spat once. Khang dropped, holding his lower leg and screaming.

I rushed the armed bum, hoping to collide into the man before he could swing the weapon back my direction. But when I was three feet away, he lunged and jabbed the cattle prod into my left side.

I crumpled to the deck in pain, writhing and moaning and fighting for a breath.

A moment later, I heard the senator's voice. "Make sure you get their cell-phones. And the sat phone as well. Then throw everything overboard."

The pain was so bad I couldn't open my eyes. I felt my pockets being emptied but could do nothing about it.

Suddenly a rod slammed into my left side again, right below my arm pit.

Every organ, muscle, and synapse shook with pain.

CHAPTER FORTY-EIGHT

BIAN WATCHED HER husband's hand shake as he poured gin into a tumbler glass.

"I've got it worked out, dear," she said. "Trust me, as always."

Bradford splashed some tonic onto the gin and downed the contents in two large gulps, then turned to her. "It didn't go exactly as planned."

"We had doubts we'd get everyone aboard the Striper. Right? That's why I had a backup plan. You'll be fine. We'll be fine."

He sighed. "You're positive this won't come back to implicate us?"

Bian nodded. "I'm using someone I've never used before, somebody I have no history with, so don't worry about it."

She gestured at the Bombay Sapphire. "Now pour me a drink, and then let's go over our story."

The senator did, then poured himself another. After that, he walked over and handed her the drink.

Bian took a sip while her husband downed his drink. She noticed his hand still shook a little.

"You don't have to do this, Bradford. You don't have to go through with it. If you don't, we'll just have to be super careful, incredibly diligent for the foreseeable future."

He shook his head. "No, I need to do this. It's what's going to win me the election. It's a cost—albeit with unknown implications—but it's one I'm willing to pay."

Bian nodded. "You're a brave man, always have been."

He walked back to the bar. "Alcohol. That's my secret, love." He smiled, though Bian knew it was forced. "That's what makes me brave."

CHAPTER FORTY-NINE

I WOKE TO an orangish-yellow light flooding my vision.

For a second, I thought maybe the heavens had opened up and I was on my way home. But then my eyes focused and I realized it was the sunset light cascading across the yacht's deck.

I lay on my right side, facing the stern. My back was to the saloon. A deep ache radiated from my left side. I couldn't move very well yet, and I didn't dare try. I heard voices behind me, which were Bradford's and Bian's. They were deep in conversation.

I closed my eyes and listened, which was all I could do at the moment.

Bian was saying, "This is a bold move, hon. I understand. Before you go through with this, we need to make sure the story is tight."

"Right," Bradford said. "And we'll need to go through it after as well. Once I've recovered and we're on our way back to port, you need to walk me through it again. I don't want the pain and trauma I'm about to incur to affect my memory."

"Absolutely," Bian said. "Now how'd your departure go at Khang's office?"

"Good," he said. "We left in a hurry. Khang didn't call up the chain or tell his secretary. Chase texted his boss, but before we threw his cell overboard I saw the text exchange. No details at all."

"So what do you tell the detectives and feds then?"

"I went to Khang's office because I knew Garrison Chase was making a false claim that I was faking my blindness. And—"

Bian interjected. "Don't forget to tell them about the YouTube clip showing Chase fake stumbling into you. I uploaded it to your phone."

"Right, I will. So I show up to the office to prove I'm indeed blind, but it turns out they're preoccupied with this missing agent, Karla Dickerson. While I'm at the office, Chase gets a call from somebody saying they have Karla and are willing to exchange her for Chase since it's Chase who they really want. And they want to do the exchange at sea so there's no chance of being spotted by the public."

"Don't get too much into details," Bian said. "Avoid the weeds, dear. Remember, they wouldn't loop you into this, at least not all the details. Just say that you were there and overheard them talking, that they quickly needed a boat, so you jumped into the conversation and offered your fast fishing boat. Mention to authorities that you kept hearing the name the Rat, and references to the Rat's men, but didn't really understand what it all meant."

"Got it," Bradford said.

I heard glasses clink and assumed they were toasting their success. My breathing had turned shallow. I had to stop them. I had to do something. What, though?

Bradford continued their conversation. "I'll also tell them that Chase was desperate to save Karla since he'd do anything for her. But the man wasn't stupid, so he contacted his boss and the Coast Guard for backup. But he couldn't wait for them to show up, for fearing of losing her."

"Perfect," Bian said. "That explains the calls and texts. How do you end the story?"

He cleared his throat. "We loaded into Schuberman's vehicle and I directed them to the yacht club. After giving them the boat keys, along with the registered Makarov, Khang and Chase took off while Schuberman and I stayed behind. Next thing I knew, I woke in a car's trunk in Compton, tied up and sporting a massive welt on my head."

"Good. Explain to the cops that the Rat's hitman was probably going to kill you, like he did with everyone else, but he realized you were blind and couldn't identify him, not to mention didn't know much."

Bradford added, "And that I'm a presidential candidate—"

"On second thought," Bian interrupted, "forget all that. I think we should say nothing about why you weren't killed like the others. Let the police and feds come to their own conclusions. Let's not speculate, let's feign ignorance wherever and whenever we can."

"Sure, you're right. I agree." A brief pause. "Okay, I'm feeling a little better about all this. Have you gotten a call from the Rat's hitman? I'd feel even better if I knew Jimmy Schuberman and Hans have been taken care of."

"Me, too, but that confirmation isn't going to come until later. Jimmy's surely dead by now, but the Rat's former hitman is waiting for later tonight to infiltrate the hospital and take out Hans. Then he'll connect with your bodyguard for final payment, except he'll get a bullet instead."

Bradford added, "My man will make sure the hitman's body is easily found, so he can be linked to the Rat quickly."

When they paused their conversation, probably to down their drinks in celebration, I realized my heart raced as I listened to my own demise. My mind spun in a million directions, thinking of any way to stop them. But I was currently weaponless and in bad shape and without a plan.

"Let's get on with it then," Bradford said. "I want to get it over with."

Next thing I heard was movement in the saloon. What was Bradford up to? What exactly were they doing?

Since I had nothing to lose, I slowly turned onto my left side and looked into the saloon. Bradford was busy fixing another drink while Bian was at a large dining table with her back to me. She was fiddling with something on the corner of a table. Both were busy and paid no attention to me.

Khang was nowhere to be seen. The deck was wet, and I saw pink striations to my right. The captain had likely hosed down the deck to clean up Khang's blood.

Thinking about the captain gave me some hope. I couldn't see the yellow-toothed man from my current vantage, and I hadn't heard his voice since coming to. Also, I realized the boat was moving slowly, so the captain had to be at the helm driving.

This was my moment to act.

I got to my feet and staggered forward, but my clumsy steps gave me away. Immediately Bradford and Bian looked over at me, though there was no concern in their eyes. And they didn't move to stop me. Or say a word, for that matter.

It took a second to realize why.

As I crossed the threshold into the saloon, clutching my left side, I glanced right. In a corner chair, behind the compressed and folded doors, sat the armed street bum. The Kalashnikov rested on his right knee; it's bayonet pointed at me. The cattle prod laid across his left thigh.

He wasn't the captain. The senator had lied about everything. I quickly wondered how many people were on this yacht.

"So," Bradford said, "you couldn't even wait fifteen minutes. I never took you as a man who followed orders, Gary." He downed the drink in his hand.

The Asian man in the corner stood. I heard the Kalashnikov's safety click off. Smiling, he took a few steps in my direction.

I ignored him and focused on Bradford. "And here you are, Brad, celebrating your treason. Unbelievable." I shook my head in disgust.

"This drink is far from celebratory." He held out the tumbler and tinkled the ice cubes. "I have something terrible I need to do. Alcohol helps calm my nerves."

The senator's wife stood five feet to my left. She spoke calmly. "Just so we're clear: you make one move, Agent Chase, and he won't hesitate to drop you." She motioned toward the yellow-toothed bum. "He's my right-hand man; he goes by Ke Tra Tan, which in my native language means the Torturer. It would be his pleasure to take you out."

I ignored Ke and stared at Bian, aka Mama Hanoi. The woman had thick, long black hair that fell straight down off her head. Her facial features were small and unassuming. For being around seventy, her skin looked flawless. It was creamy white and borderline translucent. She would've been considered beautiful if it weren't for all the tiny blue veins you could see under her skin, which made her face look like a Halloween mask.

"Where's Karla?" I snapped. "Is she here? Or did you kill her already and dump her overboard? Or I suppose you'd get your right-hand man here to do it, wouldn't you?"

"We did no such thing," Bian quickly responded. "She's here; she's been hanging out for a while." A tiny smile curled at the corner of her mouth.

My heart sank as I realized what she was saying. I kept looking at her but addressed Bradford. "Let me guess: your wife here isn't the operative. She's the torturer and human trafficker. And you're the spy. Right, Brad? You're the one feeding intel to the commies."

He walked around the bar and stood beside his wife. "Heavens, no, definitely not me. Haven't had one interaction with the Vietnamese government since we finalized our adoption all those years ago. Like I told you, it's Bian. We've—"

"Like you told me," I said, cutting him off. "Like anything from your mouth was true. Please. There was no truth from you, just lies and acting. You're a hell of a better actor than politician, that's clear."

He reached into his jacket pocket and pulled out his pill bottle. "Well, I can't take credit for acting, so perhaps I'm bad at both." He laughed and jiggled the bottle. "These little guys are fluoroquinolones, which I'm allergic to. Taking one gives me nausea and vomiting, almost instantly as you witnessed in Khang's office." He motioned at his wife. "She's the operative, Gary. We've kept her undercover life entirely separate from mine, and totally under the radar. Twice a month Bian travels out to international waters on this yacht to provide any communication to her government. Never while on land in America. Never. Far too risky."

"Dear," Bian said, looking back at her husband. "Don't waste your breath with Agent Chase. We have work to do."

"Right," Bradford said. "He's old school anyway; he'd never understand what change needs to happen in our country, internally and externally. America does no wrong. Isn't that right, Agent Chase?"

I didn't respond.

Bian waved dismissively my direction. "Old schoolers like him will be left behind, wondering what the hell just happened to their America, when the changing of guard occurs."

I gave a hard laugh, throwing my head back; couldn't help it. "Come on, really? You two are doing this to usher in a new school of thought, some new America, is that what you're alluding to? Please, like that isn't the cliché of the year. Are you guys actually buying your own cheesy campaign slogans?"

I kept at it before either could interrupt. "And like I can't understand something as basic as treason, as selling out your own government." I motioned to Bradford, then pointed at Bian. "Selling out the country that took you in and provided everything for you for the past forty years."

Bian stepped forward. "Whether you understand it—or even like it,

Agent Chase—is not my concern. A new school of thought is pervasive in this country. And it's being led by our youth. The idea that America is the leader of the free world, and gets to act as the global moral authority, is dying. America has its own internal problems that need fixing and attention. It can't afford to keep messing in other country's affairs and exerting its will on others. It never worked in Vietnam, Iraq, Afghanistan, and that's just to name a few. People are finally waking up to the truth; just so happens it's by a much younger generation than any of us could've imagined. And my husband is going to lead the charge to a more peaceful America, to a much more calm and measured response to foreign affairs. To a—"

"Sure," I interjected. "He just has to get in bed with foreign countries, sell his soul and betray his country to accomplish it."

Bian frowned. "There's certainly a cost. There's a cost to everything in this life, Agent Chase. But come on, is Vietnam really our enemy or a threat to our way of life? So what if we feed them some intel every once in a while, if that's what it takes to win an election, so be it. Bradford and I need their money. It's that simple. We evaluated the risks and costs, and concluded it was worth it. Because we believe in what we're doing."

I shook my head. "Do you even realize your insane hypocrisy? You're championing a more peaceful America, an America that doesn't exert its will on other nations and make moral judgments, yet you're orchestrating killings and torturing women in your own charity. You—"

Bian tried to cut me off, but I held up my hand. "You've already proven to be fond of clichés, so please spare me the ends justify the means. Do me that favor."

"Communism is about the community," Bian replied. "About what's good for everybody, Agent Chase. I took those women from poverty and prostitution in Vietnam and gave them a new life. And asked for nothing up front, just five years of service. I laid out exactly what would happen if they disobeyed. A few of those women made bad choices and paid the consequence. The consequence had to be severe for the greater good of the community, to keep it intact."

"Spare me the rhetoric and twisted justification."

"It may be cliché, Agent Chase," Bian said, "but clichés have a foundation in truth. Wouldn't you do anything possible to get information from a known terrorist? A terrorist that has plans to kill hundreds or thousands of innocent American lives? Or are you too soft to make those kinds of tough decisions?"

I didn't respond.

"I thought so," she continued. "Because the ends do justify the means. Because your community, your fellow Americans, are collectively more important than the individual that's threatening their existence. So you'd do anything to protect them."

Not wanting to respond and give Bian any satisfaction, I remained silent.

Bradford stepped in. "Like you said, hon, he's not worth our time."

"Agreed." She motioned at the dining table. "It's time, dear."

Bradford finished his drink, then reluctantly walked to the table.

Bian proceeded to the bar and reached underneath for something. She pulled out a long, narrow syringe, then drew some clear contents from a small vial. While she did, she carried on talking about America and its problems.

I tuned out and watched Bradford ease onto the large dining table. Four wide straps had been affixed to the corners of the table, and the senator was closely inspecting each one. I hadn't a clue what was happening.

Bian motioned at her man. "Take Agent Chase out of here."

The man called Ke jabbed the bayonet toward the open doors.

"Actually," Bradford said. "He should watch. See if he can stomach this. He'll also see the lengths we're prepared to go to."

Bian thought about it, then nodded.

"I'm fully aware of your murderous, treasonous lengths," I said. "And what you two are capable of." I looked at Bian, then Bradford. The senator met my gaze but seemed to be looking right through me.

His diaphragm worked hard, pumping up and down. He broke the gaze and fixed the Velcro straps tight around his ankles, then laid back. Bian secured the Velcro straps around his wrists. The man called Ke now stood in front of me, slightly to my right, just to make sure I didn't lunge toward the couple.

"Tighter," Bradford said.

Bian nodded and re-tightened the wrist straps.

Though he kept silent, the senator's rapidly rising chest said everything. He was freaking out.

Bian pulled her husband's hair back off his forehead. "You sure you don't want something for the pain?"

"I have plenty of alcohol in me," Bradford said. "Just get it over with. Remember, just on the sclera."

"Got it, dear, I know," she said.

What on earth? My chest started rising and falling, almost as fast as the senator's.

In Bian's right hand were an odd-looking pair of glasses. As she put the glasses on her husband, it became clear they were medical-type glasses that held a person's eyes open.

After the glasses were set in place, Bian pulled out the syringe and plunged it slightly. A micro-thin stream of liquid squirted in the air. She flicked the syringe to make sure there were no air bubbles. Then she took the syringe and dropped a pinhead-sized drop on the table to the left of Bradford's head.

During that time, the only sound in the room was the senator's rapid exhalation from his nose.

Bian leaned forward and kissed her husband gently on the forehead.

I held my breath and wiped some sweat from my brow as I understood what was about to happen.

Bian leaned over her husband's face. With one hand she braced her husband's forehead. She held the syringe over his left eye with her other hand, less than an inch away.

"Cross your eyes, dear," she said. "Look inward. Stay as still as you can."

A moment later, she gently depressed the plunger, squirting a micro-drop of some horrific liquid into his left eye.

The senator's screams were so loud I had to cover my ears.

CHAPTER FIFTY

I WATCHED BRADFORD writhe on the table. Because his extremities were fixed to the table, his midsection was the only body part that could move freely. It banged up and down on the table. His fists were red, clenched, and shaking in unbearable pain. I couldn't see his head or eyes from my position, and I was glad for that.

The screaming stopped after twenty or thirty grueling seconds.

When the senator's body went limp, I knew he'd passed out from the pain.

While her husband had been writhing in agony, Bian calmly walked over to the bar and poured herself a drink. She walked back and set her drink on the table, then picked up the syringe and proceeded to squeeze another tiny drop of liquid into her husband's right eye.

Then she tipped back her drink.

In shock, all I could muster was, "Why? Why, Bian?"

She looked up. "What do you mean why?"

I cleared my throat and gestured toward her husband. "I mean, I heard your plans before stumbling in here. It's clear you're pinning everything on the Rat and killing everyone who knows about your involvement with Second Chances. Why actually blind him then?"

"It's more of a disfigurement than blindness," she stated flatly. "I made sure to avoid the pupil and iris and harm only the sclera. The amount I dropped wasn't enough to burn through the limbus and permanently affect the sclera." She walked to the bar and grabbed a blood pressure cuff. "Though it will look horrific."

I stood with my hands out. She hadn't answered my question. And I didn't necessarily expect her to since there was a good chance I'd be dead soon.

While she checked her husband's pulse and affixed the blood pressure cuff, she said, "This part was all my husband's idea. Initially, I was opposed to it. But then he convinced me it was worth it, because of the narrative he could tell."

She looked up at me, but I didn't say a word.

Bian continued. "Think about how the story will sit with the public, Agent Chase. Prominent men in the federal government accuse him of faking his blindness, which forces him to reveal his disfigured eyes to prove they're wrong. I'm not sure if you're aware but there are no public pictures of Bradford's eyes. Every picture is of him wearing glasses."

She was right. There were a lot of photos of Bradford in Slim's dossier. Not one of them showed the senator's eyes.

"Once the initial redness and trauma has dissipated," Bian said, pumping the blood pressure cuff, "probably right before the election, we'll finally show America his disfigured eyes. Think of that picture. Here's a man that lost his vision in enemy territory by friendly application of Agent Orange; a man fighting in a controversial war because he believed in his country, which he ended up being tortured because of. A true Marine, through and through. Then he's accused of being a liar over it all. A liar! Can you believe it? And—"

I held out my hand, finally getting it. "Understood. Your husband has risen to power mostly because of the sympathy vote. This story takes it over the top, way over the top. And may even help him secure the presidency."

"That's the hope," she said, releasing pressure on the cuff and looking at the dial. A moment later, she looked up. "And I think it's attainable. We never wanted pictures of Bradford without his glasses for fear of scrutiny, simply because his eyes didn't appear blind anymore. Now we'll finally reveal a picture of his disfigurement, which I believe will bring his past into stark reality. Not to mention, speak to the character of the man and what he's sacrificed for his country. Make it incredibly real to the voting public."

"A grand narrative of lies," I said, scoffing. "Which can't be farther from the truth."

Bian shrugged. "No one will be alive to say otherwise. Only my husband will be around to narrate the story. The best part—aside from the Rat taking all the blame, of course—is Bradford will recover from this impromptu eye surgery. Sure, it will take a while and he'll be temporarily blind, plus he'll have small scars on the sides of his eyeballs, but it won't ultimately affect his vision. And—"

"Let me guess," I said. "When the medical company he's in bed with finally gets human trial approval, he'll be the first to enroll in the experiment. And voila, sometime in the distant future, he can see again."

She winked. "We're banking on it. Pardon the pun, but we'll also bank a lot of money from investing in that company. Now, if you'll excuse me, we have to double-time it and get back to port, to put the finishing touches on our story." She motioned at Ke, who walked up to me and nearly jabbed the bayonet into my chest.

I turned and took a step toward the stern, then stopped and looked over my shoulder. "Tell me, have you been working with the Rat and you're double-crossing him? Or did you take over his human trafficking enterprise, and the Rat's truly been out of the game the past few years?"

She took a drink and said, "Being a woman from Southeast Asia, I'd certainly heard of the Rat's exploits, but I've never personally met the man or worked with him directly. I didn't even know he'd been captured."

I tried to turn all the way around to address Bian, but Ke jabbed me in the left side with the cattle prod, though it wasn't turned on. I staggered forward a couple of steps, clutching my side. I said, "How'd you find out then?"

Ke told me to shut up and kicked me in the back.

Bian intervened. "It's okay, Ke. You'll have your moment soon."

I turned toward her while crouching on one knee.

Bian said, "When Hans filed his second Freedom of Information Act request about Second Chances, I knew he was a dogged and persistent one. And I certainly couldn't have him find out anything. So I sent my men to his house to discourage his curiosity. They also bugged his house when they were there. Like a good husband, Hans came clean to his wife about why he thought he was being targeted. I listened to the recorded conversations. He told her everything had to do with his upcoming testimony against the Rat. Which was perfect for me. Absolutely perfect. It set everything in motion."

I sighed. "Now you could take out Hans and it would point back to the Rat as the obvious suspect. And then me as well, since you assumed he told me everything."

She smirked. "Not to mention Karla, Khang, and your lawyer. But the real ace in my pocket is the restaurant/nail salon."

Ke had enough. He commanded me to my feet. I didn't move. Instead, I said, "How so?"

By this point, Bian was by her husband's head, stroking his hair. She didn't look at me. "Years ago, when the Rat became a changed man, word on the street was he wanted to sell the adjoining businesses, but in an under the table all cash deal. Officially selling it would require lots of paperwork, a city inspector of the grounds, et cetera. And he didn't want that."

"Right, because of the torture chamber. In case they came across that."

She looked up. "Since the businesses included a nail salon, I sent one of my associates to buy the place, with a cash offer he couldn't refuse."

"Got it. So the Rat still officially owns the place."

"Indeed," Bian said.

"He'll vehemently deny everything, of course. Say he had absolutely nothing to do with this."

"Should that really be a concern for me, Agent Chase?" She laughed. "The man certainly isn't a trustworthy source. Technically, the man owns a torture chamber, one that's recently been used."

The yacht suddenly slowed. Ke commanded me to my feet again. When I didn't listen, he pressed the tip of the bayonet in my back, which got me moving. The shallow cut on my back distracted me from the pain in my left side.

Ke addressed Bian but kept his eye on me. "What's the plan? Waste him now and dump his body overboard? Then send Khang and Karla overboard to join him?"

"No," she said. "That's not the plan. If you want you could shoot him here, but then you'd have to drag or carry his body to the Striper. Remember, we have to get rid of the boat and the bodies, so it's best we load them into the cargo hold at the stern. We don't want their bodies floating to the surface and being discovered. We burn and sink the boat and get rid of everything."

"I like it," Ke said.

A door on the other side of the saloon opened. An aged Asian man stepped in and looked at Bian. "We're currently over the Monterey Submarine Canyon."

Damn. The Monterey Canyon was one of the deepest canyons in the ocean. Not a chance the boat or our bodies would ever be found.

"Good," Bian said to who I assumed was the captain. She motioned to her husband. The senator was stirring on the table. "Give him something for the pain."

The captain went behind the bar and pulled out a large medical kit. He grabbed a syringe and injected Bradford with something.

"The woman next," Bian said to the captain. "Take her to the Striper, then get this boat underway." The captain hurried into the head. I held my breath as I heard him fumbling around in the bathroom.

Was Karla in there?

Moments later, the captain carried Karla out over his shoulder. I breathed a little when I heard her make a groaning sound. She was still alive, though not in good shape. Her wrists, hands, and feet were swollen and a few different shades of purple.

Looking back, I saw that Bian was by her husband's side. Bradford appeared to be waking. "You know," I said, "you have a decent story going here. I'll give you that. But you won't get away with it. My boss, Frank, or Karla's boss will poke a hole in your story. They're smart, and relentless for the truth. Or maybe Hans will survive another hit."

"I don't think so," Bian said. "Nope, I don't think so." She cradled her husband's head with one hand and stroked his hair with the other. Moments later, he struggled to sit up. Bian helped him by undoing his straps.

In desperation, I said, "You'll never get away with this. Never." It was far from intelligent, but I had nothing else to add at the moment.

The senator was now sitting upright. He smiled as he fought to open his eyes.

I tried not to react when he finally held open his eyelids and I saw his eyes. Both pupils were basically gone. All I could see was a glazed, milky film over that typically colorful part of the eye. And the normally white sclera which surrounded those parts was flaming red and already weeping some sort of clear liquid. It was beyond awful looking.

He swallowed twice, then cleared his throat. "Oh, we'll definitely get away with it, Gary. We definitely will."

CHAPTER FIFTY-ONE

I WANTED TO charge Bradford and Bian and clothesline them both; dump their bodies overboard and watch them sink to the bottom of the Pacific. That was where my mind was at.

But I couldn't move. One step in that direction and I'd have a bullet through my head or back. Ke prodded me in the other direction anyway, toward the stern.

I looked left and right, straining through the diminishing light to spot another boat or any signs of help. As I desperately searched the horizon, Ke ushered me down the port staircase and onto the lower platform. The captain had laid Karla, who was still unconscious, on the Striper's deck, right beside a bleeding and unconscious Ethan Khang. Currently, the captain was tying the Boston Whaler to the back of the fishing boat.

When he finished, he looked at Ke. "Need help putting them in the hold, and with him?" He motioned my direction.

"I'm fine," Ke said. "You need to get the yacht back to port. Just open the cargo hatch for me and pour that can of gas over the cockpit and bow. I'll take care of the rest."

The captain did. After unmooring the fishing boat, he raced up the yacht's starboard staircase.

Ke directed me onto the fishing boat, keeping a safe and reasonable distance behind me. I moved as slowly as I could. My hope was to piss him off enough that he'd get closer, maybe to push me or poke me with the bayonet to speed up my steps. Perhaps I'd then get an opportunity to get my hands on him or the Kalashnikov or the cattle prod.

But the man was patient. In fact, he waited for me to shuffle past Karla and Khang and make my way to the motors before he climbed aboard the bow. When I reached the stern, the yacht's engines fired up.

As the yacht pulled away, my eyes flicked all around, looking for some-thing, anything, an edge, or a weapon of sorts. For weapons, all I saw was the gaffing hook mounted on the gunwale and the anchor to my right. While Ke proceeded toward me, my eyes searched the boat. That was when I noticed Khang's right eye flicker open. He looked at me, gave a near imper-ceptible nod, then quickly shut his eye.

Since Khang was face down on his left side, with his feet pointed toward the bow, Ke didn't see the interaction. Ke motioned me toward the open hatch. In moments, he'd fire some rounds into my chest. My body would crumple back into the hold. That was how I'd do it.

Ke tossed the cattle prod onto the deck, on the opposite side of the boat from where I was standing. Then he used his free hand to dig a Zippo lighter out of his pocket. He flicked it open, then ran it up his cargo shorts to light the metal wick. He tossed the Zippo behind him. It landed in the cockpit area and, WHOOSH!, the wheelhouse lit up.

Stepping forward, Ke glanced down and to his right, at Khang's body. The Kalashnikov followed his movements. I realized the man wasn't stupid. He wouldn't walk by Khang without shooting the man first and ensuring he was dead, or at least immobile.

As Ke approached Khang's body, he said, "Good day, Mr. Khang."

When I saw his trigger finger tightening, I knew it was now or never, so I shouted, "Now!"

The U.S. attorney blindly kicked back with his good leg, connecting with Ke's shin. At the same moment, I dove forward and tapped the bayonet just offline, which sliced open my right palm. The Kalashnikov roared to life, spewing forth a barrage of bullets. Luckily, the line of fire tracked left of Khang. The bullets tore up and over the Striper's transom and into the bow of the Whaler.

I'd landed on the deck, right beside the gunwale. I reached for the gaffing hook as Ke corrected his line of fire. Since I had a decent reach with the pole, I beat Ke to the punch, gouging the hook into his left side. I gritted my teeth and jammed it deep into his fleshy hip.

He cried out and dropped to his knees.

A gaffing hook only works by pulling the object toward you, so I yanked with all my might and pulled Ke toward me. We crashed into each other. Immediately I wrapped the man up in a bear hug, compressing my arms around him as hard as I could, staying super tight so he couldn't shoot me. Then I stood and jumped forward, bringing the man crashing to the deck on his back.

I flattened the air out of him. On impact, the Kalashnikov skidded backward toward the bow, which was currently aflame. While on top of him, I realized how close the fire was. The heat from the flames singed the small peach fuzz hair on top of my head. Half the boat was now engulfed in flames, and the boat started listing to starboard. The fact that we were listing meant the Kalashnikov's bullets penetrated the stern's hull.

I turned my attention back to Ke. To my surprise, he had some fight left in him. As I leaned over and began pummeling him with my fists, he suddenly thrust his head straight up under my chin. My teeth jammed together as my head snapped back.

I saw stars as I fell off to the right, but I managed to brace my body with my right arm, which prevented me from falling over.

Ke wheezed and fought for a breath. With the gaffing hook still dug into his hip and dangling off to the side, he came at me. As he did, I planted my foot as hard as I could into his hip, directly into the spot where the hook was dug in.

He howled and staggered back, tripping over Karla's body. I wanted to jump on the man and finish him off, but I had to save Karla first since her body was close to being consumed by the raging flames, which had now advanced to the middle of the boat.

I dragged Karla toward the stern by her ankles. Ke was still dazed and holding his hip, so I dragged Khang backward, too. Then I raced to the cattle prod. As I did, I saw Ke moving toward the Kalashnikov, which was behind him and partly in the fire.

I reached the prod before he got to the gun, but just barely, so I had no time to turn it on. I improvised and swung the prod like a baseball bat, connecting with a fierce blow to the left side of Ke's face. The man buckled and fell to his right.

While the man's eyes fluttered, I knew I had to subdue him. Unfortunately, I couldn't shoot him since the Kalashnikov was now fully engulfed in flames. I grabbed the anchor, instead, and dragged it, along with the chain, toward Ke. When I reached him, I quickly wrapped one end of the chain around his torso a few times, making sure to pin his arms at his side. Then I dragged him backward until he was near the hatch.

I fired up the cattle prod and shocked him repeatedly until he toppled into the open hatch. Then I dropped the anchor into the hold after him. His body and anchor made a splashing sound, telling me the hold was already filled with water.

Working quickly, I tore off the lower part of Khang's pants, below the gunshot wound, and used the material to tie a crude tourniquet just above the wound. Following that, I grabbed a life jacket, put it on Khang, and wrestled the lawyer's body overboard.

With zero time to spare, I checked on Karla. She was still breathing, though unconscious. I put a life jacket on her, then scooped her up. When I looked at the Whaler, I clenched my fists.

Its nose was slowly sinking. I could spot at least five bullet holes near the hull's water line.

Feeling the flames on my back, I laid Karla between the motors. I looked back in hopes of spotting more life jackets, but the only thing I saw was Ke's head and upper body floating to the hatch opening. Since the chain was long, the anchor didn't keep his body under water. I saw the man's eyes flicker open. Then I saw panic in his eyes.

The Torturer would soon meet justice face to face. And the worst part for the man wasn't drowning to death. It was the fire raging toward his floating head and torso. In moments, he'd go up in flames. If he managed to avoid the fire somehow, or if the fire was put out by the rising water, then he'd drown.

He looked at me with wide eyes.

I wouldn't save him. Even if I wanted to, I couldn't. Not without sacrificing Karla and Khang.

I hopped into the transom area and scooped up Karla. As the stern sunk into the ocean, pulling the Whaler down with it, I climbed atop one of the outboard engines, clutching Karla tightly.

I turned at looked at Ke, making sure our eyes met. Then I shouted over the raging fire: "Good day, Mr. Ke."

With that, I plunged into the water to meet my fate.

CHAPTER FIFTY-TWO

THE CHILLY OCEAN temperature brought Karla to life. She sputtered sea water from her lips.

Panic filled her eyes.

"It's okay," I assured her. "I got you. I won't let you go."

Still weak, she couldn't speak. All she could do was wiggle in my arms. I released my hold on her body.

"Can you float?" I asked. "Try and float, don't try to tread water."

While she nodded, I held her head above water. I waited to see if she could remain calm and float on her back and let the life jacket do its work. I knew her hands and feet were weak and super painful, so she couldn't tread water on her own.

Ethan Khang drew my attention. He floated on his back about fifteen feet to my right. I slowly treaded over to him.

"Come on, Ethan, stay with me." As I approached his body, I saw his eyes were open, but they were glazed and staring straight up into the dusky sky.

"What's going on?" he asked weakly. "What's happening?"

"You've been shot, Ethan. Just try and stay calm and float in this position."

"I don't feel like I've been shot," he said.

"Just float, that's all you need to focus on."

A blood curdling yell echoed across the water.

I glanced at the Striper, which was three quarters underwater. The flames must've reached Ke's body. I couldn't see since the boat listed heavily to starboard and most of the underside faced me.

Ke would drown soon, if the flames didn't get to him first. Whatever happened to him was no worse than what the man had planned for me. And definitely no worse than what Ke had done to the Vietnamese women as Mama H's right-hand man.

Turning back to Karla, I focused on keeping her upper body above water. It was challenging considering the open ocean swells took us up and down six or seven feet at a time. As we crested each wave, I glanced to the horizon, in different directions.

Red and orange striations streaked across the darkening sky. It was a thing of sheer beauty. Any other time, I would be admiring the amazing sunset.

Now I was just trying to stay alive. And will my legs and feet to keep treading water.

For the next few minutes, I kept one eye on Karla and one eye on the horizon. My right hand was clamped underneath Karla's neck, to keep her mouth above water, and so her body didn't drift away. The current quickly pulled us away from the Striper, which had now turtled. The flames had sizzled out, too. It'd suddenly turned darker and more ominous in the open, empty ocean.

If the waves didn't batter us, the wind did. It howled in my ear and pelted me with water from the waves. Over the next few minutes, Karla fell in and out of consciousness, which probably helped her float a little better. I'd been so focused on her and the horizon that I hadn't noticed Khang drifting away.

I slowly treaded toward him, making sure to keep Karla's mouth above the water. When I reached him, I pulled him close. His eyes were closed, but I could see his chest rising.

The three of us suddenly shot to the top of a particularly large wave. When we descended into the wave's trough, I fought to keep Karla's head above water, and to keep Khang close.

I had to hang on. Just a little bit longer. I had to.

Every twenty or thirty seconds, I turned my head and looked in a different direction, but it felt useless. I couldn't see more than fifty or sixty feet away.

As the minutes passed, my eyes flicked from the horizon to Khang's chest. The man kept breathing, but there were long pauses between each breath. I tried not to think about his open, bloody leg wound and how it may be attracting sharks. I also tried not to think about taking his life jacket off, using it for myself, and letting him drift away. Khang was a good man, and his actions on the Striper saved my life. If he hadn't kicked Ke, none of us would be here. I owed him. I wouldn't sacrifice his life for mine, not until his chest stop moving.

Soon, even my eyes darting around was tiring, so I closed them and gave up on watching the horizon. Instead, I focused on keeping everyone above water, including myself.

Some time later—maybe four or forty minutes, I didn't know—just as my head started bobbing under water and I fought to move my legs faster, I heard something.

At least I thought I heard something. In the distance. Like a boat motor.

Whether I was hallucinating or not, it didn't matter, because the hope propelled me out of the water. The noise grew louder. I opened my eyes. When the sound got closer, I confirmed it was the unmistakable sound of an outboard engine racing toward us. At least I hoped it raced toward us.

I swear I held my breath for more than a minute, until I saw the hard-bottomed inflatable boat at the periphery of my vision. The boat sported the distinctive black and red colors of the Coast Guard. I finally breathed. The approaching boat drowned out all other sounds. As the boat slowed and the bow sank level with the water, I watched a man race to the front of the inflatable. He had a huge smile on his face.

Jimmy Schuberman.

I never thought I'd be so happy to see my lawyer's face.

He leaned over the bow holding out Karla's cell. "Tracked you all the way until losing the signal about twenty minutes ago."

All I could do was smile back, thinking about the GPS system I'd bought at Target to track Simon.

The Coast Guard members fished out Khang first, then Karla, then me. The two guardsmen were deeply concerned about the bullet wound to Khang. Before the inflatable took off, I told one of the guardsmen the direction and destination the yacht was headed. The man relayed the information through a hand-held radio. Then I asked him to have someone call Long Beach Medical and put double guard duty on Hans Schlimmergaard, just in case.

Once underway, Jimmy and I sat at the bow with our backs to the wind. I had a blanket draped over my wet body.

Jimmy narrowed his eyes at me. "How'd you know someone would come for me?" He took out the Kershaw folding knife. "This saved my life, by the way. There's still blood on the blade; sorry about that."

"No worries, Jimmy. What happened?"

His eyes lit up. "Some creepy dude followed me out of the bathroom just after you guys took off. I'd pulled out the knife, but kept it hidden in my palm. When the creep got close and reached for me, I jammed it into his thigh and screamed for help. Totally surprised the man. He chased after me, but he couldn't run fast because of the thigh wound. Your boss, Frank, showed up and took him down."

I grinned. "Best news ever. The knife saved your life, and you saved all ours."

"It was all your plan, Chase. What tipped you off about the senator anyway?"

"I suspected Bradford may be lying about everything, but I wasn't sure."

"Right. But why'd you suspect him?"

I thought about the crime scene report I'd read. "His dog, Jimmy. It was his dog."

"His dog?"

I nodded. "Absolutely."

CHAPTER FIFTY-THREE

TWO DISTANT BOOMS filled the evening air. One came from the bow's direction, the other the stern. Bian hung her head as the yacht slowed to a crawl.

Her husband, who had been recuperating on the couch to her right, struggled to sit up.

"Why are we stopping?" he asked. "What's going on, Bian? What were those sounds?"

"I'll go speak with the captain, dear, and find out. Lie down. Keep resting."

Bian didn't speak with the captain, however. In fact, she didn't even head to the bridge. She knew exactly what was going on.

Bian left the saloon and walked onto the aft deck. Two Coast Guard cutters flanked either side of the yacht. One cutter had sent a warning shot across her bow, the other one had sent a shot across her stern. She imagined her captain was on the radio with the Coast Guard right now.

And she figured they were demanding to commandeer her yacht. Or sink it if the captain chose to run.

Bian knew her hired man hadn't killed Jimmy Schuberman, but she didn't know how they'd managed to track the yacht.

Moments later, she gave up thinking about it. Her run had ended. Everything was ruined. It was over. She clenched her fists and thought of Garrison Chase, who somehow had gotten the upper hand.

Bian Bollinger didn't wallow in defeat for long. She couldn't. She had work to do. It wasn't about her anymore. Her love of country, and fear of being captured, outweighed her desire to fight.

She couldn't—wouldn't—allow any of them to be captured alive.

Moving quickly, she headed to the bridge and confronted the captain.

"I'm sorry," he said, bowing his head. "They came out of nowhere."

"Not your fault," Bian responded. "You know they can't take us alive. Right?"

He swallowed and nodded.

"You know what to do then?"

Again, he nodded, reluctantly this time.

Bian made her way back to the saloon. As she walked, she contemplated telling her husband what was about to happen. But when she saw him resting peacefully on the saloon couch, she made up her mind not to.

"What's happening, Bian?" Bradford lifted his head. "Everything okay?"

"It is," she said, sitting beside him and stroking his hair. "Just a far-off naval exercise the captain isn't worried about. Radar shows the ships heading away from us."

He nodded and laid his head back.

"The captain gave me your next painkiller. Open up."

Barrington Bradford Bollinger III opened his mouth. Bian kissed her husband on the forehead. As she placed the capsule on his tongue, she felt a deep, sudden pang in her soul.

Bradford readily closed his mouth and swallowed.

Then he immediately gagged. Bian clamped his mouth shut with her right hand. Her husband frothed, then shook, then ceased.

Bian held him tightly in her arms as he squirmed. When she felt her husband's life finally give, she released her grasp.

She took the final sigh of her life, then said, "For country."

Like ill-fated, star crossed lovers, Bian popped a cyanide capsule in her mouth. Her final thoughts before collapsing in a convulsing heap atop her husband concerned Garrison Chase, and exactly how he'd managed to get the upper hand.

DAY FIVE

CHAPTER FIFTY-FOUR

E Willow Ave.
Long Beach Medical Center

KARLA, SLIM, AND I were back in the ICU at Long Beach Medical. I hoped this was my last visit to the place. Ever.

Karla was the patient this time. After an overnight treatment of fluids, her hands and feet were back to normal size. They were, however, still black and blue. Plus, her back was killing her. Nothing a round of pain meds couldn't handle, however.

Slim had graduated from a hospital bed to a wheelchair. He was still pretty weak on his feet. They were both eager to hear my story. Karla's memory was extremely vague at best.

"So the dog, huh?" Slim wheeled to the foot of Karla's bed. "The dog was the key?"

Karla shifted in her bed until she sat completely upright. "Tell us what happened there."

"Good 'ole Ranger," I said, turning my orange plastic chair to the left so I could face both of them. "It started when I was inspecting the torture chamber and noticed a urine spot in one of the corners. The spot was still fairly wet. On our way to the yacht club Karla received an email from the Long Beach crime lab. I immediately zeroed in on the urine sample to see if they made out a DNA profile. To my surprise, it wasn't human. It was animal urine, more specifically, a domesticated animal."

"A cat or dog I guess," Karla said.

"Right," I replied. "The technician was going to perform further tests to distinguish the exact type of animal. But I knew it must be a dog because of the amount of pee, and that the pee pattern proceeded up the wall. Never seen a cat lift its leg."

Slim slapped his knee. "Ranger and his faulty bladder. You assumed it was Bradford's dog, and that the senator was present during the torture of Pham Van Lu. Therefore, he knew all about his wife and what she was into."

"That was my initial assumption," I said. "The dog never left Bradford's side; the senator even confirmed that when I directly questioned him about it on the dock before leaving. Plus, that dog was a nervous pee-er. So, it all made good sense."

Karla asked, "Did you consider taking him down then?"

"I did, but only for a few seconds. I didn't know for sure it was the senator's dog, so I didn't want to make my entire case on an assumption. After all, lots of people have dogs. Bian couldn't have lifted Pham Van Lu's body that high onto the hook by herself, so I knew she had help. That helper may not have been her husband, and that person could've brought a dog with them. But most importantly, I figured you," I pointed at Karla, "were on that yacht. I needed the senator to lead me to you. If I took him down early . . . "

She nodded.

Slim said, "And you didn't tell Khang your assumptions either?"

"Nope, I wanted to keep my cards close. Didn't want to tip off Bradford to any skepticism, or anything out of the ordinary. If I told Khang what I thought might be going on, who knows, he may not have been able to play it cool."

"How's Khang doing?" Karla asked.

"Just stopped by his room on my way here. He's doing well, though he won't be walking for a while." I looked at Slim. "You guys can wheel around the hospital together. Anyway, the bullet went clean through and missed bone, so no serious damage."

"Good," Slim said. "What about Jimmy?"

"What about him?" I asked.

"Since he didn't go on the boat, did you tip him off about the senator lying?"

I shook my head. "No, I didn't, since I wasn't positive Bradford was playing us. I mean, the man had done a great acting job. He even puked over his supposed anxiety and shock of what his wife had been up to. Of course, I didn't know he'd taken pills for that. He also gave me a gun, which I thought was loaded at the time, so I was having doubts about his guilt. I did tell Jimmy, however, to keep his wits about him. Turns out one of the Rat's former hitman hired by Bian tried to get him, but Jimmy stabbed the man with the knife I gave him." I pointed at Slim. "And that man was supposed to circle back here and take you out."

Slim slapped his knee again. "Jimmy. My pal came through! I told you he was good people."

"Incredible," Karla said, shaking her head. "And that cheap GPS tracking system really worked."

I nodded. "Best thirty bucks I ever spent. So thankful you hooked it up to your phone." I looked at Slim since he didn't know this part. "The GPS system came with two thin trackers. I put one tracker in Simon's shoes, and kept the other in my wallet. It worked for Jimmy, right up until I hopped off the sinking boat and the wallet got wet." I looked over at Karla. "Holding you in my arms."

She mouthed, 'thank-you.'

"Of course," I said. "While bobbing in the water holding you tight and trying to keep Khang close, I had no idea if the GPS tracker had actually worked, or even if Jimmy was alive to use it. I just waited and hoped. And almost lost hope at the end, if I'm being honest."

Karla said, "I can't believe you kept Khang and me afloat."

"Awesome story," Slim said. "So disappointed I missed everything cooped up in this stupid hospital."

"Me too," Karla added, smiling. "I was there and barely remember a thing. And what I do remember, I want to forget."

We were interrupted by a knock on the door.

"Come in," Karla said.

To our surprise, Jimmy Schuberman waltzed in. But it wasn't the lawyer's presence that shocked us, it was the presence of Ranger the German Shepherd.

The dog's hackles went up. Jimmy bent down to soothe him, only to sneeze violently. A big chunk of Jimmy's slicked back hair fell out of place.

"Darn allergies," Jimmy said. "I can't believe they let this dog in a hospital. Apparently, he's a therapy dog. But he's the one who needs therapy."

Jimmy laughed at his own joke.

Ranger cowered, then tinkled on the floor beside Jimmy, which splashed onto his shoes.

"Oh, man," Jimmy said, picking up his feet. "That's twice this morning."

Karla laughed and called the dog to her bedside. Ranger didn't respond.

Slim was in hysterics by this point.

I motioned at Ranger. "How'd you end up with the pooch?"

Jimmy took a seat beside me. Ranger side-stepped his urine and laid on the floor beside his mess.

Jimmy tried to comb his hair back into place with his fingers. "Ranger was the only one alive on the yacht when the Coast Guard boarded. Bian, the senator, and the captain were all," Jimmy made a slashing motion across his throat, "Kaputz. All three dead by cyanide poisoning. Anyway, when we got back to the harbor, I was the last one holding Ranger's leash, I guess. The guardsmen were too busy to attend to the dog, and everyone else was being carted off to the hospital. Guys, I can't take Ranger. I'm deathly allergic to canines."

Slim called out to Ranger. "Here boy, good dog." Ranger was more interested in licking the floor than obeying.

"Crazy, crazy, crazy." Jimmy said, shooting looks between the three of us. "Can you believe all this? I mean, what a story. The senator and his wife are like Claire and Frank Underwood. Am I right?" He nodded fast and looked around.

"Who are you talking about?" I asked.

"Never mind," Karla responded. "When I get out of here, you and I will binge watch the first season of House of Cards. You'll understand then."

I waved her off. "Whatever."

"You think the story's going public?" Slim asked.

I shrugged. "I can't tell you how many stories I've seen the government bury."

"Not this one," Karla said. "Hornsby was in here earlier. They know they can't bury this one, and not just because we're dealing with a dead presidential candidate that needs explaining. It's because of the Coast Guard. There were two full Coast Guard cutter crews involved. No way they can keep what happened under wraps."

Jimmy continued wrestling with his hair. "Wow, this is going to be beyond huge news. Massive."

Slim added, "Set the country and election in turmoil, that's for sure. Who the hell knows what's going to happen?"

"I don't want to be around the next week," I said. "Probably two weeks, actually. Maybe I'll take Simon away for a while."

Slim pointed at me. "Not just yet, pal. You may have to testify; the doc hasn't given me clearance yet."

Karla leaned forward. "You guys are still considering testifying?"

"Of course," Slim shot back. "Right, Chase?"

Karla glared at me. "But the Rat had nothing to do with what happened to us recently. Like I thought, he's a changed man and just trying to avoid the death penalty."

I knew where Karla stood on the matter. Since I was in no mood to argue, I smiled in an effort to relieve the tension. "I'll cross that bridge in a day or so, once we figure out what's happening with Slim."

Slim held up his hands. "Boy, pal, these politicians have really rubbed off on you."

"Seriously," Karla said, "talk about avoiding the question."

To continue avoiding, I called Ranger over. To my surprise, the dog actually listened. He trotted over and placed his head on my lap. Licked my forearm a few times.

Everybody cooed and carried on.

Jimmy threw the leash at me. "He's all yours."

"No way," I said. "He's yours, Jimmy. You guys have the nervous peeing thing in common. You're made for each other."

"Come on, Chase," Karla said. "You have a fenced yard and a young boy. Simon will be ecstatic. Every little boy needs a dog. And he just lost his . . . Sorry, I shouldn't have brought that up."

I blew out a deep breath. "It's fine, Karla. It's the truth, after all."

I ran my hand over my head as reality set in. I still had to tell

Simon about his mother. After checking out of the waterpark hotel, my mom brought Simon to her house. I was headed there after the hospital.

The phone by Karla's bed suddenly rang.

She picked up the receiver and said, "Yeah. Oh, hi, Frank. Yup, he's right here."

Karla handed me the phone. Ranger followed me to the bedside.

No pleasantries from Frank. He simply said, "Can you get away now?"

"I guess," I said. "What for?"

"We have to talk."

"Uh, okay, about what?"

"Not over the phone. It's serious. I'll see you at Giuseppe's in twenty minutes."

"Sure," I said, hanging up.

Karla was the first to speak. "What's that about?"

I shook my head. "Not sure, but it doesn't sound good."

"Good seeing everybody," I said, "but I have to run."

As I made my way to the door, Ranger trotted behind me.

"Don't forget your dog," Jimmy said. My ex-lawyer grabbed the leash and handed it to me.

I looked at all the eyes in the room staring my direction.

Karla shrugged. "You're the only one he's responded to."

"You guys are kidding me, right?" I handed the leash back to Jimmy.

"Don't be a stick in the mud," Slim said. "Wait till you see Simon's face light up when he meets sweet 'ole Ranger."

"If it doesn't work out," Karla said, "you can always find him a new home. C'mon, Chase."

I looked at Jimmy. "I'll take him from you if we call it even. Forget sending me that bill."

"What? You're kidding? You know how much that would cost me? That would mean Ranger's like a ten-thousand-dollar dog."

I shrugged. "Keep him then."

"Or," Jimmy said, reaching into his pocket and pulling out a wallet. "I'll keep the money in this and call it even. Sorry, I'm a nosy man, Chase. Couldn't help look inside when I saw how thick it was. Were you going to pay me off in cash?"

I snatched Pham Van Lu's wallet from his hand. "That's not yours, or mine."

Karla eyed me. I quickly looked away.

Jimmy waved me off. "Forget the money, Chase." He held out the leash. "You take the dog and we're even."

I reluctantly took the leash.

Jimmy slapped me on the back and smiled. "I was going wipe your debt anyway. Taking down a presidential candidate was definitely worth ten grand."

I left the room with Ranger at my side, to a chorus of cheers.

CHAPTER FIFTY-FIVE

Giuseppe's Coffee Shop
Seal Beach, CA

I ROLLED THE front windows halfway down and turned to Ranger, who was sitting in the middle of the back seat, though his big head was protruding into the front seat.

"No peeing, understood?" I patted his head and left the vehicle.

Frank was already in the coffee shop, and he'd ordered me my favorite drink, which was in a mug across from him, the steam still rising.

I slipped in beside him and said, "What's this all about, Frank?"

"First, I'm glad you're safe. That was quite the incident yesterday, incredible story, but I'm not here to talk about that. Maybe later." He looked away and took a breath.

"What is it, Frank? What's with the secrecy?"

He looked back. "Ah, geez, Chase, I wish we didn't have to do this." He pulled out a flash drive and slid it across the table. "The lead Long Beach detective gave me that yesterday afternoon."

I glanced at it. "And what's on it?"

"A video," Frank said. He looked up at the ceiling.

"Just spit it out, Frank. Please." I took my first sip of coffee.

"Fine. One of the wine storage rooms under the restaurant had two cameras in the room. They have a full recording of what happened in that room. I—"

I held up my hand and stopped Frank. I knew exactly what was going on. The wallet. The stupid money. The ten thousand dollars for Lu's uncle. I imagined how bad that looked to a detective or investigator.

Now I was the one looking at the ceiling.

"Listen," Frank said. "The video shows you rifling through the wallet. It's clear there's thousands of dollars in there. I don't know what to do, Chase. I'm at a loss. There might be something I could do. But it makes me nervous."

I looked across at Frank. "This is my doing. You do nothing. None of this is on you. You're going to turn that flash drive in and let me pay the consequences. Don't you dare lose that drive, destroy it, nothing like that. You stay clean. I own this."

"It's just that you're going to . . . "

"I didn't take the money for myself, Frank, so you know. I knew its exact location because the man being tortured wanted me to deliver the money to his uncle, as some sort of payment. I gave the man my word, Frank. And I'd do it all over again. It certainly wasn't by the book, but I don't regret what I did. The man gave up Mama H, which brought down the senator and his wife, and saved Karla. It was worth it. Absolutely."

Frank nodded. "I figured it was something like that. I know what type of man you are, Chase. I know what type of law enforcement person you are. I never doubted that. Believe me. But detectives and investigators, at least some of them, might not believe you. Some will think you crossed a line." He paused, then said, "Again."

I ran both hands over my head. "I know, Frank. I have a bad history, and this just makes it worse. A lot worse."

"If this was just the first blemish on your record, it might be different."

"Right," I said.

"Did Karla know? Did you at least tell her, that way she could vouch for your story?"

I shook my head. "Not at the time. I told her after, though. And she insisted I immediately return it."

"You still have the money at least?" Frank asked, a glimmer of hope in his eyes.

"I do." Suddenly I felt the wallet in my back pocket. It felt like I was sitting on a large stone.

"If you return it," Frank continued, "I'll vouch for you. Not sure how far that will go. You may be able to save your job."

I looked away. "Maybe. Maybe not. There will be another long internal investigation."

"For sure," Frank said. "And you may come out unscathed. Maybe not. But you have to return the money, Chase. You have to. Do that and at least see how far that takes you. You may as well."

I stood up. "Thanks for the coffee, Frank. And thanks for letting me know so I wasn't blindsided."

He motioned at my chair. "Just stay a little longer, let's chat and figure this out some more."

I shook my head. "You go back to our resident agency and wipe your hands clean of this. I need time to think."

I left the coffee shop in a daze. With everything that had happened in the past twenty-four hours, the wallet and money had slipped my mind until Jimmy handed it to me thirty minutes ago.

Unfortunately, I wasn't the feds model employee with a squeaky-clean record, so this wasn't going to go well for me. Far from it.

Hopping into my car, I called Ranger into the front seat and went for a drive, petting the dog and thinking about what to do. For close to two hours.

After two hours my course of action was still unclear, but I brushed the situation aside and headed to my mother's place to grab Simon.

Simon was ecstatic to meet Ranger. And that was an understatement. My mother not so much. She was more than happy when we all departed, leaving her to some peace and quiet.

Good 'ole Ranger licked my son to death while the two sat together in the backseat. Watching the joy on Simon's face through the rearview mirror took my mind off things. As the afternoon and evening progressed, my work situation drifted further away in my mind. Simon and I had a terrific day, playing with Ranger in the backyard, going to the pet store to pick up a carload of supplies, then out for pancakes. Or brinner as I liked to call it.

Or brupper as Simon did.

The day went well. So well, in fact, I decided not to tell Simon about his mom until tomorrow. However, Gina was on my mind as Simon and I snuggled together in my bed. Her gruesome death in this room would be hard to forget. At some point prior to her abduction, Karla—being the awesome woman she was—had arranged for my house to be cleaned, including new sheets and a comforter for the bed.

As I lay with my son by my side, staring at the ceiling, I knew tomorrow would be a big day. I'd likely find out if I was going to testify against the Rat. I'd definitely have to decide about my job. And I'd have to face what I feared the most: telling Simon about Gina.

Later that night, as I tossed and turned and fought for sleep, Ranger hopped into bed and snuggled between me and my boy. We felt like an instant family unit. Suddenly life felt good. Great, even.

Deep down I knew that everything was going to be all right.

I slept straight through until morning. My best sleep in months.

DAY SIX

CHAPTER FIFTY-SIX

E Willow Ave.
Long Beach Medical Center

EARLY IN THE morning, Slim called to tell me that Ethan Khang wanted to talk with us. Khang had an update about the Rat. Slim wanted me at the hospital right away.

Of course, I now had a dog and kid to take care of, so I couldn't drop everything and head straight to the hospital. I had to plan first.

By the time I got to the hospital, Slim had already left his room to visit Khang. So I walked to Khang's hospital room by myself.

I hadn't seen Ethan Khang since being transported to the Coast Guard cutter. He'd been treated in the ship's infirmary, then went straight onto an ambulance when we made it to port.

When I reached Khang's room, Slim was being wheeled out in his chair by an orderly.

"You're a little late, buddy," Slim said. "But I'll fill you in. Khang has a scheduled x-ray or MRI or something like that, just to make sure everything is healing properly."

I nodded.

Two nurses began wheeling out Khang's bed. Khang motioned for them to stop when he saw me outside the door. The man reached out and shook my hand, pumping it about five times. He wasn't an emotional person, so all he mustered was, "Thank you, thank you."

I appreciated his brevity. The way he looked me solidly in the eye said everything.

He cleared his throat. "Sorry, these guys have me on a tight schedule. Hans will fill you in on the update. They're going public with the senator's story today. It's going to be messy."

"To say the least," I said.

As they began wheeling him away, he said over his shoulder, "When this all blows over, say a month from now, I'm taking you and Karla out for dinner. Non-negotiable. I'll even bring Hans if he's still on the West Coast."

I nodded, then followed the orderly back to Slim's room and took a seat beside the hospital bed.

By the look on my friend's face, I knew he'd received bad news from Khang.

"Oh, boy," I said. "What happened?"

"Well, I guess we don't have to worry about testifying." He looked away and clenched his good fist.

I shook my head. "The AG is taking the deal, I guess."

Slim looked at me with a deep scowl. "Khang doesn't want to accept the deal, of course, and neither does his boss, the California AG. But the top attorney general, of course, trumps both those guys. The president and his AG conferred yesterday. They want the situation with the Rat handled quietly, super quietly. Especially in light of the firestorm they're about to incur when the senator's story goes public. That's what tipped the scales against us, buddy. They have no desire to spin both these stories at the same time."

Slim shook his head.

I said, "So the Rat admits guilt for the Long Beach massacre and will languish in prison for the rest of his life. No extradition to Texas."

"Yup. No private trial, no sentencing phase. Nice and tidy in their minds. But justice isn't truly served. Certainly not for the victims in the Texas massacre."

We sat in silence for a minute or two. I can't say the decision surprised me. But I didn't want to keep discussing it because I knew it would depress Slim further.

Instead, I changed the subject. "Listen, this is going to come out of left field for you, but I wanted to ask about a job."

Slim perked up. "A job? What? You mean with me?"

I reluctantly nodded.

"Wow, what's going on? That is out of left field. Why the sudden interest?"

"Just inquiring, buddy. Exploring my options now that I'm a full-time dad."

Since I hadn't made up my mind concerning my work situation, I didn't feel like telling Slim about the ten thousand dollars and potentially losing my job.

"This is perfect, pal," Slim said. "I turn down quite a bit of work on the West Coast. If you come aboard with me, you could handle everything west of the Mississippi." He looked around, thinking. "You'll have Simon full-time, so you'll have to figure out help there, but you could work like ten days a month, be home for twenty. Pull in about fifteen to twenty grand a month, too. You and I in the PI business would be great."

He smiled and nodded, kept nodding.

I held up both hands. "Just inquiring, don't get so excited."

We chatted for another half hour, then I left the hospital and drove to Garden Grove. I had one last piece of business before I moved on with my life.

Whatever that was going to look like.

The convenience store owned by Lu's uncle was right where the hitman said it was. I stood out front of the store with a fat envelope of cash in my hand. I waited until the two patrons in the store left, then went in through the jingling door.

Pham Van Lu's uncle was a sprite old man. He quickly hustled over to me. I wasn't sure if this is how he greeted everyone or if he thought I was lost.

"How can I help you, sir?" he said.

The man was stooped a little, likely from decades of stocking shelves and picking up heavy boxes. It appeared he was the only one working. On my way in, I noticed the place was open twelve hours a day for seven days. I imagined the man worked every one of those hours.

"I'm here on behalf of your nephew Lu, Mr. Pham."

He narrowed his eyes. Though he was in his late seventies, early eighties, the man had bright brown eyes that hinted at years of wisdom.

"Lu," he said, waving his hand, "he's dead to me."

I cleared my throat. "I understand. The thing is, and I'm sorry to say this, sir, but he did pass away a few days ago. I was there when he took his last breath."

He took a moment to eye me, then said, "You're a cop, aren't you?"

"Sort of," I said.

"Are you, or aren't you?"

"I'm a federal agent."

He scowled. "And I'm sure Lu was in trouble, Mr. Agent, and you were after him probably."

Again, I said, "Sort of."

The old man sighed.

I cut to the chase, thrusting out the envelope. "Lu wanted you to have this. Made me promise to give it to you, in fact. Said he owed you this."

He shook his head. "Don't want it. Won't take blood money. Want no part of it."

He walked away.

I called after him. "He was a bad man, sir. I certainly get that. Really bad, in fact. But he tried to make amends in the end. He did a good thing on his death bed, something he didn't have to do. And it led to good things happening. Very just things, actually."

The old man turned back. "It doesn't make up for his criminal life, which I begged him not to pursue. As the saying goes, 'Everyone believes in God in a foxhole. Doing something good on your deathbed." He waved his hand. "Doesn't mean much. Not to me. Forget it."

The stubborn old man turned and walked away again.

"Sir," I said. "Lu said he'd fallen on the 'wrong side,' but that he'd crossed back over, and always intended to. He wanted you to know that. That was one of the final statements of his life."

The man stopped, but he didn't turn around.

I prodded. "What does that mean, sir?"

He waved his hand to the side.

"Please, sir. I need to know what that means."

The old man reluctantly shuffled back. When he reached me, he pinched his wrinkled fingers together and held them up in front of my face. "There's a thin line, Mr. Agent, sometimes a very thin line between good and bad, between what's right and what's wrong. Even as a small child, Lu walked that narrow line. Some people are prone to living life that way." He squinted at me. "Know anyone like that?"

I swallowed and didn't respond.

"It's like a tightrope," he continued. "Those who continually walk the line eventually fall off, everybody does at some point. And when you fall off a tightrope, you can't control what side you fall on. Can you? You fall on one side or the other. And it just happens, all of a sudden, with little warning. Morality is like a tightrope. There's a good side and a bad side. Lu fell on the wrong side, the bad side."

I nodded.

He put his left hand on my shoulder. "The point, Mr. Agent, is to stay away from the line. Don't flirt with it. Don't approach it. Stay far away from it. When you do, you avoid so many problems. You're far less likely to fall on the wrong side. Trust me; I know. It's what I tried to teach Lu growing up, but he never listened."

"Understood, sir," I said. "Trust me, I certainly understand the thin line between right and wrong. I've walked the line on too many occasions."

He pointed at me. "I can see it in your eyes. You've faced many tough decisions."

I thrust the envelope forward. "Take the money, please. I promised Lu. Sounds like he spent most of his days on the wrong side, but when you fall, sir, you can get back up and cross over to the other side. Right? It's not like you're stuck on one side forever. You can change. You can make a conscious decision. That's what Lu did, and what he wanted you to know."

He patted my shoulder. "You're wise, too, Mr. Agent. I also see that in your eyes."

"Then take the money." I smiled. "From one wise man to another."

"Let me ask you, was my nephew working for you? Maybe an informant or something similar? Maybe trying to bring down the criminal enterprise he was working for? Something good like that?"

"Well, no, sir, he wasn't."

"Exactly. He hadn't changed. You were after him, and I don't care to know what for. He was caught and panicked, I imagine, and he wanted to do what was right in the very end. And he may or may not have been sincere. That's for God to decide. Not me. I don't want the money, Mr. Agent, you keep it. Or the police can keep it."

He patted my shoulder one last time, then walked to the back of the store.

I shouted after him, "It would be better used by you, for your store, or for your community."

He waved his left hand over his head at me, then disappeared into the stock room.

I went back and sat in my car. Placed the wad of cash on my lap and stared at it. I wasn't sure how long I sat and contemplated things.

I thought about returning the cash, coming clean to the police department and the feds, then fighting for my job. I also thought about not returning the cash. Losing my job over it and working with Slim as a PI. Could I possibly find fulfilment as a private investigator? What if I used the money to start Simon's college fund, something noble like that?

What was the right thing to do?

My fingers incessantly tapped the steering wheel. Ten minutes ticked by.

I suddenly found myself out front of the convenience store, looking through the front window. The old man was helping an elderly lady on the opposite side of the store from the cash register. I jammed open the door and made my way down the aisle closest to the cash register. When I reached the register, I placed the ten-thousand-dollar envelope on top of the till and said to myself, "To a new life." I turned and walked out without looking back.

I was a man of my word.

Always was, always will be.

ALSO BY CRAIG N. HOOPER

Fallout (FREE!)

The Greatest Good

A Thin Line

All the Good Men

The Garrison Chase Series (Books 1-3)

AUTHOR'S NOTE

Dear Reader,

Thank you for taking the time to read my book. I hope you enjoyed A THIN LINE. If you did, I'd be grateful if you'd consider leaving a review on Amazon.com and/or Goodreads.com. Reviews are extremely helpful!

If you'd like to learn about ALL THE GOOD MEN—book 3 in the Garrison Chase series—or sign up for my newsletter, please visit my website at:

www.craignhooper.com

I'm also giving away a free ebook to all my readers! FALLOUT, the prequel to the Garrison Chase series, is FREE when you sign up for my newsletter. Please visit my website to get your free copy.

If you have any questions or comments, please don't hesitate to reach out. You can reach me at craig@craignhooper.com. I love hearing from fans!

Thanks for being a reader.

P.S. Flip the page for a preview of Chase's latest adventure, *All the Good Men.*

A GARRISON CHASE THRILLER

CRAIG N. HOOPER

CHAPTER ONE

I SLID A Walther P99 handgun from under the driver's seat and thrust it toward the United States senator sitting to my right. The senator had been sipping a cup of joe from one of DC's finest establishments, Compass Coffee. When he saw the pistol coming at him, he sprayed a mouthful of coffee across the dashboard of the compact rental car.

"What the hell, Chase?" The senator batted the gun away, then wiped his chin with the back of his left hand.

I dangled the gun by his chest. "If you insist on going to this meeting alone, then you should at least take this. I know it's overkill, sir, but I'm super cautious with all my clients."

He huffed, his breath filling the tiny car's interior with a pleasant coffee aroma.

"Please, Senator." I placed the Walther on his lap.

He brushed the gun off his thigh dismissively. Senator Felton Byrd wasn't a stranger to firearms, and he certainly wasn't the scared type. The fact that I was sitting next to him right now and not the cops or feds proved the latter.

"You're paying me a lot, sir. Since you won't let me tag along on this meeting, I'd feel much better if you were carrying. Just as a precautionary measure."

Felton didn't pick up the gun or glance at it. We sat in near silence. The only sound was the car heater pumping hot air in a winless battle against the December cold.

He cleared his throat. "Listen, I appreciate your cautious nature, Chase, but like I said, Morse is going to clear everything up at this meeting and tell me what's going on. It's probably all a big misunderstanding—"

"A misunderstanding? Really, sir? Yesterday we confirmed the threats came from his computer." I jabbed my finger at the condominium complex we were parked in front of. "From the very condo you're about to enter—alone, I might add. If you hadn't told me Morse Cooper owns more guns than socks, that the man's a total gun nut, then I wouldn't be so insistent."

Felton held up both hands, signaling he understood my misgivings. He looked at the Walther for a moment, then out the passenger window.

Approximately a week ago, Felton Byrd received two death threats via email. Threats weren't that out of the ordinary for a prominent US senator like Felton. But these particular threats came from Felton's friend and fellow senator, Morse Cooper. Ironically, Morse Cooper, one of the Wyoming senators, chaired the Senate Select Committee on Ethics, which Felton was also a member of. Morse was supposed to be the ethical gatekeeper for his ninety-nine colleagues.

Washington. Its hypocrisy never ceased to amaze me.

Felton turned toward me and swept up the Walther. "Fine, I'll take it to appease you, but I won't need it." He stuffed the Walther into the right pocket of his black Patagonia jacket.

"I take it you still know how to use that, sir?"

Felton looked away and sighed. His warm breath steamed against the passenger window's cold glass.

"Just checking," I said.

When Felton looked back, my eyes drifted to his nose, which I couldn't help. It was so long and thin I swear you could pick a lock with it. The joke, of course—which social media had a field day with—was that his last name was Byrd and he had a beak.

Felton opened the door and climbed out. A frigid East Coast breeze poured into the car. Being born and raised in Southern California, I never felt prepared enough for the cold. I zipped up my waxed trucker jacket as high as it would go. A beanie would've been appropriate to warm up my bald head, but I was in a rush this morning and left it at the hotel.

Before closing the door, Felton leaned in. "Sorry about the coffee. I'll bring some paper towels from Morse's condo and wipe up when I'm back."

I shook my head. "No need, it's a rental. And the coffee aroma masks the stale cigarette smell."

Felton nodded and pulled back his jacket sleeve to reveal a watch. "This will be a somewhat quick meeting. Morse and I need to be at the Capitol in forty-five minutes, so I'll be back here in twenty, maximum twenty-five. Obviously, we can't be late to this healthcare vote. Probably one of the bigger votes in the Senate's history."

"I'll drive you, of course."

"You can drop me off at my office and I'll take the Senate subway into the Capitol."

I furrowed my brow. "Senate subway? What do you mean? There's a subway just for senators?"

"Sure," Felton replied. "Two lines for the Senate side and one for the House of Representatives."

"You're kidding me, I hope."

Felton looked quizzically at me. "No, been around a hundred years. Ferries us around the heart of Washington."

I shook my head. "I'd rather be ignorant to the perks you guys have."

The senator smiled. "Keep the car warm for me."

As he turned, I called after him, "Be safe, sir."

He waved me off and didn't look back.

I watched Felton Byrd slip into the old building and out of sight. Seeing him wave me off like that got me thinking. Maybe I was being too protective. Felton certainly wasn't concerned about Morse after the two spoke yesterday and agreed to meet today. Drumming my fingers on the wheel, I thought about the threats.

Both emails from Senator Cooper, which came two days apart, were vague. Originally, we assumed Morse's email had been remotely hacked. Just yesterday, however, we verified the emails were sent from his laptop. They warned Felton not to screw up their long and productive relationship. The first email told Felton to drop it or die. The second one said pursue it and perish. Neither email elaborated on what to drop or what not to pursue, though. Apparently, Morse was going to explain everything and clear the air at this meeting.

Settling into the seat, I wondered if Morse had too much scotch those nights—which I'd heard he had a propensity for—and fired off the drunken death threats because Felton opposed him on the recent healthcare bill. Maybe Morse felt terrible about that and was about to apologize. Or perhaps this was a last-minute attempt to persuade Felton to vote with him today.

I rubbed my hands together in an effort to warm up. When Felton hired my buddy Slim's private security firm to investigate the threats he'd received, I finally felt a twinge of excitement for my recent career choice, which was subcontracting some security work for Slim's firm. The firm specialized in investigating members of Congress. When I accepted the Felton job, all I wanted was to uncover some deep-seated Washington corruption. That excitement faded throughout the week, however. Now I feared it would die a quick death if I found out this was all a silly drunken mistake.

Suffice to say, investigating members of the Washington elite had been a snooze fest the past year. Most of my clients were congressional folks who hired me to dig up dirt on themselves. They wanted to know what could be found out about their past so they could get out in front of it during their next re-election campaign.

Not exactly my dream career.

I shut off the rental car and decided to distract myself by getting coffee. I knew if I sat here for the next twenty minutes all I would do was ponder my questionable life choices. So I took two deep breaths and ventured into the cold, heading toward a Compass Coffee shop I knew was three blocks from the condo complex.

The line was five people deep. By the time I got my Americano and walked back, I expected Felton to be standing by the rental.

He wasn't there.

I fired up the rental and cranked the heater. Since I had two keys, I locked the doors and left the car running, then slipped into the condo's lobby to warm up. A rotund security guard sat behind a counter-height desk to the right of the elevators. He looked jovial enough, so I smiled and gave a courteous wave.

"Good day, sir," he said. "How can I help you?"

"Just waiting for a senator," I responded.

"Which one," he said, chuckling. "This complex is a who's-who of congressional delegates."

"Felton Byrd, the senator who came in about twenty minutes ago."

"Right, he's visiting Senator Cooper."

I nodded and turned my attention to the Americano in my right hand; I was never much for chit-chat. After five minutes of waiting and sipping and avoiding the security guard's stare, I pulled out my phone and called Felton to prod the man along.

The call went to voicemail after four rings. Not bothering to leave a message, I flipped the phone shut and walked to the security desk. I stuck out my hand.

"Garrison Chase. Nice to meet you"—I glanced at his nameplate— "Chuck."

"Likewise," the chubby guard said with a genuine smile. The heating vent for the room was directly above the security desk, so strands of the guard's wispy blond hair swirled around and distracted me.

I blinked and cleared my throat. "Listen, Chuck, do you have a way to buzz occupants of the building? Maybe an intercom system in each unit." I looked at my watch. "The senators are pushing it. They have an important vote in about twenty minutes they can't miss. And Senator Byrd isn't answering his cell."

"Sure thing, Mr. Chase." He glanced at his watch. "You're right, they really have to get a move on. I heard the vote's at ten this morning. I'll buzz Senator Cooper's place."

The buzz was louder than expected and reverberated through the small lobby. We waited in silence for a response.

After twenty seconds, the guard tried again.

"Maybe they're on their way down," I said, turning toward the elevator. However, the elevator numbers weren't lighting up on the panel above the doors. "Maybe they're in the stairwell." I walked to the stairwell door and opened it. After listening for a few seconds, I walked back to the security desk and shook my head.

"Try again," I said to Chuck.

He buzzed a third time, but no response came.

I looked at my watch and took a deep breath. Leaning over the counter, I said, "You have security cameras back there? Maybe they went out another exit. Did you see anything?"

The only thing behind the counter, however, was an intercom system and a laptop.

"Naw," Chuck said, "this is the only entrance and exit that people use." He thumbed over his shoulder. "There's a service stairwell at the other end of the building that leads out to an alley where our dumpsters are kept, but it's not used as an entrance."

"But it can be used as an exit?" I asked.

"I guess," Chuck said. "But that's not common. Plus, there's a silent alarm on the door that buzzes up here if it's opened without the code punched in. And it hasn't gone off."

"Hold tight," I told him. "I'm going to circle the building. Maybe the alarm is busted and they went out the back exit."

Before Chuck could respond, I hustled down the long corridor toward the back door. When I reached it, I pushed it open with two hands and stepped into a standard-looking alley. Glancing around, I spotted no people. To my right, the alley dead-ended into the back of some business. I walked quickly to my left until I reached the cross street.

As I rounded the corner to circle the building, I looked to my right. I noticed two people walking toward me and a cable man crossing the street and walking away. No sign of Felton or Morse, however. I continued around the next corner, expecting to see the senators standing out front, or at least Felton by the rental.

Nobody was there.

When I entered the lobby and saw Chuck sitting by himself, I ran my hand over my bald head. "No sign of them?"

He shook his head.

I listened in the stairwell again. No sounds. The elevator numbers were dark, too. I looked at Chuck. "I take it you have a master key for the condos?"

He hesitated to respond.

I glanced at my watch again. We were now a full seven minutes past the maximum time that Felton had laid out. Thinking about the death threats and the Walther P99, I was definitely feeling uneasy.

"Do you, Chuck?" The question came out a little too forcefully. I took a breath. "Please, it's important."

The guard eyed me, eventually asking for ID and a business card.

After studying my license and a business card Slim had made for me, he reluctantly nodded. "I do have a key."

"Let's go then," I said. "We have to get those two moving. What floor is he on?"

Chuck studied his watch. "They're gonna miss the vote, aren't they?"

"Not if we hustle, Chuck. What floor?"

He sighed. "Three. In condo 322."

"You take the service stairwell at the back," I said. "I'll take the front stairs. Don't want to miss them if they're on their way down. Bring that master key, just in case."

I waited until Chuck squeezed out of his chair, then I ducked into the stairwell and proceeded to the third floor by taking two stairs at a time.

There was no one on the third floor. There were three condos on each side of the hall. The walls were made of beautiful red brick and at least ten feet high. The floor was worn hand-scraped planks about eight inches wide. My footsteps echoed loudly against the wood as I hustled to the senator's condo, which was second down on the left.

I rapped on the door as soon as I reached his place.

Close to a minute later, after no response or sounds of movement inside, I used my palm and banged hard on the door. Waited another thirty seconds. To my right, I heard Chuck's shuffling footsteps.

When Chuck reached the door, I motioned at it. "You have to open it. Something's wrong. I know it. I feel it."

He held up both hands. "Whoa, whoa, slow down. I'm not going to just open up and barge into a senator's place."

"Listen, I'm a former FBI agent working for Felton Byrd. For security reasons I can't go into now, I need you to open that door."

He looked reluctant, so I put my boot on the door. "Either you open the door, or I kick it in. That's how serious I am, Chuck."

He eyed me. "You said you *were* an FBI agent?"

I nodded quickly and motioned at the lock.

"This is on you then," he said, reaching for his keys.

When the door opened, I let out a deep sigh. My hope was to see the men in the living room, or at least hear voices somewhere, but the condo was eerily quiet.

Way too quiet.

I turned to Chuck. "Do you know the layout of this place?"

"Sure, they're all pretty much the same. Living room and kitchen are in the front. Down the hall on the left is the master. On the right are two bedrooms with a Jack and Jill bathroom between them. I think the senator uses one of those bedrooms as an office."

"Stay here," I told him.

The first bedroom door on the right was open, so I rushed into the room, which was empty. Another door was located at the back-left side of the room.

While standing in front of what I assumed was the bathroom door, I said, "Senators? Felton. Morse. Anyone in there?" When I didn't get a response, I barged in.

Empty.

As I swept across the bathroom toward the far door, which opened into the other room, I stopped. The door into the second bedroom/office was ajar, by about an inch. Lights were on in the room and a solid beam of light flooded the dark bathroom. Overtop of my heavy breathing, I heard a dripping sound in the background.

It wasn't raining or snowing outside, however.

The hairs on the back of my neck stood to attention. Something was terribly wrong.

Instead of busting into the bedroom, I gingerly prodded the door open, which creaked on its semi-circular path until it touched against the wall with a dull thud.

Then I stepped into the room. And into a bloodbath.

Made in the USA
Middletown, DE
22 February 2023

25400372R00179